rec·og·nize:

the voices of bisexual men
an anthology

edited by robyn ochs and h. sharif williams

Bisexual Resource Center
P.O. Box 170796
Boston MA 02117-1026
United States of America
www.biresource.net

Printed in the United States of America.
15 14 13 12 11 10 09 08 07 06 05 9 8 7 6 5 4 3 2

ISBN 9-780965 388177 PRINT; 978-9-9653881-8-4 EBOOK

Library of Congress Cataloguing-in-Publication Data

Ochs, Robyn and Williams, H. Sharif, editors.

RECOGNIZE: The Voices of Bisexual Men / Robyn Ochs and H. Sharif Williams
1. Bisexuality 2. Gay and Lesbian Studies—bisexuality

The publisher of *Recognize: Voices of Bisexual Men – The Anthology* is the Bisexual Resource Center, a 501c3 nonprofit. The BRC is the oldest national bi organization in the United States that advocates for bisexual visibility and raises awareness about bisexuality throughout the LGBTQ and straight communities. The BRC envisions a world where love is celebrated, regardless of sexual orientation, or gender identity or expression. The BRC publishes print and online resources for the community, provides support to bi community members, and works in coalition with other bi groups to enhance a bi presence within the LGBTQ movement.

A version of "While I Still Go to Pride Events" previously appeared on the Good Men Project website (goodmenproject.com) as "Gay Day at Disney Meets the Promise Keepers," June 25, 2012. An earlier version of "The Worst Feeling" was published as "Journeys of an Intelsexual" c. Forbidden Light, 2013. "Conversation with Parents" was first published in *Trikone Magazine* V. 20/21, No. 4/1 (March 2006) and is reproduced with permission of *Trikone Magazine* and the author. "Ocean's of Love Letter" was first published in bimagazine.org and is reproduced with permission of the publisher and author. A version of "A Day at the Free Clinic" was first published in *Conjuring Black Funk: Notes on Culture, Sexuality and Spirituality, Volume 1* (Vintage Entity Press) and is reproduced with permission by the publisher and author. All other works contained in this anthology are property of their creators.

Photo Credits: Robyn & H. Sharif Williams by Ellyn Ruthstrom; Cameron Kude by Chase Person Photography; Seth Fisher by Lydia Hudgens; Juba Kalamka by David C. Findlay; James Hawkins Howard by Victoria H. Williams. All photos appear by permission of their subjects.

Cover design by Jewel Hampton. Interior design by Kena Ravel.

contents

identity

challenging labels

liminality

institutions

anger, angst and critique

bodies and embodiment

religion and spirituality

traveling

relationships

resources

preface

by h. sharif williams

rec·og·nize ˈrekigˌnīz,ˈrekə(g)ˌnīz/ verb

1. identify (someone or something) from having encountered them before; know again.

2. acknowledge the existence, validity, or legality of.

Synonyms: acknowledge, accept, admit.

It can be difficult to recognize all of yourself, particularly if you haven't yet encountered all of your parts, facets and nuances. For me, the difficulty was not because I hadn't encountered all of me but rather that I didn't see anyone in the world like me. When it came to love and desire, I didn't recognize myself in others. Before I entered the second grade of elementary school, I had a boyfriend and a girlfriend and had experimented sexually with both of them. I had no name for what these experiences meant for me. I could only recognize how they made me feel—good. But that's where my recognition would remain for some time.

It can be harder still to get the world around you to recognize all of you when there are parts of you it has yet to encounter. But once you have put together a substantial body of who you are and demanded the world acknowledge and accept your existence and validity, they had better *recognize.* Or there will be consequences. The sites in which these consequences manifest include bedrooms and boardrooms, street corners and salad bars, conferences and cabins. For a bisexual man, those consequences can be experienced as microaggressions and assaults on his humanity that daily slice away at the spirit. They crisscross along the contours and perturbations of the body, in some cases creating reservoirs of mistrust, guilt, resentment and rage and, in other cases, the promise of redemption and transformation. I was nearly 20 years old when my spiritual teacher, a father figure to me for nearly a decade, attempted to marry me off to another student, a woman, to ensure his "son won't become one of those homosexuals." The engagement didn't last but my capacity to love and desire people across a variety of genders did.

Recognition is an unfolding and continuous process that requires us to remember the parts of ourselves that we have lost, forgotten or had silenced. Being a bisexual man in a world dominated by straight or gay thinking, I continue to resist the pressure to conform to one or the other way of being even while I continue to question my own sensibilities. Are my sensibilities bisexual enough? Am I a straight/gay man in bisexual drag? Oftentimes, like when I first agreed to co-edit this anthology, I will have an experience that reminds me of the capacities for love and desire that I have carried since I was a child. Those moments bring the recognition and with it the dynamic tension I have with a world that does not truly recognize the complexities of being bisexual and male. To recognize ourselves as bisexual men, therefore, is a queer reclamation in that it frequently means that we are reclaiming lost or forgotten parts of our stories, our desires and ourselves.

But how can you lose or forget yourself? In a world that leaves little room for you to exist, it can be very easy, albeit painful, to get lost or forgotten even within your own gaze and to collaborate with forces that have pushed you aside or rendered you fabrication, foil or folly. Living every day in the between spaces of the sexual landscape, the walls that have been built and policed to maintain the just order of sexual conformity can crowd out the space needed to love and desire as one is moved to do.

I invite bisexual men to consider the name of this anthology—*REC*OG*NIZE: The Voices of Bisexual Men—An Anthology*—as a call to recognize ourselves as well as a demand that others recognize us. Hopefully, you will recognize yourself in your brothers even if their voices don't exactly match yours. Let the voices contained within the book call us to recognize who we've been, who we are or who we are working on becoming. Let the voices call us to be vigilant in recognizing each other. The next voice you hear will be your own. RECOGNIZE.

introduction

by robyn ochs and h. sharif williams

Opening the Way: The State of Bisexuality and Politics of Language

Introductions are interesting fabrications of human convenience. We assume or hope in providing an introduction to share with others our way of encountering and framing the things we introduce. To the degree that such commonality exists, it is rooted in shared experience, perspective and worldview. When introducing a work such as this anthology, the assumption and experience of commonality become so much more apparent, complicated, conditional and subverted. That is, in part, because bisexuality, a complicated and contested framing of sexual, erotic, romantic and social life, provides both a space where the queers among queers have found each other and a target for people who advance false dichotomies and binaries. Therefore, in this introduction we will expose our thinking to you as a way, hopefully, of letting you into our process and providing you with our context for the development of this work.

This anthology comes on the heels of a historic gathering in the United States of bisexual activists, organizational leaders, and scholars at a White House forum on bisexual public policy on Bisexual Visibility and Pride Day, September 23, 2013. Both of the co-editors and three of the contributors were among those present at the forum. The forum was the extension of decades of work by various people to bring the unique needs, experiences and locations of bisexual people to the fore in public policy advocacy. We mention this gathering not as a way to reinforce United States-centric framings of the work, but to be transparent with readers about the sociocultural environment and moment within which this work developed.

This is a particularly energized time for bisexual organizing in a number of different places. There has been an explosion of labels, monikers, handles, representations and identities for people who identify with non-binary, non-monosexual or middle sexualities: bisexual, pansexual, omnisexual, polysexual, panromantic, fluid, queer, questioning, heteroflexible, straight-with-a-twist, gayish, same-gender loving (which doesn't necessarily preclude simultaneous different-gender loving), MSM (men who have sex with men) or, as Robyn likes to say, PSP (people who have sex with people), and so on. The possible ways to describe the middle sexualities are as limitless as our imaginations. Concomitant with this trend is the simultaneous dismantling of gender binaries with various possibilities such as transgender, genderqueer, genderfuck, gender fluid and agender.

With these trends comes the subsequent challenge of finding language to communicate succinctly and meaningfully about the very complex and generative ways people are living their lives, loves, embodiments and desires. On a meta level, lives, loves, embodiments and desires are located within and informed by the intersections of cultural genealogies, socioeconomic statuses, geographic locations, ages, temporal contexts, relationships to global phenomena like colonialism/imperialism and a host of other factors. Because of all of these ways that differences are present for us as co-editors, it is clear to us that there is no one singular or universalized experience of being bi/pan/poly/fluid, and therefore it is important for us to reflect that in our work.

This perspective had an enormous impact upon our work as editors—informing our decisions about soliciting material, selecting contributions and organizing the text. Because of that reality, we think it is important to share with readers the following considerations. We hope sharing them with you in this way will serve the goal of orientation that is common for introductions but in a way that invites you into the opportunity to be disoriented in the sense of not being quite so sure where you are, where you end and another begins, where the boundaries may be or where home/not-home is.

Some of the contributors will be speaking to/with you. Some will be speaking to/with someone else. As an audience involved with co-creating the anthology as an experience, we get to participate in these simultaneous discourses together and consider the ways in which we find (dis)comfort, (re)cognition and identity in what is familiar/similar and unfamiliar/dissimilar. Some of the contributors' perspectives may not align with yours and you may even feel offended by their perspectives. We, the editors, intended to create space for people of like mind to speak with one another and also for people of different perspectives to learn from one another across difference. We believe each of these perspectives speaks to someone's experience. An example of a perspective different from our own can be found in those authors who speak of same and opposite sexes and/or genders. Neither of us view sex or gender as binaries, understanding both to be complex continua. However, we recognize that many—indeed, most—people use this framing.

The contributors come from varied backgrounds. Some are deeply rooted in queer communities. Others have no contact with LGBTQQQIKSGL (i.e., lesbian, gay, bisexual, transgender, queer, quare, questioning, intersex, kweer and same-gender-loving) communities. Some—not many—are connected with a bisexual organization. Some find community online or through reading. Others are not at all familiar with LGBTQQQIKSGL worlds. Some are involved in queer politics and indeed may be leaders of same; others not. Thus, there is no shared set of values or agreed upon standard of language, beyond that which we—as editors—provided in our call for submissions and commitment to finding ways to use language that is respectful, complex and simultaneously representative of the various perspectives of contributors.

This approach is not inherently neutral or even benign. It has meant that in our practice of respect for the voices of contributors—even when their politics may not correspond with either of ours—we have included perspectives that oppose or challenge perspectives with which we have been publicly associated either individually or together. We have done so because we believe that diversities, mixities and complexities are powerful. We hope you experience them as powerful, too.

Who We Are and How We Came Together

This project began as the brainchild of co-editor Robyn Ochs. Robyn has identified privately as bisexual since 1976 and has been an out-and-proud bisexual activist since 1982. Her first publications were twelve editions of the *International Directory of Bisexual Groups* and three editions of the *Bisexual Resource Guide*—essential tools in the pre-Internet age. In 2005 she co-edited with Sarah Rowley a 32-country anthology, *Getting Bi: Voices of Bisexuals Around the World*. In 2009, they released a second, expanded edition of this book, with representation from 42 countries.

Since 2005, Robyn has served on the Board of Directors of MassEquality, the statewide LGBTQ equality organization that helped Massachusetts become the first state in the United States to win and secure marriage equality back in 2004, and that is now engaged in supporting LGBTQ youth, seniors and people with HIV and AIDS and with bringing an LGBTQ voice to the larger social justice table. While she cares deeply about many social justice and environmental issues, much of her activism has focused on giving voice to the experiences of those who identify as bi or with one of the other middle sexualities, because there are so few resources available. As a speaker, Robyn's work takes her to colleges and universities, and to youth, community and professional audiences across the United States and beyond.

Robyn is also the editor of the *Bi Women Quarterly*, a publication that provides a platform for the voices of women who identify as bi or by some other label (or no label) within the middle sexualities. After her speaking engagements, audience members have often asked whether there exists any similar publication for bi men. Sadly, she has had to answer that there is not. After having been asked this question for what felt like the thousandth time and seeing the crestfallen looks on the faces of the men with whom she was speaking, Robyn decided to put together a one-time special issue of the *Bi Women Quarterly* featuring the voices of bi*[1] men. By making this available online, at least there would be a place to which to refer bi* men. She drafted and distributed an initial call for submissions.

H. Sharif Williams, a.k.a. Dr. Herukhuti, saw that call for submissions and contacted Robyn to learn more about the project and how he could contribute. After co-editing a special double issue of the *Journal of Bisexuality* on spirituality with another iconic woman of the U.S. bisexual movement, Dr. Loraine Hutchins, he was primed for another such opportunity. Certainly, he thought it would be important for a man to be on the editorial team for an anthology of men's writing and as a man of color he could open up certain discourses about the diversity of voices across various racialized experiences.

Dr. Herukhuti is a clinical sociologist, cultural studies scholar, performance artist and neotraditional African shaman who focuses on sexuality, gender and spirituality themes within Africa and the Diaspora. He is the founder of the sexuality-themed cultural center, the Center for Culture, Sexuality and Spirituality (formerly Black Funk); author of *Conjuring Black Funk: Notes on Culture, Sexuality, and Spirituality, Volume 1*; and co-editor of *Sexuality, Religion and the Sacred: Bisexual, Pansexual and Polysexual Perspectives*. Through the Center, he provides individuals and groups information and education for sexual empowerment, decolonization and liberation. He is a faculty member at Goddard College, one of the nation's oldest institutions for progressive education, where he works with undergraduate and graduate students. He is also a member of the editorial board of *Journal of Bisexuality*.

A scholar-activist-practitioner in the tradition of Dr. Frantz Fanon, Dr. Herukhuti's work has always taken a revolutionary and community-oriented approach to radical social transformation at the intersection of culture, sexuality and spirituality. His early work included using Tai Chi Chuan, Yoga and bodywork as alternative health practices with people living with HIV, facilitating erotic workshops for men and hosting educational sex-themed play parties. His work has been published and anthologized in various academic and popular contexts including *Sexualities, Journal of Bisexuality, ARISE Magazine* and *Ma-Ka Diasporic Juks: Contemporary Writings by Queers of African Descent, Black Genders* and *Sexualities*.

1 Bi*" (pronounced "bi star") is used here to encompass the constellation of identities used to describe nonbinary or middle sexualities, e.g., bisexual, pansexual, queer, fluid and omnisexual.

After Dr. Herukhuti contacted Robyn, we discussed the possibility of working together on the project as co-editors. Robyn enthusiastically embraced the idea, welcoming the opportunity to add Dr. Herukhuti's valuable experience and perspective to this project. Dr. Herukhuti was honored for another opportunity to work with a significant U.S. thought leader and bisexual activist. Prior to this project, we met at a PFLAG awards and fundraising dinner in Queens, New York, where Robyn was the recipient of the 2011 Brenda Howard Award. The award recognizes an individual or organization whose work on behalf of the bisexual community (as well as the LGBTQ community as a whole) best exemplifies Howard's political spirit.

To mark the new collaboration, we drafted a new call for submissions using the original call as a base. We created a schedule of editorial meetings that would include video chats and weekend retreats at Robyn's home in Boston. We exchanged email and worked on shared documents online. We cooked meals together and dined out. We shared stories of our childhoods, professional lives and activist careers. We found moments at conferences and other gatherings to share meals, take pictures, discuss our progress and check in with each other about our lives.

Each time we met, we (re)connected with why we were interested in this project, the meaning it held for us and the potential meaning it would have for others. The sense of importance that we felt for the project was not merely ours. We received a tremendous response from around the world of men who wanted to contribute to the text or who were simply glad for the promise of its existence. As we reviewed the submissions, it soon became clear to us that we needed to expand the original vision from a special issue of the *Bi Women Quarterly* to a book-length project. We approached the Bisexual Resource Center (BRC) with the intention of partnering with them as the publisher of the book. They agreed and we set out to expand the project.

Why? The Purpose/Aims of The Book

There are not nearly enough resources available. People with identities that are non-binary or non-monosexual are simply not seen enough, and men are even more underrepresented, even among bisexuals. Many *of* the leading, prominent texts on bisexual identity have been authored or edited by bisexual women and fewer than half of the voices within existing all-gender anthologies are those of men.

Thanks mostly to the efforts of Ron Suresha and Pete Chvany, there are a few bisexual men's anthologies in existence. Bisexual men are also the focus of some articles in the *Journal of Bisexuality* and men share their stories in anthologies such as *Getting Bi: Voices of Bisexuals Around the World* and *Bi Any Other Name: Bisexuals Speak Out.*

This need is perhaps even more urgent for non-binary or non-monosexual men of color. Many gay men of African descent have been moved by anthologies like *In the Life* and *Brother to Brother* but no similar anthology has spoken to the needs of bi* men of color.

Non-binary or non-monosexual men are a population under stress. The negative stereotypes facing this population are legion, and indeed the very fact of their existence is challenged.

And they are likely to lack access to safe and supportive space. There are few organizations or support groups for bisexual men, and non-binary or non-monosexual men who seek support from the larger LGBT community often receive a less than warm welcome. Here we must also take into account the compounding effect of minority stress on those who are members of more than one marginalized group, hence the importance of making sure that a wide variety of men are represented within these pages. There is an urgent need to create opportunities for people—particularly bi men of color—to recognize themselves and to bring their entire selves to the table.

A 2013 Pew Research Center report on lesbian, gay, bisexual and transgender Americans found that bisexuals were far less likely to be out to important people in their lives than lesbians and gays. "[Seventy-seven] percent of gay men and 71 percent of lesbians say most or all of the important people in their lives know of their sexual orientation, while just 28 percent of bisexuals say the same. Bisexual women are more likely to say this than bisexual men (33 percent vs. 12 percent)." The huge disparity between out gay men and out bi* men—77 percent vs. 12 percent—is clear evidence of the need for further research and resources directed at this population.

There is a prevalent myth that bisexual men living in the closet are taking "the easy way out," that lack of disclosure results in an easy path. But the small amount of research that makes an effort to look at bisexual men as a group distinct from gay or straight men suggests otherwise. While in some regards bisexual men fare worse than straight men and better than gay men, bisexual men appear to engage in some risk behaviors at a higher level and have poorer health outcomes along some dimensions than men who identify as gay or straight, indicating a higher level of minority stress. For example, in 2010 the United States Center for Disease Control's National Intimate Partner and Sexual Violence Survey collected data from 16,507 adults aged 18 and older and found that bisexual men have a higher lifetime prevalence of rape, physical violence and/or stalking by an intimate partner: an incidence of 37.3 percent compared to 26 percent among gay men and 29 percent among heterosexual men. A 2002 study of 4,234 Australian adults found the bisexual group highest on measures of anxiety, depression and negative affect. The San Francisco Human Rights Commission's 2011 report, *Bisexual Invisibility: Impacts and Recommendations*, found that bisexual men were 6.3 times more likely and gay men 4.1 times more likely than heterosexual men to report having had suicidal thoughts or attempts.

Silence and invisibility are extremely costly. Rather than disparage bisexual men who are closeted, we should examine why bisexual men are less likely to disclose their sexuality to others and also recognize the emotional costs of being passed over, of having their very existence invalidated.

There is an urgent need for even more representation and for a wider range of voices and experiences to be heard. There is power in speaking our truth. In so doing, we validate ourselves and we validate for others by offering them an opportunity to recognize aspects of themselves in the written word.

This book provides another stage to give voice to some of the many and varied experiences of non-binary and non-monosexual men. Each person has multiple identities: race, ethnicity, political, age, geographic, social class, educational status, occupation, nationality, ability, sex, gender, religion/spirituality and so on, and each of our identities informs the experience of each of our other identities such that there is no singular "bisexual experience," let alone a single word with which to name it. Our intent is to show these men not as a singular group, but in their complexity. The stories contained herein demonstrate the amazing diversity of experience, background and demographics as well as the common themes and experience shared by many of the men who answered our call for writing.

This book will serve as a life preserver for some, and for others as a survival guide.

How Contributors Were Recruited/Selected and Their Demographics

We made a commitment from the start to attract diverse voices, specifically including men of color, trans*[2] men, youth, elders and men outside the U.S.

To blur the line between "the authorized voice" and "the rest of us," we sought to include a variety of writers, ranging from experienced writers to those previously unpublished. We are pleased to say that a

2 "Trans*" is used here to encompass the constellation of identities used to describe nonbinary or alternative gender identities or expressions, e.g., genderqueer, transgender, transsexual, agender.

third of the contributors are seeing their words in print for the first time. Others have been published online, in periodicals, or in books, and—indeed—nine contributors have authored their own books.

We also wanted this anthology to comprise a variety of writing styles: short fiction, poetry, creative nonfiction, reflective essays, critical essays—and visual images as well.

Using social media, we put out several calls for writing, and we are thankful to the many people who helped us in this process by emailing, re-posting, reblogging and retweeting our calls. We issued personal invitations to bisexual men who are seen as opinion leaders and who represent identities and perspectives often absent.

Many men responded to our calls for writing, and what you will find in these pages is only a fraction of those received.

We asked authors to provide demographic information, with the understanding that it would be used to understand contributors as a group.

Here is what we learned about the men whose work appears in this anthology:

Ages. Our 63 contributors range in age from 20 to 77, with 19 men in their twenties, 15 in their thirties, 15 in their forties, 7 in their fifties, 5 in their sixties and 3 in their seventies. The large number of younger writers can be attributed at least in part to Robyn's huge network of current and recent students due to her campus speaking and also to generational differences in comfort around being out as anything other than heterosexual.

Locations. These men currently reside in at least 22 different states within the U.S., and in Australia, Canada, Chile, India, Spain, Sweden, Turkey and the United Kingdom. Two were born in Brazil and South Africa, though they live elsewhere now.

Sexual Orientation Labels. Fifty-one of the sixty-four who responded identify as bisexual or include bisexuality as one of multiple identities. Other identities reported include: fluid, pansexual, queer, Two-Spirit, sissy, faggot, butchqueen, polysexual, freak, sacred whore, Bodeme, "Bisexual in a Same Gender Loving Relationship," pomosexual, straightish, "not specified" and "I don't give a fuck."

Ethnicities. When asked to name their ethnic identity, the complexity of this aspect of our identity became clear. Responses included "Caucasian," "Northern European Disapora—American, African ancestry Maafra descent," "African American," "Person of African Descent," "Asian Indian," "Asian American," "Latino/White," "hispanic," "White," "African-American mixblood," "Mixed," "Caucasian/1/4 Spanish," "American Mutt," "Native American/ Scottish/English," "Dutch," "Polish," "Welsh (Race = White)," "Estonian," "Anglo-Saxon," "anglo-saxon/caucasian," "Hispanic/ Slavic," "mixed race hispanic/white," "Pakistani," "Jewish (Askenazic)," "Anglo," "Thai," "White South(ern) African," "German-American," "Honkey," "White-British," "mixed: Ethiopian/South Asian (Indian) via the Caribbean/First Nations (undocumented Tsalagi)/Andalusi" and "I am having an African American experience." Twenty-two identify as men of color.

Religious/Spiritual Identifications. Self-reports of religious/spiritual identification also revealed a wide variety of responses: "Agnostic," "Atheist," "agnostic atheist," "Spiritual Humanist," "Christian," "christian," "Hindu Agnostic," "spiritual," "None," "Pagan," "United Church of Christ," "N/A," "Interfaith/Mystic," "Pagan/Buddhist," "mixed Sufi/neo-Hasidic/shaman/yoruba initiate/tibetan buddhist initiate," "radical christian (post-Catholic)," "Syncretist," "neotraditional African/Disaporic," "Unitarian-Universalist," "Wiccan," "Buddhist," "unsure," "Protestant," "Christian," "Jewish," "Humanist Buddhist," "Atheist as fuck," "agnostic, Jewish, Catholic," Buddhist Christian," "Jewish by background, Pagan in practice," "secular humanist," "Jewish/ Agnostic/Unitarian Universalist," "Unitarian/Native Spirituality, "Episcopalian" and "Episcopalian Christian."

Gender Identities. We asked "Where do you identify on the gender spectrum (for example: cisgender, i.e., your gender identity is the same as that which was assigned to you at birth), genderqueer, transgender, transsexual, etc.)?" The majority of our contributors identified as cisgender and/or male. There was a strong showing of other identities along the gender spectrum, with twelve contributors reporting other identities including trans*, transgender, transsexual, transsexual F-T-M, transguy, Two-Spirit, bigender, gender questioning, unsure, cis-genderflexible, genderqueer and soft butch.

Relationship Status. When asked their current relationship status, here again there was a wide range of responses: single, dating, celibate, engaged, domestic partnered and married. Some described their relationships as monogamous, some non-monogamous, polyamorous or polyfidelitous, and even "monogamish." One answered the question by writing, "I live with cats."

Occupations. Answers to the question, "What is your occupation?" were no simpler:

Many have a link to education, as students, university professors, higher education administrators, scholars, diversity educators and consultants. Several are in health care and the helping professions, including a massage therapist, two psychotherapists, a minister, a pastor, a sexologist, a social worker, and someone who works in senior care. There are writers, an editor, a writing consultant and a translator. Four work in information technology.

Other careers or occupations include (in alphabetical order): artist, attorney, activist, barista, biological anthropologist, biologist, client advocate, comedian, corporate/managerial communications, cultural organizer, electrical engineer, fundraiser, linkage and retention specialist, marketer/fundraiser, mechanical engineer, model, national anti-violence speaker/performer, performance artist, photographer, property manager, public health bioterrorism response planner, public health professional, researcher, risk manager, sales manager, sex and relationship whisperer, sexologist, shaman and TV writer. One self-reports as unemployed, two are on disability and two are retired.

And finally, one describes himself as an "Ochs-ologist (Robyn Ochs's assistant)."

Editorial Process: Practice, Decisions, Events and Milestones

Do you know what a gift it is to receive someone's writing, artwork or story and to be asked, "Please help me share this work with the world and help me to make it better so that when it is in the world it can live without me, nourishing other people's hearts, minds and souls as it has my own? That is editorial process. Like doulas and midwives, editors help others to carry preciousness to term, give birth and recuperate from the process. Editing calls for a number of the same skills: patience, insight, sensitivity to the energies of others, watchfulness, compassion and engagement.

Co-editing with someone else adds another level of complexity, support and challenge to the process—particularly when you have not previously worked together. In our case, we were coming together as co-editors across genders (cisgender woman and man), ethnicities, classes, geographies (Boston and the Republic of Brooklyn, New York) and generations. We had to reach beyond our well-crafted biographies, the stereotypes about the Other that worldly people like us learn to blithely dismiss in favor of our politically correct personas, and our fears of the very public failure to which our inability to work together would amount.

Technology was there to help us. And we used it. It is unimaginable how we would have worked together without being able to see each other through video chat windows—even as we acknowledge the many co-editors who completed similar projects before the existence of video chat. Most of our meetings occurred while Robyn sat in the second floor office of her quiet home nestled among friends who have become neighbors, neighbors who have become friends, and Dr. Herukhuti sat in the bedroom/office of his apartment in a noisy and busy apartment building inhabited by people living with mental illnesses, economic distress or intergenerational roots in the community. We peered across our computer screens into each other's world and talked about writing, art, voice, intention, audience and logistics. Those meetings were punctuated by retreats in Boston where we met for several days to work on aspects of the project that required our being together in the same place at the same time benefiting from the other's presence and energy as well as precious moments we carved out of the largess of the Creating Change Conference (Atlanta 2013 and Houston 2014) schedule for editorial meetings.

We read each submission we received and discussed its possible inclusion in the anthology. When we both agreed that a submission should be included, we moved it to provisional acceptance and assigned it to a co-editor for further development. When we both agreed that a submission should not be included, we informed the writer that their piece had not been selected. Submissions about which we had an initial difference of opinion were set aside to be reconsidered after the supporting co-editor had an opportunity to work with the person who submitted the work to develop the work further. Each of us worked with a set of submissions that we provisionally accepted, giving our collective feedback to the submitters and working with them to develop their work. At editorial meetings, we discussed the progress of the works.

The work of engaging contributors on the aesthetic, artistic, conceptual and/or theoretical aspects of their work was intense. We were not seeking to make them conform to a specific construction of or school of thought on bisexuality, pansexuality, polysexuality, fluidity or non-monosexual queer identity. Instead, we engaged in a practice of noticing and witnessing for the contributor aspects of their work, including apparent and underlying questions embedded in the work, as a way of being in conversation with them about their perspectives, intentions, ideas and feelings, and through that dialogue giving space for the work to change as needed into its finalized form.

Our work affirmed the wisdom that necessity is the mother of invention when, in contemplating the enormity of the task of proofreading, we decided to seek volunteers through our social media networks and personal relationships to help. In this way, we were able to identify 23 people interested in supporting us through their volunteer labor. We thank the following people who generously donated their time as proofreaders: Jessica Carballo, Marcia Deihl, Dragonfly, Renee Fitzsimmons, Heron Greenesmith, Rachelle Hademenos, Andrew

M. Humphrey, Charemi A. Jones, Tony Laing, Chas Mitchell, Holly Mitchell, Mindy Mitchell, Eleanor Moss, Philippa Neville, Arielle Schecter, Rachel M. Schneewind, Archana Somashekar (a.k.a. Archie), Pete Sturman and Eric A. Thomas. We are especially grateful to Katelynn Bishop, Catherine Rock, Ellyn Ruthstrom and Ron Suresha, who—in their role as final proofreaders—reviewed the entire manuscript. Their work was an invaluable contribution to the production of the anthology.

The Organization of This Anthology

We recognize that readers will come to this anthology for different reasons, in different settings, and with a different history, for example: academics seeking bisexual content to enrich their syllabi; curious or questioning people seeking to recognize themselves within the pages of a book; activists seeking inspiring and informative stories to share; allies wanting to learn more and challenge their prejudices; people who love the diversity and accessibility of anthologies seeking to add to their collection; journalists and researchers wanting to learn more about a segment of the population they are beginning to cover in their work. Those differences will inform how each of you approach and engage the work. Therefore, we've chosen not to force a particular frame on the structure of the anthology but instead provided just enough support to help you in making decisions for yourself about what contributions are related and the sequence you use to encounter and engage the contributions.

Although we created sections of work related to what we believe are common themes, we did not create introductions that provide commentary for each of those sections. We have left the commentary for you to produce. Although we ordered contributions within each section based upon their tone and relationship to one another, we were clear to keep in mind that readers will choose what contributions they engage with and in what order.

We have also provided readers with a topical index that groups contributions based upon the type of writing, generation of author (under 30, 30 to 60, 60-plus), sociocultural identity, gender identity and topic. We hope this index is useful to you.

Conclusion: Desired Impact

It is our hope that this book will serve your needs.

To those young, old and in-between who are beginning to question your sexualities or opening yourselves up to new sexual possibilities in your lives: May you find in these pieces of work a place of reflection, representation, affirmation or consideration to nurture you on your journey. May you find your own experience reflected in some pieces and may you also find writing that introduces you to entirely new concepts and framing.

To those engaged in the work of education: We hope you will find within these pages tools to use in schools as well as in community settings such as discussion groups, religious/spiritual institutions, etc. to promote dialogue and further inquiry. The experiences of bi* men are rarely included in course materials, and it is our hope that those teaching gender and sexuality studies will look here for materials to enrich their syllabi.

To the bisexual movement: May this book contribute one more building block to the ongoing body of work documenting and reflecting on the lives of bisexual, pansexual, polysexual, fluid and non-monosexual queer people and sparking further conversation.

And finally, to you, the reader: We hope that you find these readings to be educational, thought-provoking and, not least, enjoyable.

Peace, Pleasure and Passion,

Robyn Ochs and Dr Herukhuti (H. Sharif Williams)

identity

"nobody knows," efrain gonzalez

two peas in a pod: letter from a bisexual son to his bisexual dad

by abilly s. jones

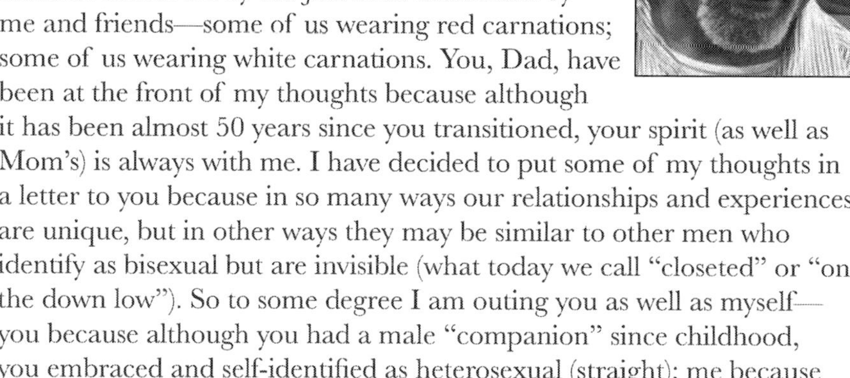

June 16, 2013

Greetings, my loving Dad:

Another Father's Day has just been celebrated by me and friends—some of us wearing red carnations; some of us wearing white carnations. You, Dad, have been at the front of my thoughts because although it has been almost 50 years since you transitioned, your spirit (as well as Mom's) is always with me. I have decided to put some of my thoughts in a letter to you because in so many ways our relationships and experiences are unique, but in other ways they may be similar to other men who identify as bisexual but are invisible (what today we call "closeted" or "on the down low"). So to some degree I am outing you as well as myself—you because although you had a male "companion" since childhood, you embraced and self-identified as heterosexual (straight); me because although I have been in a same-gender-loving (SGL) relationship for thirty-five years, I self-identify as bisexual but am perceived by most as homosexual (gay).

Using terms that will make sense for you is a challenge because what sexual minorities call themselves and identify as today has evolved over the years. Many of the "labels" we use today had not emerged during your lifetime or my youth. You were born in 1913 and I was born in 1942; so if you were still alive you would be one hundred and I am seventy-one. For me as a kid, I heard persons known or thought to be sexual minorities discussed with labels such as punk, sissy, fairy and bull dyke and always used in a degrading manner. Of course, "polite" persons would whisper comments like, "There's a lot of sugar with..." or there would be a shaking of a hand to indicate that someone they were discussing was different, not heterosexual. Unfortunately, negative labels are still bestowed upon persons perceived to be sexual minorities and we are still at risk of being beaten, killed, incarcerated and subjected to unwanted and unnecessary therapies and denied basic human and civil rights.

While I do not know for sure, given your progressive stance on most social and political issues, I feel confident that you would embrace the LGBT community's demand for equality and social justice and be proud of my being a part of it. I have recently revved-up my involvement with the bisexual community and organizations in part because I am tired of individuals and organizations giving mere lip service to bisexuals, in part because we bisexuals are often excluded from important issues and events that impact our lives, and in part because of the biphobia that comes from individuals as well as organizations. To the same extent that people of color and women have had to fight multiple forms of oppressions from within their ranks as well as outside, so too must we bisexuals confront biphobia within LGBT communities and organizations as well as within straight communities and organizations.

So, Dad, you might be wondering when the realization occurred to me that you were bisexual. (I am tempted to say "are bisexual" but I don't know how that works after transitioning.) Actually, it was Mom who turned on the light bulb. Soon after your death, I decided to have the same conversation with her that I had had with you by revealing that I was sexually attracted to men. After my beating around the bush and finally getting it out, without a moment's hesitation Mom exclaimed, "Oh, you are just like your Dad, two peas in a pod!" Moving closer to me and holding my hand, Mom proceeded to tell me about Dad's friend from childhood who was respected in our household as an "uncle." When I inquired how she knew, she waved her hands and said, "Wives and mothers know these things." And when I asked how she dealt with Dad's relationship with "Uncle," in her usual comic fashion, Mom replied, "Son, with ten children to care for and a demanding career, I was glad for all the help I could get. He was a good husband and a good father." I often wonder, Dad, if you and Mom ever discussed your intimacy with "Uncle" and if "Uncle" had discussed the relationship with his wife.

Mom's advice to me was very much in line with the advice that you had given to me when I had the same talk with you, Dad, about my sexual attraction to men: a) be discreet and do nothing to embarrass the family, community or race; b) protect yourself from diseases; and c) get married and have children. Because I was also dating and sexually attracted to women as well as men, the discussion from both of you was also about not getting a girl pregnant. While my sisters were repeatedly told to not have sex before marriage, my brothers and I were given mixed messages—sex was a rite of passage for males but we were not to get a girl pregnant. Sex was freely discussed in our household and the boys were actually given condoms while the girls were just told not to give up their virginity until marriage.

I pretty much adhered to the advice you and Mom gave me—pretty near. I did not get a girl pregnant before marriage; I got married (and remained so for 14 years), and have children (one biological, two adopted and two with a lesbian couple and my same-gender partner). Unfortunately, you transitioned before I married, but I did marry someone you met and really liked. I do wish you had been able to meet your five grandchildren, nine great-grandchildren and three great-great-grandchildren, and that is just from one of your ten children.

I continued experiencing sexual intimacy with women and men during my seven years in the U.S. Marine Corps (four years enlisted; three years active reserves) and four years of undergraduate university studies (I was president of my junior and senior class as well as the Student Government Association). I married in my junior year of college pretty much because we were following the lead of my best friend who married. Peer influence can be powerful and for years the four of us had done practically everything together. In college, my best friend and I became sexually intimate and lovers, but we never talked about our feelings or same-gender-loving passion. We dated girls at the college but had our "serious" girlfriends at home whom we eventually married. We became godparents to each other's children. We are still good friends but our lives have taken a very different path—especially in politics where our views are on opposite ends of the spectrum.

Although I had had several fleeting affairs with men and women prior to college and the Marine Corps, none felt meaningful until my fourth year in the Marine Corps when I met the woman who was to become my wife. I had a pattern of dating women for an extended period while having an affair with a guy just once, or at most, off and on. In my teens and early twenties I did not consider my sexual encounters with men to be serious, while with women I was always inwardly questioning, "Is this the woman I want to settle down with; is this the woman I want to have children with; is this the woman I want to introduce to my family?" It was in college that I really fell in love with a man, the first man for whom my feelings went beyond sexual passion, the first man I wanted to be with on a regular basis. One of my childhood girlfriends (you did not care for her) attended the same college and we resumed dating after having been apart for several years while I was in the Marine Corps. Turned out we were using one another as a front; however, that façade fell apart when she was expelled after being caught having sex with another woman in her dormitory. I lost track of her for years until we reconnected on Facebook and confessed our bisexuality to each other.

For many years, Dad, in many ways my lifestyle was looking very much like yours—I was married with three children and I had a male companion who I loved very much (very much like your relationship with "Uncle"). However, our careers took us on very different geographic paths—the man I loved and his family went further north in pursuit of career opportunities; I went west with my family in pursuit of career opportunities.

It was in Minneapolis, while on a new job and waiting for my wife and children to join me at the end of the children's school year that I began to explore and cruise the underground gay male culture. I had never been to a gay club or seen female impersonators. I had never been to an adult bookstore or seen magazines depicting men with men and women with women. I had never been to a bathhouse or seen men parading around with nothing on but a towel (if that). I had never experienced a gay nude beach where women paired off with women, men paired off with men, and men and women paired off with each other. I had six months in a city where no one knew me to explore these new adventures. I met a man who was not closeted or on the down-low about being gay. I spent all of my free time with him until my family relocated to Minneapolis.

I tried very hard to wean myself from this new male lover when my family arrived, but to no avail. So I tried to follow the path you had taken, Dad, by introducing my male lover to my family. "It had worked for you; why would it not work for me?" I thought. Turns out that he had fallen as deeply in love with me as I had with him, but he was not willing to be closeted about his being gay, and I was having a difficult time acknowledging that I was in love with a man. So he took the noble path, severed the relationship, and took a job in Key West; he said he did not want to destroy my marriage and that he needed to move as far away from me as possible so that he could "get on with his life." I was devastated, depressed and for weeks not a nice person to live with. Finally, one night after an exhausting discussion to get to the cause of my moodiness, my wife confronted me and flat-out asked, "Are you in love with him?" There was a prolonged uncomfortable silence. In my head I was thinking, "Should I lie and deny that I love him? If I confess that I do love and miss him, will she leave me?" She very patiently waited. I finally said, "Yes, I love him and miss him." Tears flowed from both of us as we embraced and comforted each other before she asked, "Do you still love me?" This time I answered without hesitation, "Yes!" We agreed to keep talking and to try to work it out.

The expectation for both of us was that I would stop having sex with men. For a while I did, but the desire was still within me. Another career opportunity presented itself, this time in California. Now how does a bisexual or gay man live in California and not encounter opportunities to be sexually intimate on some level with other men? It really was "raining men" in the San Francisco Bay Area and I was in hog heaven. I became active with a gay fathers' group in which a few men declared themselves to be bisexual. There were several political organizations that presented their views as being for gays and lesbians, but I do not recall the mention of bisexuals. Of course there were bisexuals in the various organizations, but we were often quiet about our attraction to men and women; in fact, if we were bold enough to openly declare our bisexuality, we would be subjected to ridicule and accused of "sleeping with the enemy." At this time the only woman I was sexually intimate with was my wife; however, I could connect with a man for a quickie anywhere and anytime. I worked hard at being a good husband and father, but finding a bisexual mentor or role model was difficult to impossible—especially for a Black man of African and West Indian descent.

However, miracles do happen and I found a role model in the form of an African-American Episcopal priest who had been married for many years, open about his bisexuality to his wife and active in several progressive political and social organizations within the LGBT community as well as the African-American community. He was also a member of the same Greek fraternity I had pledged. One obstacle in the way of my being comfortable about my sexual attraction to men was the hell-and-damnation messages I had heard so often from ministers and religious zealots during my childhood. The Episcopal priest gave me a copy of Reverend Troy Perry's book, *The Lord Is My Shepherd and He Knows I'm Gay*. Just the title was an eye opener. Once I got it in my head that God loves me just as I am, I stopped being concerned about what others thought about me.

Another career opportunity (this time for my wife) brought us back to the East Coast where we settled in a progressive community in Howard County, Maryland. I worked as a youth counselor for runaway and homeless youth in Washington, D.C., and later opened a counseling agency for persons in non-traditional relationships and families. You would be amazed, Dad, at how many persons are not in what our society defines as a "traditional" or "wholesome" family structure. This agency managed several telephone hotlines and Gay Married Men's Association (GAMMA) was one of them. GAMMA attracted men who defined themselves as gay or bisexual and were in heterosexual marriages. In some cases, the wives knew about their husbands' sexual attractions to men; in other cases, the men had not yet revealed their sexual desire for male intimacy. It was through GAMMA that I met my current partner of 35 years when he called inquiring if the men of GAMMA were married to men or to women. This was in the early seventies, so he was ahead of this year's ruling by the Supreme Court that the federal ban on same-sex marriage is unconstitutional. Eventually my partner and I did meet face-to-face at a GAMMA meeting, but both of us were in the arms of other men. Good fortune eventually brought us together several months later in 1978 to put together a series of workshops for a retreat.

My wife and I remained married for fourteen years, seven of which I was also in a relationship with my male partner. While my wife and I never discussed the fact that our marriage had become poly and non-monogamous, the behavior of both of us dictated otherwise. Eventually she met someone who was more settled than I was ready to be at that time, and she filed for an amicable divorce—no drama and open visitation with our three children. I was a little sad but not devastated. We are still very good friends, attend family events and call upon each other from time-to-time for advice (especially pertaining to the kids).

My male partner and I are talking about getting married. While marrying a person in an SGL relationship was not even on the radar during your lifetime, Dad, now SGL couples can legally marry in 17 states and the District of Columbia (where my SGL partner and I live). Attitudes regarding SGL couples are changing rapidly worldwide and remind me of the 1967 Supreme Court's ruling that state miscegenation laws were unconstitutional. There are also federal and state laws that prohibit discrimination in housing, employment, public accommodations, schools and universities; laws to protect individuals from discrimination based on race, ethnicity, sex, national origin and religion. Unfortunately, in many states there are no laws to protect persons who are sexual minorities. As in the past with race, one who self-identifies as a sexual minority (or is perceived to be one) can be denied housing, employment and admission to a university and can be excommunicated from a religious faith. But times they are a-changing! Just as you were on the front lines to end Jim Crow laws by marching, sitting at lunch counters, going to jail and getting beaten, I have followed your lead and tried to stand up for freedom and justice wherever it is being denied. Our greatest moment together was the 1963 March on Washington for Jobs and Freedom. Neither of us had a clue that 1963 would also be the year of your transition.

The Aries in me drives me to keep fighting for progressive social and political changes. Where there is no organization, leadership or clear direction, I am known to step in and make things happen, very much like you did as a civil rights activist, community organizer and someone not afraid to speak up for social justice—even when the KKK burned a cross on our front lawn. That was the scariest night of my life. I have not had to endure the battles and danger you endured, and thankfully my children and their children will not have to endure the injustices of my generation.

If you are looking down upon us (and I believe you are), you know that we have an African American as a two-term President of the United States, 43 African Americans in the House of Representatives and one Senator and one on the Supreme Court (whom I am sure you would rather not be there). Progress has also been made for those of us who identify as sexual minorities. However, there is still an incredible amount of stigma for those of us who identify as bisexual. Your spirit is always with me, and I find myself often asking, "What would Dad do in this situation?" I think you would tell me to step forward and be visible, to organize and speak out and to mentor the youth who will carry the bi pride banners as we continue to stand up for LGBT equality on all fronts.

Your loving bisexual son,

ABilly

A bisexual in a same-gender-loving relationship for 35 years, ABilly S. Jones is a founding member of Gay Married Men's Association and Gay Fathers in Washington, D.C., and the National Coalition of Black Lesbians and Gays. A former co-chair of National Association of Black and White Men Together, he is currently a board member of SAGE (Services and Advocacy for GLBT Elders) of Metro D.C., serves on the advisory board of D.C.'s Rainbow History Project and is a member of the Bisexual Leadership Roundtable and AMBI (the Alliance of Multicultural Bisexuals).

by anonymous

i am

I am a Child, like everyone else. My hair is the messy hair of a little boy. I run to recess and stroll back to class when the bells ring. I study hard, or just hard enough. I get nervous about tests and I am thrilled by the last day of school. I am also the kid who doesn't play sports. I'm the one who pulls the pigtails out of a misunderstood feeling of jealousy. I feel myself growing differently, and I feel quite alone.

I am a Teenager. I find my own friends and my parents don't always like my choices. I study harder, look to college and freedom. I feel those new feelings for him as well as for her. I think I am gay. I swear I am straight. I find new friends to match my changing sexual temperatures. I am bold, I am shy, I am a social being, and I am a hermit. My confusion hides in plain sight, the irrational whims of a teen hiding my experiments and excitements. And when I get closer and closer to who I think I am, it is met with the dismissal of peers and the condescension of parents.

I am a Veteran. I run away to the Marines to escape who I really am, only to truly find myself. I serve proudly, standing side by side with equals. I talk of dark green, light green, women Marines. Race and gender blended in that understanding that we are all Marines, and we serve with honor. Hard work, long hours, first true homesickness, and many trials and tribulations forge our patriotism and friendships. And then they ask. And I tell. A slice through my heart when I think of leaving after only four years. But in the end I am proud of standing up and proud of being myself, regardless of consequences. But I will always have the dreams that wake me in the night only to realize I'm no longer in uniform. That the best and hardest work I did is taken from me for finally saying, "I am bisexual."

I am your Husband. I buy you the perfect Valentine's Day gift one year, and a not-so-perfect one another year. I celebrate our anniversary in a nice restaurant with you, awkwardly handing you the card and gift bag over the table. I kiss you every morning and every evening. We make love—more before and less now. I settle into you on the couch and we grow old together. I can see nothing but our future, finding new aches and pains together, and it thrills me. You understand my story, you hear every last word and yet you love me. You understand that sometimes I feel the need to go out, and sometimes I need to stay in. And when I say I want to come out, it is the shame in your face that makes me sad. That you would be uncomfortable with the questions of others, their suspicion and confusion. Our love will survive the bump, but it feels like a betrayal. But I will give you that silence just as you give me your personal acceptance.

I am your Father. I put the Band-Aid on your cut after kissing away the salt of your tears. I hold the back of the bike and see you fly away from me. I dance with you when you are a tiny little girl, and know it will be moments before I give you away at your wedding. I explain the birds and the bees to you as a young man, both of us uncomfortable but working together to understand one another. You are my little princess. You are my little man. I hope for everything for you, and for nothing I experienced. But I know that when it comes time for you to state who you are, I will be there with you. And if you tell me you're gay, you're straight or you're bisexual, you may ask about me. And I will hold you and say, "I am." Or I will hide and let you find yourself during those confusing years without thinking about what your father did before you. And you will find it hard to understand why I defend "the gays," since it seems very apparent I'm not one of them.

I am your Neighbor. I attend the barbeques, the block parties, the neighborhood watch meetings. I attend the funerals of the older residents when they pass away. When the siren stops close to our block late at night, I am on the front lawn with everyone else hoping for a glimpse of excitement, hoping nobody is hurt. I look with jealousy at the lesbian couple down our block. They're accepted as another family in the area, congratulated and celebrated during Pride week. They are something solid, and I am not.

All of these things make me who I am, force me to be someone I feel I'm not and allow me to feel as if I don't belong. But no matter what, for better or for worse, I am who I am. I am bisexual.

"Anonymous" is a seemingly normal father, husband, neighbor, friend and co-worker, just another one of the many invisible bisexuals hiding in the conventional world.

by rodney mcgruder brown

say it loud, i'm a black bisexual male and i'm proud

Being born a Black male in America automatically puts me in the category of a stigmatized minority; add bisexuality and you have one of the most disenfranchised, underrepresented demographics in our country. There is a huge burden that comes with these intersectional identities. First, there's understanding and accepting what it means to be Black in America. Historically, Blacks have been second-class citizens who sacrificed their lives and freedom for inalienable rights bestowed upon them by the American Constitution. Their struggle for equality has been met with raging opposition including negative stereotypes of Blacks as lazy, dumb and worthless. Now add male to that description. Black males in America have been portrayed in popular culture as hyper-masculine and overly sexual. Add bisexuality into the mix and now we have a dumb, lazy, over-sexualized, indecisive, hyper-masculine individual.

Living in a heteronormative society that embraces hegemonic masculinity takes courage because most, if not all, aspects of society are developed in contrast to the identity of Black Bisexual Males (BBM). For instance, the Church is supposed to be a place of refuge, love and acceptance but instead it has become a breeding ground for hatred and intolerance. Specifically for me, the Black Church offered no sanctum, no positive foundation for a male who identified as bisexual. Being bisexual challenges several religious expectations such as monogamy, the role of a man and sexual, physical and emotional attraction. It should be noted historically that the Bible approved of practicing polygamy but this was within the context of a heterosexual relationship. Even the American government offers no legislative support or initiative for BBM even though this demographic is affected by the HIV/AIDS epidemic at a disproportionate rate. There should be an initiative by government-funded agencies such as medical facilities that promote positive sexual behavior and identity. The education system also fails to meet the needs of BBM in the area of sex education. If the state has a sex education course it is dedicated to a superficial understanding of heterosexual sex, limited to vaginal and oral intercourse. Without support from society at large, creating a positive identity is a journey. And yet, this journey is imperative to one's happiness and well-being.

Coming out as a BBM is one of the most important things that I have ever done in my life. My process of coming out of the closet began when I was about 13 and I realized that my attraction to guys was the same as my attraction to girls. This attraction included emotional and sexual attraction. I even began to fantasize about having committed relationships with males just as I did with women. In the years preceding this realization of attraction, I always made excuses about my physical and emotional responses to other males, interpreting them as extreme admiration, but never admitting to a genuine attraction. Puberty opened up a different way to express my sexuality. I had been physical with girls, kissing and touching in a very sexual manner, but this was never the case with guys. The closest I had come to being physically intimate with a guy during middle school or my early high school years was limited to homoerotic activity in the boys' locker room. I was taught that simply being attracted to another male was enough to send me to Hell for an eternity. The realization of my attraction to men led me to resort to suppressing my feelings and urges. As a result, I became ashamed and demonized my identity. I hated who I was becoming. Confusion in my mind came as a result of being taught that sexuality is black and white, gay or straight. I began to ask myself whether I was attracted to men or women. I did not want to identify as straight and I did not want to identify as gay. I had trouble with identifying as gay because I was still very much attracted to women.

One day in high school I was on the school bus and I overheard two girls discussing the dating habits of a classmate. One of the girls yelled, "He's bisexual?!" In my mind something clicked and I came out to myself as bisexual. I was familiar with the term, but had only heard it used in a condescending manner. I believe at this moment being bisexual finally resonated with me because I realized that I was not alone. I felt there were other guys just like me who had an attraction for guys and girls. After that moment there was an exponential amount of clarity, something that I had never felt before. Internally I began to ask myself a different question: "How am I going to deal with being attracted to both men and women?" The answer to that question was to eliminate the hatred and shame that I had internalized from external forces. I realized that my thoughts about myself and my sexuality were not my own. I had learned my attraction to men was wrong. I had learned there was no such thing as bisexuality. I had learned that no woman would love me if I disclosed my sexuality to her. As soon as I eliminated the biphobic ideas that I had learned and internalized I was able to hear my voice. I was in a space where I began to listen to my heart.

I began the next phase of my coming-out journey by coming out to family and friends. This transition happened my senior year of high school. That same year, I was outed to my mom by a friend. After that moment I felt betrayed and paranoid; I thought every person I knew had somehow found out about my sexuality and was judging me. In the fall of 2008, I attended Jackson State University in Mississippi. JSU was a great institution but for me it was not an environment where I felt safe to come out as bisexual. There was no space in which I could flourish and nurture my identity. There was a subculture of openly gay males but they embraced being effeminate, which as a form of expression is not me. There was another group of males who embraced what is known as "down-low culture." This did not encompass who I wanted to be, either. I wanted an environment that would embrace and challenge my identity, so I transferred colleges.

I enrolled at Westminster College in Fulton, Missouri. It was a small liberal arts college that embraced diversity of all kinds. Westminster offered me another chance to introduce myself. I soon found a group of friends who were open to an array of lifestyles. It was a place where I had a forum for dialectic exchanges and debates. I nurtured my voice and gained strength because I was being challenged on all fronts. These exchanges could take place anywhere from the confines of a dorm room to my pointing out hypocrisy at a fraternity. A situation that comes to mind took place in a room full of straight guys in a fraternity house who questioned me about "flaunting my sexuality." It was Halloween and I decided to go as Sexy Malcolm X. A member of the house accused me of flaunting even though 15 feet away on the dance floor a guy and a girl were making out. I viewed moments like this as an opportunity to affirm my identity and to educate others.

My sexuality is something that is not completely obvious. It is something that I could hide and keep a secret. The same cannot be said for my race. When I walk into a room the first thing most people will notice is that I'm a Black male. Being educated in institutions that were not predominantly Black proved to be a challenge. Oftentimes I was in situations in which I was the only Black guy, and in situations when I was not the only Black guy, I did not fit the stereotypes or ideas that people have about Black guys. Just as with my sexuality, my race was being attacked because once again I did not fit into a box that society had built for me. My race came into question because I was not the stereotypical pants-sagging, gun-toting, unapproachable guy that our culture has unfairly labeled Black males to be. I'm very intelligent, articulate, well-dressed and college-educated. I found myself having to defend my Blackness to Blacks as well as to people from other racial backgrounds. My heroes and role models were not limited to to Black entertainers in sports or the music industry. I have a deeper connection with my racial history. I admired people such as James Baldwin, Bayard Rustin and

W.E.B. Dubois. These were the men that I wanted to become. And since most people are not familiar enough with Black culture outside of the realm of entertainment and pop culture, I was always seen as somewhat of an outsider.

The image of the Black male in America has been a peculiar one. The stereotypes that have been assigned to Black men have evolved. The later portion of the 1930s and 1940s saw the development of Sambo used as a slur. Sambo was an ignorant, jolly and docile creature who represented White America's perception of Black men. Characteristics such as hyper-masculinity, over-sexualization and violence have always been a part of America's view of Black males and have been used historically as fear-mongering tactics. Currently this image is glamorized. This combination of traits and ideas proved disastrous because it symbolized, in White America's view and in the view of some Blacks, what it means to be a Black male in America. This characterization is problematic because it is not an accurate portrayal of Black men. Black men are viewed by the dominant culture from a monolithic perspective. When people encounter a dimension of Black culture that doesn't fit with familiar images they often dismiss the Blackness of the subject. In the words of Henry Louis Gates, " . . . if there are 40 million Black Americans, then there are 40 million ways to be Black."[1] Blacks face a unique challenge because the dominant culture doesn't value Black culture or view it in a positive manner, but any attempts to redefine Blackness or exemplify traits that do not correlate with societal expectations of Blackness are met with resistence. These attempts at confining Black culture happen from outside as well as within Black culture.

It was through silencing negative distractions that I was able to hear my voice, a voice that knew bisexuality was not a conflict between my attraction to men and women but rather a realization of the beauty in both sexes. By defining what being Black meant to me I was becoming the man that I wanted to become. I was letting go of a dangerous trend of letting people define me. Once I began to seek self-affirming experiences, I no longer needed society's permission to be myself.

Who am I? I am Rodney McGruder Brown. I am a proud Black Bisexual Man.

1 Touré, Who's Afraid Of Post- Blackness: What It Means To Be Black Now. New York: Free Press, 2011, p. 5

Rodney McGruder Brown's lifelong goal is to create a space for ethnic minority males who identify as gay, bi or as MSM (men who have sex with men). He wants this to be a creative space that encourages their well-being through education and the promotion of positive sexual behavior.

by ben atherton-zeman

me, myself and bi

Fifteen years ago, I met the love of my life, Lucinda Atherton. Then, as now, I was a spokesperson for the National Organization for Men Against Sexism, an organization that is pro-feminist, gay-affirming and anti-racist. Then, as now, I worked to stop men's violence against women, drawing the connections between homophobia and sexism. A proponent of marriage equality, I had a crisis of conscience when I realized I wanted to marry Lucinda. My internal monologue at the time may have sounded something like this:

Me: Why are you getting married? You're a feminist—you know traditional marriage was the transfer of ownership of a woman from the father to the husband! Participating in this institution buys into historical sexism, and thus supports it.

Myself: That is the historical root of marriage, but both the meaning of marriage and the ceremony have evolved. Marriage is an evolving institution, and there are feminist weddings performed by feminist ministers. Plus, I really love Lucinda and I want to spend my life with her.

Me: Then call yourselves "partners" like all the other feminists do! Have a commitment ceremony, not a wedding!

Myself: It won't mean as much if it's not a wedding. Lucinda really wants a wedding, and her family wouldn't understand a commitment ceremony.

Me: Oh, so you're saying commitment ceremonies don't mean anything? How nice for you that you have the privilege of even having this choice. You both have friends in same-sex relationships that don't have the option to marry. And you have hetero friends who are refusing to marry until the law changes. Why not stay true to your politics and choose that option?

Myself: I know, and I respect that. I even felt that way myself for most of my life.

Me: Then you are being hypocritical by choosing this privileged option. Because you happened to fall in love with a woman, you have access to this option that many do not.

Myself: I really am in love with Lucinda! I want to get married. I promise to work hard until marriage equality is the law. I have a feeling it's going to happen soon in my home state of Massachusetts.

Me: Okay, fine. Go ahead. Bask in the glow of power and privilege. Congratulations to the happy couple.

Myself: Um. . . . thanks. I guess.

Me: At least, if you're going to get married, use it to help dismantle homophobia and heterosexism. Instead of "just another bisexual guy," you can now present yourself as a fantastic Married Heterosexual Ally!

Myself: Uh. . . .

Me: You've been working for marriage equality! You know that married hetero allies get more airtime and are taken more seriously. Oh, this is perfect! I've changed my mind. Get married! Be the new poster child for Married Heterosexual Allies for Marriage Equality!

Myself: Um . . .

Me: Let's see—we could start an organization. MHAME—isn't that a great acronym! Hmm. . . . I've got it! How about SHARE Marriage? Straight Heterosexual Allies Respecting Equal Marriage. Okay, for our first press conference, let's invite—

Myself: I'm not heterosexual.

Me: Oh, come on! Technically, you're not. But you're not going to have sex with anyone but Lucinda again. Ever.

Myself: That doesn't mean I'm heterosexual. I'm bi.

Me: You're splitting hairs! How many guys have you had sex with?

Myself: You know it's only one. Well, unless you count. . . . Okay, maybe three.

Me: So why not change your label? It'd do so much good for marriage equality.

Myself: Because it feels wrong. Even having a conversation where I'm thinking of saying, "I'm heterosexual," feels wrong in the pit of my stomach. I feel like I'm lying.

Me: Oh.

Myself: Remember when my friend heard about my getting married, and said, "I'm glad you've stopped pretending you're bisexual?"

Me: Yeah, that was pretty biphobic.

Myself: I can still work for marriage equality, and I will.

Me: Sigh. . . . It would have been such a great group. SHARE Marriage—

Myself: Too bad that real life is sometimes more nuanced—

Me: —than a bumper sticker.

Myself: I guess sometimes, when the question is asked—

Me: —and the answer is "I'm bisexual—"

Myself: —it's not the end of the conversation.

Me: It's the beginning.

Ben Atherton-Zeman is a spokesperson for the National Organization for Men Against Sexism (www.nomas.org). He uses humor as a tool for violence prevention, and performs a one-man play internationally (www.voicesofmen.org). Ben lives with his amazing wife Lucinda in Maynard, Massachusetts. They have no children except for themselves.

unconventional

by joshua turner

This is the story of the two conflicting forces of my sexuality and my romantic ideals. For some it may not be hard to fall in love, but for me at least, love is something I would dislike either falling into or living without; I'd rather take the approach of finding someone functionally compatible and then working to see if there is an emotional and trustworthy basis to the person.

First I should share a couple things about myself. I am an African-American male who identifies with the masculine pronouns, and if I were to place myself within the grand scheme of the LGBTQ continuum, I am simply a bisexual bear. In my down time I enjoy exercise, a good book, the Good Book (yeah, I am fairly religious), poetry, quoting famous people, and all things that have to do with people in the social sphere (because I'm a Sociology major). That's all I shall share for now because this story isn't only about me, it's about my quest for love.

When I was younger—seven or eight—I knew that I was a little bit different from the other kids in my school because I started having class crushes on not one but two people. There were two people who caught my attention and I knew I had to spend time with them. One was the fiery, snaggle-toothed redhead Natasha, who kind of made me think of Nancy Drew herself with her red hair and inquisitive manner. The other was Andrew; he was a very relaxed boy with a monotonous voice who reminded me of your average Joe without a care in the world. In elementary school the three of us were very close and we spent most of our days coloring and talking about kissing during recess. I remember these two well because they were vital parts in my understanding of the word "unconventional." We were unconventionally married to each other under the big slide—which was a great location for our "wedding"—one warm day at recess.

Looking back, I wish I could go back to that jungle gym and have that as the venue for my actual wedding to show the innocence of love: what better place than a playground? But that wouldn't work out because now I'm six feet eleven. Most people didn't know about our relationship because to them we were just your everyday ragtag group of kids playing childhood games. To me, though, I saw it as my first polyamorous relationship, even though it ended abruptly after about seven months when I moved to the city's east side. I haven't spoken to Natasha and Andrew since because most kids my age still didn't have cell phones.

There were many things in my childhood that I later observed as being out of the status quo; for example, the fact that I lived in a predominantly Caucasian environment and was part of one of the three African-American families in the town. One would think I'd keep to myself. However, I managed to be best friends with a Caucasian female and a Hispanic male. To this day I'm still colorblind when it comes to dating.

You're probably wondering why I would want to share such a simple story about my first crushes and the sad truth of my first marriage's demise. I found myself conflicted about the idea of deciding between Andrew and Natasha. This conflict could only be solved by my dating multiple people at once instead of choosing one or the other. Polyamory was something that I had understood from a fairly young age, but I never wished to identify as poly. As I got older, I fought the feeling of wanting to be with a male and a female at the same time, not because I thought poorly of the community that "loves many," but because to me it was "unconventional." This word haunted me and restricted me from trying many things that I knew I wanted to try.

By the time I was in college—around 19 years old—I decided I was going to explore polyamory, and I did. It started with my asking out a male friend I had met at a small-town bar nearby. As time went on, the numbers would fluctuate between my dating two guys and one girl and one guy and two girls. At other times I'd be dating only males and other times it was only females. It was beautiful to accept the love of another human being, but it was euphoric to have the hearts of more than one. As long as I remained in a relationship with at least one female and one male, I felt that I hadn't been able to reach the end result of having a soul mate within one person with whom I could share my secrets, passions, sadness and love. Needless to say, my relationships didn't last long. I attribute the downfalls to the fact that I didn't feel true intimacy with numerous people at once. I should have known it would be difficult to do it with multiple people if I couldn't achieve love with just one person.

After long deliberation I asked myself why it was that I had been seeking something as convenient as the Natasha/Andrew mash-up. I knew after some thinking that monogamy was what I wanted, but the bisexual identifier that I correlated with was, in my mind, the conventional idea that a perfect bisexual will always want to be with a man when with a woman, and vice versa.

This perception of what it meant to be bisexual made me feel as if I had to prove my bisexuality to others by always having both, even though my feelings shifted between my wanting one or the other. The logic behind that was that if I wanted to be known as a bisexual, I thought that I would have to want to be in a relationship where I had a male and a female at the same time. Stupid, I know, but this was my time of early misconceptions.

As time went on since my initial coming out at age sixteen, I started dating people, but with some restrictions. I wouldn't date someone who was shorter than five foot ten, and I wouldn't date a feminine male or a masculine female. The lines were very clear-cut. The problem with dating with restrictions was that I tended to not be interested in the people I found. So I told myself that I would search for someone to date who sparked my interest, not for the physical or superficial things they put on the table. I was on a search for a female who had a sense of humor and a good head on her shoulders. My ideal male would be the same. I don't always go by these guidelines, but most times things turn out well.

Of course after meeting a suitable candidate for my heart, the person had to meet my family. Every time I met someone new, I would come home with a person of a different race. To my mother's surprise, I managed to date African-Americans, Caucasians, Hispanics, people of Mediterranean ancestry, and many other cultural backgrounds. She felt that all I needed in my life was "a strong Black woman," but when I introduced her to Xavier, my multiracial boyfriend, the family dinner conversations became much more interesting because he wasn't female, nor was he Black.

My mother told me she just needed time to adjust to my "new lifestyle." My mother is a kind woman who is very involved with the Church. She had many religious conflicts when I came out because of the Southern Baptist belief that if you aren't straight, you're a sinner. Growing up knowing this information made coming out larger than an act against my parents; it was now an act against God. When I came out to my mother, I followed it with the fact that I identified as a Buddhist as well, so she was even more confused and even hurt. Daily, she would question why I had decided to go the route of Buddhist instead of Baptist, and I would say that it felt like I could be at peace with myself instead of fighting a battle that got me nowhere. When all of this information was being put on her shoulders, she initially looked at it all as a burden; luckily, with time and some heavy conversation, she has come to feel that as long as I am happy and safe, she will support me. It's nice that she came around; it makes loving her a bit easier.

Taking a more laissez-faire approach to my relationships will hopefully allow me to find my diamond in the rough. This change was good for me because I was no longer looking for the perfect person that I had in my head. I met many people and landed a total of 28 broken hearts, one of them always being mine. I haven't managed to figure out whether or not the love of my life is out there, but I will continue searching for him or her and meeting as many people as I can, and hopefully, whomever he/she may be, I will love that person because we're compatible and willing to make it work. I think I could qualify as a good catch. I'm a nice guy; I am Joshua Turner. And at times I am described as unconventional, but I don't mind being unconventional because . . . well . . . that's just me.

Joshua Turner is a third-year student at Hiram College with a focus in Sociology and Gender Studies. He is President of the student group, Presence and Respect for Youth and Sexual Minorities (PRYSM) and he attends peace rallies and marriage equality events. He hopes to do graduate work in the field of Social Sexology and to stay active in the LGBT community.

genderfuzz, or, how i learned to stop worrying and love bisexuality

by ron j. suresha

Growing up in the 1970s in a northwest suburb of Detroit, Michigan, I became aware early on that I was different from other boys my age. I felt a much stronger attraction to men than to women, though I regularly enjoyed fantasies of heterosexual acts. The implications of having a homosexual orientation then were bleak, given the stereotype of the doomed queer: gay men were considered deviants and perverts who lived pathetic, solitary lives because they could not express their attractions openly.

A scrawny, artistic, somewhat feminine nerd, I was often a target of homophobic taunts and bullying. But the stigma of my sexual orientation became most clear at age twelve. I came home from school one day to discover a letter from my father to my mother telling her he was leaving her and our family. In his letter he expressed his extreme discomfort with my being gay. It was easy to blame myself for my father's departure.

I struggled through my early teens and, with the guidance of a friend several years older, I began to explore gay life in Detroit. As I had started growing facial hair quite young, I could pass already for older. At age 15—when Michigan's drinking age was 18—I went to my first gay bar. I connected with a larger community when an older friend took me to several Gay Liberation Front meetings, where I met other gay men who were struggling with their own sexual identities.

In 1975, between my junior and senior years in high school, my friend and I attended the first Detroit gay pride picnic. I was certainly the youngest person attending among the couple dozen men and women at what seemed at first a fun and low-profile event—except for the presence of a local TV news crew. That evening my friend and I—and my mother—watched as footage of a line of men at the picnic aired at the end of the local evening news program. I was among them.

Apparently plenty of my classmates and teachers saw it too. School days became hellish: I was verbally taunted almost every day and at times physically threatened. I was one of the most unpopular kids in class because I was gay and now everyone knew.

Following a suicide attempt in November of my senior year in high school, I spent six weeks in a rehabilitation hospital, where in therapy I began to learn to tame the shame of being gay. My classmates were kinder when I returned to school, but because I had been in a hospital I felt even more stigmatized.

One day, soon after my return to high school, I was hanging out with three of the nerdiest kids at my school outside the school library. As we chatted, we all came out to each other as gay or bisexual or lesbian, and so we formed a core support group. Having a handful of pals who helped each other out as we struggled to navigate school and family, and sometimes love and lust and coming out—perhaps with just a gay joke or a bit of gossip—made all the difference to me. I learned the importance of queer community early in life.

Since puberty, I entertained occasional masturbatory fantasies about sex with both women and men. Sometimes I felt confused or guilty about these private erotic desires, thinking that a man should be either straight or gay, so I kept those feelings to myself. In high school and in college I had a few limited experiences with women. Though I knew my primary attraction was to men, I rejected the misogyny and vaginaphobia expressed by so many gay men. I never really understood why being gay meant that you had to hold your nose and make nasty jokes about fish anytime desire for women came up in conversation.

Despite my understanding that sexuality is a spectrum—a line strung with billions of points—I was not ready to out myself as bisexual, because I knew that biphobia in the gay community—even among more mature men such as bears—was often senselessly vicious.

In my early twenties I experienced a spiritual breakthrough that led to a shift toward asexuality. Several years earlier, my mom had been killed unexpectedly in a car accident, and I'd quit college to settle her estate and recover emotionally. Now living in a Western yoga ashram, I voluntarily observed a non-masturbatory celibacy for two years.

For eight more years after that I had limited sexual contact of any sort. Since romantic relationships with both men and women baffled me and I couldn't understand why anyone would want to have sex with me, I wouldn't let anyone get close. During this time, I developed nomadic habits and moved an average of twice a year. Like most gay men I knew personally, I continued to struggle with finding acceptance and a vocabulary with which I could positively describe my personal expression of gender and sexuality.

Once the subject of sex was removed from my daily life, I saw how powerfully my desire for sexual contact had driven my interactions with others. When I stopped relating to people based on their potential to fulfill a passing sexual desire, I developed a sense of humanity and equanimity that allowed me to see the essential androgynous divinity in everyone regardless of their gender or sexuality label. At times during meditation I experienced myself transcending all physical limitations and egoistic personality traits, including my maleness and masculinity. This spiritual worldview became my foundation for a new understanding of bisexuality and gender equality.

Eventually, the power of my sexual desire proved too attractive a force for me to ignore or resist. I left the ashram in 1986 and moved to San Francisco where I lived until 1993, making dozens of friends and sex partners, then losing them to AIDS in the midst of that awful onslaught of disease and death. My period of asexuality had the effect of protecting me as it effectively eliminated my risk of exposure to sexually transmitted infections.

Yet amidst all this sickness and death, something creative, sex-positive and life-affirming was awakening in the local queer culture. Two friends of mine, Richard Bulger and Chris Nelson, started a photocopied 'zine that focused on the kind of men to whom I'd always found myself most attracted: older, hairy, bearded, bulky and mature. They called their publication *Bear* magazine, with the tagline "Masculinity – without the trappings." My personal involvement with the original *Bear* magazine—and with Chris, who became my lover, and Richard, who became a friend—established the basis for my involvement in the bear community, even after I left California to move back east.

Once in Boston, I put together my first book, *Bears on Bears* (2002) in which bear-identified men explore many aspects of the worldwide bear subculture, including queer masculinity, coming out and self-image issues.

My interviews in bear communities revealed that one might come out more than once in one's life. So by the time the possibility of coming out again—this time into bisexuality—loomed large in my own life, it was much easier to find the inner strength and self-acceptance that the process required.

But the topic of bisexual bears did not make it into the anthology. This was not because I didn't find bisexual bears of great interest; rather, it had not been apparent to me how many of my bear friends were bisexual. After an interview with local bear and bi activist Pete Chvany, it became clear that not only was there a lack of information about bisexual bears, there was virtually nothing published about bisexual men in general. Research quickly revealed that most of the published writing about bisexuality—academic as well as popular—was written by, for and about women.

With support from pioneering bi activist Dr. Fritz Klein, Pete and I collected three dozen highly personal essays in a 2008 book, *Bi Men*:

Coming Out. That collection and a companion anthology of erotica I edited, *Bi Guys*, were named Lambda Literary Award finalists.

In my own essay for *Bi Men*, I detailed the personal evolution of coming to terms with my bisexuality. For years I had had many short-lived sexual encounters and romantic relationships with bi men, and I had basically stereotyped them as married men who cheat on their wives with other men. Yet I knew my own story was quite different and as I started to read about the lives of other bi men in their own words it became clear that this was an irrational prejudice that I had held for too long, and one that most people I'd encountered—gay and straight—seemed to hold as well.

In my forties, along with several other midlife crises (it might be fairer to call them midlife developments), I finally came out as bisexual. This life passage eventually proved much more provocative and positive than my first arduous teenage process of self-discovery as gay, but just as much a rollercoaster.

Within a two-year period I experienced the death of my father, sold my house, moved three times, lived in four different cities, published my first two books, underwent cancer surgery and radiation treatment (entirely effective, knock on wood) and met and fell in love with my husband. It is hard for me now, even ten years later, to separate coming out as a bisexual man from the numerous challenges facing me at that time.

I experienced shifts in perception of how my body functions and relates intimately to others. My experience with cancer changed the way I looked at my mortal body. I felt I no longer had the luxury of time to deny *any* aspect of my sexuality, including my occasional but very strong feelings toward women. I realized that many of my favorite erotic fantasies involved active sex with both men and women, and I stopped feeling guilty about having them. As I moved past cancer into healing, I affirmed my bisexual potential.

In October 2003, 12 days after surgery and two weeks before I started radiation, I attended a queer literary conference in Provincetown, Massachusetts where I met Rocco, a family physician who writes poetry. He came into my life during a period of crisis and offered his devoted care, unselfish support and his love. To this day, I'm grateful for such a blessing.

Though I feared Rocco would respond negatively to my bisexuality when I came out to him, he completely affirmed, embraced and supported my identity. Although I've experienced many curious and dubious reactions when I've mentioned my bisexuality, every person in my life *who matters* has validated me. What ultimately matters, though, is how I perceive and bless my own process.

Coming out—whether as gay, lesbian, bi or trans—is a complex process of self-discovery and life-actualization. To declare any manner of non-heterosexuality queers one's world in a truthful, positive way. Some men who—like me—move from gay to bisexual identity are coming out a second (or third) time and expanding the way in which we queer the world. For me, this ongoing process of transformation, in which I continually fuzz or queer my understanding of gender and sexuality, is an undeniable and welcome reality. I sometimes think of my personal journey of sexual transformation as "genderfuzz," perhaps not quite as radical as genderfuck, but a term well-suited for a mature, hirsute ambisexual man whose sexual identity has been blurred over time.

I have found purpose in advancing the rights of bisexual people, and especially in giving voice to bi men, who are arguably the least understood and most stigmatized gender and sexual minority. BGLTIQA is not just alphabet soup; it is a chain that represents millions of lives, linked in myriad ways and only as strong as the weakest link. As queer pundits like Dan Savage have begun to acknowledge, married bisexual men are the ones who most urgently need to hear the call to come out. Bisexual men experience greater misunderstanding and stigma than the general population—more than gay men and even more than bisexual women—and it is my experience that gay men convey much of that prejudice.

An additional aspect of my identity has shifted as well: over time I've considered myself not so much as gay or bear or queer but as wolf, an animal with which I have identified for many years. According to my research, wolf was considered a twentieth-century gay slang term for sexually available bisexual males (think: "wolf whistle"), sometimes referring to bisexual females. Wolf is not as well-recognized in the same way that bear later came to refer to a certain type of sex-positive, masculine, mature male, but for me it fits.

Although it may be that closeted bi married men in primary relationships with women are the most important bi-identified subpopulation to be identified and convinced to come out, gay men coming out as bi are also a significantly underrepresented population. We must develop unique outreach approaches and make special efforts to educate and recruit leadership from each of these communities of bisexual men.

I would not have predicted that coming out multiple times as gay, asexual, wolf/bear and bi would be part of my life's journey, but perhaps my journey is no more unusual than that of many others. At this point

I am unwilling to accept the notion that my sexuality is fixed in any way whatsoever.

Men such as myself coming out (once again) as bisexual are expanding the way in which we queer our world, creating our own unique sexuality, because we can. And why shouldn't there be as many sexualities, as many ways to love, as there are humans, or stars in the sky?

Ron J. Suresha is a three-time Lambda Literary Award finalist for his three anthologies on bisexuality and a former board member of the Bisexual Resource Center of Boston. He participated in the 2013 White House Roundtable on Bisexual Issues and is a member of the editorial board of the Journal of Bisexuality.

why it matters

by gregory lindon smith

You might well ask why it matters. If I am homoromantic and only date men, why do I come out as bisexual? If I never find a female partner, why does my sexual orientation matter at all?

It's certainly not the only thing that matters. It matters that I'm trans. It matters that I have a mental illness. It matters that I have an older brother who makes me think. It matters that my mom is advancing through the stages of Alzheimer's disease. It matters that I take a walk almost every day with my dad. It matters that I write letters to political officials.

I feel the need to come out as bi in all of my groups and relationships. Usually, people say nothing in response. Occasionally, someone will make a remark about people who come out as bi and change their minds (although people can change their minds about any identity). Once, a boss asked me what my position was on monogamy. (She would not have asked this of a gay or straight employee.) But usually the conversation moves on to other things.

Part of what matters is that it took me a long time to accept who I am, and that hard-fought journey is part of what defines me. It's not something I figured out in my ostensible girlhood, although I liked boys and my Barbies were sexually active with each other. I was 27 when I admitted to myself that I was sexually attracted to a woman, 29 when I accepted that I am bisexual and 31 when, after a period of questioning, I realized I am not a woman myself. Now I'm almost 43 and starting to come to terms with the possibility that I might not meet the man of my dreams, even after all the fighting we've done for my right to marry him.

But there's something more than history that tells me that being a bisexual man is an important part of who I am. I have a deep love for truth and a yearning to be known and accepted as the person I really am. The details may require a conversation, but the truth is that I'm bi, and I want people to know it. I want them to know that they know someone like me.

Even though I only have romantic feelings for men, not a day goes by when I don't see in advertisements or encounter at the grocery store both men and women I find attractive. This isn't something I can turn off because I only date men or because I'm alone. It's always there. It's part of who I am.

Some of the people whom I want to know are also bi people. I want them to know there is nothing embarrassing or less than or necessary to hide about who they are. It matters to me that they know they are not alone and that I know I am not alone. At a bisexual meeting, someone suggested that I wouldn't need to meet other bi people if I'm not poly. I disagree. It's essential to know we're not alone.

Today, my bisexual day involves going to breakfast, going to church, writing, sorting, communicating online, listening to the radio and watching TV. None of these things are very sexy, I'm afraid. I wish all of the people who think bisexuality is extreme could know about my day today. I wish they could know how deeply I fall for a man when I fall. I wish they could understand why all of it—questioning and coming out and starting to date again—is worth it after all: because it is liberating to be who we really are. It matters. It matters very much.

Gregory Lindon Smith is a bi trans guy living in Bellingham, Washington. He offers occasional trainings on gender diversity and sexual orientation and is starting monthly potlucks for bisexual and pansexual people, their partners, families and friends.

notes from a unicorn

by seth fischer

I started jerking off when I was nine. I still remember my favorite fantasy. I pictured everyone in my third grade class, standing at their desks. Everyone took off their clothes because they got in trouble for something. It didn't matter what. My imagination zoomed in on some boy or girl. I wouldn't think about sex with them, really. My knowledge of sex at that age came from watching *Looks Who's Talking*. I thought you'd kiss someone and then have a baby. I'd just think of them naked, boys and girls, and maybe I'd think of kissing them, and sometimes I'd think about their butts. I'd touch myself, and it made me feel good.

It wasn't until I'd moved in with my dad up in Boston a couple years later that I let it hit me that anything was different. I was running the mile in gym class, and our teacher brought us over to the high school for that because there wasn't a track at my school. It was 1990 or 1991. My mom wanted me to look cool, but she was from Los Angeles, not Boston, so she had me dressing like some kind of weird White preppy surfer member of the hip hop group N.W.A, with terrible neon green shorts that went down to my knees and a bright orange hyper-color shirt that got brighter as I sweated on it. No one would talk to me, obviously, but I kept pace with two kids who would at least let me run near them.

One of their uncles had just died. "He was totally a fag," said the nephew. The other kid said, "But that's your uncle you're talking about." "Yeah, but he was a fag, and that's what happens to fags, with AIDS, you know?" He wasn't saying it to be cruel to the uncle—there wasn't an ounce of cruelty in his voice, even though he was saying fag. It was just the word he knew. He used the same tone I'd heard him use when he told me the story about going into that one overgrown house where there's supposedly a hunchback inside. And it was then that it hit me, as I was jogging, even though I already knew, really, but I hadn't let myself think about it.

"Fags like boys, so I'm a fag."

When I got home, I ran to one little section of carpet in my room near my desk and my dresser with the trap door I would always write stories on, and I knelt there, and said over and over to myself, "Fags like boys, so I'm a fag," crying and crying, not once thinking about that page from a magazine hidden in my desk, three feet from my head, with the naked women sprawled in impossible positions, the one I'd been beating off to every night for the last week, and not once thinking about the girl I'd kissed on the lips, my first kiss ever, a few weeks before, when my heart went pitter-patter and did all the things hearts are supposed to do during a first kiss, the girl whose heart I later broke because I thought I was a fag. I didn't want to bring her down with me because being a fag was this cancer that would grow inside me and eat up the straight part of me until I'd die of AIDS and never be able to do anything with my life.

A year later, I sat at my desk with a knife, poking at my wrist. I had an impossible crush on a boy. Frank Martin and I were on the same basketball team. His locker was two over from mine, and I couldn't help it—I was twelve or thirteen years old. I had twenty boners a day. When he changed, I kept sneaking peeks because I just wanted to see, because I could smell him, and it was amazing, and was it too much to smell and see?

And he caught me looking. But when he caught me, he wouldn't look right back at me. Instead, he looked at the locker in front of him, and said, quiet enough so no one would hear, "I don't give a fuck if you're gay. I know it's not your fault, but you better not fucking look at me like that ever again."

I decided that day that I would choose to grow the part of me that liked women and kill the part that liked men. I poked at little parts of my wrist until they turned bright red, then I pulled the blade up and watched my skin turn back to its normal color, and then I pressed down again harder. But I couldn't make myself do it hard enough, because I couldn't stand blood, because I was too afraid to die right then. I tried to spell out words with the little red dots but they disappeared too quickly. I tried to spell out "Frank." I tried to spell out "tired." I took out a pack of stolen Kools and snuck outside and smoked cigarette after cigarette after cigarette.

I earned a graduate degree and started a career working for various Democratic politicians during the Bush era, absolutely convinced that if I was going to be able to change anything, the closet was the best place for me to be.

In the years I spent working in politics pretending I wasn't bi, I learned a lot of things, but the most disturbing thing I learned was how to win: What you do is find the simplest possible message that resonates with people—and when I say simple, think, "It's the economy, stupid" or in local races just, "Bob for State Senate"—and then you repeat it *ad nauseam* and get other people to repeat it *ad nauseam* and then ask them to get other people to repeat it until every front lawn and bulletin board and door hanger and public space in the place you care about is filled with your message.

Somehow, in the last half-century, LGBT activists have pulled off one of the biggest public relations coups in history while dealing with one of the most complex issues. It was less than forty years ago that the American Psychological Association agreed to stop saying non-straight people were sick. Today, I work at a school with a program that was created just to train therapists to be sensitive to the needs of LGBT people. Ten years ago, in Lawrence v. Texas, the United States Supreme Court stopped states from prosecuting people for sodomy. Today, 17 states allow same-gender marriage.

Here's the thing I want to tell Human Rights Campaign and Equality California and all the gay rights groups who have done such incredible work, who now have their own buildings in Washington and are thinking in terms of talking points and "ramifications" and focus groups and public polling: The gay rights movement has been so successful because activists like Harvey Milk encouraged people to come out and tell the truth to their families, to their friends, and to their coworkers, to be everything they were, to say "We're here, we're queer," yes, but also, implicitly, to say, "We're here, it's complicated, and probably it'd be good if we talked about this over tea."

Which talking point would you rather use?

Recently, on OkCupid, a woman messaged me: "Are you truly into ladies, and if so, what type? Finding a truly bi man is like finding a unicorn."

If I'm a unicorn where I live now, in Los Angeles, then I was a unicorn Rocky Mountain oyster when, at 25, I moved to the old rustbelt city of Syracuse, New York to escape my political career, go to grad school and live for the first time as a fully out bi man.

There was one other mythical bi man in the entire city, but try as I might, I never found him. At the gay bar, I sometimes got called a "half-breeder." Straight people treated me just as shittily as they treated gay people. Three times gay men hit me in the back of the head when they saw my head turn for a woman. For the most part, straight women wouldn't date me because, as one said, "You're just gonna leave me to go suck a dick." For the first time in my life, frat boys called me fag. My professor said, "The world just isn't ready for gay marriage." I emailed him "Letter from a Birmingham Jail." Then I went out with friends and my gay friends didn't know what to do because I got drunk and flirted with a lesbian. A friend said she thought bi people didn't exist. I said, "I'm sitting right here," because that was my answer, but I was starting to believe her. I stopped telling people what I was. I let people think what they wanted, which was usually that I was like them.

About a year into being there, I thought, "Why don't I just call myself gay?" I would see if I could do it before I told people, I thought. I mean, except for the occasional straight porn, and that one girl, and maybe that other one, I was only dating men. I made it a point. No more straight porn. No more thinking of women. No more dating women.

A few months later, I found myself in bed with a guy. I'd been doing well making up for lost time. No women, no women at all, except for a tiny bit of porn. I was almost ready to just say, "I'm gay. You guys were right. That bi thing was bullshit." I was getting better at the whole blowjob thing. I was tied to the bed because I love being tied to the bed. I couldn't move. I moaned and screamed and made all the right noises, but then it was time, and he started to expect an end because it was getting late—dogs needed to be fed and teeth brushed and homework finished—but I just couldn't come. I just couldn't. He was getting tired and starting to look around but he didn't stop, thank god, because it would have ruined it, because I was right on the edge. Right there. So I did what everyone does but no one admits to their lovers: I closed my eyes and let my mind wander to other people. I thought about men. I was sitting there forcing myself to think about men, only men, men men men men men men, and then it slipped in there, like when someone says don't think about rhubarb pie and you think about rhubarb pie. I thought, for a second, about Willow from *Buffy the Vampire Slayer*, because I'd watched an episode earlier that day. Then I fucking erupted. I came so hard I was worried about getting enough air. I hope Alyson Hannigan doesn't take out a restraining order on me for admitting that, but it's important. Not because I came like that, and not because it's ridiculous, which it totally is, but because I'd tried to make a choice to be straight but it wouldn't work and now I'd tried to be gay and it wouldn't work.

I wanted to join a team so I wouldn't have to answer any more questions, so I wouldn't have to say that I preferred one or the other or whether I exist or if I'm a unicorn or how I can ever hope to be monogamous if I'm attracted to more than one gender. But I failed to choose a side, so now, for once, I'm going to answer all of these questions honestly:

I don't know. I can't speak for other bi people, but only for myself. I just don't know.

I don't know because I can't get all the voices out of my head, the ones that ask all the wrong questions. The ones that tell me I must be one thing or the other—for whom, or why, I don't know. The voices want a neat fit, but I can't accommodate them. I've tried, and I can't, and I shouldn't.

No one will ever make this go away. No one will ever make it simple.

And maybe, just maybe, that's how I win.

Seth Fischer's writing has appeared or is forthcoming in Best Sex Writing 2013, The Rumpus, Pank, Guernica, Gertrude *and elsewhere. He teaches and tutors at Antioch University Los Angeles and Writing Workshops Los Angeles. Find more writing from him at www.seth-fischer.com.*

by josiah harris-adam

for some reason

For some reason
it's OK for me to be bi–
like girls and guys–
while I'm single.
With my lover on my arm they say
"Oh well, I guess that one is straight"
or "I guess that one is gay"
or "I guess that phase is over."

Well guess what?
I fell in love because
My lover is smart
and my lover is kind
and my lover feels lucky to have me
and I don't give a fuck
what's between my lover's legs
just what's behind my lover's eyes

As long as I see understanding there
my lover doesn't care
if I stare
at some movie star's
ass or tits or chest or legs

As long as I see passion there
my lover doesn't care
where my gaze drifts
cause my lover knows
where all my loving goes

As long as I see love there
my lover doesn't care
about nothing but me

And if my lover doesn't care
which labels I wear
and which I choose to lose
Why should you

Josiah Harris-Adam is a musician, poet and counselor working in higher education.

challenging labels

"classic tracks nasty," gymnos alithiea

labels

by ian wilson

Every item in a grocery store has a label. Drug bottles have labels. The ports on the back of your computer have labels. Vending machines, buffets, restrooms, fax machines, underwear: all have labels, often more than one. We humans love labels. It's even a crime for some labels to be removed! And while the information age has seen an explosion in labels, they are certainly not new to humanity. Labeling is an ancient and universal practice. Not all labels are stitched in, nor printed on. Some are virtual, held in tribal knowledge. The force that holds these labels is stronger than any glue.

In a previous life, when I worked for a sound company, I would often have some deep conversations with the company's owner while we were on the road. He was a good guy, a smart guy, with some well-formed and carefully thought out opinions on various heavy topics. But every time I tried to apply a word to him that ended in -ist or -ian or -er, he would bristle and reject it. My attempt to voice a word to validate his position would be taken as labeling, and that to him was a terrible thing. Confining and insulting, he hated labels and hated being labeled even more. When I called him an anti-labelist, he shot me a look that labeled me as an ass.

The thing is, I get this; I really do. Labels can be heavy as well as sticky. Labels are for bottles, bins and bus routes. Humans should be above such material things, right? Labels on humans can imprison and marginalize. People resent being reduced to flat characters.

But like it or not, we need labels. Labels help us sort things out. We need them to communicate and by communicating we can learn, grow, connect and share. Whether we admit it or not, hate it or not, we label ourselves in order to build bridges. But the bricks from which bridges are made can also be used to construct walls.

American, husband, male, man, boy, Christian, Lutheran, son, programmer, geek, photographer, father, ginger, redhead, eccentric, stubborn, introvert: all these describe me. (Pay no attention to the order. My wife would insert a few more; so would my friends.) Who doesn't have such a list? Social media expects these things, and we happily supply them. Facebook, Google+, Twitter, Tumblr, Flickr, most any online forum has personal "about" sections. Heck, the whole concept of a hashtag is to label a piece of content online so that search engines can efficiently index that content.

I am free to choose labels that describe me. And yes, it is obvious that others can apply labels to me beyond my control. But a more insidious problem is that the meanings and definitions of the labels evolve, morph and are abused. Labels are words, and their meanings are rarely (read: "never") static.

Who decides what words mean? An elected body? A deity? An election with ballots? Nah, it's better and worse than any of that: everyone decides! In our English language what words mean is the ultimate democracy, more democratic than our nation's government. Or in a darker light: it's a popularity contest. I am no authority on linguistics, but my understanding is that words mean what we mostly agree on. Makers of dictionaries research sources of writings and count up the various uses of words and choose the most common ones. But we laypeople rarely open a dictionary. It is really an amazing process that we exchange words, words that have complex and varied meanings, and still do not carry dictionaries with us at all times.

Think about it. You might hit words like *somnambulist*, *pochette*, *ratiocination* and have to look those up. But there are so many words that fly in and out of us, as easily as breathing. Even words that can have special meanings, read-between-the-lines meanings, or words that conjure memories good and bad, we love them, we speak them, we hear them. Think of all the pictures you can draw in your mind when I say *thirsty*. What about *beer* or *tea party* or *naked*?

The OCD geek in me loves to label so that I can sort, categorize and study. But I do hide one label. I am not out, loud and proud as a bisexual because I absolutely loathe the idea of being a foregone conclusion. I pass for straight, especially with my wife and kids around me, but I also wear kilts full-time. I do this because I am proud of my Scottish heritage and, more importantly, kilts are very comfortable. Yet it is not uncommon for my perceived straightness to be called into question because, after all, a kilt does look like a skirt. I enjoy the confusion in some when they see the kilt and my wife and kids all together. However, if I were flying the bisexual flag high, those same muggles would think, "Oh, well of course!"

I know what *bisexual* means for me. I am OK with that label, because for me it means that I find some women attractive and I find some men attractive. Period.

However, the associations that come with the label *bisexual* make me rather uncomfortable. "Anything that moves" is one, with its presumption that a bisexual must be attracted to everything and anything and further, must be promiscuous. I have heard gay men dismiss bisexuality in males as a "phase" in the coming out process. I have been told that I am not being fully honest with myself. The typical straight male hears "gay male" when "bisexual male" is said. I guess I can label myself as a unicorn, often read and talked about but presumed nonexistent.

In addition, U.S. standards for masculinity are bound up in sex. A man can only be a "manly" man if he has sex exclusively (and often) with women, or at least one woman. If a man has any sexual inclinations beyond that, then suddenly he is no longer a man. He is labeled feminine or weak or gay—as if those are synonyms. To the heteronormative man, "gay" is an indictment.

Yet the same standards are not applied to women. Bisexual women are seen in a completely different light. A woman who steps outside of the heteronormative standard might be seen as empowered and taking charge of her sexuality, free to experiment without losing her femininity. Katy Perry can kiss a girl and like it and sing a song about it. And many will applaud her for it. All this at a deep level speaks to just how fragile our culture's sense of masculinity is for all males, but that is another talk show.

As with so many things in life, we need to have balance and show respect. We cannot throw away all labels because this will impede education. Education leads to empathy, and empathy to peace. Yet at the other extreme, we cannot apply labels so thickly and heavily that we suffocate beneath them, and we must constantly be mindful of our audience. For example, not everyone would be helped by the 15 different sexual orientation distinctions for males made by sexologist Joe Kort in his Straight Guise blog.[1] Yet reading through that list could be illuminating for many. Definitions are fluid, so avoid clinging too tightly to them. Most importantly: be respectful. Know that people are more than their hashtags. Know that you are more than your labels. Do not take a label's value and impute that on the person. For example, do not let your negative opinion of lawyers or vegetarians lead to a negative opinion of a lawyer or vegetarian you've just met. Better yet, put their name before their label. Remember everyone's humanity. Labels can be any color, but the blood flowing beneath is always red.

1 http://www.joekort.com/articles91.htm

Ian Wilson has three kids and an awesome wife. He loves photography and all things Scottish and Celtic.

by joshua hutchinson

speak on it

When it comes to my sexuality, I am probably the last one to ever speak up about it. It isn't because I am confined by a severed tongue, both of the figurative or the literal kind, as I find being an advocate of such matters tiresome. I don't mean to suggest in any way that my sexuality isn't worth advocating for. It is. It most certainly is. However, there are so many people out there nowadays willing to charge onto the proverbial battlefield bickering on semantics of the subtlest of these details alone that it makes the real fight worth fighting for not really worth fighting for at all. Especially when at the end of the day we are practically saying the same thing, just in a different way. Oftentimes with the differences lying in the spelling and pronunciation of the word, not the real core meaning.

Case in point, the submission call for this particular anthology project; these wonderful and gracious editors painstakingly sifted through every known label and non-label related to bisexuality or the act in kind to appease every possible contributor. Categorizing every brand, be it named or not, a substantial bona fide word found in the dictionaries or the hottest new catch phrase of the season, to make every male-identified being who has ever engaged in sex with another man as well as another gender feel included in this particular group of brethren. Bisexual. Anthrosexual. Ambisexual. Fluid. No Label. Multisexual. Omnisexual. Pansexual. Pomosexual. Polysexual. And, just in case you didn't feel like you hadn't made roll call yet, non-monosexual (a self-explained cosmopolitan way of saying that if you whore around with more than one sex, this includes you, too).

I am not saying that each phrase does not have its own validity, its own merit as its own form of community. I am saying that just as I am sure that the editors have gone out of their way to try to accommodate everybody out there, there was probably some lone individual(s) that probably happened to ream them out because they failed to mention their label(s) as well. So by the time we as a community (that is considered the minority even under one name) once again sift through this continuous growing list to give ourselves some kind of unique identity, isn't it understandable that when it comes to the real battle at hand, the real one worth fighting for, I honestly find myself too battle-scarred from friendly fire to tread back out there to fight the real fight? Too exhausted to dispute the ignorant class with my words to thoroughly believe that I may influence them in some way that some other predecessor hadn't articulated better or confused them even worse. Notwithstanding the ravaging effects of drugs, hypocrisy, fanaticism and other ignorance that plague the human mind and community in turn from the processes of reason and rationalization different than our own.

Of course, an exception is given to friends and associates I come across on a regular basis. I don't necessarily believe I have as much power to change their minds (if they chose to be so staunch in their mental stance with my words) as I may have with my actions working on them at a much slower rate. My ultimate goal with these individuals is for them not to think or say some ignorant shit that I have to heavily correct them on later. Nothing personifies this more for me than a recent trip to my local barbershop. I am fortunate to have two to call my home: one shop where I actually get my haircut from barbers who measure their experience in scores and another where I hang out sometimes to get my intellectual shit-talking perspective on.

I was thoroughly enjoying the latter when a patron by the name of Miguel came strolling through the door. He made himself known not because the place was yea big but because he caused a major infraction by stepping into the male-only sanctuary with a woman by his side. The master barber grunted his unusual pass of acceptance, permitting everybody to follow suit. If he hadn't, Miguel would've kindly been asked to come back some other time. I guess the master barber permitted this indiscretion because just like everybody else, he remembered when Miguel's great uncle used to bring him in. I remember clearly when the little boy would sit in the chair busting eardrums, annoyed by the motorized sound of the clippers rubbing against him. And now, looking at him, a junior in college, drinking age with a girlfriend, almost made me feel ancient in my 30 years. Almost. It was quite obvious Miguel still had a lot to learn about the ways of the world, bringing his girl into the shop.

After a brief interlude of silence, they took their seats and we resumed talking like we usually do, paying very little mind that either of them were even still there. Miguel wasn't much of a talker. So when he spoke up to impress his girl, we gave him his pass. It seemed that every intelligible sentence he spoke was rewarded by a come-hither look of seduction and a pat on the knee. Then the boy started getting a little too mouthy for his own good. Suddenly he became a know-it-all on everything under the sun although he had never experienced life substantially to comment on the things he chose to speak on. We had been around to know that the kind of arrogance that he was displaying wasn't so much for the benefit of the girl as it was like that of a guy that just popped his first piece of trim or an expectant father expediting the road of manhood too soon onto his offspring. Seven months later, we proved to be right on both accounts.

We might've let Miguel continue to have his King Shit moment for his girl if it wasn't for his girl mistaking our un-objecting stance for the freedom to inject her own. First, by self-righteously talking about the promiscuity of her generation, and then by toying with this meticulous dance revolving around sex and sexuality, before going in for the kill she was originally after. I knew where she was heading even before she got started as there was this well-dressed male patron with this unusually high-pitched feminine voice that had just left the building. Because there are such a large number of Black women who fancy themselves self-appointed experts of men who mess around with other men on the down low because of some played-out perpetual stereotypes or a few lines they read in some book, it never once occurred to her that the man with the high-pitched voice could after all be heterosexual, which he actually was. Much like the big brute of a man sitting across from her in his city work uniform, whom she was teasing by opening and closing her legs, was actually an openly gay power bottom, although he was well-equipped with a very deep baritone voice and a natural masculine demeanor that bucked the stereotype of his disclosed sexuality.

"I just don't get it. How can a man go that way?" she sucked her teeth after the high-pitched man left.

The master barber looked across the room hoping that somebody would stand up and defend the man with the high-pitched voice since it was common knowledge around town that he skillfully managed a wife, a girlfriend, two mistresses and another woman on the side.

Of course, I felt like I was slightly put on blast when the master barber deadpanned me and the macho power bottom, as the unofficial spokesmen of the sexual alternative in the shop.

Like I said, I didn't entertain such foolishness nor was I in the mood to make a valuable exception. Besides, I wasn't going to play that game. I knew a boatload of men who had women coming out of their asses to also have a male piece on the side to call upon too.

"I don't either, sistah," the macho power bottom responded garnishing laughter. "A man got one dick. He doesn't need others to play with!"

"Exactly," she agreed against the muffled snickers.

"Sistahs out here already having a hard time scoring one good Black man, and you guys have to compete with him and the likes of him? Shame—just a damn shame!" He shook his head like he genuinely meant what he was saying. "Not only that, you got to compete with the White girls and just about every other nationality for a good Black man, too."

"You seem like you understand what I'm talking about. You're married or have a girlfriend?"
"Hell no," he barked. "There are too many women around town to settle down like that! Black. Latin. Chinese. Japanese. Other Asian. Australian. European. Plain White. Exotic White, and whatever else that can be thrown in the mix of the human race."

The room roared with laughter as a seasoned few probably remembered hearing him say that in his 44 years on earth he had never once slept with or had the desire to sleep with a woman.

"At least it's all women and Black women are at the top of your list. No men. I can't stand a man that plays both sides of the fence. Or one that pretends to play on one side and actually plays on the other."

The master barber eyed me again, with a look of Don't Start, as the macho bottom has always wanted to coax me into a duel over my gender-unbiased sexuality.

Our sexuality inside the barbershop was sort of treated like the family secret. Everybody knew about it, but it wasn't discussed unless some misinformation about it needed some major correcting.

And since I never willingly jumped on any soapbox unless I absolutely had to, both the guy and the girl were still safe from my lazy wrath.

"Well, sistah," the macho power bottom hawed. "You can't have it both ways. You can't get mad at a man that don't want you, be it because you're Black or because you're a woman. People have a right to like what they like, and be damn what anybody else thinks."

"Easy for you to say," she snapped.

"Easier for you to do," he retorted. "Black women outnumber Black men in most places. If the few [men] you got recognize the choices they have, why not you guys?"

"Because we want what we want."

"So why fault that man if he wants what he wants be it another man or another woman of another race, and goes after it?"

"I can . . . for the struggle of Black women everywhere," she said, garnishing laughs from the room.

"What struggle, young lady? Your momma and grandmamma might have struggled, but you haven't even begun to put in the work to complain at the tender age of what?"

"Twenty," she filled in.

"Twenty? You wouldn't know what struggle is, little girl."

"I have three kids. Trust, I know what struggle is."

"No. Struggle is when you're fighting all odds because all odds are stacked against you, honey. You chose to spread your legs three times to bear three children before you are old enough to take a sip of the real struggle. And unless you come from a mega-rich family or something, my taxpaying dollars are the ones struggling to house and feed more mouths that I didn't bring into this world. So you're adding to my struggle."

The woman paused for a moment, hopefully feeling the ridiculousness of her argument, and then responded with, "I don't know how we got off on this subject. I was just saying that I am fed up with these men trying to be women and don't know where the hell they are going. Don't know if they want to use their dicks or not . . . on everybody or nobody."

I guess I should have stuck with the urge not to entertain such foolishness but I didn't. "I hate to tell you. Sex and sexuality isn't nearly as cut and dried as you might want to think."

"True." The woman agreed with a hung head, not knowing if she had personally offended anybody, perhaps me, in the way I suddenly perked up.

"You look like you're quite happy with Miguel. You look like you found a man who will stay the course with you. So why are you worried about what some other guy does or doesn't do?"

She paused again, letting my words graciously seep in.

It was obvious to me that she had been associating with a bunch of negative women, that she chose to inherit their anger and attitude and mistook their bitterness and hatred for her own. So I couldn't let her go without saying, "And I'll tell you something else, too, about struggle. Keep your own car in your own lane, and you might find that you can drive it a lot better and without so much of a struggle than trying to drive everybody else's car from their position, okay?"

Her face turned from thought and reflection to a reddish fit of huff and puff as she stormed out with Miguel trailing behind her.

I had so much more I wanted to say. So much more that I wanted to teach her before she left.

"You were wrong for that," the master barber said jokingly. "I appreciate that, but you were wrong for that."

"I hadn't really even said anything," I commented.

It was the truth. I hadn't really said anything. Though, my words may have carried a far stronger force behind them than I was aware of them intending. She was the one who was offended by the guy with the high-pitched voice, assuming that he was gay just because. She was the one blabbing her mouth off in front of an openly gay man and a bisexual man because we didn't fit into her small-minded mold of what she thought we should have looked like.

If she had the time and the ears, I would have even broken down to her why sex and sexuality wasn't nearly as cut and dry as she made it out to be.

I may be rogue in my way of thinking. But I have been around the block enough to know that when it comes to men that have sex with men, overtly or covertly, it doesn't necessarily equate to those men being gay or bisexual or any or all of the other labels I mentioned before.

Not to justify the discriminations that oftentimes come with those various distinctions, but it is the truth as I see it.

What most women fail to understand and what most men fail to tell these women due to simple mortification as well as fear of losing their sexual privileges with them is that most men can get a hard-on from a gentle breeze in the wind, if not resort to other measures to achieve that same end. That is, it is really nothing distinctly special about a woman (or a man or a transgender individual) in particular for them to achieve that end unless it does involve an amorous affair of some kind. And even then, it can still be a natural occurrence that his body reacts to on its own or by some other sexual stimulant.

I stress this because I hear all too often that a number of misguided women honestly believe that a man's erection, when presented to them, only awakens in their presence. That it is their gift to unwrap at their convenience when biologically that couldn't be further from the truth. Just about every grown man living and dead can relate to some time during his pubescent years of having an unwarranted erection at an inappropriate time that they couldn't easily discard with immediate thought.

While this phenomenon is most common with young teenage males and possibly with those in their early twenties (and sometimes beyond), it isn't uncommon for men to be attracted to one gender or another to brandish an erection for the "other" team. Just like I've known confirmed gay men to have an erection looking at a woman, I've also known heterosexual men to sport an embarrassing erection in the presence of another guy. It doesn't always translate to either of them being sexually attracted to those individuals as it might be something about that person that they might find attractive in some way or their thought process drifted to a totally different memory or event or some kind of unawareness altogether.

So a heterosexual man isn't made gay if his body reacts to a man; nor is a gay man made straight if his body reacts to a woman.

To further my point, if I am to be ever so crass, a wise uncle once told me that the difference between a young man busting his nut and an old man busting his is that the young man wants to arrive at the destination as quick as possible while the old man wants to enjoy his journey from start to finish.

So, if most, if not all, men and a great number of women know that their man can or has reached this climatic end by use of the palm of his hand, regardless of his sexual experience or inexperience, what exactly constitutes a grip that is off-limits?

Think about it. Seriously.

A hand or a mouth or even an anal cavity has no gender distinction since it is not unique to the sex of the person. And let's not talk about the many sexual devices that are out there on the market to take care of a man's sexual needs when his partner won't suffice.

I am not suggesting nor do I want to imply that all men want or need to take the license of thrusting their penis inside anything they choose as a means to an end. The pun "different strokes for different folks" should definitely apply here. What I am articulating, or trying to at least, is that sexuality, even with its growing labels, isn't nearly as cut and dried as the actions they engage in. Hence the reason for the various labels as a whole to begin with.

Are we going to start calling people who masturbate "hand-sexual"? Are we going to start referring to people who engage in oral sex, via performer or receiver, as "mouth-sexual"? And what about people who engage in anal intercourse, are they going to be known as "butt-sexual"? Then, if we are going to go that far, what are we going to start calling men who use sexual devices with no fleshly or living ties? "Machine-sexual"? "Silicone-sexual"?

As a bisexual-identified person (and perhaps someone who can be defined by some if not all of the other labels mentioned in the second paragraph), I accept my bisexuality. Not for the ease of society to place labels on me. I accept it is as my truth because my attraction to the sexes generally flows like tides in the ocean, buoying from one gender to another, with the occasional tsunami that pulls strongly one way for a while before its force changes direction.

As I mentioned before, it is far more an emotional element rather than anything else because my attraction lies strongly in my want of the individual rather than their gender. So for me, it isn't hard to have sex with either gender because everything sexual (on the physical plane) is rather doable since most body parts have no gender. Whether they factor in or not, the sexual agreement can often be reworked to benefit both parties. Mental and emotional factors must be considered as well as factored in with a strong sexual desire.

I fully understand that gender is a large part of the individual, but it is not their entirety. Nor does it guarantee that whatever want that person might pursue will be granted.

For example, if my goal in life is to produce a family biologically, as a man I must find a woman to carry out this deed as my sperm needs to pursue her egg. But what if the woman I choose is infertile? Then what? I did everything biologically possible to pursue this dream short of medical intervention. I could go out and find another woman, but wouldn't that discredit my choice of the woman I had already chosen? What if childbearing were her dream, too? Based on the doctrines of societal and religious organizations, a woman is supposed to bear children. Then what? Throw up two fingers and tell her I'm on my way out the door because she is unable to deliver what biology told me she should? And what if I'm the infertile one; would that make me a less credible contributor to my manhood or my society?

The same thing applies if I only pursue a relationship with another man in the hopes of having a certain kind of sex. It could possibly be that he doesn't fancy what I want and isn't willing to entertain it though the relationship itself is substantial in other regards. Then what? Choose the sex that I want or the relationship?

I guess that is why it is such a foreign concept for me to grasp that societal norms, for what they're worth, put the utmost value on a person's plumbing as a determining factor in engaging a person in a sexual relationship.

Logically, I get it. Through centuries of religious and other societal standings we have been taught to hold onto this belief in the continuation of a civilized culture. Everything else in the sexual spectrum that is also a great part of our mores was swept under the rug while not erased by history as "There is nothing new under the sun," just the amount of shade we give it.

If we were to thoroughly and honestly investigate some of the age-old items put before us and really start to question them, wouldn't we be left with a lot more questions than we initially had? If being attracted to the same sex is first regarded as a sin and then later rephrased as being some kind of "phase," why is it that we treat it more like an incurable disease than a natural occurrence, since that is precisely what a phase implies? Also, if a man is to sow his wild oats before he is asked to settle down and expects the woman he settles down with to be chaste, and for most of the human spectrum men outnumbered women, then who exactly was he sowing his wild oats with? Were all men sowing their wild oats with the same women, or were there also some men and transgender individuals involved?

Then, every so often, some "great" mind comes along in society to tell me that my sexuality and that of my peers in our struggle for recognition and equality is wrong. Sexuality, according to some religious teachings, is strictly for procreation, with pleasure taking a distant second in the dance. But these same people who condemn us will turn around and greatly fancy those same sexual acts that they condemn. Sex and sexuality aren't cut and dried even by the confines within which most of us are brought up.

In our teens, growing up, in the short time I lived with my cousin, he was never without a girl to make it with and kept nearly 300 condoms of the same brand and color stashed away at all times in several places in my auntie's house. More startling than that, other than him going through them like water, he knew when I grabbed a few and demanded that I replace them immediately. Like Condoms #258 through #261 were missing, as there were as many coming in as there were going out to really notice. Even in all his poking around, I don't think making it with a man ever entered his mind. So am I to believe that because he is now behind bars that he decided to take a strict vow of celibacy? Particularly when the terms of his sentence are life in prison with no possible chance of parole? I seriously doubt that my cousin ever had any homosexual tendencies. But I also doubt seriously that he isn't above being the first one to jam his penis into some gender-free orifice, be it by choice or even by force, as a way to get off. While I hope "by force" isn't the case, knowing his logic like I do, he probably figured he is in prison anyhow. What are they going to do? Lock him up and throw away the key?

Or to paraphrase my poem "Revelation Five" from years ago, if he couldn't keep his pants on while he was out of jail, what in the hell makes you so sure that he's going to do such a good job keeping them on in jail?

To take it a step further, what about the guy in prison or elsewhere who is raped? Does that guy become gay because of actions he can't control or do things that he may not otherwise do as a free man but has to do in confinement that may be critical to his survival in such a dire situation? What if that man gets an erection during said event, as has been well documented can occur: does that means he is gay and warrants such a sexual assault?

As for the situational circumstances, I'm not sure if one of the men at the barbershop, George, fits the bill, as to me he is sort of in the gray of gray areas. George is one of those devastatingly handsome Black men with his intellect geared towards getting over on others in the street. He confided in me years ago that he too had sex with both men and women. He wasn't gay, of course—a line I'd heard too many times over the years to count. Nor did he dare classify what he did as being bisexual. I must admit that it took me a long time to figure out that for George, having sex with another man wasn't nearly a social taboo for him as it meant not worrying about creating another mouth to feed and still have the freedom of unprotected sex. His crooked smile and streetwise demeanor always guaranteed somebody would be willing to throw caution to the wind, as many of his male and female conquests complained that he only takes them doggy-style while grumbling obscenities on his way to execute his climax, treating both men and women like less than a disposable cum wipe teetering equally on both misogyny and homophobia.

I would agree that he isn't gay or bisexual even though his actions speak otherwise. I wouldn't say that he was even heterosexual either in spite of fathering nine children with eight different women. However, society would because his many offspring are quite visible while what he does behind closed doors indiscriminately with both sexes isn't.

I have a transgender friend who, once she had her surgery, never bothered to mention to her partners that she was really born a man. There is absolutely nothing that would ever suggest otherwise, even on the occasion I might feel free to call her out to other unsuspecting people (doing this with her prior permission, of course). So does that make the men who assume they're making it with a naturally-made woman newly gay? Let's not forget the woman who might entertain a threesome with another woman for her man. While there might be a handful of women that might classify themselves as part of the "sexual alternative," most will fight for others to recognize their heterosexual identity as well.

As we can go through the tiresome motion of trying to figure out how we would label this man or that woman or the lot of them to ease our simplistic thoughts in this complex world, the truth of the matter is that we can only go by the information given to us, nothing more or nothing less, unless we have personal knowledge of it, like the preacher who might openly condemn homosexuality to his congregation but be the first one to engage in it behind closed doors or the openly gay advocate who might've made the exception of sleeping with a particular woman or two.

Even as it relates to myself, I often accept being called gay rather than battle for my proper identity as a bisexual man because the effort, for the most part granting few exceptions, is pointless. I feel sometimes that I'm damned if I do and damned if I don't as it relates to people that I could honestly not give two good shits about. If I do, it can be perceived as trying to minimize the fact that I have sex with other men. And if I do stand up and acknowledge my dual sexual attractions, it can also be perceived that I am undecided, which is far from the truth. If I pursue something exclusively with a man for a certain period of time, I am labeled gay with no wiggle room. If I pursue something with a woman for a while, I am perceived as "trying to be straight." If I pursue a polyamorous relationship with people of both sexes, I am playing stereotypes about bisexuality. Labels and assumptions are put on me by others at every turn.

Another reason I don't necessarily advocate my sexual orientation, as with the various labels I mentioned in the beginning of this essay, the real argument gets lost sifting through the smoke and clouds in search of something tangible.

It is also the reason why I take the rogue stance I do. Because although people are able to perform various physical acts of sex, that too can easily be discredited as most people are going to do what they think they have to do to be accepted, either by society as a whole or even by themselves.

Like the closeted gay men or lesbians who have heterosexual relations with their partners. Although they can move their bodies to have sex, their lust and heart might be with members of their same sex. Or the man who might go down to a gloryhole, not concerned one way or another who may be fellating him, only wanting to be satisfied with the end result.

But if we put more emphasis on the emotional connection, however it resonates with the individual person, I would think that we would find it even harder to use the labels we create and find them as useless altogether rather than to take a stance on what we are or what we think we are along with those who accept us for just that reason.

Joshua Hutchinson is a freelance writer. He is far better known under one of his many pseudonyms than his own given name.

ocean's of love letter: is one black man loving another man the revolutionary act of the twenty-first century?

by dr. herukhuti
(h. sharif williams)

In *To Be Young, Gifted and Black*, Lorraine Hansberry proclaimed, "For some time now—I think since I was a child—I have been possessed of the desire to put down the stuff of my life . . . And, I am quite certain, there is only one internal quarrel: how much of the truth to tell? How much, how much, how much! It is brutal in sober uncompromising moments, to reflect on the comedy of concern we all enact when it comes to our precious images!"[1]

Telling the truth of one's life can be a complicated and dangerous endeavor, especially when you are young, gifted, Black and queer (in this context I use queer to mean having experienced something other than normative Eros). It may mean that you destroy the hopes, dreams and expectations constructed for you to fulfill—only to have new ones built in their place. This is why the concept of coming out is so limiting as a way to explain what happens when someone puts "down the stuff of [their] life."

Social media booked, tumbled and tweeted itself into a frenzy in response to R&B and sometime Hip Hop artist Frank Ocean's Tumblr posting. Who is Frank Ocean and why should you care? Ocean is set to release his debut studio album this month after seven years of hard work in the music industry including writing for Justin Bieber, John Legend, Brandy and Beyoncé; joining the deliberately provocative Hip Hop collective Odd Future; touring North America and Europe performing and promoting a successful mixtape album; and appearing on Jay Z and Kanye's most recent album as a writer and featured artist.

In the post of a December 27th, 2011 journal entry, written while on a plane ride from his birthplace of New Orleans to Los Angeles, Ocean eloquently explores his experience of love toward/with/for an undisclosed man. Travel gives us time to reflect on the things we've done, should have done, and wanted to do. The solitude of certain forms of travel, like the anonymity of an airplane with its recycled air and pressurized environment, can bring us closer to the immediacy of our

1 See: Hansberry, L. *To Be Young, Gifted and Black: An Informal Autobiography*. New York: Signet Classics, 2011

needs—needs like love, unconditional and reciprocated. Media sources have alleged that the self-disclosure was precipitated by a music reviewer noting instances in Ocean's forthcoming debut studio album in which the singer/songwriter uses male pronouns in expressing love and Eros toward someone.

By the intensity of the widespread clamor, you would have thought that one of the major male figures in Black music rumored to have experienced same-sex desire had posted this journal entry online. I will not name any of them but the rumors are out there and truths are waiting to be put down. In fact, unlike these other artists, Ocean is at the early stages of what seems to be a promising career in the music industry, an industry that in recent years has been transformed by changes in technology distribution and access—changes that have given artists and consumers more opportunities to own, control and share music. So what does it mean for Ocean to have both fluidly written homosexual and heterosexual desire into his album and shared with the social media world his experience of love of a man—his first love and a love that was "malignant" and "hopeless" and yet he gratefully credited with changing his life?

In choosing to communicate through the simile, "I feel like a free man," rather than saying he was a free man, Ocean provided us with a painful truth for Black men in, what Ibrahim Farajajé (formerly Elias Farajajé-Jones) in his essay "Holy Fuck" called a "dominating culture [that] expends incredible amounts of time, money and energy controlling and policing our bodies and the ways we decide to use them."[2] By not definitively claiming and owning freedom in the journal entry, Ocean acknowledged the task at hand for him and other Black queer men, as Farajajé described, "the physical/spiritual/psychological process of making our bodies and our desire our own." It is a process—rather than a destination to which we arrive and reside—that will not allow for easy definitions of who we are or interpretations of our artistic or life choices.

Supporters and detractors of Ocean have made the themes of his album and his Tumblr post mean much more than Ocean himself may have intended. In 2012, some folks find it more provocative that a Black man has loved another man than if he had done violence against one. Joseph Beam once wrote, "Black men loving Black men is the revolutionary act of the eighties."[3]

Honoring our capacity to love other men and women in a society that makes it easier to use and abuse others is the work of making our

2 See: Farajaje-Jones, E. "Holy Fuck." *Male Lust: Pleasure, Power, and Transformation*. Eds. Kerwin Kay, Jill Nagle, and Baruch Gould. New York: Harrington Park Press, 2000.

3 See: Beam, J. "Black Men Loving Black Men: The Revolutionary Act of the Eighties." *Gay Community News* [Boston] 20 April: 1985: 5.

bodies and desires our own. Ocean clearly seeks to put the work into that project, at least for the time being. But one young, gifted Black man does not a revolution make, particularly if he is still understanding his relationship to that revolution. Revolutions require many committed others working "in sober uncompromising moments, to reflect on the comedy of concern we all enact when it comes to our precious images!" Where's your love letter? How much truth does it tell?

Dr. Herukhuti (H. Sharif Williams) is founder of The Center for Culture, Sexuality, and Spirituality, author of the book Conjuring Black Funk: Notes on Culture, Sexuality, and Spirituality, *co-editor of* Sexuality, Religion and the Sacred: Bisexual, Pansexual and Polysexual Perspectives, *high priest of the Shrine of Sekhmet and Heruhet (Brooklyn, New York), and faculty member at Goddard College (Plainfield, Vermont) and Fielding Graduate University (Santa Barbara, California).*

This essay was first published in bimagazine.org *and is reproduced with permission of the publisher and author.*

by josh bergeleen

this bi phase

Coming out is hard. Coming out as bisexual and being told, "You'll get past that," makes the process even more confusing and even more frustrating.

My biggest surprise when I came out was how aggravating my queer friends were—my identifying as bisexual seemed to be their cue to start talking about how long their own bi phase lasted, or to proudly exclaim that they didn't need a bi phase. That would make sense if you viewed establishing your sexual identity as a race, where we run through identity models to see how quickly we can get to that end goal of a six on the Kinsey scale and win a trophy.

Being stubborn to a degree that only Germans can be, every time I was told I was gay, I identified more and more strongly as bisexual. So, by the 754th time a friend/drunk guy at the bar/student in my class/casual passersby pulled me aside to have a conversation about how it would "be okay" to "finish coming out," I was feeling militantly bisexual.

At this point, I began to experience my identity as a restriction rather than a word that felt like home and represented how I understood my romantic and physical attractions. Being bisexual seemed to be one of the first things I would mention in conversation, followed quickly by a summary of my love life. You know, just to reinforce how bisexual I was, having dated and loved members of same and other genders. I had become so used to people judging or mislabeling my identity that I felt I had to preemptively and emphatically define myself.

Now, a few years later, while I may still be in my "bi phase," I no longer take such offense when an enlightened stranger tries to explain how my identity is temporary. I have realized people hold these beliefs because bisexual guys are fairly invisible. Either we are out being fabulous and people assume we're gay, or we're wearing a suit to work and people assume we're straight. Either we walk down the streets holding our boyfriends' hands and we're obviously gay, or we're holding our girlfriends' hands and we're clearly straight. And since we're not really recognizable, people think they don't have a lot of experience with bisexuality, and they don't really know what to do with those of us who declare our identities.

To me, there are two distinct steps to coming out as gay. One is to admit your same-gender attraction. The other is to acknowledge that you don't have the other-gender attraction that, throughout your entire life, people have expected you to have.

In the process of coming out as gay, many people do use a bisexual identity as a temporary steppingstone. In my head it's like trying to walk a perfectly straight line: you deliberately put one foot in front first, before taking step two to catch up. I am the guy who gets in the pool slowly to let my body adjust, so this strategy totally makes sense to me. While some people just jump right in despite the fact that the water is often freezing; that is not my style.

This line of thought is why I just want to say that if you identify as bisexual I hope you enjoy your stay.

For however long you are here, I hope this label and our awesome community make you feel as safe and as treasured as it has made me. You may later believe that "gay" describes your romantic and physical feelings or that you're actually straight and just happened to fall in love with your best friend. Maybe you just end up being amazing and coming up with your own unique label to describe your identity. All of those labels are equally beautiful and deserve to be celebrated.

However you identify, I promise to respect whatever label currently describes your identity but, please, return the favor.

Josh Bergeleen is currently a senior at Emory University in Atlanta, Georgia and President of Emory Pride.

liminality

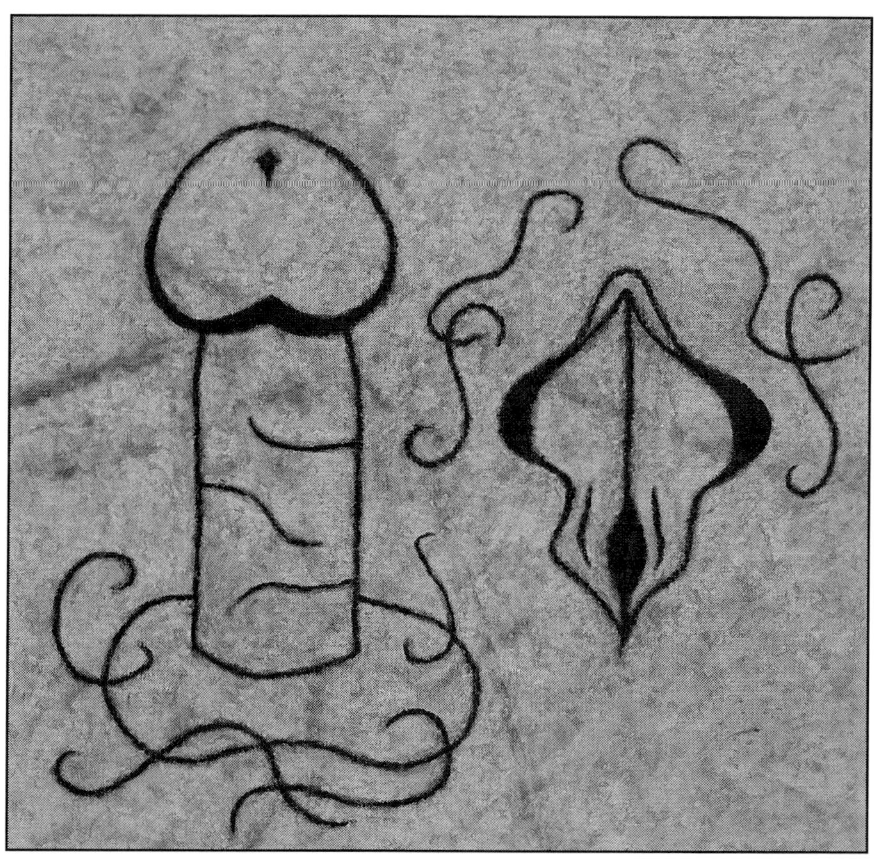

"sex symbols," hew wolfe

ambidextrous in a righty world

by kye b.

For me, being bisexual is a lot like being ambidextrous, which I happen to be to some extent. As an ambidextrous person, I sometimes feel out of place because I do not fit into the norm. I am seen as different instead of being recognized as a person with two perfectly working hands. My dominant hand is my left hand so little things like using scissors or writing in a notebook can be difficult for me and other lefties because they are designed for right-handed people. Just like right-handedness is presumed and right-handed people are more accepted than left-handed people because there are more righties than lefties, heterosexuality is presumed and heterosexual people are more accepted than non-heterosexual people. Bisexual and nonconformist sexual identities are often ignored, ridiculed and misrepresented.

It took a lot of time and self-reflection for me to understand my sexuality and gender identity. At the age of 14, I thought I was a lesbian. The idea of having sex with a man who has a cock was not very appealing to me at the time, but the label *lesbian* did not fit me either. Until that point, it never occurred to me that I could be attracted to more than one gender at the same time.

Perhaps I should explain something else about myself before continuing.

By the time I was 16, I had realized I was not a lesbian because I became aware that I had an interest in both women and men. I also came to understand that I was a man born into a woman's body. I was assigned female at birth even though I am male.

In two years, I had gone from identifying as a lesbian to identifying as a bisexual man. I had already come out to my grandparents as a lesbian so I had to come out to them again, two years later, as transgender (female-to-male). My mother's parents raised me from the time I was an infant. They are the people I have always been closest to in my family, and their opinion mattered the most out of everyone I know. This made them the hardest people to come out to. After I told them I was a lesbian, my grandmother said, "Oh, you'll grow out of it; you're just confused," and boy, was she right! My grandfather said, "Be who you need to be. I may not agree with your decision, but I will support you. I just want you to be happy.

"The next time I came out to them was not as pleasant. When I told my grandparents that I was transgender—that I was actually a guy—Grandpa ignored the issue. He did not understand what I meant by it. In fact, he said, "I love you and you'll always be my granddaughter to me." My Gram took it even harder and did not talk to me for three days. Eventually they both came around and accepted me as I am. There are still issues with using the proper pronouns and the proper name, but we get by. They try their best and love me for who I am.

At the age of 18, I started hormone replacement therapy. As of this writing, I am 27 years old and have had a full hysterectomy. I am still waiting to get my breasts removed through a double mastectomy. I have legally changed my name and gender marker.

Looking at me, no one could ever tell that I was born female. I keep my chest flat and (thanks to testosterone shots) my voice has gotten deeper and I can grow facial hair. I am fine with people not being able to tell what my gender used to be. When I go out into the world, I am perceived and treated just like any other guy. It is not that I am ashamed of my gender identity—I am actually very proud of it—but it is just safer and easier to blend in with everyone else. The fact is that I am emotionally and socially male, and it feels right.

I am fine with people not knowing that I am transgender. What I am not fine with is when people presumed I was straight when I was in a relationship with a girl. I also do not like it when people now see me as a gay man because I am in a relationship with a (wonderful) guy. When I tell people I am bisexual, I get asked certain questions. The one I am most often asked is, "How can you be attracted to more than one gender?" I reply, "How can you only be attracted to one gender?" The response to that question is "That is who I am." Exactly! Me being attracted to more than one gender is who I am. This question is even asked by my gay and lesbian friends— people from whom I would expect understanding.

I have an acquaintance who is a gay man. He said, while I was in the room, "I don't believe bisexual people even exist." He then went on to ask everyone in the room (all of whom were gay men or lesbians, except for me) if anyone knew of any bisexual people. I raised my hand and said, "Me. I'm bisexual." He looked very surprised when I said that. Maybe it was because I did not have a woman draped over one shoulder and a man over the other.

It is at moments like that in which I feel I am isolated from the very community I am supposed to belong to the most: the GLBTQQIA (gay, lesbian, bisexual, transgender, queer, questioning, intersex, asexual) community. Since I identify as bisexual and not gay, I am often denied my sexual orientation by the same people who are so gung ho to make the case that everyone should be accepted as they are, no matter what they may be. The B in GLBTQQIA often gets overlooked, I believe, because Western society demands that things must be black or white, not gray.

Well, I am gray. Just by being alive, people like me break that black-and-white mold. Insisting on a black-and-white standard is like saying a person must be either right-handed or left-handed, with no variation. It really is possible for people to be ambidextrous, just like it is possible for some people to be bisexual instead of gay or straight. Most events that I have attended for the GLBTQQIA community are largely geared toward gay men and lesbians. I often feel as if I were the only ambidextrous person in a right-handed person's world, out of place and unaccounted for.

I am writing this essay in the hope that it may open at least one mind to the idea that it is okay to be bisexual or to have a nonconforming sexual identity and that I, as a bisexual person, am not confused about what genders I am attracted to. I am a person who is proud to be in-between the sexual black-and-white and to have a gender that is also part of the gray area. I hope you feel proud of the person you have become. Remember that it is okay to be ambidextrous. Be proud of your individuality. Go out into the world and be proud and happy about the differences that make you, you.

Kye B. is originally from central Maine. He has been living in northern California since February 2010 with his fiancé, Aidan (who is also from central Maine), their two cats, Paige and Samhain and two rats, Sage and Ezra.

by victor raymond, ph.d.

with my feet in several worlds

"You don't *act* Indian!" she snarled at me.

We were on a metro transit bus, headed for my college campus. "I'm Indian enough just as I am!" I countered. "I don't need to live up to your ideas of what is 'American Indian!'" Still, I felt uncomfortable. Another native student at the same small liberal arts college, she looked like a "skin": long, straight black hair, copper-red complexion, dark-brown eyes. She sounded Indian, too: that slight accent that comes from living with other Native people, speaking both English and their own language.

I was from a different tribe. But I had grown up in the inner city, in a multicultural setting. My father—whose own looks were far more visibly Native than my own—was a university professor and, later, a consultant. My mother, however, was White, making me biracial. So while I had black hair, my skin was light in complexion. When I was around other people of different ethnicities, I spoke with an upper Midwestern urban inflection. I didn't act the way that most people expected Indians to act. Did that make me not Native?

"Whatever! Be *more* Indian!" she shot back. We lapsed into an uncomfortable momentary silence, broken by the bus's arrival at our stop. We got off the bus and quickly separated from each other in the snow, heading to different classes in different buildings on campus. My father told me when I was younger, "Son, there will be people who won't accept you for being what you are. Don't let that stop you. You're Indian enough—you don't need them to validate you."

But besides being biracial, I was different in another way: I was—and am—bisexual. I also identify as a *two-spirit* person, but that's not the same thing. I knew from when I was quite young that I was attracted to boys and girls, and one of those attractions was okay to talk about, the other, not so much. It wasn't until I was older and I learned more about my people that I understood what *two-spirited* really meant. Even the term *two-spirit* is an English gloss of a more complicated set of identities that vary from tribe to tribe. Historically among my people, a *winkte* was a medicine person—someone with a special connection to *Wakan Tanka*, the Great Spirit—who was biologically male, but whose gender roles and relationships were not the same as those of a tribal warrior. Even writing this, the English description is uncomfortable in its approximation; the nuance of the meanings in Lakota is lost. And it's also something I can only distantly relate to—I grew up in a different age, a different time. Being bisexual and *two-spirit* was a touchstone for me; it gave some greater meaning to who I was and where I came from. That didn't mean that other people, Indian or White, could always see clearly who I was.

As a kid, I grew up with the feeling of always having feet simultaneously in two worlds. I was Indian—and I was White. I spoke some Lakota, but my primary language was English. My family went to church *and* to pow-wows. I lived in the city, but we went to our land in South Dakota, too. It was something akin to W.E.B. DuBois' concept of *double consciousness*. There was always a sense of *both/and* in how I viewed the world; nothing was ever simple.

That made things easier when I realized I was bisexual. I had a model for understanding it. I could be attracted to women and to men. My self-awareness evolved over time: I would later amend that to "being attracted to more than one gender" and then to "gender is not a determining factor in my attractions." (So clinical in tone! It is still evolving!) Along with that came the need to affirm myself to others, to come out as *bisexual*, even if people didn't believe such an identity existed. As I entered adulthood, I slowly grew comfortable with this process.

When I talk with White people about being a tribal member, I sometimes get in reply, "Oh, I can see your high cheekbones!" or something similar. This may or may not be true, but it's often intended as an affirmation. When I interact with other Indians, there is sometimes an unsaid sense of "Well, he's an *iyeska*—not full-blooded, that's for sure." It's not meant as an affirmation, but as a questioning of who I am. A similar process happens when I say I am bisexual. Among straight people, I sometimes get a response of "Oh, so do you have a boyfriend and a girlfriend?"—again, this is sometimes meant in a positive way. But among some gay and lesbian people, my queer identity is sometimes only conditionally validated. In few, if any, of these cases does it mean that I am fully accepted for who I am. I can understand all this—having feet in two worlds means I often have insights into why things are the way they are. Because I see things simultaneously from different perspectives, I frequently figure things out more quickly than someone brought up in a single culture.

All of this also has meaning for me as a man. I used to say that I was definitely a "guy"—as if I was clearly on the "male" side of the gender line. When I was younger, I was acculturated to a very White sense of what it meant to be male: be strong, be tough, don't show emotion and don't admit to finding other men attractive. I also ended up being transphobic; I didn't know what to make of transgender identity, much less transgender people themselves. It took years and the patience of my transgender friends to come to grips with my issues as I worked to overcome my prejudices. As this was going on, I started reading about gender much more critically. I read John Stoltenberg's *Refusing to Be a Man*, and slowly realized there was a lot about being a "guy" that did not work for me. Over time, I had unconsciously moved away from traditionally WASP ideas of masculinity to something . . . different. Being *two-spirited* made increasing sense to me as I got older.

As an older adult, I have sympathy for my younger, college-aged self. Defensive about being labeled as "not Indian enough," I wasn't quite ready to see the connection back to being bisexual. Trying to fit in, using someone else's ideas of what it meant to be Indian, was like getting caught between the sharp edges of racial category boxes on some cosmic identity form. I wasn't ready to do that, but I had not yet realized that I did not have to—and did not *need* to—fit in that way. The sometimes uncomfortable gift I've been given by the Creator has been to see things from more than one point of view. I could take another path with my feet in two worlds.

Now I find that my identity as both bisexual and two-spirit is a different kind of touchstone. I see how gender and sexuality are not—and can never be—either/or, black/white, up/down issues. It also has revealed how these labels—*bisexual, biracial, two-spirited, male, White, Indian, gay, lesbian, straight, transgender, queer*—can be oversimplified to keep me apart from others, or considered in all their complexity to bring me closer to *mitakuye oyasin:* all of our relations. This journey across many worlds is not done.

Victor J Raymond, Ph.D. is a Rosebud Sioux/Scottish/English bisexual/two-spirit man. He lives in Madison, Wisconsin and works as a Sociology instructor, writer and activist.

why i still go to pride events

by justin cascio

During the years I lived on the Gulf Coast of Florida, we didn't have any kind of gay parade. I went to high school in rural Florida, in a small town where to admit to not being either a Christian or a heterosexual was to become an instant outcast. I was already an outspoken atheist; I didn't yet realize I was queer.

After high school, the closeted ones and I made our way to Tampa, the nearest big city. I know because I found them there when I arrived, a few years after them. LGBT people had our own coffeehouses, dance clubs, churches and activist groups in the big city. On campus, at work and in the mall there were Pride beads to help us find each other. I put on my rainbow-colored beaded necklace in 1996 and didn't take it off again for years.

Some of us also had a gay family reunion in the annual Gay Day event at Disney. This was and remains an unofficial event, not sanctioned by the park officials. Starting in the early nineties, someone put up a website, and would post the date months in advance. Central Florida LGBT folk, and more from out of state, even from out of the country, would show up. We would all buy our tickets like everybody else—only when we arrived at the gates, we would be wearing red shirts or something rainbow or gay-themed, like t-shirts that said "NOBODY KNOWS I'M GAY," or more parade-like attire, to whatever extent that didn't violate the dress code of the park. (No assless chaps are permitted in the Magic Kingdom.)

I'd been to Walt Disney World before going to Gay Day. I went as a child, taking my first airplane trip with my parents and little sister for a family vacation. When we moved to Florida, we went to the park again, driving the hundred or so miles for a day in the Happiest Place on Earth.

In high school, I'd gone to Grad Nite at Disney twice—once as the date of a senior and again in my senior year. Grad Nite was held every year in the late spring. After the park was closed, we were invited with other Florida high school seniors for a night in the Magic Kingdom. It was an all-night party for students at Disney, so there were many safety rules in place: everyone had to arrive via the buses, not drive there. On arrival, our attire had to meet the semi-formal dress code: no doubt an attempt to keep us all behaving like ladies and gentlemen. We submitted to "Mickey's Friendly Frisk" for drugs and firearms. Then we had the park to ourselves for the night: all the usual attractions, plus big-name music acts. In 1991, I saw The New Kids on the Block and C+C Music Factory perform at Grad Nite.

When I went to my first Gay Day, it was my first time back in seven years, and the first time going to Disney I dressed not to please school or park administrators or my parents, but for gay visibility.

Driving into Disney World is an orienting experience. First, there are hundreds of miles of billboards. Then there's Radio Disney. There are several miles of topiary Disney animals and palm trees. Halfway between Tampa and Orlando, we began spotting each other on I-4 by our rainbow bumper stickers, and by the growing numbers headed east with us. Our excitement grew as our numbers swelled and we came closer to the park entrance. By the time we were in Walt Disney World, we were already pumped up: Disney Happy.

Hundreds of people in the park that day wouldn't know we were going to be there until they saw the sea of red shirts and inquired about them. Walt Disney World is full, on any given day, of people who have made the trip of a lifetime. Many had planned for months or years, like my parents had for my first visit, and had traveled from all over the world, to delight their children and enjoy the park that day. By random chance, some of them were wearing red. If a guest got upset about all the gays and complained to a park official, Disney would give them a pass to visit Epcot Center or one of the other Disney parks in Orlando that day instead.

In 1998, Operation Rescue protesters showed up for Gay Day at Disney, and their people made it all the way into the park, buying admission the same way we gay redshirts did. I saw a couple of them inside, talking to other park guests, but most visible were the protesters who stayed outside the park to be seen on the way into the park. The Operation Rescue protesters, standing on the immaculate grass with their grisly anti-abortion signs, in front of the beds of foxgloves and tulips in the shapes of Disney characters, were just part of the orienting experience that day.

I'd seen an enormous anti-abortion protest once when I was in high school. Bradenton, the city next to our small town, had the nearest shopping mall. As my blithe and unchurched family drove to the mall one Sunday, we rode past hundreds of people lining the streets from the city limit at the river's edge, down U.S. 41 to the mall and beyond, stretching, for all we knew, all the way out to the beaches 20 miles away. Many had their children with them. They were all dressed in their Sunday clothes and holding signs like these.

In 1999, I would face off against another Christian army, Love Won Out. You wouldn't think a group with such a nice name would need to run protests, but they had poured a lot of money and resources into my sun-stroked Gulf Coast community to educate public school teachers, administrators, social workers, lay ministry, Sunday school teachers, church members, parents and every other interested party in how to counsel youth who might come out to them as questioning their sexual orientation or gender identity and need coaxing back onto the "right" path. In the course of the protest, I found myself pulled into a group of people on the LGBT side who were chanting, "Love thy neighbor," more and more loudly and at close range with a group of counter-protesters, until I was filled with mob rage, screaming these words. I stumbled away in confusion. How could I yell these words with so much hate?

By the late eighties, the liberal, New England college town where I now live had a gay protest parade. I've heard from our town's archivist of gay history that people would march through downtown with paper bags on their head to keep their neighbors from recognizing them. This year, I went downtown with my husband to see the Northampton Pride Parade, when we ran into my girlfriend, Carolyn. I wasn't expecting to see her there—I'd tried to make plans to meet her at the parade, to watch together, but she wasn't sure she would go. But she was there, and she wanted to talk, so Kevin left us together on the footbridge over Main Street to talk, while he went down to the street level to see the parade up close.

I realized, standing up there over Main Street with my arm around her waist, that Carolyn and I would look like tourists, or allies, to all of the people gathered below, not like two queers who live in this town. Our queerness becomes invisible at times like this. It's not even as simple as saying that this is an experience of passing trans men, or of bisexuals in roughly half their relationships, or, even more complicatedly, of lesbians who sometimes date men. My farmer has seen me at the farmer's market on different days, kissing Carolyn or holding hands with Kevin. He knows who I'm married to: we've been to his house to buy meat and eggs. I wonder if I should come out to him about my girlfriend.

On Mother's Day this year, Carolyn bought me a card. It was one of those cards that are blank on the inside, sold for times when there just isn't a card. For even more complicated reasons that have nothing to do with trans identity, she deserves a Father's Day card, so the following month I did the same thing. An experience we share is that the kids we're thinking of don't send us cards on those days. We love them, and they love us back, but we don't get to see them. So we're sad when we're around kids, and on those days when parents are honored and well-intentioned people try to get it right, wishing us a "happy." It's a kind of invisibility, too, similar to having the relatives you haven't come out to ask you if you're thinking about settling down yet.

There are so many aspects of our lives that we don't flag or hold up a sign about. You can stud yourself with markers of your religion, politics and cultural identities, or you can walk around in a plain white t-shirt, like I usually do. Whether it is a matter of survival to appear anonymous, or of sanity to put on the rainbow-colored beads of your resistance depends on where you have stood lately, who you have had to stand up against and whether you are free today to be yourself, where you are.

On the bridge over Main Street in Northampton, Carolyn and I stand close together and cheer for each of the marching groups as they pass beneath us. I've marched in other Pride parades—twice through the Village in New York City—but I'm done for now. I figure the parade is for the ones who need it: young ones who need to be loud about it, old ones who have never done this before. Carolyn, Kevin and I have each done our share of marching. Maybe we'll be down there together on Main Street some year in the future. In my dream for us, we're all there with our overlapping families of partners and lovers, our friends and neighbors, all cheering, all smiling and happy and proud and gay. They can all see us, finally, and we can see them, and there's no one left to come out to or fight with about who we are.

For now, though, we cheer, especially for the kids. Today, it is enough just to be here.

Justin Cascio writes about the intersections of lifestyle and social justice.

trade

by cedric maurice

"An object used only for its purpose, then set down or discarded, often traded, loaned or sold."—Cedric's definition

"Objectification: to present as an object, especially of sight, touch or other physical sense; make objective; externalize"—Dictionary.com

"Trade: the business of buying, selling or exchanging commodities; synonymous with 'swap"—Merriam-Webster

I knew I was bisexual at eight years old. I didn't know what to call it, but I certainly liked boys just as much as I liked girls—you know, in that stomach-churning, eye-avoiding, can't-talk-much kinda way. Without role models, I gravitated toward gay community, in spite of having read the one paragraph explaining bisexuality in the first edition of *The Joy of Sex*. Responding physically to boys at 12 didn't require access to community. It only required a consciousness of my emerging sexuality, uninhibited by the fact that I was just as responsive to girls.

It wasn't long before I ended up in Atlanta and met the first guy with whom I would have a genuine sexual experience. I was 14 or 15. Sam was older, probably in his early twenties. I met Sam at a church dance event. The church had hired a band and laid out food. My best friend and I met Sam, who invited us to leave the church to attend a radio set party where a well-known DJ supposedly hosted music celebrities. Being interested in meeting music celebrities, we accepted the invitation. After being driven to a nondescript high-rise building downtown, Sam said the party had been canceled and we should stop at the home of Sam's friend Melvin, the manager of the band, himself at least 30, to smoke a little pot. We acted cool and tried not to let on that we had little to no experience with drugs and alcohol. After beer and a couple of joints, they separated us and each made their move. I remember pretending nothing was going on, afraid to move or break the silence and yet not wanting to disappoint.

I trusted Sam and enjoyed the fact that an older, mature guy had taken some interest in me. There weren't many men in my life, including my absent father, and I wanted Sam to like me. I wanted to be an adult and I wanted to experience the world. Sam seemed to offer me those things. He had a van and would call me, come to my house, park outside until I came out and then drive me around town while we drank beer and smoked pot—until he would reach over to fondle me. I thought Sam liked me and I enjoyed feeling liked. I accepted that sex was expected, which wasn't bad since I readily enjoyed the experience of orgasm. Something was missing, but I didn't know it then. Sam had never met my mom. He had never come inside the house. He was a ghost, really. He only spoke to me and only showed up when he wanted. It never occurred to me that Sam might have been apprehensive because of our age difference. I was definitely in unfamiliar emotional and relational terrain.

Sometime during this time, I met a crew of older gay students who hung out at an older drag queen's home. This became the spot where we would cut class to smoke pot and drink beer. It also became the spot where many of us minors were taken advantage of by older men far beyond our age. This is where I first heard the term "trade." I wasn't sure what it meant, but it was a status they certainly applied to me. It seemed that trade was masculine, expendable, worthy of f*cking, not worthy of keeping long term. Trade seemed a novelty, a whimsy, someone to "have" and dismiss as "had." Most of us, the young men in my crew, were underage, a little thuggish, not yet socially sophisticated, and to some degree, needy. We needed attention, guidance, money, drugs, homes and, yes—love. What we got, mostly, was used.

For years after this, I found myself searching for love, imagining that sex, being the core of my power and my only value, would somehow attain it for me. I found myself seeking attention and validation, from men and women, through my sexual talent, only to be ultimately discarded, rejected and dismissed by those who I thought cared about me. The gay community was fertile ground for fly-by-night relationships, where empty, meaningless sex was always available. My quest for sanity, salvation and soulmates was clouded by an inner sexual philosophy for which I had no words, model of fulfillment or roadmap.

I sought help and guidance from older men, often men in church leadership roles, but these men took advantage of my sexual availability and distorted sense of trust, rendering church just another spot to trick and hustle. These men were everywhere—in the justice system, youth programs, schools, driving the streets, clubs, workplaces—and some were even friends of my mom. It felt as if the only thing anyone wanted me for was sex, and yet sex proved barely enough to secure any semblance of genuine love. My hunger for love and pursuit of it through sex with anyone who gave me the slightest attention left me feeling unworthy, damaged, empty, angry and powerless.

Eventually, I reached my bottom. Drugs, alcohol, jail and broken relationships brought me physically and spiritually to my knees. I could see the double life I led as I avoided being my authentic self. I came to realize that I needed to be more than honest if I was ever to find myself, let alone my partner or partners. Anyone could be *a* partner, if I remained willing to mold myself to fit other people's needs over my own. *My* partner(s) would value me for living in my truth. I needed to risk being unapologetically authentic, even in the face of potential rejection. I began to heal through the support of people who understood what I was going through, and I began to find my way through the maze that was me. I came to realize that the only thing wrong with my sexuality was the destructive way I had expressed it. The shame and guilt I had come to know so intimately were simply results of my secrecy, confusion and misguided need.

As I learned to develop boundaries, values, principles and self-confidence, I learned that some people actually saw value in me beyond my sexual potential. This was a long time coming. Soon I began to search for people of like mind. I decided that with two and a half million people in Atlanta, there had to be at least a few more like me. I placed an ad in a local paper and started the Bisexual Atlanta Resource Network, Atlanta's first bisexual support group. Within a few months there were hundreds of self-identified bisexuals meeting in small groups in my apartment. It was inspiring to find others who could relate to the inner experience of bi- or pansexuality. Not long after, I heard about the Fifth International Bisexual Conference to be held in Boston.

The Boston conference was a turning point for me. I had finally found people, from literally all over the world, living the dream I had long ago tossed aside as a fantasy: where I walk down the aisle of a cathedral hand-in-hand with my soon-to-be husband and wife bound for matrimony. Yes, it might have been a far-off dream, but at least I knew that people lived these commitments daily.

My experience at this conference gave me the confidence to continue the work I had begun, and upon my return, I founded Atlanta's second bisexual support organization, Colorbinumbers. Colorbinumbers was my response to the amazing kinetic energy I felt during the Boston conference when the bisexual people of color broke off to form a contingency group, which included Dr. Elias Farajaje-Jones (now Ibrahim Farajajé), among others. It revealed my need to connect with others who shared my cultural and sexual experience.

My personal growth as a therapeutic professional and educational specialist has included counseling and coaching many men and women in meeting the challenges of reconciling their intrapersonal sexual natures with their interpersonal spiritual, social and familial roles.

As a recovering person with a respect for all spiritual traditions, I have sought to share my life experience with others as an atonement and a healing offering of what I didn't have in those early days. Today I recognize that the love I share with men and women is precious and to be cherished. I welcome intimate, honest, accepting people into my life, while appreciating the strengths and depth of "Being" within me.

Today, I am loved for me, not for sexual favors. Sex is not central to my life. It is an important part of who I am, but it is not the sum of me. My value today is as a multifaceted spiritual human being whose inner experience is complex and joyfully mysterious. I am no longer traded from one lover's hands to the next like an object used and discarded, with no consideration of my humanity. Most recognize who I am long before we make it to the bedroom. In fact, today it is because of *who I am*, rather than *what I can do sexually*, that we make it to the bedroom at all.

Cedric Maurice strongly supports bisexual community. Lifestyle coach, counselor, speaker and trainer, he facilitates integration of the authentic self into practical life choices and can be reached at cmauriceinquiry@outlook.com.

the queen

by derrick rice

I ordered a blackberry mojito, savoring the sweet sting, rolling the delicate fruit across my tongue. The lights pulsed and stretched across the room, blending reds with blues and greens with yellows. A large wrinkled hand gripped my right shoulder, fingers spread pointing down towards my chest.

"You're new around here."

"How can you tell?"

"Come on, darling. This is my natural habitat. We can always tell when there's fresh blood lurking about."

His pink shirt with thin white stripes fit snugly around his protruding stomach, his long gray dress pants fell down to shamelessly scuffed brown leather shoes. Frail gray strands of hair were gelled and slicked back across his square head. "Let me buy you a drink."

"Alright."

He called out to the bartender, "Hey, Mitch, two Pink Ladies. On the tab."

"Two Pink Ladies. Is it 'Take Your Son to the Drag Show Night,' Francis?"

He burst out with crude laughter. "I think that's next weekend, Mitch. I was just getting to know my new friend—umm, what's your name, kid?"

"Alex."

"I see you know him so well, Franny."

"Oh, shut up."

The bartender handed us the two drinks, the same bright pink as his shirt. It was a damn good drink. A drag ensemble began singing "It's Raining Men." The whole bar seemed to roar out in celebration, sweaty boys without shirts making it wherever they could find a place.

"Look, Francis. It's been a good time, and this is some place you've got here. But my friend is ready to go, and I'm his ride."

"Give me your number. We can do lunch."

"I'm not looking for a date."

"Neither am I. Don't be so vain. I'm looking for a friend. All of mine are either dead or straight. Do I look like I'm here picking up?"

He held his head up with a long blotched arm scarred through with surgical precision, and let the other rest over his bulging stomach. I gave him my number.

Francis called me to set up lunch on Sunday morning, after his service at the gay church in the city, at a café in the artsy part of town with some members of the choir. The café had wooden chairs pushed into the sidewalk without tables and a single bar resting behind white brick where a thirtysomething with spiked black hair made drinks with an easy smile and told the chef that it was going to be a slow morning. Francis was there with two men dressed in carnation-colored robes with golden sashes who were already squawking away.

"Now, honey, I told you the first time and I'll tell you again. If he wanted to stay with you, he woulda treated you better."

I walked up to the group and was at first admonished by the man to Francis's left.

"Is there something wrong, sir? Don't just stand there and look at me like I'm some kind of freak—if you have a problem say something!"

"Slow down there, Bunny. He's a friend of mine. Say hello, Alex."

I raised my hand to wave and was run through the introductions. Bunny was William, former soldier and woman about town, criss-crossing the whole U.S., leaving boys with broken hearts and sometimes-arched backs still sore in the morning. Allen had worked at the embassy in Switzerland for 15 years until he was outed by a coworker after being seen with an Italian ambassador in the back alleys of Zurich. They sat me down and shouted to the bartender for another round of red wine to be brought to them, as well as one more for their new friend. They were all gray- or white-haired, and had attuned to the same conversational frequency after years of telling the same canned stories.

"So let me tell you about the love of my life. Let's face it, girls, we're far too old to be of use to this young man for anything except maybe this," Francis let out after finishing his glass of wine, yelling at the bartender for another.

"Oh, come now. I don't imagine this kid is looking to be put through that so suddenly. It's such a nice day today. Don't go ruining it with your stories," offered Bunny.

"No, no. It's fine. I'll listen," I said. What else is there?"

"I knew he was a listener. I have always been able to pick up on these things."

"Oh, God save the queen! Whatever sort of planet would we have without you and your infinite wisdom?"

"You're always making me out to be some kind of ego."

"And all of the dukes and duchesses will gather to hear the words of our royal majesty. Share with us your story, oh beloved mademoiselle."

He rolled his eyes and began, his friend giggling all the while.

"I was living in Florida with a Cuban businessman I had met in New York. He smuggled for a living so money was always coming through. It was beautiful. No strings attached—I was as free to love as he was, and we both took advantage of that. One day I noticed a black patch formed up on his right hip. Something that looked like it would be pierced if you pressed into it hard enough. Like the Black Death. That night he tried to come onto me and I turned him down. I don't know why exactly—I just felt strange about those spots on him. He got drunk. Mean. Ended up kicking me out. But—he didn't make it past that winter. No one knew about the sickness or how serious things could become without some sort of restraint. I wish we had. Ricardo treated me right. I would have liked nothing more than to stay with him forever."

"You don't mean that. You're blowing smoke because there are no consequences. From what you've told us, he was a loose cannon and if you had real friends back then they would have told you to leave him."

"None of you knew each other back then?"

"Allen was too busy chasing after married Swedes to ever have to deal with that. There is a certain tragedy to married men, don't you think? If they drop their wife and kids for you, all of a sudden they're everything you don't want."

"As good as you. How many faceless boys did you fuck in the pursuit of liberation?"

"That's where you're wrong. I wasn't pursuing anything. I was liberated. I fucked who I wanted to fuck, whenever that was possible. I was never at odds with myself chasing straight boys in back alleys. I just moved on to the next catch."

A well-dressed uptown bear took a seat at the bar, ordering a tall glass of beer which he sipped slowly, letting the foam stick against his lips without licking it off. Each queen at the table sent signals his way in deliberate glances that had come from years of practice. Francis pushed himself up from the table, almost knocking over the wine glasses, and smiled greedily.

"Not so fast, girls. He's mine first."

He strutted over to the man and they began talking.

"Well, damn. Francis is standing in front of him—we can't see how it's going."

"I'll bet you he's in. You know how he is."

"Does he get around a lot? Do you know if he's got the sickness?" I asked, suddenly uneasy at the implications of this question, intended only to find common ground between us.

"Oh no, honey. Cancer, most likely. Something benign now, but he had to shave his head a couple of years ago. It looked awful. He never told us, but between pills and doctor's visits you can't keep that kind of thing a secret."

"Pipe down, you two. He's coming back now."

Francis and the man shook hands and put their phones back in their pockets, presumably having exchanged information, and he now walked back to the table with the dumb grin of a teenager. His whole frame shook with each step, as if it presented a great difficulty. The heels of his scuffed shoes clicked against the cement evenly, and when he returned to the table, Allen raised his glass.

"To another conquest, your majesty."

"Shut up, will you. Don't blame me because you're lonely."

"What did you say to get him to go out with you?"

"A lady never reveals her secrets," he said, taking a long sip of wine, calling out to the bartender for another.

"He really is a good one, Fran."

"I know. I like his genes."

The whole group laughed and ordered many glasses of wine instead of bottles to avoid feeling diseased, squawking across the bar like loveless birds. So the words flowed easily and the afternoon sun was lazy in the sky, hiding behind casual clouds that filtered out the harsh rays, still leaving the spring breeze blowing fermented red kisses that stung like real love.

I saw a young woman walking down the street, short dark blonde hair twisted wildly, white shirt with the sleeves rolled up walking proudly, long pale legs left to air out and make the day more beautiful. I was a child. Meek and smiling and there she was walking—but she caught my cast-net eyes (I must have learned something being around those old queens) and called me over to her with a wave. Without looking back at the table I found her, each of us maintaining that connection without a name, her face made clearer with each step, a stud over her lip, ring through her nose, full rosy cheeks holding green eyes that trapped me.

She spoke first.

"Who are those guys you're with?"

"Just some friends I met. As good as anyone else."

"They're old."

"They've got stories to tell."

We walked over tightrope details, put names to faces, voices to words. I was full of liquid confidence, slightly slurred but not shattered. She was new to town, looking for someone—no different from anyone else in that regard—studying culture in her spare time; her wrist held portraits of saints she didn't believe in as aesthetic ideals, reminders of the great whys—people throwing themselves into the pavement like madmen. I could have kissed her, but did not.

She bit her lower lip.

"Do you want to get coffee or something?"

The proposition firmly planted set root and branched out towards her. She wrote her name and number down on a notepad she kept in her back pocket.

"See you around, Alex."

"You too, Lilly."

"Oh, and for the record, if you ever make my name into some kind of cutesy pet name—Lilly-Pad, Lilly-Billy, any of that shit—I'll never speak to you again."

"Duly noted."

I raised an invisible glass to her as she walked off, leaving me alone there as quickly as she had come.

I took a second, eyes closed with the wind caressing my face, and walked back to the table.

"Well, what in the hell was that?"

I lit a cigarette and took a sip of wine.

"What do you mean?"

"You know goddamned well what I mean. You're not one of us?"

"I'm not gay, if that's what you're saying. Bisexual. I don't see the problem here."

He obviously didn't approve and was floating on too much drink to hold back his thoughts. "I don't believe in that. Bisexuals are just gays who sometimes sleep with girls."

"Or vice versa. That's kinda the whole point of it. I never said anything about your gay church ignoring those passages calling for you to be stoned to death."

Francis stood up from his chair. Allen intervened.

"Calm down, girls. I was married once. Two kids came from it. Obviously it can be done, and being with a girl isn't some kind of cardinal sin, even I enjoyed it a few times. If you're not at odds with yourself, young man, there's nothing to discuss. Do what makes you happy. Fran, he's from a different time. Young gays are so fickle these days—most of them are either cutters or druggies, and the deniers must really spoil the pot, that's how it was back then, at least. I can see how it would be a pain. We lived it. You had to struggle to be recognized once, pay him some respect. And you, Al, just because you don't believe in what we do doesn't mean it can't be done. I've read the gospel, and I will live and die for the message of love and equality. That's what we believe in. That's what we sing about."

Everyone finished their wine glasses and tipped generously, realizing that we had consumed too much for a Sunday afternoon. Francis bummed a smoke from me, each of us apologizing for the misunderstanding, though with what sincerity it was hard to say. The silent cab ride back to my apartment scrambled the optimism of a newfound beauty. Francis could have called me a breeder. I've never heard the term used, but the thought still lingered, unable to be cast away into the passing gray streets.

Derrick Rice studies Creative Writing at the University of Houston. He is currently revising the first draft of his first novel.

cooking from scratch: learning queer from the kid's menu

by andrew salman

When I first came out as gay, I was finishing my first semester of college (in the Army ROTC, no less) and being bombarded by stories of Tyler Clementi's death and the still undecided repeal of Don't Ask, Don't Tell. The only things I knew about queerness were taught to me by Lady Gaga, porn and news stories of queer-bashing-spurred suicides of lonely kids whose profile looked a lot like mine. Crafting queerness out of such a limited exposure is the equivalent of baking a cake that is all cocoa, no flour or sugar. Yet even with a recipe as incomplete and imperfect as it was, I made my damn cake and left it for the world to devour.

And there I was: Kinsey-six gay with a painted-on, ultra-campy and hyper–poppy "Fuck you" attitude and a rainbow bracelet. It didn't fit. My super-gay friends were pretty unlike me. They scoffed when I expressed mere aesthetic appreciations of people who weren't Sean Cody actor-lookalikes. I was the capital-O Other when discussions of marriage equality came up because, oppression as it was, I wasn't particularly that put out by not being personally offered marriage. I just completely did not understand catchphrases from men's dating websites such as "masc4masc" or "no femmes." Not knowing the alternatives (or even that there were alternatives) left me looking for that one conventionally masculine boy to sweep me off my feet, be mine and mine alone and to presumably have really vanilla sex with for the rest of my life. Can you imagine eating only cheese pizza for dinner every day until you die? I don't even like cheese pizza.

It took an intervention by an older queer for me to realize how much bullshit this presentation of myself was made up of—my new fabulously gay wardrobe was as ill-fitting as the Army-issued gym shorts from mere months ago. She followed this up with how limited my worldview and scope of understanding of queerness was. Had I ever once questioned the gender binary? Compulsory monogamy? The entire culture behind sexism and its many derivatives, like transsexism and heterosexism?

I hadn't, and never would have without her prompting. I can no longer say that social pressures or exclusions keep me from liking the people and bodies I want to like in the ways they did before. I've spent my time knowing and loving men who reminded me why we call hairy gay guys "bears" (though the one I'm thinking of more resembles Mama

Bear than her relatives), women who liked tying me to the bed with pretty pastel ribbons, boys who rocked the skirts and shirts they tailored themselves, and those whose gender and its expression could be as variable as flavors of ice cream.

It shouldn't have taken me years upon years to be taught that there is far from one way to be queer. Despite not identifying as such, and demonstrating some pretty clear deviations from the common definition of "gay," the binary of straight/not-straight has people from stranger to friend calling me and those like me gay. It's as much the fault of queer cultural leaders as it is of straight ones. I mean, if my queer college peers have never sat down and thought through these dimensions for themselves, how can they think to explore them in people they interact with? To them, there is one and only one way to be queer.

And it's not their fault. In no small part, it's the homosexual agenda's fault. Gay pride's fault. The fault of LGBT equality. I have criticized them as harshly as I have Dan Cathy of Chick-fil-A, or Fox News. The rigidity with which people within these circles espouse "traditional" values, such as biphobia and erasure, monogamy, sex-negativity and restrictive gender expectations, leaves little space for those who are queer in more ways than in the desired gender of their romantic partners. It's this mass-produced, peachy-keen message that "love is love" and "we're just like you" that are to sex and romance what "colorblindness" is to race. This "we just want gay marriage" bullshit spouted by the Human Rights Campaign and most major cities' pride festivals has bargained and sold out the diversity of queerness out to make "gay okay" in the hopes of a slightly quicker victory for those who still identify nicely with the new, smaller definition.

This discourse exists at the expense of every other identity or the option to create our own, distinct from the clusterfuck of alphabet soup that is LGBTQQIAetc.etc.etc. The Acronym—which makes me cringe in all of its iterations—has limited me to gay; conflated my sexuality, romantic ventures and gender expression; and kept the public from understanding what I want and what I don't, or thinking in any sophisticated way about what they want and what they don't.

This agenda is in the business of selling the world a breakfast of bacon and eggs when all I want when I wake up is a bowl of whiskey-soaked Cheerios. This agenda is telling me that I can't love getting tied down and beat up by a woman whose biceps are bigger than my thighs or suck the dicks of guys who are straight-except-for-with-me while their lustful, lonely eyes linger on their fraternity brothers. This agenda sells a single sex-love-identity deluxe package ("Everything you need in one place, for your convenience!") to the whole world with an insane markup in social cost, all the while hiding that infinitely-long *à la carte* menu that holds everything you desire while not forcing anything you don't down your throat.

This agenda, the homosexual, LG-sometimes-B-almost-never-T agenda won't have anyone examining and developing a sophisticated understanding of their love, their sex, or their self, and I'm over it. Post-gay. Post-LGBT. Post-suffocating, hetero/homonormative bullshit. I want my à la carte relationships, because my sex is nothing like your sex, my goals are nothing like your goals, and it's not about who I love unless we're talking about loving ourselves.

Language limits us. The different ways of interacting that work for us are as infinite as we are. Even those with the most seemingly simple sexualities and searching-for-a-soulmate romantic drives would benefit from eschewing the heteronormative relationship model. The penetration-as-king guide to fucking admonishes navigating those murky waters for ourselves, discovering our own desires in the process.

There's no need for cookie-cutter, mass-produced relationships when homemade cookies are better, no matter how they end up—even if that's just like the mass-produced ones—because *you* made them. Shortcuts make our experiences shallow. When you're ready to give experimentation and diversification a try, make some damn cookies. I'll be waiting for you with a glass of milk, or coffee or whiskey, and can't wait to chat about how we're navigating this mess of love and sex for ourselves, and the benefits you're reaping from it. After all, I still haven't tried all of the items on the menu and would look forward to your recommendations.

Andrew Salman is a Western Kentucky University undergraduate and Radical-in-Training. He's still grappling with perceptions of "radically" queer identities, mental illness and broader anti-assimilationism in society and is going to stick around in academia until he's got it all figured out.

by james donald ross

cooking longer than others

First memories are tougher to recall as we get older, and I'm no exception to this phenomenon. My childhood was actually nice and positive for the most part, free from major issues that can complicate growing up. Then, in 1973 my mother became part of a very conservative religious organization, the Jehovah's Witnesses, completely changing my world. No more holidays, birthdays or the usual things I had become used to.

As I got older and moved to a small Montana town from a very large California city, my world became smaller. It was fun and exciting but the changes my body experienced at puberty made me aware of things that others my age didn't talk about.

Then we moved to a city in Washington State, and that is where—at age 13—I started to become aware of my attractions. All of my other friends in school were discussing the newest supermodel and I also enjoyed the conversation and resulting daydreams. Still, I also did the same dreaming about a few certain boys at school. We never had a term for this at school other than "gay—no bisexuality, pansexuality, etc. We didn't even have LGBT yet in the late 1970s. Added to that, the religious pressure I was under kept me from even asking about. So I hid it away. Every day.

Although I deceived myself and kept things hidden, I most certainly had those men and women from my early years as fantasy and romantic material. I remember vividly being in love emotionally with Cary Grant and Grace Kelly at the same time with both still in my heart and soul today, although the first time I felt sexual stirrings on my gay side was in the mid-1970s with Michael York after the film *Logan's Run*. That was a very poignant time for me, with York later being surpassed again by Grant. Ah, youth.

In 1994, I married a delightful woman and began my new life with her. Even today she is my bride and I love her more than ever. But I harbored a desire for men that never subsided, even as I remained ingrained in my religious organization and moved up the ranks in duties. It was not easy to live every day with this desire and attraction to both males and females and not act on it.

Then in 2008 my father passed away and my wife and I made the split from the church and flew free to be our own selves. I came out to my wife and told her my long-held secret. Fortunately she showed how loving a heart and soul can be, accepting me as the bisexual man I truly am.

Things improved dramatically from there when in 2011 she too came out as bisexual. We began to share sacred thoughts and dreams together as a bisexual couple, hoping to experience the freedoms we had long wanted. Although it would be another two years before we would take action on these long-held desires, I had prepared myself for this eventuality by researching everything I could from others in similar situations. When that time arrived, I was prepared. The experience of being with another man who shared similar experiences and desires was more than I'd hoped for and proved to me that I *was, am* and *will be* bisexual. Once I read a phrase that applied to me:

"Some of us simply take a little bit more time to cook, but eventually we all get to the dinner table to share."

That was perfect. My years of cooking might have taken longer than some, but once finished, it was well worth the wait.

James Donald Ross is an American bisexual man of 47 years who finally had the courage to come out after 33 years of religious, social and familial pressure to conform. He thanks his wife, Ann, and his partner, Liberty, for all their support.

by rich conrad

the gift

Of all you learn here, remember this the best:
Don't hurt each other, and clean up your mess.
Take a nap everyday, wash before you eat.
Hold hands, stick together, look before you cross the street.
And remember the seed in the little paper cup:
First the root goes down, and then the plant grows up!

—*John McCutcheon ("Kindergarten Wall")*

The inner well of my sexuality is as inseparable from my essence as the quality of knotting is inseparable from the rope. No choices here—just a dawning perception of what has been there since the beginning. When I was ten and masturbation, recently discovered, was becoming a favorite pastime, I remember watching a Tarzan movie with Johnny Weissmuller and Maureen O'Sullivan. Which one would I blaze with? Both. In fact, being the meat in a T and J sandwich or sharing T with J were the fantasies that brought the most satisfying self-induced orgasms. And then when Boy came along, a remarkable vista of possible combinations presented. Haley Mills (from *The Parent Trap*) was another player in those early fantasies, and although intimacy (not only sex) with the male players was prominent, my first real crush was on Haley. Once when 11, thinking of her, I sat on my bed and wept.

I could arrange the cast of my fantasies in any way I chose, but please note that no actual actors were importuned or had any idea of what I scripted for them. I'm sure they would have been mortified! The rarity of desire for boys and girls together as sexual partners is what placed me in a small, lightly inhabited circle. When I hear the term switch-hitter used to describe me, I know that some monosexuals cannot imagine batting from both sides of the plate at once. They see me as a pendulum, but I'm more like the quantum mechanics notion of the electron. We all look at each other through the lenses of our own natures (but seriously, some of my best friends are monosexuals).

This never seemed strange to me because my root system was well-nurtured, although I did absorb the standard fifties and sixties take on being queer: a *Diagnostic and Statistical Manual of Mental Disorders*-listed disease. I want to be clear that, while I didn't see anything wrong with me, I clearly knew that others would. Anxiety about discovery, leading to hiding such a wonderful part of my nature, produced a wound. As the son of divorced parents raised by a mostly single mother, the Freudian explanation for my semi-queerness would have been clear in everyone's eyes, including my mother's. To her credit, whenever she knew that I had heard people trying to demean "queers," she reminded me that during the war, as a Red Cross canteen supervisor in North Africa and Italy, she had worked with a lot of homosexual performers and that like all people they were worthy of respect and freedom from fear and, like all groups, they consisted of both the admirable and otherwise. She had no idea how profoundly that message affected me. Had my fantasies been public, my poor mother would have been the scapegoat for my nature.

I never met a young boy comfortable discussing sex with his mother. Mine had given me a very thorough book about sex, including puberty, and told me to ask if I had any questions. That wasn't going to happen. The book said that youthful experimentation among boys was normal so long as it was followed by the equally normal change to adult heterosexuality. How comforting to someone not quite bent at a right angle but certainly not straight. Now, I was happy with Kinsey's suggestion that sexuality occurred on a continuum. In adolescence I imagined not a one-dimensional linear scale, but a bell curve where I lived dead in the middle, attraction- and behavior-wise. I didn't feel odd, so maybe this was normal and the others just hadn't wakened to their true natures yet! I later learned that I live in the center of a bimodal curve with the very unequal modes at both extremes of the distribution, bobbing in a very shallow trough between two waves, both of which I see cresting above me–a minority within a minority.

In America, you can recover from almost any defect, but suck one cock and you're a cocksucker ever after. Recent social research seems to indicate that for younger men that attitude may be waning. For me, I'm happy to say they were like the Lays® potato chips slogan ("You can't eat just one!"), although I would have preferred to share them with a girl. But then, as far as I could see, it didn't matter that I lusted after Mary or Sandi or any of the others. As long as I also lusted after Johnny or Dean, the deal as to my real nature was apparently sealed. My stigma bonded me in a narrow way to others who were stigmatized.

I remember one poor effeminate boy in elementary school who took unending shit about being queer despite lack of any clear evidence. Fifty/fifty chance he was straight and late to puberty, and if so, certainly straighter than the martial arts student that I was at the time. Gender fluidity may incite homophobia more than gay sexuality. Gender was never my issue, and my clear affinity for girls protected me from derision from many of the jocks with whom I played intimately (I don't mean baseball). When I heard girls or boys ragging on him, I asked them, "Why does he frighten you so much?" The old man, my jujutsu teacher, was helping me to see fear beneath churlish behavior and bravado. The fearful, above all, crave power, and men, though not above all, long for and fear intimacy with other men. I saw their fear, and usually they lowered their gaze. I still do not suffer impoliteness gladly. Gay, straight, in between, transgender, whatever, I hope you made your way, Jimmie.

I was never confused, as many people think bisexuals are. I liked to eat pussy as much as I liked to suck dick (both at the same time is the sweetest spot). I liked to fuck girls and boys and be fucked by both. I wish my clarity about what I was had extended to knowing how to live what I was. I would have benefited from role models. Either sex could set me aflutter and I suspect that I could have made a life journey with someone of either sex. The physical and the spiritual intimacy I have shared with Ann, my partner and wife, was born of my early explorations, of lessons in trust and ease of caring in the midst of fear, with boys and girls. Through all of these experiences, I learned that sex was only one door to intimacy and not always the end of a chase.

I also learned that people are anxious to be themselves with someone who listens and won't punish them for asking uncomfortable questions. I loved people of both sexes, but I have only been interested in marrying one person, because I feel the tug of a fundamental disposition to pair bonding. It's just that simple. I was to learn that I was liminal, at a threshold and just beyond reach from either side, seen as betraying both by many heterosexuals who thought people like me could only be gay and deceiving, and by many gays who thought I could only be gay and in denial or passing (no one thought I was straight and just kidding).

Sometimes I felt as if I aroused more fear in both camps than did members of either in the other's camp. I remember meeting Jon's friends in St. Louis. Jon is my brother-in-law who, along with many other fine qualities, is gay and to whom my wife and I were out. His friends looked at me like an accidentally caught coelacanth; they couldn't quite see what use I had in the modern ecosystem. This is hollow complaining for someone who looked so straight from the outside and was never bashed or bullied (well, I guess if you're breaking bricks with your bare hands a certain deterrent factor exists).

When you are a kid and the other, you feel isolation. You hide, and only in the shadow do you show yourself. If bisexuals can be out, we're now out to the people who matter. People's usual reaction, before they talk to her, is to worry about Ann. Unlike Diogenes, over a lifetime my lamp discovered a few bisexuals like me, out to wives and in happy heterosexual marriages. Even coelacanths stumble on each other. When I finally talked to my dearest male cousin about my sexuality, he told me he had known a long time and loved me.

Our natures pose questions—some we hide from and some we embrace. My sexuality is a gift that allowed me to explore the bounds of my humanity and, finding answers, to move joyously beyond either/or. I love my place in the world, even though I'm not normal!

But then, who is?

Rich Konrad lives in Vancouver, Washington, with his wife of 42 years. He and his wife have managed a very happy marriage that celebrates his sexuality as well as hers.

by mitch kellaway

energy can never be destroyed

Hundreds of eyes stare out from the wall. Though they're all plastic, the effect is still unsettling—just as the dorm's residents intended it, I suppose. I spot several plush tentacles discarded on couches, their stuffing protruding where they lack a suture; when my eyes adjust to the dim light and haze of smoke, I notice more littering the corners. I get it: this room is the belly of a beast. My mind does the mental work to piece the rest of a story together, as I stare at the hall's residents—some listless, some hyper-charged—strewn about, smoking pot, doing whip-its and who-knows-what else. The dorm's inhabitants had apparently decided to make their common room into a monstrous art project, and gave up halfway through. It seems fitting, somehow, and just the kind of avant-garde and nonchalant that I am not.

"I am so out of place here," I think bemusedly for probably the eighth time this night. Nonetheless, I settle down next to a girl who'd been friendly when I walked into the party. Her glazed eyes don't seem to recognize me though, so I sit silently and observe the others for minutes that seem endless. I'm looking for something in this anything-goes space, so different from my day-to-day—but I'm not sure I'm going to let myself grab it if I even find it, whatever it may be.

Uneasily, I get up and drift to the next room. Its lights are out, but I can sense the darkness seething with human shapes. I have no idea what they're doing. Drugs? Sex? Sexy drugs? Drugged sex? I move on to the next doorway, but pause outside. I've heard that this room, unlike the others, is a dedicated space: leather and S&M. I've been clued in by Milo, one of the few people I am actually friendly with here. A friend of a friend of a friend, he's a short, rail-thin White gay man who takes delight in shocking a wound-tight lesbian like me. He told me to stop by for the hour he'd be up on a rack getting paddled, but I'd forgotten until now.

Serendipitously, he saunters out of the room just then, shirtless and grinning like a Cheshire cat. Our eyes meet past the bodies trailing between us and, perhaps sensing my aimlessness, he crosses the hall.

"Hey, what's up?" he gives the standard greeting, and I return the standard response.

"Nothing much."

"Having a good time?"

"Yeah," I reply, but I'm pretty sure we both know it's untrue. Though I'd seen many others who looked like me walking around—butch dykes with equally baggy cargo pants, no-frills t-shirts, and tightly cropped hair—I'm out of place. I feel as if I'm exuding introversion and home-body-ness from my pores.

"You want to go someplace more quiet?" His intense blue eyes twinkle mischievously. I nod, relieved. I trail behind him as he weaves between partygoers, leading me to his bedroom. For the first time tonight, I'm genuinely anticipating what comes next. When we get there, I sit on a desk chair and he stretches out on the narrow bed; we're surrounded by edgy art posters and loose pieces of paper scattered about. He cuts to the chase bluntly, clearly more versed in talking sex than I. "I'm not attracted to you." In turn, I stare at him dumbly.

"But do you want to have sex?" he asks.

"Yes," I assent, surprising myself with how true it is. With a silent smirk, he gets up and turns out the light. We share an unspoken understanding that this exchange is a one-night stand, meaningless. I presume that includes a guarantee that it won't shake the core of our sexual identities.

Except it did. At least for me. The confidence with which Milo pushed our tryst forward had me convinced that he remained unchanged—but that's just an assumption, because I never spoke to him again. If I think about it harder, I have to admit I never fully understood his intentions for, just moments after we'd settled down, he hastily left the room to retrieve something. High as a kite, he probably never figured out exactly what he was looking for. Maybe he was content with the satisfaction of luring a lesbian into his bed and couldn't wait to tell his friends; maybe he just had the munchies.

After an increasingly humiliating ten minutes, I left the room, my chest heavy with self-disgust, my mouth and head feeling as if they were filled with cotton. I realized how drunk I was. I left the dorm and resolved to sober up at a cafe across the street, then head home on the first train at five a.m. But after 15 seemingly interminable minutes, I backtracked dizzily across the way, heedless of oncoming traffic. I just had to know what this all meant.

"Which room is Milo's?" I asked anyone in my path, until I knew I was pointed in the right direction. When I got to the doorway I'd fled less than an hour earlier, I barged in with righteous fury.

"Why didn't you come back?" I threw the words at the blanket-covered lump on the bed, putting all the anger I felt at myself behind them. He didn't stir. I flung the covers off to make sure I had the right culprit: the man to blame for stirring these conflicting feelings, then leaving me to pick up the pieces of my shattered sexual identity. It was him, all right; the same mussed brown hair, impish face and gangly limbs. I knew if he awoke right then and invited me to lie beside him, I would. It enraged me.

"Milo? Milo!" I shook his lifeless form carefully, then with greater force as he failed to awaken. Then I caught myself. I reviewed the evening's experiences—getting wasted with strangers, random (though ill-fated) sex, putting hands on someone in anger—and could barely recognize the person I'd momentarily become. I hurriedly restored the covers over Milo's frame and left his room for good, unsure whether his faint grin meant he'd been feigning sleep all along or he was pleasantly dreaming, unaware that the world had changed overnight.

Sometimes I dig that memory out of my mental vault with wonder; I play and rewind the images as if watching a movie of someone else's life. While plenty has changed over the ensuing seven years—I've matured, stopped partying, gotten married, transitioned to male, and treated my social anxiety—I can still transport myself back to the overwhelming feelings of helplessness and shame. I'd spent years as an activist fighting for everyone's right to love any gender, and I just couldn't afford myself the same latitude.

In retrospect, I can see it had everything to do with my actually being a man. But at the time I agonized over being a lesbian imposter, believing my self-betrayal was fundamentally rooted in sexuality rather than gender. I quickly threw myself into a relationship with a woman, but in quiet moments I would envision how I could tell her I thought I was really bisexual. The guilt of not being true to her restarted whenever I quieted the guilt of not being true to myself.

So much of my adult identity was wrapped up in being a gay woman; it's what had given meaning to my high school years and helped me find belonging in college. It informed everything from my clothing choices to my movie choices to my class choices. What would it mean to do the same things with a man by my side?

I buried those questions, rationalizing that I just didn't have the time to focus on them with all of my university classwork and extracurriculars. Curiously, I'd done the same with the lingering thoughts about my gender identity—"Am I actually a man? How do I go about transitioning?"

that I'd been having periodically since I first discovered the word "transgender" as a teenager. In truth, I shelved a lot of self-work during those first few years as a college student and not-quite-independent grown-up. It all felt, to put it simply, too much.

There's no easy way to summarize how I gradually stuffed such monumental revelations down until I could ignore them completely. I don't quite understand it myself. All I can say for sure is: just because something is underground doesn't mean it disappears. As an adult, I've heard the same idea from alternative healers: energy can never be destroyed, it simply takes another form. All of my self-denial—my half-uncovered gender and sexuality, unprocessed pain about a lover I'd lost and crippling anxiety—bubbled up a year later unbidden. By the end of my third year in college, I filed paperwork for a much-needed hiatus that I ended up renewing for the next three years.

"So, I'm finding that I'm really just a straight dude," my friend Gray informs me incredulously. We're sitting across from each other in a cavernous restaurant booth, nursing the last of our beers. The rest of our group—fluctuating between five and eight trans guys each month—have departed to their partners and young children. For the past half year we've been meeting up regularly over pizza; I've never missed a Sunday, save for the week I had my chest surgically reconstructed. This time only three of us show up and, once we've eaten our fill, we're now down to just two. Perhaps Gray, like me, is holding out for the rare, intimate opportunity to talk one-on-one, away from staring eyes and jocular banter, inhibitions mellowed by a couple drinks.

"You know what I mean?" he raises his eyebrows, but I let him finish his thought before I respond.

"Joanna was so worried that I'd start only being attracted to men, like so many guys do after they transition . . . but nope. I'm really, really straight." We share a smile at how silly that sounds coming from a former out-and-proud lesbian.

"Actually," I answer quietly, "I am quite attracted to men. I find that I'm very physically drawn to them, but more spiritually attracted to women." He nods knowingly.

"I've heard that a lot."

Ten years my senior and ten times the extrovert I will ever be, Gray's probably met every kind of queer there is; perhaps I feel safe knowing nothing could surprise him. He's the first person I'd revealed my range of desire to besides my fiancé—a cisgender woman, just like the partners of every man in our group, curiously enough—and my brothers, who are my two closest friends. My relaxed posture and tone don't speak to what a milestone this moment is; then again, it feels right that it's hardly earth-shattering. The second time I'd come out as bisexual to myself, shortly after beginning my transition to manhood, hadn't shaken me, but rather reconfirmed that I was on the road to accepting my whole being.

Little over a year earlier, I finally allowed myself the space to become a man, consequently resetting my defaults on virtually everything that asks one to relate to other bodies in this world. I started revisiting questions I had long ignored or settled: who is Mitch the sibling, the son, the partner? How would I relate to my future children? What does it mean to be a man attracted to both men and women, but happily committed to being with only the latter? Gradually, in aligning my physical form with my spirit, I gained clarity on why certain kinds of interactions—especially ones involving spontaneous socializing or relating sexually to men—resulted in panic. There's probably more to it than I'll ever know, but I'm convinced it has something to do with being seen.

Everyone needs to be seen for who they are to self-actualize, and gender—in all its physically and socially constructed complexity—is part of that. As an emerging adult, the inklings I'd been having about my gender nonconformity, coupled with my nascent embrace of queerness and feminism, crystalized into a lesbian identity that I held onto fiercely. I rejected anything within me that resembled a heterosexual or patriarchal status quo; my narrow-minded self, fresh out of high school, threw bisexuality and male-ness in with that lot. At the same time, I isolated myself socially more and more. I dove headlong into schoolwork, deeply convinced that no one "got me" and plagued by a feeling of inauthenticity.

To get by day-to-day, I buried the contradictions—my desire for people of any gender, my need to embody masculinity through physical interventions, my lively inner life that could translate into a relatable personality—under a prudent, studious facade. But for the final months of my initial college stint, I could feel their weight as a dark force unavoidably growing within me.

If its viscerality sounds beyond belief, it's because it was; I literally sensed something heavy and alien take up residence in my chest. Sometimes it frightened me with its strength. It distracted my attention and drew the life out of the one uncomplicated, joyous identity I had left: scholar. My depression, as it was eventually labeled, seemed to strike with intent.

Today, I imagine it as the redirected energy of habitual self-denial coursing upwards through my neck and jaw, settling shadow-like on my brain. Insistently, it hijacked my attention until I took notice of the parts of me that I'd been ignoring. The process was messy and meandering, but eventually I got it.

Sitting in my new apartment's kitchen one morning, I finally heard the message loud and clear: living my true gender will allow me to be present and accountable in relations with myself and others. Instantly, I connected the dots: the wrongness I'd felt as a lesbian trying to sleep with a man wasn't about betraying my queer sisterhood. It was about betraying that I was truly attracted to being with men as a man. I sat up straighter as a fresh energy flowed through me, liberated; my head felt clearer than it had in years.

Mitch Kellaway is a Boston-based transgender writer and activist. He is co-editor of the anthology Manning Up: Transsexual Men on Finding Brotherhood, Family & Themselves *(Transgress Press, 2014).*

by declan wiffen

the right to confusion

At 25, I moved back to England from France to finish my Ph.D. Simultaneously, I decided that I would no longer deny my bisexuality. I have done the latter more effectively than the former. I hardly knew any LGBTQ people, and I didn't know a single self-identified bisexual person. I hadn't done so much as to even kiss a member of the same sex and I was very slow and tentative in coming to terms with my attraction towards men.

I began this exploration of my sexuality by reading as much as I could. My search for information on bisexuality didn't yield much to begin with. I really wanted a memoir written by a bisexual person to help me to process my sexuality. But I couldn't find any, so I read memoirs by gay men and lesbians. These were interesting and informative, but they didn't speak to my experience, and if they did it was as a challenge to and/or a denial of it. In order to find out more about bisexuality, I turned to the Internet. It wasn't as easy to find information as I thought it might be. I didn't really know where to look. So I trawled through random blogs, newspaper articles and Tumblr. Reading these was often helpful, but one thing that kept coming up was the common statement from self-identified bisexuals, that they were bisexual and weren't confused!

As someone new to exploring and admitting their sexual preferences, I found this more like a goal to achieve than a sentiment I could readily embrace. I did find some encouragement in it—an affirmation that my sexual preferences were accepted and valid. But predominantly it made me feel like I couldn't be bisexual, as it didn't seem that bisexuality and confusion could co-exist. And this only added to my confusion, because I felt like I was bisexual *and* I was confused.

I respect those who are un-confusedly bisexual. I'm even a little envious. I also understand how and why those who use the phrase above do so to respond to a culture which has told them that they are "just confused" when they're not. It's important.

But I feel the need to claim for myself and other bisexuals in a similar position the right to avow and speak about our confusion, without it being stigmatized. People's experiences are different.

I assume that many people who are attracted to more than one sex are somewhat confused when they first start to explore and avow their sexuality—and possibly also somewhere, or in various places along the line. But I didn't hear about this type of experience in the resources I found. Most of us live in a society that tells us to be attracted exclusively to the "opposite sex," but even if we're lucky enough to live in a less homophobic environment, then heteronormativity is still present in the belief that it's an either/or situation. If it's not, then you're lying to yourself, or going through a phase ("It's normal, everybody does it"), or, God forbid, just confused!

BUT IT IS CONFUSING.

Some days it just doesn't make sense. Other days I think I'm just open to the world in a different way. On Tuesdays and Wednesdays, someone's gender really isn't an issue for me, but then the following 24 hours I can be obsessed by wanting the specificities of a male or female body. It becomes exhausting, and I decide I will refuse to think about it any longer, which is inevitably impossible.

Just saying this out loud makes me feel better. Trying not to be confused isn't worth the effort. From childhood to my mid-twenties, I believed that you should be attracted to the "opposite sex," and if you weren't then you must only be attracted to the same sex. Straight or gay were the only categories of sexuality I had language for. Realizing that I fit into neither category is going to take a while to get used to. And it's an ongoing process. I feel unsure about my sexuality some days—but I'm trying to embrace this feeling of confusion because it's to be expected in the environment I live in, it's quite normal when exploring one's sexuality and it's valid.

Perhaps it won't last forever. On bad days I really hope it won't. I hope that it will fade into the past and allow me to get on with my life. But this is just a ruse to a notion of normality. I'm new to exploring my sexuality and I can feel like I have to get it figured out, specifically when talking to people about my experiences and desires.

People are often used to the prevalent discourses that exist about sexuality, and if you don't fit into these, then they can try to force you to "pick a side," or deny how you feel because they don't understand. This has caused me huge anxiety and has only hindered the process of exploring my identity and sexuality. I've found that these negative emotions—from myself and from others—are really more about fear than about confusion: a fear of confusion.

By admitting my confusion, I'm realizing that I don't have to yield to these outside pressures to fit into a pre-defined space. Being able to say, "I'm bisexual, and I'm confused," enables me to get on with my day, to refuse anxiety and fear of the unknown and allows me to stay open to the possibilities that confusion in bisexuality offers me.

So I'm living with confusion.

Why?

Because we have the right to be confused.

Declan Wiffen is 27, based in the United Kingdom, and trying to complete a Ph.D. Wiffen blogs at www.malebisexualqueer.wordpress.com.

institutions

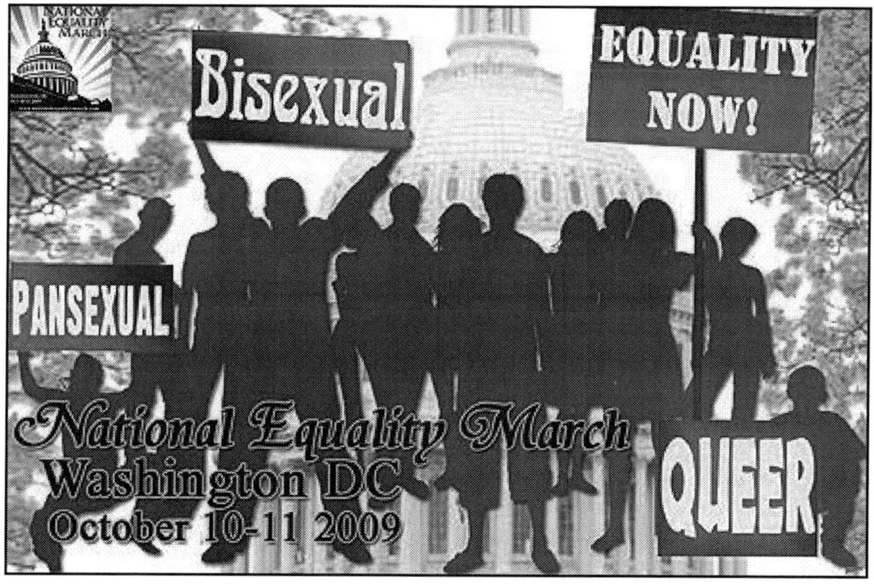

national equality march poster,
new york area bisexual network

greedy

by samati niyomchai

It was 2012. I had the privilege of a graduate degree in social work and a respectable job in my field. The city I lived in had protections against anti-LGBT discrimination in the workplace, and the state was working towards lifting its ban on same-sex marriage. Yet, I was still not entirely comfortable being out to everyone. I was careful at first to whom I came out in my graduate program. Even in the field of social work, it never hurts to be pragmatic. Not only was I one of the few men, I was one of the few queer people in the program. It became clear that some of my fellow graduate students were unaware of having met a gay person before, much less a bisexual person and even less a bisexual male.

One of the many comments I remember hearing at school, sitting at a table with all-female colleagues was, "Where are all the hot men?" I am no underwear model, but I would like to think I am decently good-looking. Another common comment was, "Where are all the straight men?" I would always imagine replying, "Well, I'm not straight, but I date women and I'm available." But I never did. Clearly, my female colleagues assumed that I was not attracted to women, despite my never having claimed this. Maybe it was because of presumed gendered behavior or other social cues, but a few weeks into the program, labels were already assigned.

When I told a straight man from graduate school that I played video games, he responded with pure shock. "You play video games!" he blurted, "I didn't think you were a gamer! You never talk about it!" He was an avid gamer and it seemed he had labeled me "feminine," making me, by his logic, uninterested in video games or other "masculine" things, or unable to do them at all. We became close friends and embraced our mutual interest in science fiction and video games. I thought of him when I stood in the comic bookstore for my weekly trip for the newest issues of *X-Men*, listening to the *Glee* soundtrack on my iPod.

In the interview for my first job after finishing graduate school, I was pushed to come out. My résumé has a lot of LGBT-related work on it, so one of the interviewers asked how I gained the trust of LGBT people I worked with as clients. She stated, "This group has issues concerning trust especially with what and how they disclose aspects of their personal life." I thought to myself that if I came out and they decided not to hire me, it would be okay since I would not want to work in a hostile environment anyway. I explained that I was a part of this "group" and trust was not an issue in the work I did. I then gave an answer about LGBT people and the importance of trusting their healthcare provider. I got the job. My agency had assigned me to a local hospital to work with patients there, which I knew would mean coming out at work a second time.

The agency work environment was not as friendly as I had hoped. Evidently, my supervisor, one of the folks from my interview, had outed me, incorrectly as gay, to everyone at the agency. A number of strange follow-up questions came up as I shadowed my new co-workers. When one asked me if I was seeing anyone, and I answered that I had a girlfriend. She then asked if I was straight. When I told her I was bisexual, she then asked, expectantly and intrusively, if I had a boyfriend too. The presumption that if I were bisexual then I must also be polyamorous was just the tip of the iceberg.

Things became even more uncomfortable a few months later when my coworkers and I gathered for a casual lunch. We started discussing our relationships, updates on who people were seeing, upcoming dates—typical office talk. I stated that my previously mentioned girlfriend and I had broken up and that I had started seeing a man. A co-worker, whom I did not know very well, blurted out very obtrusively, "You need to pick one and stop being greedy. The rest of us pick one or the other. It's not okay, being indecisive and hogging everyone." She went on like this for what felt like a few minutes. I had assumed she was joking, but after lunch another co-worker shared how uncomfortable she, too, had felt during this conversation, reinforced by our co-worker's pattern of intolerant behavior.

The accusations of greed came up again later when the co-worker who had issued the earlier diatribe backhandedly asked if I was still being "greedy." She then implied I knew "all about" the movie *Magic Mike*. The fact of the matter was I had—and still have—no interest in seeing *Magic Mike* and, aside from knowing it is about a male stripper, I really could not care less about it. The fact that I date men does not mean I will jump at the opportunity to see a film about male strippers. At least I got paid to work at this agency.

The hospital where I did most of my work was another story. I was relatively sure most of the staff assumed I was straight as heteronormative comments popped up a lot in our conversations. One man frequently looked over my shoulder and one day saw me reading an LGBT-related article and he made a comment about how "the Democrats always bring up gay marriage." In a dismissive tone of voice he said, "They say it's the next Civil Rights Movement."

Coming out to him as bi was going to be fun, I thought.

Of my own choice, I wear a rainbow bracelet and I never hide it, but I think some of my hospital co-workers had chosen to completely ignore it. On a few occasions, patients have noticed. One actually gave me a high five. Two queer female co-workers noticed the bracelet and asked about it; they knew I identified bisexual. With almost everyone else, I kept my identity to myself and allowed them to assume whatever it was they were assuming. It did not seem like it would be helpful to tell everyone that I identified as bisexual. Anyone can wear a rainbow bracelet (I know many allies who do) and anyone can be reading about LGBT news.

Even today, I sometimes wish I were gay so conversations would be easier. Don't get me wrong—it would still be difficult but at least it would confuse people less. I had mentioned my previous girlfriend before at the hospital, and therefore no one was really assuming that much. They simply heard what I said and drew conclusions from that. When I started seeing a man, I was afraid to bring it up because I did not want the questions that were bound to come up about sexual history or preferences; the looks staff would give me; the weird, amateur sociological statements starting, "Here's what I think about bisexuality . . ." and the potential harassment from them in the form of jokes about my sexuality, which I was already experiencing from members of my agency. I wanted to be able to continue to do my job and help patients, which was hard enough given that I worked with the uninsured/underinsured who were the subjects of a lot of hostility from some of the hospital staff. I really did not want to add the layer of my sexual orientation into the mix as well.

Then again, I mentioned ex-girlfriends and that I was at PrideFest. I wore my rainbow bracelet and brightly colored, fitted polos and dress shirts as part of my work attire, which were very well received. I identified as an Asian-American, male social worker in a hospital and had great rapport with patients. I challenged many assumptions some people made and I had the respect and support of many co-workers by doing my job well. Maybe some things can just be left unsaid.

I have since left the hospital. I did not come out there, except to a handful of people. One of the medical technicians started to use "gay" pejoratively around me, waiting for a reaction that I never gave.

I also reported the unacceptable attitude of my biphobic coworker and the inappropriate discussion of my sexuality to the agency leadership, which was taken very seriously, resulting in my coworker being reprimanded and a workshop being scheduled for the agency on human diversity, specifically including sexual orientation.

I did not know if this workshop changed any minds, but I was not willing to wait around to find out.

Samati Niyomchai has a Master's in Social Work. He works in the Midwest and is currently pursuing his professional license. He also volunteers with a local LGBT youth support group.

safe spaces

by andres musta

My first language was Estonian, though I grew up in anglophone Canada. Both my parents are Estonian by birth, and Estonian was all we spoke at home in Toronto. In Estonian, there are no gendered pronouns (his/her, he/she): only me and you, us and them, yours and mine. This profoundly shaped my experience of the world, my basic comprehension of identity and human relations.

Throughout my youth I explored sexually with my peers, male and female, but thanks to the Lutheran Church and the prevalent culture of immigrant machismo, this was shrouded in shame, guilt, confusion and denial. It wasn't until adulthood that I owned this.

My union, the Elementary Teachers Federation of Ontario, gave me the motivation and sense of safety to come out. Some of their training programs are only offered to people who self-identify, so that was a big incentive, just to be able to participate in leading-edge workshops and conferences. Secondly, they take human rights seriously and nurture a supportive environment and a culture of caring.

Through union activities, I met more like-minded people and it became easier to speak openly about my identity. I gradually came out as bi/queer in my late thirties and early forties. My father had already passed away when I came out, but my mother handled it without surprise, very casually. Identity was not something we discussed much as a family—there were more pressing issues to deal with.

As a teacher, though, it is important to speak up about respecting differences and creating a safe space for students. Professionally, I avoid discussing my personal life at work: I'm only "out" if anyone asks, though I do make it clear that I am an ally by wearing pink and rainbow t-shirts to work, and have several pro-gay stickers on my car that the kids notice immediately. The stickers make good conversation starters.

In various subject areas, it helps to highlight the contributions of specific LGBT people and to explicitly identify cultures where gender roles are different from what students might experience as normal, as with two-spirit "berdache" shamans in some Native American cultures, and with female-headed households in Finland, for example.

The new curriculum is especially good at helping to explore the stories we tell each other about how we came to be here from different perspectives, with a focus on personal identity and being active in the world, on making a difference.

Biographies can make abstract conditions real, and the stories of famous bisexual artists and performers are easily adapted to the classroom. Every time period in every country has examples: [1]Sergei Eisenstein, Green Day lead singer Billie Joe Armstrong, Mike "Ned Schneebly" White, Frida Kahlo, Jean-Michel Basquiat, Josephine Baker, Igor Stravinsky, Sammy Davis, Jr., Billie Holliday, Drew Barrymore, Marlon Brando, Lady Gaga, Angelina Jolie, Grace Jones, Bif Naked, Frank Ocean, Margaret Cho, Lou Reed, Jack Kerouac, Kesha, Sheryl Swoopes, Alexander III of Macedon, Azealia Banks, Cary Grant, Pete Townshend, Megan Fox, Walt Whitman, Alec Guinness, Fergie, James Dean, Freddie Mercury and Gore Vidal, who said, "Everybody is bisexual, and that is a fact of human nature." I don't go out of my way to point out bisexuals, but when haters start to talk, it is helpful to identify people whom we have been studying in relation to other matters. Sexual identity should not make a difference but ignorance needs to be schooled.

It also helps to have good resources available. An excellent book series that breaks down LGBT issues in depth for a junior/intermediate level is *The Gallup's Guide to Modern Gay, Lesbian, and Transgender Lifestyle* Series by various authors. The series provides a great introduction to the major issues of the past few decades in a language that is accessible, affirming and optimistic, with an emphasis on how people have organized to improve life. There are several excellent booklists online, for those seeking more ways to discuss LGBT issues with children. Online videos like "#OperationBeautiful—Adam Swagg" have also been an important piece in our school-based character education program. It makes a difference when youths see other people their age talking openly about what matters to them.

As adults, we must recognize that the progressive talk in schools about identity is made possible by unions, by organized labor. Much of the inclusive legislation we now operate under was first developed in our democratic unions, where human rights often carry more weight than with governmental policymakers. Workers' unions have championed inclusive language, same-sex spousal benefits, equal pay for women, anti-harassment policies and related concerns for decades and have set the standard for other organizations.

That said, unions continue to struggle with equality, difference and White privilege; there is much work to be done. The debate over designated executive positions for marginalized and disadvantaged members continues. There is still debate over how much unions should advocate for non-unionized people, on how much we should organize communities. We debate the merits of centralized decision-making. Union membership contains both hardcore activists and disengaged masses with other concerns. But, as Billy Bragg says, "The antidote to cynicism is to engage." Our democratic process has survived. We debate. We discuss. We decide as a group. All the more reason for marginalized groups to be out and vocal.

My life is more authentic now, thanks in large part to my union. With union and school board endorsement, I can openly discuss various family structures with elementary students, no matter what they may be taught at home. Insults roll off my back more because I know I have allies. My friends know who I am, and most still accept me the same as ever. When students ask about my identity I can respond freely.

Nevertheless, LGBT youth still need as much support as we can provide, so I encourage each of us to share our stories, so that we can be real together. Together we can make it better. I encourage each of you to be out as much as you can, to get involved in social justice, to join a union and to get your locals linked through regional labor councils. Form pride committees and go to local, national and international pride events. Organize and be fabulous!

Andres Musta teaches Visual Arts and is an active trade unionist. He maintains sanity by making art every day.

by dr. herukhuti
(h. sharif williams)

a day at the free clinic

I spent a day at a local free clinic run by New York City's Department of Health and Mental Hygiene to get tested for HIV, gonorrhea, syphilis, chlamydia and whatever else gets tested at these places. Here's the story of the adventure.

I walk into the large brick building reminiscent of structures of the 1940s—Industrial Revolution meets wartime functionalism. I feel the weight of bureaucracy settle onto my shoulders as I ride the metal tomb of an elevator up to the floor that plays host to the testing center.

As the doors of the elevator open, a wall painted with a mixture of what appears to be benign neglect, autocratic convenience, stale utilitarianism and pee confronts me. "Where the fuck do I go from here?" I ask myself since there are no markers for where to go next. The security guard downstairs, already busy helping to redirect someone to another facility for pediatric issues, did not bother to do more than to confirm the floor that I already knew the clinic to be on. I haven't even received one test result yet and already I feel lost, afraid, intimidated and alone.

I walk off the elevator and discover a group of "waiters" scattered in seats in an area to my right. I assume that I'm expected to join them. Their gazes—making sure they don't know me, making sure I don't know them—and their facial expressions tell me they are also here to get tested. I don't feel I can ask them if this is the right place or who I should see to sign in. I don't want to break the anonymity that we are all so desperately trying to maintain. We don't want to break the alienation we've built up in the ride in the elevator. To do so would be to confront the humanity of our lives—we have desires, emotions, feelings for other human beings; we have sex with these human beings we desire, love, feel for; and we have fears and concerns about our health as a result of those loves and desires. But there's also a specificity to our humanity that's equally present: we don't have health insurance, and many of us are poor or the working poor. Our access to the nice, clean offices of a private doctor is limited.

There are various kinds of bodies that inhabit the seats. Most are Black or Latino, though there are a few that are not. There are males and females. There's a Latino family—mother, father and four children. A cute Caribbean couple—two men, one in business casual, the other in hip-hop cool. I pray they avoid the B-boy blues of a positive test result and I marvel at the expression of love, conscientiousness and routine in their relationship—they get tested together. That's so twenty-first century American Gothic.

I sit among my fellow public health citizens. The design of the room has us all seated facing a wall a few feet away. Is this some architectural metaphor for the system's forecast for us—all headed in the same direction, hitting a wall? Mounted on that wall is a television obviously connected to a VCR hidden somewhere in the nether regions of the office. Snow and grainy noise pours out the black box, filling the room with white noise's irritating cousin, static. Someone must have hit the play button because a video abruptly begins on the screen.

This video was obviously made as the HIV equivalent to "Scared Straight." The video uses real people to tell their HIV stories in the hope of influencing the sexual decision-making of those of us sitting in the room watching it. But the video was made in the 1980s. You can tell because of the way the people are dressed, their hairstyles and the degree to which their bodies have been ravaged by drugs, disease and economic oppression. And I thought the metaphor of all of us hitting the wall was bad. Now we're subjected to face a future of HIV's past displayed on the video.

I'm already terrified about this test and the impact the results will have on my life. Regardless of whether there's a significant reason for concern, getting an HIV test always quickens the blood and creates a lot of anxiety. You don't have to have done anything. It's an irrational fear promulgated by the socially induced paranoia of decades of HIV-prevention propaganda.

I sit here at the juncture of every HIV prevention message I've received since high school and my memory of every sexual act I've engaged in since first receiving those messages. I'm trying to hold it together, not appear as terrified as I am and now I'm confronted by this ghost of the past, "HIV=DEATH," in the guise of a video. I wonder whose brainchild it was to play this video long after its dubious truth has any connection to current reality. Is it a disaffected, thoughtless bureaucrat who just follows the mandate to provide prevention messages while clients wait? Or is it a religiously inspired, dogma-supported bureaucrat with a complex mix of pity, disgust and condescension who plays the tape to scare these sinners into living a healthier=more righteous=more God-fearing life? Whatever the reason and whoever the person responsible, to me, the decision to play this video at this time in this place was a colossal mistake, and a breakdown in human empathy.

Finally, they call me in to the doctor, a fiftyish, short, pink-skinned man. He takes a brief and inadequate sexual history. He asks me about my sexual history with women. I wait for his questions about my sexual history with men. They never come. He moves on to take the samples he needs for the tests. He gives me a date to return and I'm out. But wait, where are the questions about my sexual history with men? Why doesn't he ask me about that? Is it because I present as masculine and therefore such questions are unwarranted in his mind? Masculine equals heterosexual, right? Sex with women equals heterosexual, right?

I walked into this clinic to get tested for sexually transmitted diseases and unintentionally walked into a test of the public health system's capacity to adequately respond to the sexual realities of the public they serve.

Dr. Herukhuti (H. Sharif Williams) is the founder of The Center for Culture, Sexuality, and Spirituality, author of the book Conjuring Black Funk: Notes on Culture, Sexuality, and Spirituality, *co-editor of* Sexuality, Religion and the Sacred: Bisexual, Pansexual and Polysexual Perspectives, *high priest of the Shrine of Sekhmet and Heruhet (Brooklyn, NY), and faculty member at Goddard College (Plainfield, VT) and Fielding Graduate University (Santa Barbara, CA).*

A version of this essay was first published in Conjuring Black Funk: Notes on Culture, Sexuality and Spirituality, Volume 1 *(Vintage Entity Press) and is reproduced with permission of the publisher and author.*

hot, safe, fun

by william e. burleson

We shook hands. I like to shake hands—it builds trust, especially with middle-aged men. I took my seat behind the desk. He looked around my small office, examining one poster at a time with the wide-eyed reverence of a child's first visit to an amusement park. He stopped at one poster for an extended visit; it featured two shirtless young men standing close together, one guy looking at his friend's chest, the other holding out a small red condom package and looking at the camera. The caption said, "Hot, Safe, Fun."

I opened his chart. "You're here for an HIV test?" I wondered if he would answer, his attention so focused on the poster.

"Yes."

I sorted out my stuff, a foil package, stand, lancet, alcohol wipes, gauze, Band-Aid. I arranged it so that just the right thing is at my fingertips when I need it. Hundreds, thousands of tests over the years made the task rote. "My name is TJ. We'll get the test started . . ." I glanced at the name on the chart. " . . . Bob, do some paperwork and after twenty minutes you'll have your result. Sound good?"

He nodded.

I opened the package and took out a plastic vial of developer and placed it in the stand. "We just need a little drop of blood. Won't hurt a bit." I put on rubber gloves. "Are you right-handed or left-handed?"

"Why?"

"So when I prick your finger and you get gangrene, you won't have your more useful hand amputated."

He smiled just a little, enough to assure me he understood it was a joke. He held his right hand out, and I turned it palm up. I wiped the tip of his ring finger with an alcohol swab. "Won't hurt a bit." As the last word left my mouth I realized I had repeated myself. I took a lancet and with one swift motion poked his finger. I squeezed, a drop of blood appearing. I took a tiny sample with the collection loop and placed it in the vial. I stood up and tucked his chart under my arm. "I'll be right back."

I carefully carried the stand with the vial down the hall of shiny linoleum and smelly antiseptic, past the door to the packed, noisy waiting room, past a clinician wearing goggles entering an exam room. She nodded to me. Nurses used exam rooms and prevention workers like me had offices. Nurses did HIV and STD tests, pelvic exams and more. HIV-prevention workers did HIV tests. Clinicians wore white lab coats. I wore Doc Martens, a flowered shirt, and tribal tats. Clinicians went home at 4:30. Many nights I and others like me would float between gay bars into the morning, handing out condoms, talking to potential clients, seeking out the scared and uninformed, navigating around the drunk and defiant.

In the lab I set the stand in the appropriate spot next to four other tests. They looked like home pregnancy tests, and all four had one red bar: negative. These tests were state-of-the-art: used to be a blood draw would be sent to a lab and we'd get the results in a week, but in 2008 we could get a result in minutes. I put the tester in the vial. I logged the test, the time, the code.

"Busy today," said the white-haired nurse looking over my shoulder.

"Yup."

He went to answer the phone. He worked only in the lab. He used to give tests, but his bedside manner had become short, abrupt, some even said judgmental. He had worked at the clinic for 20 years. Probably a hell of a case of PTSD: he'd seen the worst days of HIV in the mid-eighties, four or five positives a day, at a time when a positive came with the frustration that there was nothing to do. Not anymore. Now there were amazing, if at times brutal, treatments; few died, but many struggled. It was still HIV, and thus the specter of AIDS.

Back down the long hall, file folder in hand, I grabbed the doorknob but realized I had forgotten the guy's name again. I looked at the chart: "Bob."

As I entered he was reading a pamphlet on pelvic exams. He put it back in the pile of materials next to him. "How long did you say?"

I sat down behind the desk. "Twenty minutes."

I looked at him, perhaps for the first time. A bit thick around the middle, he wore a baseball cap and a sweatshirt from the Academy of Holy Angels. No one would notice him walking down the street. I knew I would never recognize him again, one more of a small army of men parading through my little office.

He bounced his knee, arms crossed. He focused on another poster, one with two young men and a young woman with their arms around each other's shoulders. The girl had a tattoo. The caption: "Know Your Status." That was my shout-out to my fellow bi folk.

I leaned back, opened the folder, and picked up a pen. "Okay, let's see.

I'm guessing male, White." I was trained not to assume, but that went out the window a long time ago in the interest of expediency. I filled in the bubbles. "How old are you?"

"Why?"

So, I thought, it's going to be like that. Sometimes when people were freaked out, they became oppositional. No matter. After eight years, there was nothing I hadn't seen and dealt with, including guys like that. "Well, largely because it asks on the form. Give me a ballpark."

He said 45, and I blackened in the bubble for "40-49."

"If you liked that question, you're going to love this one: who do you have sex with?"

Anger flashed across his brow. "I'm not going to give you their names!"

I laughed. "My bad. I said it wrong. I don't want names. What gender are your partners?"

"What do you mean 'gender'? You mean 'sex'?"

"Yes." Political correctness didn't have a prayer with this guy.

"Women." He didn't look at me; he looked at his finger with the Band-Aid.

I decided to let his lie go for the time being. "How many people have you had sex with in the past six months?"

"One."

I let that go as well, even though he had used plural not seconds before.

"Your wife? Are you married?" I asked.

He shook his head no.

I was surprised—he seemed like a married guy to me. "Prostitute?" I regretted it as soon as I said it.

"Do I look like someone who can't get sex without hiring a hooker?"

Actually, yes. "Sorry. Did you use condoms?"

He shook his head *no.*

"When was the last time you had a test?"

"Five months ago."

I filled in the bubble, and closed the file.

"That's it?" he said.

"For the form, sure. You have . . ." I looked at my watch. " . . . 16

minutes left."

His leg resumed bouncing.

"What brings you in for a test today?"

"What?"

I sensed now that it was less being oppositional and more that he wasn't listening. I asked again.

"You should know your status, right?"

For a moment I was impressed, but then I remembered the poster. I repressed a smile. "Do you have reason to believe your status changed since your last test?"

He shook his head *no*, with a bit of a shrug, making his answer less conclusive than he may have intended.

"Believe me, there is nothing you can say that will be shocking or new for me. If there is something on your mind, now's a good time to talk about it."

"There's nothing to say. I just thought it would be good to get a test, that's all."

In my job, we wanted men to talk about what was on their minds, and I was well-trained in making that happen. Too many guys carrying too many secrets; the burden is too great, the cost high. But I felt tired. Maybe too tired to get a closet case to open up, to see how much risk he is taking, to maybe see a better way. "Do you have any questions for me?"

"Yeah. How much longer?"

I looked at my watch. "About 12. Any questions about how HIV works?"

He shook his head no, then, "Yes. Yes, I do. What happens if it's positive?"

I told him about the confirmatory test and the need for an appointment to get set up with services. "Plus, there's more forms."

"That's it?"

"For now. For us here."

He looked down at his hands. His fear filled the room.

"But I got to tell you, having one woman partner in the last six months and a test only five months ago, your risk is pretty low. Very, very low, I would say." Ten years into working in HIV prevention, there were few surprises left. I might have been shocked that a client was negative, but I was never surprised by a positive. Never. I considered that maybe this guy was what he said he was, and that he was a member of the "worried well." There were a lot of worried well: guys who get tested as often as they can, even though they have little or no reason. OCD guys. Certain they have AIDS even though they've been with the same partner—or no partner—forever.

But not this guy. He liked those posters.

"Do you ever have sex with men?"

"What?" He flinched.

"Men."

"What makes you think I have sex with men?"

"You are in an STD clinic getting an HIV test. I'd say there's a pretty good chance you have sex with men."

He looked at a poster of two big guys in hard hats. The poster said, "It only takes once. Condoms."

"Look," I said, hoping to calm him. "You're not alone. You're talking to a bi guy. I enjoy sex with men as well as women. It's cool."

He was having none of it. "How long until it's done?"

I told him eight minutes. Then I sat there, saying nothing. Sometimes you have to let silence work its magic.

"You're bisexual?"

"Yup."

"Say I did. Say I did have sex once with a guy. What are my chances?"

"One guy? Once? Oral sex, pretty much zero. Anal, a good bit better than zero, but you'd have to be unlucky to have sex with one guy once and get HIV, although I've seen it." Not what I was trained to say, to be sure, but it was what I believed to be true. When you'd been in the pits as long as I had been, you cut through the bullshit.

"I thought it only takes once."

I thought how I needed to take that poster down. For high-risk guys, "it only takes once" didn't work—they may have had a hundred *onces* in the past six months, and they are still negative. "Sure. But it's like the lottery: you can hit on your first ticket, but most people buy a lot of tickets increasing their odds."

Most days I tested some guys who had had dozens, even hundreds of partners in the past six months. It can give you a warped view, if you're not careful. I saw it in my colleagues, in that white-haired RN. Pretty soon you assume everyone is hanging around the basement bars at one a.m. or the park in the afternoon, forgetting that on any given night the vast majority of your fellow MSMs—Men who have Sex with Men—are home watching TV, playing with their dogs, loving their partners.

He was a ball of nervous tics, hands wringing, knee vibrating. "Sometimes . . ."

"Sometimes?"

He said nothing.

Tired or not, I found a crack, and I wasn't going to let the door close again. "Where do you meet guys?" Time to ignore the bullshit of *once.* "On the Internet?"

"I travel a lot."

I nodded, leaning forward, elbows on the desk. My best concerned, active-listening pose.

"In Washington, there's this place."

There are a lot of places in Washington, and I had been to all of them. Bathhouses and I went way back. "It's fine, you know. You're an adult. Everyone there is an adult. The question is, do you play safe?"

He was rubbing his hands together as if he were at a sink.

"Look, it's all good, yes? Play safe, use condoms for anal sex. Give yourself a limit for how many people you'd blow, and stick to it. Get tested regularly." I said, practically carpet-bombing him with messages.

"I don't do oral sex."

We were getting someplace. "Are you a bottom?"

"I've never talked about it."

"Being a bottom?"

"I've never told anyone that I like men."

Sad, but I understood. Cruising bathhouses, as fun as it can be on a Saturday night, usually doesn't lend itself to conversation, to sharing feelings, to intimacy, to simply talking. It doesn't have to be that way, but there it is—guys are there to get off, not to have a rap group.

He asked how much longer.

I looked at my watch and lied. "A couple more minutes." This guy was not playing safe. I felt sure. There's no "Hot, Safe, Fun" for him, just shame-driven self-medication, with sex bringing on more shame. I knew that trap well, personally and professionally. "Are you seeing a counselor?"

"What am I supposed to do? Tell me, what am I supposed to do?" he said, talking to the floor.

"Is it that you're afraid you infected your wife?"

"What?"

"Your wife? Are you afraid—"

"I'm not married. I said before, I'm not married."

"Listen, I care. I do. You look like—"

His eyes shot up to mine. "You 'care'? Is that all you got?"

"You're not alone. Trust me, you—"

"You already said 'You are not alone.' Are you following some goddamned script?"

I tried to move toward soothing. "I hear your pain—"

"What's my name?"

"Wha—"

"What's my fucking name?" I tried to peek at the chart on the desk. He slapped his hand down over his name and I jumped. "Tell me what my name is!"

I looked in his eyes, which were now red, wide. "Sorry, you've got to understand—"

He shot out of the chair, hands on his head, eyes closed. "It's been more than 20 minutes. I know it has."

I looked at my watch even though I knew he was right.

"I'll be right back, okay? Right back. You going to be okay?"

"You tell me."

Carefully moving around him, out the door, in the hall, I stopped and looked at his chart. Bob. Fuck me. His name was Bob.

I really did give a shit. He had no idea. I had been in the same room. I was Bob 12 years before, a product of a homophobic world telling me in endless ways that I was sick, twisted, unable to, unworthy for, incapable of love, love of another, love of myself. You don't have to have a damaged soul to get HIV—you just have to be unlucky—but still, there were a lot of people like Bob and me visiting my little office.

Yes, I did care. But did I matter? Maybe that's what haunted me. I was trained—I believed—that by holding a mirror up to people so they can see their risk they were being helped. But was that true? Was my probing into Bob's business doing any good for Bob? I was no longer so sure.

I walked. I dreaded the walk. Seven, eight, nine or more times a day. The guy who gave me my positive took that walk. He was a bear, handsome, blue eyes and one earring—I forgot his name.

I wished I remembered his name.

What if I had had me to do my HIV test, that lifetime ago?

When did I become so casual?

That day 12 years ago, when the bear guy gave me my positive, I cried. He hugged me. He wrapped me in his big arms, and I felt a little less like I was dead. I told a couple or three guys a week that they were positive, and I never hugged one of them. I never let them in like that. It would be too much, too much to give a piece of me to all those guys. A piece of myself sexually if it were different circumstances, sure, but never a piece of me. I decided I would try to give Bob a hug if the test was positive. That's what I would do. Just like the bear.

I pushed the lab door open with my fist. It hurt and felt good.

The white-haired nurse turned and looked at me.

William E. Burleson's short stories have appeared in several literary magazines. He is the author of Bi America: Myths, Truths, and Struggles of an Invisible Community *(Routledge 2005), a book exploring the bisexual experience, and most recently the* Minnesota Bisexual Needs Assessment 2012 *(Bisexual Organizing Project 2013). For more information, visit www.williamburleson.com.*

scientific research on bisexual men: what do we know, and why don't we know more?

by brian dodge, ph.d.

Before appearing on a recent broadcast on National Public Radio, to discuss the topic of "bisexuality: what we know and what we don't," I sat down to map out a few bullet points. I suddenly realized that, despite another celebrity "coming out as bisexual" in the past week and the flurry of media coverage that conveyed this as a "new" phenomenon, I had actually been speaking on this issue of "what we know and what we don't" for quite a while now. Was anyone listening?

It had been over a decade since I had committed my own research career to focusing broadly on gaining a better understanding of sexual health among bisexual men. At the time, I felt like I was working against all odds. While participating in a prestigious postdoctoral HIV-research training program at an Ivy League university surrounded by some of the world's most renowned sexuality researchers, I encountered a very unexpected and unsettling resistance to understanding and accepting bisexuality as a valid sexual orientation, particularly among men. I had gone through what felt like a cruel and unusual merry-go-round of grant writing, review, revision, re-writing, re-review, re-revision, re-re-rewriting, re-re-review and re-re-revision, simply for proposing a small pilot research study that was intended to explore issues related to HIV risk and sexual identity among bisexual men—an idea that seemed so logical to me at the time.

By this time, in the early 2000s, we had already come leaps and bounds in terms of understanding the significance and complexity of self-identity, the negative impact of isolation and "minority stress" on marginalized individuals, the seemingly protective role of community belonging among gay men and even among other groups of "men who have sex with men" (who—as we in public health are so good at doing with entire groups of marginalized populations—are most often reduced to the sterile acronym "MSM"). We already knew that sexual behavior and sexual identity were not necessarily always, or even often, congruent with one another. We were well aware that individuals engage in a wide range of sexual behaviors with a wide range of partners (male, female and other) throughout the lifespan. Indeed, in the HIV-research world, there were some who would go so far as to say, "Men with male and female sexual partners are the driving force of the HIV epidemic from 'homosexual' communities to 'heterosexual' communities . . ." but astonishingly, in the same breath, these same people would say " . . . but bisexual men do not exist." Was it just me—or did this simply not make sense?

Perhaps I was unique in my perspectives. I hearkened back to my days as a doctoral student at Indiana University-Bloomington, where I had the unique opportunity to follow in the footsteps of others who sought a deeper understanding of sexual behavior and, in the process, had found that human sexuality is anything but "black and white." One of the most fascinating, and apparently still largely misunderstood, findings to emerge from Dr. Alfred Kinsey and his team's pioneering research on sexual behavior in the human male was that, in addition to exclusively heterosexual and exclusively homosexual individuals, substantial numbers of men reported sexual attractions and experiences involving men and women along a continuum (Kinsey, Pomeroy, & Martin, 1948). One of my favorite quotes from *Sexual Behavior in the Human Male* summed it all up, not simply in terms of bisexuality but for human sexuality, in general:

> *Males do not represent two discrete populations, heterosexual and homosexual. The world is not divided into sheep and goats. Not all things are black nor all things white. It is a fundamental of human taxonomy that nature rarely deals with discrete categories. Only the human mind invents categories and tries to force facts into separated pigeon-holes. The living world is a continuum in each and every one of its aspects. The sooner we learn this concerning human sexual behavior the sooner we shall reach a sound understanding of the realities of sex (p. 639).*

This was 1948, and even then this was not "new" (and Kinsey and his team soon expanded on similar findings and implications among women in his female study, published five years later). Decades before Kinsey, other behavioral and social scientists had already noted that bisexuality was a common and natural (if not inherent) form of sexual expression in both men and women. Early psychoanalytic theorists suggested that all human beings were inherently, and even normatively, bisexual at birth. Indeed, bisexuality was seen as essential for understanding psychosexual development. Sigmund Freud claimed that all humans naturally experienced homosexual and heterosexual feelings and he saw bisexuality as helpful in explaining later homosexual orientation. Havelock Ellis (1905/1942) expanded upon Freud and was among the first theorists to declare bisexuality, defined then as sexual attraction to men and women, as a unique and viable sexual orientation/identity category:

> *It is well known that at all times there have been, as there still are, human beings who can take as their sexual objects persons of either sex without the one trend interfering with the other. We call these people "bisexual" and accept the fact*

of their existence without wondering too much about it. . . . But we have come to know that all human beings are bisexual in this sense and that their libido is distributed between objects of both sexes, either in a manifest or latent form (pp. 261–262).

These early theories were not without opponents who claimed sexual orientation to be an essentially binary (homosexual/heterosexual) construct and believed that bisexual individuals were confused, in denial or deceptive in terms of their sexuality. The fact remains, however, that even these early scientific writings on bisexuality are now well over a century old—so why do we keep coming back to research on bisexuality as something "new?"

Back in my postdoctoral period, with each round of brutal grant reviews, and subsequent revisions of my intrepid little pilot study proposal, it became clearer to me that I was fighting an uphill battle. One reviewer, for example, required "documentation" that bisexual men exist; in response, along with a revised proposal, I submitted an accompanying letter of support from Dr. Fritz Klein, a man who became not only a constant source of support but also a dear friend at this time of my life, when we would meet for lunch in his favorite restaurant on Lincoln Center when he regularly dropped in to visit New York City. He would assure me that everything was going to be all right—after all, he had done research on bisexuality (although it was a different era and he had relied on private, rather than federal, funding for his studies). In his letter, Dr. Klein detailed his own previous research efforts which, indeed, had supported the "existence" of a wide range of lived experiences among bisexual individuals. Further, he provided documentation of a large number of informational and social networking websites for bisexual individuals, many of which were maintained by his own nonprofit organization, which included thousands of profiles of bisexual people.

In response to this, the reviewer worried that, although the letter of support was compelling, the existence of "one series of idiosyncratic websites whose members could not be verified" did not provide "sufficient evidence of the existence of bisexual men." By the time the third revision of the grant proposal had been reviewed and promptly rejected, it was clear that the institutional powers that be were not yet ready to invest in research on self-identified bisexual men.

As always, Dr. Klein encouraged me to keep going as he laughed, "When life gives you lemons, why not make lemonade?" Personally, though, I was feeling totally beaten down. My lowest moment was when I asked myself if maybe everyone else was right, if maybe trying to launch a career trajectory focused on understanding and improving bisexual men's health was "a dead end" for me. I remember being told, "There is a fine line between being a scientist and being an activist, Brian: I am afraid you may be too personally connected to this bisexuality thing." (Never mind, of course, that nearly every other researcher in that setting was a proud, vocal and out self-identified gay man who sang the praises of having unparalleled insight and wisdom in conducting "community-based participatory research" on countless samples of other gay men recruited from local bars, pride parades, community centers and even "activist" events). My biggest fear at the time was that if I did not do this work, would anyone ever do it?

At a crossroads, I had a difficult choice to make: would I listen to the naysayers and go against doing what I felt really mattered in my heart? Or would I continue to push a giant rock up a never-ending hill, only to reach the summit and be pushed back down so I would have to start climbing all over again?

Thankfully, with the patience and guidance of the finest mentor a blossoming researcher could ever hope for, Dr. Theo Sandfort, along with a lifetime of my own experiences that simply would not allow me to turn my back on what I knew to be true in my own heart, I decided (as with many other things in life) I did not need to "choose one or the other." With Theo's wealth of experience working in the research funding machine, even on issues that were far outside the "mainstream" in sexuality research, I chose to go in "under the radar" and follow a path of subversion and resistance (a phrase I later learned from another prolific mentor and colleague, Dr. Dennis Fortenberry of Indiana University, one of the most prolific and productive adolescent sexuality researchers of our time). I learned the buzzwords to avoid in the federal funding world—which, in the darkest days of conservative politics and AIDS-phobia actually included "sex" and anything sexuality-related; these had to be purged from funding application abstracts in fear of being defunded. In the environment I was working at that time, "bisexual" seemed to be one of those words—which was promptly replaced with "men who have sex with both men and women (MSMW)," knowing that the wheels of public health still moved faster when working with acronyms rather than human beings.

The whole issue of "the down-low" was in full force in local and national media by this time and I began to learn, for better or worse, that many in the "scientific community" treat *The New York Times* as one of the most sacred scientific publications on Earth. Once I was able to cite an article in The New York Times that alluded to the "existence" of Black bisexual men, it seems, there simply could not be any denying it. "And think of the risks they pose to their female partners," I was told at a meeting where peers reviewed my proposal. "Why hasn't anyone looked at this high-risk population before?" Ugh—just think.

I had learned a valuable lesson. Through subtle subversion and working within the system as it was, given all its shortcomings and limitations, I was eventually able to garner the support that I needed to launch the research I knew needed to be done. Even better, once I had the resources to take off from the launching pad, I was able to do the work I really wanted to do and use the results as a form of resistance against the structures and systems that had pushed me down so far. I could use the very same players in the system who refused to open their eyes and see us right in front of their faces to bring about scientific research on bisexual men, women and transgender people visible to the outside world. I have not looked back and, at least I would like to think, we have done some very good work since then . . . in the form of dozens of scientific papers and presentations, several peer-reviewed special issues (Dodge & Schick, 2012; Sandfort & Dodge, 2008), subsequent funded grant proposals from the National Institutes of Health and other agencies, developing community-focused initiatives and interventions for bisexual men, and training opportunities for the next generation of sexual scientists who will fill our shoes long after our brief time has passed. And there is still much more work to do.

So what have we learned thus far in research on bisexual men and what do we have left to learn? Coming back to the moment when I was brainstorming bits and pieces of my work that I hoped to cover in my short time on NPR, I ended up writing down one bullet point: *Bisexuality is not new—and we need to work on new issues now.*

This seems so simple and straightforward to me, but I really do think it is absolutely essential to reiterate every single time we are faced with a hand that tries to push us down, a pen that tries to erase us and make us invisible, a gatekeeper that tells us to "prove" we exist. That is nothing new, and we're way beyond that now. Kinsey knew the truth, and over 60 years have come and gone since then—and even more since all the others before him—and we're way beyond that now so let's not even justify that conversation by going there.

Being forced to go back and start at square one perpetuates a cycle of constant reinventing of the wheel and keeps us from asking the really new and important questions that may matter most. I also see this same cycle play out over and over again in mass media depictions of bisexuality. Insert this week's celebrity who "comes out as bisexual" or "still fancies girls" or refuses to be pigeonholed into denigrating his or her sexuality into a label that does not reflect the true beauty and complexity of their own sexuality. I guarantee you the headlines will lead you to believe this has never happened before, that this is something NEW. *Newsweek* ran a cover story on bisexuality in the mid-1990s with a subtitle declaring it "the new sexual identity." A generation before this, in 1974, *The New York*

Times featured an article on "Bisexual Chic: Anyone Goes" perpetuating without shame the stereotypes of bisexuality as being something NEW, something "trendy," something that will likely disappear until the next time that it is . . . something NEW!

The constant re-invention of bisexuality as "new," despite written records and depictions dating far back to Ancient Greece and even antiquity, subtly but very effectively trivializes bisexuality as a flash in the pan, illegitimate and unreal.

Media coverage of scientific research on bisexuality is often the worst, calling to mind the disgraceful coverage in *The New York Times* of since-debunked junk science using penile plethysmography as a "lie detector," with the take-home message that the almighty scientific research "casts doubt on the existence of male bisexuality." One really does wonder how many times this whole issue of "bisexual existence" can be played out yet again in trashy newspaper science sections and editorial columns before someone demands that we remember the wise words of Alfred Kinsey, "the sheep and the goats." We know that already.

Let's move on to the bigger questions that really *are* new. For example, as a starting point, despite all the evidence we have, why is there such a reluctance to accept the existence of bisexuality in some narrow-minded sectors of our society, including many social and behavioral science researchers? Besides all the risks and the "problems" bisexual individuals may face, are there positive aspects of their lives we could all learn from? What forms of resilience might some bisexual individuals have that allows them to flourish in a society where their very existence is often questioned or denied? What do the life stories of diverse groups of bisexual individuals have to tell us about how human beings experience their genders and sexualities and lives in different ways: how human beings relate to one another, how human beings have the capacity to love and be loved by others, beyond the boundaries of gender? How do we create environments where bisexual individuals can feel validated for who they are, where bisexual individuals can experience and express their desires for relationships with others without fear of judgment, where bisexual individuals can attain happiness and health and hope? In short, how do we help bisexual individuals to be the best that they can be?

These are the sorts of questions I hope we can begin to ask and answer in future research on bisexuality. It will only require the time, resources and commitment of other individuals who are willing to take on the challenge—and most likely a little subversion and resistance.

Brian Dodge, Ph.D., is an Associate Professor at the Indiana University School of Public Health in Bloomington and Associate Director of the Center for Sexual Health Promotion. Dr. Dodge's research has included a number of studies on sexual health among diverse groups of bisexual men and women throughout the United States, Latin America and the Caribbean, India and elsewhere. He is happy to be alive in Bloomington, Indiana, with his family and two dogs, Barney and Miles.

References

Dodge, B., & Schick, V. (Eds., 2012). Bisexuality and health. *Journal of Bisexuality*, 12(2).

Ellis, H. (1942). *Studies in the psychology of sex: Volume 1*. New York: Random House. (Original work published 1905).

Kinsey, A. C., Pomeroy, W., & Martin, C. (1948). *Sexual behavior in the human male*. Philadelphia: W. B. Saunders.

Sandfort, T. G. M., & Dodge, B. (Eds., 2008). Black and Latino male bisexualities. *Archives of Sexual Behavior*, 37(5).

by mitchell plitnick

we can be heroes

Leftists often bemoan a perceived lack of progress on the issues they work on. Fighting economic injustice, war or discrimination can feel like a thankless task. On top of the difficulty of the work, too often we fail to celebrate success and lose a longer historical view of how the world has changed for the better.

That's why the 2013 revelation by National Basketball Association major-league player Jason Collins that he is gay was so important. Collins was the first professional player in a major U.S. male team sport to come out while he was still active, and the media as well as most other athletes who have spoken publicly were extremely supportive. It's worthwhile to stop and realize that only a few short years earlier the response would have been very different.

As an avid athletics fan who often listens to sports talk radio, I can say that the worst of the responses I've heard have been measured and usually consist of asking, "Why did he even have to bring it up?" That is a very long way from the open hate directed at lesbian, gay, bisexual and transgender people that I've heard most of my life, in every social realm. Still, it's worth examining just why it is so important that Collins came out publicly.

The fact is, statements and stances by public figures can have a strong impact on people who are struggling with their identity. Hiding who you are, afraid of what those dear to you might think if they found out, is a terrifying way to live. That is an experience I know too well. And it leaves one very vulnerable to the actions, both positive and negative, of famous people who dare talk about "it."

By the age of nine, I knew I was bisexual, even though I couldn't articulate that idea even in my own mind. As I got older and moved into my teens, I grappled with shame, denial and an overwhelming fear of discovery. Though actively bi from the time I was 14, I didn't tell anyone—not even friends who were gay—let alone my family, until I was 26.

One of the things that got me through those difficult times was my favorite (to this day) musician, David Bowie. I had been listening to Bowie since I was nine, and didn't really get the whole bisexual thing about him until I was twelve or thirteen. That was, as it turned out, just when I needed it the most.

I wasn't sexually active yet, but I always felt that my interest in guys showed, even though I could honestly display a genuine interest in girls that was just as strong. I felt like people could read my "inner queer." My environment was split between a religious Jewish community and a lot of hormonal teenagers, some of whom liked to get drunk and talk about "going to beat up some fags," so external pressure reinforced internalized homophobia to make me feel alone, afraid and ashamed.

But Bowie put another feeling inside me: one of pride and a sense that this brilliant artist was just like me, at least in one way. I waited for a new album with great anticipation (even when he was in his Berlin phase and I was too young to grasp the music I would later recognize as his most brilliant work). I loved Bowie's music before it related to my struggle to accept my sexual identity, but he later came to be the one support I felt I had for that struggle.

Then, after *Scary Monsters* was released in 1980, there came three years of nothing, very little new music, as Bowie struggled with putting his life back together after overcoming drug addiction. Finally, in 1983, *Let's Dance* came out. I was 17 that year, and I waited for that record as I had the previous four. The record was a hit, probably Bowie's most successful ever in the U.S. But I was bitterly disappointed. It lacked any originality or creativity. *Let's Dance* was just a very well-produced pop LP. And then came the real heartbreaker.

Bowie gave an interview to *Rolling Stone*, and the cover blared out loud: "DAVID BOWIE STRAIGHT!" Bowie told the magazine that his public declaration of bisexuality was "the biggest mistake I ever made" and "I was always a closet heterosexual." I was devastated.

It wasn't only Bowie. In 1983, AIDS was really making its way into the headlines and hatred of gay men was rampant. Much of the progress that had been made since the 1960s' Gay Liberation Movement was being reversed. The gay culture that was so open during the Decade of Disco was being forced back underground beneath the cloud of a devastating epidemic. Worse for me, bisexual men were seen as the "conduit" through which the "gay disease" was infecting heterosexuals.

It was a tough time to be anything but straight. For the next decade, I watched as friends and colleagues got ill and died. And the one person in my life that had once made me feel positive about my sexual identity had turned his back on me, told me it was all just a publicity stunt. I had, in 1983, been considering sharing my bisexuality with some of those closest to me—my best friend, who was a lesbian, my brother, one or two others I thought might understand. But I was already terrified, and Bowie's reversal slammed that idea deep down for almost a decade.

David Bowie continued his artistic decline through the 1980s, culminating in the perversely titled *Never Let Me Down*. His meaning in my life had disappeared and so did his music, leaving me with only the records of the past, which, though I still loved them, now seemed like mere illusions.

In 1990, I found a book of short stories by a wonderful gay Jewish writer, Lev Raphael. In it was a story called "Betrayed by David Bowie," which made me weep for hours after I read it. Raphael wrote about his reaction to the *Rolling Stone* interview:

> *I couldn't buy the new album. I waited for Bowie to clarify, to say that he wasn't denying his past, that this was all just some kind of intriguing retranslation of himself, like Ziggy (Stardust) or Major Tom. I wrote angry letters in my head. Bowie was more popular than ever before and his music was the least original of his career. He was claiming to be just like everyone else; forget about 'Queen Bitch' or wearing a dress or going down on Mick Ronson's guitar at more than one concert, or singing about trade, 'a butch little number,' cruising, 'the church of man love' being 'such a holy place to be,' all of it, the obvious and the metaphorical. 'The Man Who Sold the World' was selling himself and everyone who'd believed in him.*[1]

Raphael's words mirrored my own feelings. But I also knew that Bowie didn't owe me anything. He would manage his own life and career as he wished, and that was his right. Eventually, I found my own way to come out to those closest to me. Some of it wasn't easy, and some reactions were very unpleasant. But mostly, I found acceptance and warmth and love.

What does this story have to do with Jason Collins? A lot. Somewhere out there, by the hundreds, are young men and women who love basketball, who are also gay, lesbian, bisexual or transgender. There are other gay athletes, but a man in one of the major team sports in the U.S. had now broken that barrier and come out while he was still in the league. Some of those basketball-loving queer kids will now be more able to be open about who they are, and some who still aren't ready to do that will find some comfort in Collins's revelation.

And it's important for us all to realize that 2013 isn't 1983. About a decade ago, David Bowie, who since his comeback in the mid-'90s has again produced some of the most brilliant and creative music in the world and seems (with Bowie, one can never assume what's real, only what seems to be) to have shed his various personae and decided to just be David Bowie, revised his stated sexuality again.

In an interview with *Blender*, Bowie was asked if he still thought saying he was bi was "the worst mistake" he ever made:

1 Lev Raphael, "Betrayed By David Bowie," in *Dancing On Tisha B'Av.* (New York, NY: St. Martin's Press, 1990)

"Interesting," he said. "I don't think it was a mistake in Europe, but it was a lot tougher in America. I had no problem with people knowing I was bisexual. But I had no inclination to hold any banners or be a representative of any group of people. I knew what I wanted to be, which was a songwriter and a performer, and I felt that [bisexuality] became my headline over here for so long. America is a very puritanical place, and I think it stood in the way of so much I wanted to do."[2]

I felt better, not least because I shared Bowie's view of the U.S. and still do. By that time I was at peace with myself and comfortable with who I am. But more importantly, Bowie's ever-present marketing sense reflected a changing world. The U.S. was lagging behind and still is, but even here times have changed and changed radically.

The response to Jason Collins is as solid proof as you'll get. It's a lot of hard work and difficult times, working to make the world a better place for everyone. We sometimes take a step or two backward, but we can change the world. We've done it before, and we'll do it again.

2 http://exploringdavidbowie.com/2013/02/14/dear-superstar-david-bowie/

Mitchell Plitnick is a former activist with both the New York Area and Bay Area Bisexual Networks. He has worked in Middle East peace since 2002 and currently writes at various sites on U.S. foreign policy. You can follow his work at http://mitchellplitnick.com.

This essay was originally published at Souciant.com (http://souciant.com/2013/05/we-can-be-heroes) on May 3, 2013.

by kazembe balagun

the audacity of black bisexual life: kuwasi bulagoon as queer panther

Black queer historians write on life and for life. When I first learned of Kuwasi Bulagoon, the only openly bisexual Black Panther and member of the Black Liberation Army, I was a young bisexual Black revolutionary coming into my own and out into the streets. I needed and wanted heroes and sheroes who crossed boundaries and borders and refused categorization to call my own.

Bulagoon was one of those people. From his early years growing up in Maryland to his conviction and death at the early age of 39 of AIDS-related causes, Bulagoon was radical in his self-making. At various points of his life he was in the United States Army, a published poet, a Black Panther and a soldier of the Black Liberation Army. In all those spaces he pushed the limits and demanded freedom on his own terms. At the same time he saw his own liberation bound in the fight for a social revolution and the liberation of humanity.

In this age where there is a stigma against "down low brothas" and HIV in the Black community, we need to reclaim brothers like Kuwasi as our own, in their full sense as Black, bisexual and audacious.

Early Life

Kuwasi Balagoon was born Donald Weems in Lakeland, Maryland on December 23, 1946. Kuwasi was influenced early on by a deep maternal instinct, primarily through his grandmother ("Mama Shine") and Miss Reed, his elementary school teacher on whom he described having a fleeting crush. Kuwasi was a self-described "wild child" who had once jumped out of the second-story window of his house in imitation of Superman.

Two major events led to Kuwasi's political awakening. The first was the rebellion in nearby Cambridge, Maryland. In 1963, under the leadership of Gloria Richardson, the local Student Nonviolent Coordinating Committee led a series of sit-ins aimed at desegregating public facilities. The sit-ins brought national attention to Cambridge, a town that prided itself on being able to maintain "racial peace." Nevertheless, that peace exploded when two young students were arrested for staging a pray-in. Their indefinite incarceration angered the Black community. For two days, White businesses were firebombed.

On the Maryland Governor's request, the National Guard entered and occupied Cambridge's Black community for a year, leading to more rebellions. The other event was more personal in nature. Kuwasi's eldest sister, Mary, began to date Jimmy, who Kuwasi describes as "a cool guitar player" who was "like a big brother to me." The two ran the streets together, sneaking drinks and enjoying life. As a truck driver for a local department store, Jimmy also played the role of Robin Hood, often expropriating merchandise from the store. "The Christmas I was 13 was a super Christmas for a materialistic youth. . . . Good God he liberated, we couldn't get everything under the tree."[1]

Kuwasi's friendship with Jimmy only ended with Jimmy's arrest for raping a White woman. A typical charge leveled against Black men in the South, the case was flimsy, but within 15 minutes an all-White jury convicted him. Jimmy would spend seven years in the state penitentiary before he escaped. Jimmy's exportation and prison escapes would serve as a template for Kuwasi's life.

Becoming a Panther

For a disillusioned Kuwasi Bulagoon, New York looked like a promised land. He soon moved to Harlem to get closer to the struggle and found a job as a tenant organizer alongside the legendary Black Nationalist Jesse Gray. Gray led a major rent strike to protest the dilapidated living conditions faced by Harlem residents. Indeed, as Kuwasi would later note, many of the health problems faced by Harlem residents (particularly children) were the direct result of poor housing conditions, including lead paint as well as the vermin infestations that led to rat bites.

Kuwasi's ascent as an organizer coincided with the formation of the Black Panther Party for Self-Defense (BPP). Founded in Oakland, California, by Huey P. Newton and Bobby Seale, the BPP formed as a response to police brutality. Trained in Marx, Lenin, Fanon and guerilla tactics, the BPP combined both a political program (the Ten-Point Platform and Program) with direct action including armed patrols. In this sense, the BPP synthesized the multiple political tendencies within the Black community, from cultural nationalist to communist. Soon afterwards, BPP chapters spread like wildfire across the country.

In New York, the BPP came of a previous incarnation, the Black Panther Party for Political Power, which fell apart, primarily due to interference by law enforcement. The BPP served as a catalyst for a new generation of Blacks, many of whom had moved to New York from the South and the Caribbean. This is an important point missed by many

1 Bulagoon, Kuwasi, *Look For Me In The Whirl Wind A Collective Autobiography of the New York 21*, New York: Random House 1971.

because, while many scholars and activists focus on the West Coast/East Coast divide in the BPP, it was not only a matter of personality but also of geography. Whereas Oakland faces Asia and Mexico, producing a mestizo radical politic, New York faces the Caribbean and Africa. As such, many of the transplants who come to New York carry with them what Winston James called a "majority consciousness."[2]

The New York Panthers were changing their names to reflect this majority consciousness: Assata, Afeni, Zayd, Sundiata and Lumumba. It was in this period that the young Weems became Kuwasi Balagoon, a name derived from the Yoruba people: *Kuwasi* meaning "born on Sunday" and *Balagoon* meaning "warrior."

As the Panthers slowly made inroads in the community, they were soon derailed by state repression. In 1969, 21 Panther leaders were arrested on conspiracy charges including an alleged plot to blow up the Botanical Gardens, subways and police precincts. The 21 Panthers (Kuwasi included) were held on $100,000 bond apiece or $2.1 million (an amount unimaginable in 1969 terms).

The "Panther 21" under trial were sent to separate prisons throughout New York City. Rather than surrender, the Panthers began to organize against the horrific conditions in the jails. Kuwasi and other comrades in the Queens House of Detention soon staged a rebellion that resulted in five guards being taken hostage. In Manhattan, a similar rebellion took place at the infamous central processing prison known as "The Tombs."

It is interesting to note how the Queens prison rebellion served as a catalyst for Kuwasi's later anarchist leanings. During the rebellion, his primary concerns were a consensus process for all inmates in decision-making and access to food being brought from the outside.

Fearing that the Panther leadership was too influential in the prisoners' decision-making process, Kuwasi and his comrades skipped out of general meetings in order for prisoners to "determine what was true and what was bullshit."[3] The Panthers also promised to go with the majority.

In the end, the guards were released. Kuwasi had mixed feelings about letting the hostages go, feeling that the prisoners could have "fought to the death and taken as many pigs with us as possible." Indeed, the prisoners, many of whom were locked up on petty charges and told throughout their lives that they could not accomplish anything, were able to hold the state at bay. As Kuwasi noted, "We are going to have

2 James, Winston, *Holding Aloft the Banner of Ethiopia: Caribbean Radicalism in Early Twentieth-Century America.* New York: Verso Books, 1999.

3 Bulagoon, Kuwasi, *Look For Me In The Whirl Wind A Collective Autobiography of the New York 21*, New York: Random House 1971.

our freedom and we'll tear down the jails with bars and the jails without bars and America will be unusable for the pigs and fit for the people. All Power to the People!"[4]

The Black Liberation Army

After deliberating for 30 minutes, the jury found the Panther 21 not guilty on all charges. Police repression coupled with internal fissures within the BPP left many members stranded ideologically.

Newton's release from prison marked the beginning of a moderate approach for the Panthers. Focusing on "survival programs," Newton sought to curb the image of the BPP as violent. Eldridge Cleaver, now head of the International Panther Branch in Algiers, was in favor of urban guerilla warfare. Meeting with leaders of Third World liberation struggles, Cleaver was convinced that the time was right for armed struggle.

The ideological battle turned bloody as Black Panthers both on the East Coast and West Coast were killed in the intramural battles. Without a doubt the conflict was escalated by the Federal Bureau of Investigation Counter Intelligence Program (COINTELPRO) that sought to destabilize the Panther leadership with a combination of local repression, misinformation (in the press and amongst members) and mass imprisonment.

For the NYC BPP, the formation of the BLA units was in response to particular crises facing the urban Black community: police brutality and drugs. As the revolutionary fervor and activity of Black people increased, there was a growing drug epidemic. In addition, police killed several people, including ten-year-old Clifford Glover. The BLA led campaigns against drug dealers and their suppliers while sabotaging the ability of the police to wage war on the Black community. Expropriating banks, damaging patrol cars and attacking station houses were seen as an offensive measure against years of brutality.

Kuwasi was in the BLA mix from the start. After being convicted of sniping a police station, he and another comrade escaped from the Brooklyn House of Detention. Between 1971 and 1975, Kuwasi would lead a number of actions to "liberate" funds for the movement.

Brinks Robbery and Prison

The fever pitch of 1960s radicalism ended during the 1970s. The combination of repression, burnout and political disorientation led to a collapse of movements. While some moved towards non-profit work,

4 Ibid.

others dug in their heels and became participants in the growing New Communist Movement. The BLA suffered major defeats after arrests and killings of leaders such as Twymon Myers. By 1975, the BLA's fighting capacity was decimated.

During this period, Kuwasi lived underground, taking assumed names. Although he could have stayed underground, Kuwasi re-emerged for the Brinks job in 1981. While the plan called only for disarming guards and taking the cash from the armored truck, the result was three officers dead and five members of RATF arrested: Kuwasi, David Gilbert, Sekou Odinga, Judy Clark and Kathy Boudin. Marilyn Buck and Mutulu Shakur were also arrested for their involvement in the Brinks job as well as the liberation of Shakur. Kuwasi, who was wanted by New Jersey police for escaping prison, eluded capture only to be arrested later. During the trial, all of the RATF comrades took the stance that they were prisoners of war and did not recognize the jurisdiction of the court. Kuwasi was particularly articulate. In his opening trial statement, he linked his actions with the 400-year history of Black people being brutalized in this country. This served to turn the tables and place the entire system of United States oppression on trial:

> *The United States doesn't intend to make fundamental changes, it intends to bully New Afrikans forever and maintain this colonial relationship based on coercion, or worse, a "final solution." This means that some New Afrikan soldiers like myself must make our stand clear and encourage New Afrikan people to prepare to defend themselves from genocide by the American nazis—study our mistakes; build a political program based on land and independence . . . and be ready to fight and organize our people to resist on every level. My duty as a revolutionary in this matter is to tell the truth, disrespect this court and make it clear that the greatest consequence would be failing to step forward.*[5]

For having the audacity to act as prisoners of war and not be shamed as criminals, the judge gave Kuwasi 75 years to life in prison. Kuwasi wrote in a letter, "As to the 75 years in prison, I am not really worried, not only because I am in the habit of not completing sentences or waiting on parole or any of that nonsense but also because the State simply isn't going to last 75 or even 50 years."[6]

As Anarchist

The 1980s represented an ebb in the overall revolutionary movement. As conservatives continued their assault on the poor, many on the Left were bewildered by the new circumstances.

5 Bulagoon, Kuwasi "Brinks Closing Trial Statement" from Harper, Clifford, *Kuwasi Balagoon, A Soldier's Story: Writings by a New Afrikan Anarchist*, Montreal: Kersplebedeb Publishing, 2001.

6 Bulagoon, Kuwasi "Anarchy Can't Fight Alone" op. cit.

In prison, Kuwasi was politically principled, maintaining a revolutionary position, but worried about the future of the movement Looking for answers, Kuwasi began a study of anarchism. He was not the only Black Panther to do so; Frankie Zitts and Ashanti Alston also began to read anarchist literature and apply the theories of Wilhelm Reich, Emma Goldman and others to the Black Liberation struggle. This was an outgrowth of the organizing work put forward by anarchists in the prison system, particularly groups like Anarchist Black Cross.

In looking back on his Panther days, Kuwasi saw shortcomings in the model of centralized leadership, particularly in its relationship to the rank and file. While Kuwasi embraced anarchism, he did so as a constant nationalist. Looking squarely at the reality of American racism, he still maintained the correct position that Black people were oppressed as a nation and had a right to self-determination. This was in direct refutation of anarchists engaged in a pure class analysis such as the late Freddy Perlman, the target of Kuwasi's critique "The Continuing Appeal of Anti-Imperialism."[7]

It would be a failure to simply read Kuwasi's embrace of anarchism in purely political terms. Anarchism was a theoretical framework for Kuwasi's abiding individualism. Within the context of movements, individualism is often seen as a vice, and indeed Kuwasi did commit serious errors because of his refusal to abide by collective decision-making. Nevertheless, individualism also means choice. The Russian nihilist Nechayev once wrote, "The revolutionary is a doomed man."[8] In Kuwasi's sense, the term "doom" refers to choice: either die a quiet death obeying the dictates of an oppressive system or give up one's life to fight for freedom.

As Bisexual

One of the silences that engulfed Kuwasi's life was his bisexuality. According to his comrade and current political prison Judy Clark: "Did Kuwasi get AIDS from his transvestite lover, who he persisted to love and insisted entrusting despite pressures and conflicts from the rest of us? i would like to say 'from those others' in the revolutionary movements who hardly celebrated that part of his life. But having called for an honest accounting i have to look at my own bourgeois moralism, hypocracy and self-hating anti-gayness."[9]

7 Bulagoon, Kuwasi "Anarchy Can't Fight Alone" op. cit.

8 Nechayev, Sergey, *The Revolutionary Catechism* (1869). http://www.spunk.org/library/places/russia/sp000116.txt

9 Clark, Judy "Remember the Fallen" from *Kuwasi Balagoon, A Soldier's Story: Writings by a New Afrikan Anarchist*, op. cit.

The official eulogies offered by the New Afrikan People's Organization and others omitted mention of his sexuality or that he died of AIDS-related complications. These erasures are a reflection of the ongoing internal struggle against homophobia and patriarchy within the larger society in general and the movement in particular.

The Black Liberation movement has had a complex relationship with the question of sexuality. Black people's sexuality has always been defined from the outside. In the media, Black men and women are portrayed as sexual deviants. As such, protecting the image of Black people as firmly masculine and feminine was a project of much of the Black Liberation movement.

Adding fuel to the fire are the inroads by conservatives, particularly the Christian Right, in creating a wedge between Black, feminist and queer movements. The Christian Right's moves have manifested in a number of ways, from accusing queers of benefiting from the Black blood spilled in the civil rights movement to the meme of the "down low" brother infecting Black women with AIDS.

Of course, homophobia is a cover for a larger push to enforce "traditional" family structures, including condemnation of single-parent households. Since the Moynihan report of 1965 that linked Black oppression to the "pathologies of single mothers," money from "faith-based" initiatives has flooded people-of-color communities encouraging abstinence instead of safe sex and forcing single mothers to marry the fathers of their children in order to receive benefits.

Unfortunately, some in the Black Liberation movement have been taken in by these arguments, although the work of the Combahee River Collective, Audre Lorde, bell hooks, Marlon Riggs and Dorothy Roberts, among others, has fashioned space for queer/feminist thought within a larger Black liberation framework. Still, Kuwasi's life as a queer man presents the Black Liberation struggle with the fundamental question of what kind of society we are fighting for. Many feel that there should be unity at all costs and therefore there should be a pragmatic focus on jobs, healthcare and housing. I agree these are key demands and needs in our community; however, it's important not to forget the goal of revolution is not only to lay hands and seize state power but also to smash the state. This means fundamentally dismantling the social relationships that reproduce oppression, including homophobia, sexism and patriarchy. This is what we can conclude from Kuwasi's sexuality.

Kazembe Balagun is a writer and cultural activist who lives in the Bronx, New York.

anger, angst and critique

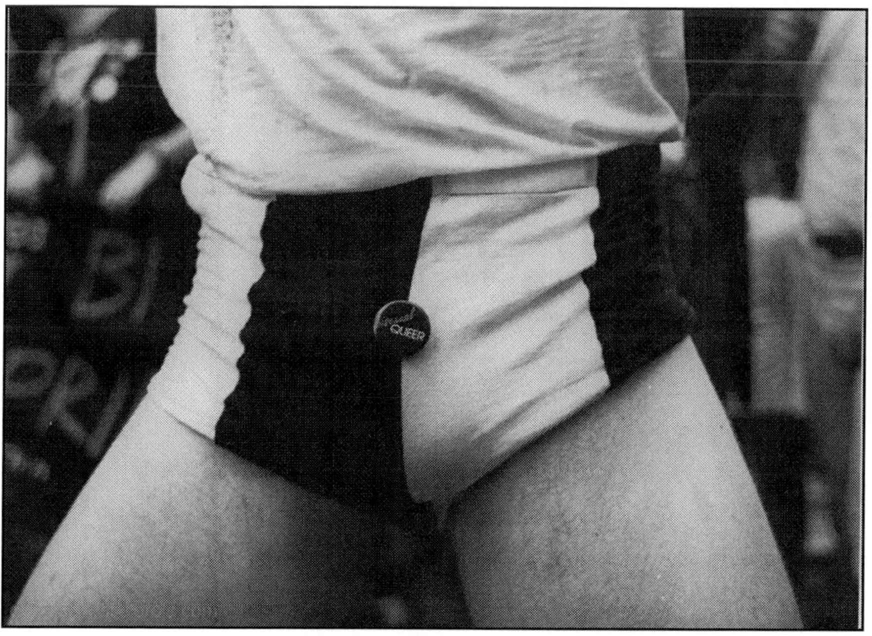

"bisexual queer," efrain gonzales

skydiving without a parachute

by david houston

I have long wondered what it might be like to be able to take it all off—to remove completely the mask of me, to reveal to others what's really hiding inside. For most of my life, it has seemed clear that this is one of the "rules" we cannot violate. We're almost required to build walls around our true self, and in turn around our psyche. I no longer try to understand why this is; I just accept that it is.

Coming out, for me, was a long, difficult, and seemingly unending process, shrouded in mystery, enveloped in a sort of mystique and very painful. The real mechanics of coming out didn't even start until long after I had the faintest inkling of my own bisexuality. For most of that time, I did not even have a word for what it was I felt. I had no one at all to talk to about it—no male friend or acquaintance, no female friend, no parent or relative. Despite being so bottled up, it didn't really seem to hurt, at first.

It didn't seem to hurt, that is, until much later in life. After all the girlfriends, the social acquaintances, the marriage, the kids, I began to realize that these strange feelings never went away. It started to sink in that all the years of hiding the outward (but very private) manifestations of those feelings were taking a serious toll.

It was then that I began to understand that this odd part of me—this strongly sexual, demanding, often wild and adventurous side that, day in and day out fueled these crazy urges and completely ignored gender—had been grinding me down. After being held in check for so long and hidden away through an odd mix of shame, giddy delight and fear, these same feelings were taking a serious toll on my psyche. I also recognized that I was making a huge effort to try to expel these feelings, to kill them completely. As someone whose early social life was frequently marked by painful encounters around sexuality, I remembered that in an awful lot of those instances, much of the hurt seemed to stem from being on the outside, from feeling different and never letting anyone know about it.

As I struggled with the issues of coming out, I realized that I had to come out to myself first: without coming clean inside there was no way I was going to be able to come clean with others. While I can say I've been a lot better about this recently, I'm still not entirely there. I still hide myself away from time to time.

I don't believe that matters of sexual identity, particularly those that depart from a normative baseline, are easy for any of us. Anyone who struggles with this goes through their own individual pain and must find their own path that works for them. There is no one-size-fits-all here. While I rarely share a lot of this, in part because I know that my issues and problems are insignificant compared to those of some others, I find that not being forthcoming, not being out, serves to reinforce existing belief systems, the same beliefs that I want others to at least move past far enough to accept difference. The problem for me was that the whole process of coming out and accepting my own sexuality drove me further and further into a black hole. Along the way, the depression never really stopped. It just got displaced. The number of times I thought I was making progress pales in comparison with the many times I felt that a cold steel barrel or a bottle of pills was a better answer. But that's so messy, really. I kept plugging away, hoping to find some resolution, some relief. In the ensuing years since I first ruminated on this side of myself, I've come to a far more peaceful resolution and finally have moved away from the cold steel barrel theme.

Some things have changed less than others. Sadly, too many social venues continue to be little more than carefully maintained cliques. In spaces where I would have dared to hope for more than just simple conversation, I'm often left feeling very empty. It often feels to me, when I go to an event where sex-positivity or kink or some other aspect of identity is the central theme, that I (and others) are somehow not part of the mainstream, that to really be accepted means one also must conform fully to the standards and expectations that serve only to define a new set of socio-sexual norms.

A lot of this is about physical feeling: it has taken a long time to recognize that this drive is not immured solely within the boundaries of a loving relationship. It's there, period. Should I be so strong as to deny it or is that a fool's religion? I like how I can feel when I am explicit with my presence, my appearance and my sexuality. I've since learned that many others feel the same way.

Oh yes, the self-pity. I nearly forgot. The many who have struggled, who have persevered, who are ensconced within their community like a caterpillar in a cocoon, have little use, much less interest, in an interloper, especially an acey-deucy like me. To be bisexual is not even to be marginalized; it is simply not to be.

It's not clear to me whether there are answers to some of this. It may well be true that bisexuality and bisexual persons aren't as stigmatized as they were, say, 20 years ago, but the number of hostile exchanges online and in real life has slowed only a little, to my reading. It used to be that I did not hope for much. It didn't seem so much a matter of resignation, but rather that I was okay about having this inside of me and having only me know about it. Stay hidden, stay safe.

In the course of the past ten years, I've found places and groups that, when I'm present there, are my tribe. It's not a twenty-four/seven kind of thing, but it's enough to keep me sated, and helps me to retain a perspective on the sexual being I am that is, I think, the real me.

It seems likely that the depression will ebb and flow. I've since consummated my desire with action, and while not every experience has been stellar, most have been positive, and all have led me further along the path toward self-understanding. Along the way, I had some stones thrown at me from all sides when those pitchers realized that I'm not their image of what they believe I should be. I have learned to accept all of this.

I still realize that if it all becomes too much, that I can always go skydiving with no parachute. What a clean, thrilling finish and no one the wiser. But having come this far, and having had such pain, I hold out the hope that this too will be a pleasurable experience, one of wind and sky and a soft landing. That's something I'm working toward for everyone in the work I'm now doing in sexuality and teaching.

David Houston is an educator, teacher and healer who believes in the right of every person to achieve self-actualization that includes their identity and sexuality.

by james hawkins howard

that boy'z cute

"That boy'z cute…do you think he's gay?"
(All the hurtful things they will say)
"Chill the fuck out, James, I didn't mean it that way. Must you always go and misinterpret whatever I say?"
Then what do you mean when you ask if he's gay?

"It's an initial reaction and all I can think to say when I see those lips lookin' oh so thick; my most sincerest wish that man's lips locked with mine. For there's nothing quite as hot as a gay man's kiss."

(Then what did it mean to you when our lips and eyes and tongues and hands and feet all met? This man's lips and your man's lips. Are gay men the only kind of men who can share a kiss?) Tell me. I truly don't know.

"The band was really good. All of their girlfriends were there, so I guess they were all straight. I thought the one was gay." (Me) "Well there are other explanations." (Eye rolling). "A man having a girlfriend is no more indicative of heterosexuality than a man having a boyfriend is indicative of homosexuality." "Well I guess he could be attracted to men or women." (Me) "Or he could be attracted to both men and women." You took a deep breath to show me you were angry and annoyed. You exchanged a look with our friend in order to make the same statement of annoyance. I am very hurt.

"They always seem to save the rain for the gays."

Are gays the only ones in this fucking parade? I thought this was a parade for our gay and lesbian and trans brothers sisters and siblings. Men who are trans, women who are trans, who are also gay, straight, bisexual, queer and asexual. Those who fuck with gender. People who are intersexed and their allies. Pansexual and many more people who are invisible from our privileged vantage point. I thought all of us were standing under the same rain. These are the words that I meant to say as I pushed back my hair and looked up to the rain; water falling onto my face, my uni-brow, my glasses. Silencing myself and many others into the invisible margins of straight and gay.

I feel your words deeply. What you choose to say and what you choose not to say.

As we converse 'round the fire, I can tell you want a break from the questions that I raise and the things that I say. I'm being misunderstood not knowing how to connect what I'm saying with what I'm feeling.

I'm hiding behind the theory.

The truth of what I've heard you say, and say, and say (sometimes to me) about people like me burns vividly in my mind (like the red, orange and white flames before me) but is too painful for me to bring up when I anticipate the invalidation I will experience from defensive remarks thereafter.

I feel your words deeply. Own them. But this plea will remain deep inside of me (burning). It won't attach itself to the lips, the teeth or the tip of the tongue. It won't reach the ears of my friends who are answering the questions I asked to the other.

"I don't know any bisexual people. Well, I mean other than you, James." That statement is beyond absurd to me. I've challenged heterosexual people when they have tried to deny your visibility in the very same way. I defend you because I love you. The hurt of my silence burns deep inside of me like the red orange and white flames around us.

As I went to the bathroom to cool my flames, the only thing I was not confused about was how much I would like a break from the assumptions of gayness and straightness I experience in my own life. I wish I could take a break from being hurt by the simple words that friends say. I wish I were not always left to defend myself (totally alone). I struggled not to cry when I heard you say, "I guess they could be bisexual but it doesn't usua—" You didn't finish. I didn't ask you to clarify.

Walking inside was my best attempt at giving us all a break. I came back outside and allowed my mind to crawl into the deepest flames of the fire.

James Hawkins Howard is an aspiring multi-issue activist and writer. He is a self-identified queer feminist bisexual faggot and a proud sped.[1] *James studied Women and Gender Studies at Wells College. Some of James' interests include singing, dancing, interrogating his privileges, yoga, nature and love.*

1 A mentally disabled person. From "SPecial Education" (Source: The Online Slang Dictionary)

by matt slade

# of anger and empowerment

My throat is so choked up I'm physically unable to speak. I choose to chat rather than Skype. I type in the words. It's done. Oh, fuck, what have I done?

At first it was hard, then it got even harder. I didn't get any bad reactions, as I had expected from knowing the people I've told. What I didn't anticipate was my own reaction. I felt ambivalence: relief dampened by a deep sense of shame. The first time was hard, and the second time was even worse. The first time I was ready to explode and desperately needed to get it out. But the second time I already knew shame, I already knew what it felt like standing naked, vulnerable and exposed in front of somebody else. And I knew the crippling self-doubt would only get worse the more I moved forward with this. Consequently, I moved forward very slowly. Months and months and months to tell a handful of people. Always accompanied by the nagging feeling of making the wrong choice and the notion that it wasn't too late to crawl back into the closet.

At one point something happened, something changed. It took some moving around in bi, queer and feminist space on the Internet keeping my eyes wide open, attuned to the details of everyday life, but it happened. Something clicked, my perspective shifted. I began to notice things, and to question. The misogyny, heterosexism and gender expectations—they were all there! Actually there, in plain sight, if you just looked, not just theoretical constructs. The bus stop at the corner, upon seeing me, starts derisively telling me that gender-inappropriate deodorant will cause my armpit hair to twist itself into a braid, implying that one shouldn't let that happen. I see a father explain to his six-year-old son who just fell off his bike that crying is for little girls, not little boys. I give a man I've known for over a decade a hug and he pulls away, uncomfortable. None of this is directly aimed at me and these are just a few examples, but over time it seeps in. From boyhood teasing to the ads that confront us as we walk down the street, we're constantly bombarded with the message that the worst thing that could happen to a man is to be like a girl. And we all know, the closest you can get to being like a girl without actually being one is to be a faggot.

Most of the time mixed-sex relationships are presented as the natural and, in fact, the only option. And any hint of same-sex attractions or behavior is immediately read as completely, 100% exclusively gay. I've actually heard someone say that the phrase "gay boyfriends" is redundant (because if two men are boyfriends they're obviously gay), and everyone present agreed, at which point I was kicking myself for being in the closet. I can also count the positive portrayals of bi men in media with one finger. These are the micro-aggressions or micro-invalidations, if you will, which we have to deal with constantly as bi men.

I realize that it's not my fault. I have been carrying these feelings around for a decade, I've "always known" and done nothing about it, and that's not my fault. The insecurity, shame, self-doubt—none of that's on me, it's something that has been done to me by our sexist, heterosexist and monosexist society. (Some might say I have a victim complex, but that's not it. I'm not playing the victim, nor shirking responsibility for where I go from here. I'm merely acknowledging some of the forces that have influenced me and brought me to where I am now.)

This makes me angry. And that's empowering. I don't have to beg for crumbs anymore. I grow ever more comfortable with my fluctuating attractions and the uncertainty of who I may be noticing tomorrow. My confidence has increased, and thus also my resolve to define the meaning of my own queerness for myself. No more apologizing.

Angry queers, I have joined your ranks!

Matt Slade is a U.S. graduate student currently residing in South America.

by ibrahim abdurrahman farajajé

fictions of purity

"Bisexual Men should be put in concentration camps. Showered with gas." REALLY?

Sometime today,
28 August 2012,
someone chose to write
the following on Facebook: *"Bi-sexual Men should be put in concentration camps. Showered with gas."*

Sometime today,
28 August 2012,
the anniversary of the Great March on Washington
(28 August 1963), led by the Rev. Dr. Martin Luther King, Jr.,
Sometime today,
28 August 2012,
someone chose to write
the following on Facebook: *"Bi-sexual Men should be put in concentration camps. Showered with gas."*

but sometime today
28 August 2012,
the anniversary of the assassination of Emmett Till on this day in 1955,
(when I was only three years old)
someone chose to write
the following on Facebook: *"Bi-sexual Men should be put in concentration camps. Showered with gas."*

Today, at the age of 59, I read a sentence and a phrase connecting bisexual men and being showered with gas in concentration camps. Even though Holocaust Studies scholars hold before us the distinction between "concentration camps" and "extermination camps" (or "death camps," built by Nazi Germany to systematically kill millions), someone did think that it was somehow acceptable to link bisexual men and gassing.

"Bi-sexual Men should be put in concentration camps. Showered with gas."

In cultures that prioritize either/or thinking, either/or monolithic/oppositional definitions of sexualities/genders, in an either/or world, anything that occupies a liminal, an intersectional, an interstitial location is seen as a threat. Whether it be in terms of racial/ethnic mixities, religious mixities, etc., those who inhabit interstitial spaces, those who move between worlds, those who are literally fringe-dwellers, are seen as the ultimate threat. Sometimes the mixities are denied ("Well, you are not really bi: you are just a gay man."), or mocked ("Blatin@?" "We all know you are just a Latin@"). The person who occupies the space on the border, the space in-between worlds cannot be trusted precisely because zhe does not owe loyalty to one or the other of the worlds. Furthermore, the threat is perceived as being lethal: the very existence of those border-dwellers threatens the very existence of those who clearly identify with one world or the other. For some, the very existence of bisexual men means that they are out to destroy gay men and heterosexual women (and what about other genders?)

"Bi-sexual Men should be put in concentration camps. Showered with gas."

Someone felt that it was all right to post these words on Facebook with impunity. These few, heavily-charged words, speaking of executing people who subvert essentialist paradigms, speaking of executing genderqueers, racial criminals, border-bandits, vectors, shapeshifters . . . .

OR

How the demonizing of the bisexual man and especially of the bisexual man of color is rooted in fictions of purity.

LIMPIEZA DE SANGRE/PURENESS OF BLOOD/UNMIXED IDENTITY/FICTIONS OF PURITY:

In fifteenth-century Iberian Peninsula, the fear of a Jewish/Muslim Other becomes inscribed in the very heart of the West's self-definition and internalized by Muslims and Jews in a variety of ways that lead ultimately to a broad spectrum of reactions. The Reconquista (the re-establishment of Roman Catholic rule in the Iberian Peninsula after approximately 700 years of Muslim rule) constructs a "pure" identity that must be protected at all costs.

One of the ways that subsequent fictions of purity were preserved in post-Reconquista Spain and its colonies was through the establishment of the concept of *limpieza de sangre*, of pureness of blood, blood that was identified and defined as the blood lines of Old Christian families (i.e., families that had no Jews or Muslims in their ancestry), meant to protect Old Christians in Spain and elsewhere from having their blood contaminated through contact with Muslims and Jews who had been forced to convert to Spanish Catholicism.

The fear of the *Moro*/Moor (which becomes the fear of the Turk in Europe outside of Spain) dominates Western history up through and including the present. When certain members of the European Union talk of Europe's "Christian heritage," they are forgetting a major part of what makes up the cultural and religious heritage of Europe.

The erasure of the importance of Islam and Judaism from Europe's religious history (as well as that of earth-based religious traditions) creates a paradigm that is monoreligious. Once the monoreligious paradigm is created, there can only be monoreligiosity. In a similar way, the monosexuality paradigm (which says that people are only either "gay" or "straight") erases the very existence of alternative ways of conceiving of sexualities.

In yet another way, bi figures in queer history are very often "gayized"/"lesbianized": they are not described or defined as *bi*, but as *gay* or *lesbian*. It becomes a very circular argument: how can one talk about bi contributions to queer history when everyone bi has had their bisexuality erased? And then, some people simply say, "Well, that just proves our point that there is no such thing as bi people!" Or, "Well, they are all really lesbian and gay!"

Sometime today,

28 August 2012,

someone chose to write

the following on Facebook: *"Bi-sexual Men should be put in concentration camps. Showered with gas."*

We live in a world that is obsessed with fictions of purity and struggles over authenticity. Fictions that say: "Pure feminism will only deal with certain matters and only in a certain way." Struggles over authenticity that say: "Only lesbian and gay people have true integrity." Struggles over purity of religion that say: "Only 'real' practitioners of this religion will be able to understand why biphobia is the@logically 'justifiable.'"

In a world of fictions of purity, the bisexual man, the man who "troubles," must be removed. The source of impurity must be removed so that the body's sense of wholeness can be restored.

The bisexual man, especially the bisexual man of color, is constructed as the *diseased other*, one who interrupts the ease of the public, the one who is vector and carrier of *dis-ease*. That *dis-ease* is not just physical, but it is also psycho-spiritual: the bisexual man, through zhir very existence, threatens and calls into question rigid definitions of identities.

This "Other" challenges the discourse of purity: whether it be of fictive heterosexuality or enemies in the midst of the "gay" men's community. Whether it be in personal ads that repeatedly stress, "no bi men."

"Bi-sexual Men should be put in concentration camps. Showered with gas."

In recent history, we have witnessed, for example, in Rwanda, Bosnia, Bangladesh, Myanmar, Sri Lanka, the ways in which people have raped, destroyed, massacred and erased those whom they considered to be interrupting their fictions of national purity. Once impurity is connected to health, the icon of the bisexual man (of color) as vector/transmitter of HIV/AIDS becomes larger than life. If people of color were already carriers of disease, then it was not surprising that bisexual men of color would be carriers of HIV/AIDS.

This obsession with the@logies and fictions of purity (around gender, race/ethnicity, sexualities, embodiment, class, language, national identities, etc.) leads to a religiously based obsession with ferreting out the "impure," that which will "contaminate," for example, the purity of the United States. This, then, leads to a dangerous linking of citizenship and religion, in an already hyper-nationalized United States civil religion. The Other must be killed and/or driven from the land, erased; expelled/ extracted so that "innocence" may now be restored and "rediscovered." But the process does not stop with the Expulsion: it is carried over into the virtual erasure of any awareness of this history. The fears of the present are cast back onto the past.

The existence of bisexual men, especially the existence of bisexual men of color in the United States, challenges the monosexuality paradigm and means that there is not a clear, "pure," strong line between two clearly-separated worlds of sexuality or sexual identity. It is not even clear what most people who do not identify as "bi" mean they use the term "bisexual." Bisexual identities or bisexual questioning of identities challenge and confound fictions of purity, fictions of pure identities.

The fictions of purity and struggles over authenticity say that people who exist in the interstitial spaces, in the in-between spaces are, by definition, wrong and are probably "carrying" something bad from the "bad world" into the "good world." Those engaged in these struggles attempt to make categories more rigid and establish more rigidly defined identities, and as part of that, they challenge the right of many of us to be in the world.

We witness ever more horrific vanguards of violence rooted in these fictions of purity, enacting their deeds in the name of the Divine or of some notion of a sacred mission to purify the world, leading to degradation of humankind, especially of those who are considered to be disposable people, and furthering the abuse and destruction of our Mother Earth, of the environment. Literal walls of separation are built; "globalitarism" runs rampant, with no input from the peoples of the world.

Whether it be the wanton murder of poor transgender people in the United States,

the rape and massacre of people of all genders in
Rwanda,
Bosnia,
Myanmar,
Bangladesh,
Iraq,
it is done
in the name of
using human bodies
as lines of demarcation,
re-establishing clear lines of purity,
of separating a fictive "us" from an equally fictive "them."
We live in a time of contraction
and expansion of notions of religions, genders, race,
embodiments;
with Nation-States blurring into all-consuming and self-absorbed Empire.
And Walls
and fences
and drones
to keep out the
threat of the unknown
the scent of the impure.

28 August 2012,

someone chose to write

the following on Facebook: *"Bi-sexual Men should be put in concentration camps. Showered with gas."*

Eighteen months after reading these toxic words, I am still just as upset by them as I was when I read them in 2012. I am still traumatized by that kind of in-your-face hate speech, by that kind of lethal application of fictions of purity. Believers in fictions of purity find border-banditing so unsettling of the social fabric that they need to erase those who unsettle that very fabric. That can lead someone to saying that bisexual men are just problematic, and need to be gassed, whether because they are perceived as vectors and spreaders of dis-ease, or people who are really crypto-gays and therefore also fundamentally dishonest, evil and not trustworthy.

If our either/or
thinking continues
to tell us to
divide the world
into "us" vs. "them,"
"pure" vs. "impure"
that "they" are "evil"
and
"we" are "good,"
that it is OK
to kill
"others," then
maybe
it is time
for us to
say, "NO!"

28 August 2012,
someone chose to write
the following on Facebook:
"Bi-sexual Men should be put in concentration camps. Showered with gas."

Professor Dr. Ibrahim Abdurrahman Farajajé, provost and professor of Cultural Studies and Islamic Studies at the Starr King School (Berkeley, California), is a pro-womanist/mujerista green anarchist muslim who pioneered work that helps faith communities of color shape compassionate responses to people of all genders and sexualities in the HIV/AIDS pandemic. He is currently engaged in disability issues, counter-oppressive multireligious spiritual guidance, transgender intersectionality, green and accessible natural burials, work with the dying and the dead, food justice and the dismantling of the prison-industrial complex.

by juba kalamka

m(aa)f (do you figure?!?)

This song's title is a pun on the Swahili word *maafa*, which loosely translates as "great disaster" and has been used by Afrocentrist scholars to describe the Transatlantic Slave Trade.

M[AA]F developed out of conversations I had in the early 2000s about the particulars of African-American men's code switching as an emotional and psychological coping mechanism. When I moved to the San Francisco Bay Area from Chicago in 1999, I immediately found a community of Black, mostly monosexually-gay, men with whom I began to create and share artistic work. Many of these men struggled with what seemed to be a politic of authenticity within this community. The overwhelming majority were Ivy League or private school educated, and what they learned socially and academically was clearly integral to who they were. Just about all of them appeared to find the notion of saying so problematic ("I went to school on the East Coast," for example.), as in their minds it seemed that speaking aloud about their relative privilege would at best complicate their identities as Black queer men and at worst render them inauthentic.

LaZarrick DuShawn Abercrombie (the fictional narrator/subject of the following song) is a composite of myself and other Black men I've known or been told stories of throughout my life. ("Two Foot Dushawn Nigga" is the nickname of a person encountered by a childhood friend of mine.) LaZarrick's complicated series of selves—hood escapee, scholarship student, bisexual, bookworm, elite athlete—find him navigating queerness inside of queerness which exacts a psychological, emotional and ultimately physical toll.

Jumpshots for bloodclots/And who got beef?
If you believing Bocephus/you'll be relieved of your teefus
My inner demons they speak/of the weak and the weeks
Trading Kon-Tiki for freaks/I fill the seats in Division Three
"LaZarrick!" You hear it/They scream, but laughter ceased
I penned a master's thesis/on the abuse by police
I cheated death of my breath/'cause I could fake to the left
And passing tests with my write/is how the brother took flight
In light of light-skinned crushes/blushing rushing the topic
Was my better set of options/'stead of slanging, I'm stopping
Off the dribble I pop it/and I'm filling the lack

Instead of hanging on corners/In dorm rooms banging his back
And still my manhood's intact/but doubt, it lingers on days
When I can't feel my fingers/but still my record for treys
Has paid for stays in Venezuela/bail and tail through the mail
I stand in lines of linea/and make a snail up a love trail
For assailants accused/I give up 22 clues
Because my halo is phtalo/you see, my greens are my blues
It's cause I'm used to being the only show pony in the stable
Fed the stale and day old/the crouton the poupon,
zesty the pesto mayo
If he fails, his mama wails/the trade and boosters stay home
While we lament about potential through the glass on the phone
And so he's seizing the season/daddy gives you a reason
All the smiles and fake cheesing/Hoping pains it be easing
It's all a part of the plan/"You'll understand when you're bigger"
It's the killing of wills/but sans the pulling of triggers

Chorus (x1):

(sayin "How in the fuck do you figure?)
('cause I'm Two-Foot Dushawn Nigga, Nigga.")
fractions caught up in my everyday actions
fractions caught up in my everyday actions
fractions caught up in my everyday actions
pointfive's equal to your real satisfaction
I'm now a pro at prorating/the jock has doctored his fate
I got to working at the café/and the seitan was great
Grating taters on a plate/and shaving steak, I feel fake
Avie May she asks what "J" means/I say "jump in the lake"
I've trouble hiding from deriding/ride the gravy boat home
Because I miss it and it miss me/I'm the sissy with poems
Cause I know 'em from the listings/saw their names in the forum
I'm getting jollies in Raleigh-Durham/I'm whoring on tour and
Meeting Obies and Yellow Springers with things in my bags
We sequester for questions in a semester that lags
Anecdotals in totems and dissociative motives
All disappear now there's fear and the loathing shone by the votives
Switching codes in the kitchen/and yo. It's killing my brain
Unhooking booksense and sentiments, "said it meant down the drain"
There a coping mechanism that's imbedded in schisms
Cause I'm scholar, Gene LaMar who's popping collars and jism
so bring your scissors for the sister/and the system we'll scissor

Chorus (x1)

And so it's gotten right down/to those inaudible sounds
Of the twisting in the wind combined with shifting of ground
You feel it moving yeah, but how the hell to prove what you feel
When the course requires your corpse and horse for making it real?
Crying over their dead, he sips the red wine and nibbles steak tartare
("It's all required, you know who we are")
then a tape of the martyr's voice starts
a throat clears—we're here for art
a cater waiter lunges and stabs you in the heart
he's shot by a security guard who's only doing his job
and there's a doctor who tries to stanch the bleeding from there
but yo there's nothing but air/and Air LaZarrick? he lies
in a pool of his own au jus, and he cries
"It got to be too much/keeping up face in this space"
("So many sodas and sandwiches/food was going to waste")
"All this po pimping and primpin/how I been limping along."
"I thought that somebody'd listen/(—Oh well I guess I was wrong.)"
And as it faded to black/the way he hoped it would be
Administration saved the scene for future students to see
All you Inglewood bourgie, all you Williamsburg wiggas
Zarrick's work and his purpose is lost in smirking and sniggers

Chorus (x1)

Chicago-born Juba Kalamka is an intersectional multimedia art activist focused on HIV/AIDS healthcare and prevention education and sex workers' rights. He lives in Oakland, California with his partner, their daughter and a neurotic standard poodle, practicing polyamory both globally and locally. His music can be found at http://jubakalamka.bandcamp.com.

kink and violence

by richard m. juang

I love pinwheels.

I don't mean a spinning toy on the end of a stick. I mean a thin wheel of spikes made of surgical-grade steel, attached to a handle about five inches long. Steel is essential; it has the right weight for balance and control. It's prettier and stronger than aluminum.

Pinwheels are designed to roll across skin and muscle, almost piercing, but not quite. In my world, they don't draw blood. Rather, they tease, arouse and antagonize my bound flesh.

Being pinwheeled is an exquisite release. Not orgasm—that comes from different circuits. Pain tweaks my body-mind connection, and the pinwheel's sharpness sets in motion a freefall from anticipation to alertness to delirium. And from delirium comes my submission and release. Typically I'm high-wire taut, mentally and physically. Submission breaks me in like leather being made soft. Good tops are attentive to that transformation. They remind me to breathe . . . and then push me off the cliff.

Because of how I'm wired, the only lovers I allow to top me are those who take me in hand like patient trainers of skittish horses. They coax and force me into complete submission through the conscientious mixing of pain with pleasure.

Kink is part of my sexual reality. I incorporate it into the rhythms of my relationships and I enjoy the communicativeness about boundaries and consent that good play requires. I'm at ease with kink as part of my sexual habits and at ease among kinksters.

At the same time, however, I do not identify as kinky. It is not a label I adopt publicly or privately. Kink—unlike the other characteristics whose labels I gladly assume—has not become part of my identity. The reasons for my dis-identification with kink are partly practical and partly political: I feel no inherent affinity with kinky folks. I do not consider myself part of a kink community. I do not subscribe to any listservs about kink or BDSM. I do not even take part in any BDSM discussion groups or meet-ups. (Boston, my hometown, is a very intellectual city; everyone has a discussion group.)

It would be easy, but fundamentally inaccurate, to attribute this dis-identification to some kind of personal or cultural shame. I'm not a particularly private person. And frankly, I have no shame. I also don't feel guilt.

My culturally Buddhist heritage, unlike Christianity, puts no positive value on either of those emotions. Nor are my kinks therapeutic. My attraction to kink is not based on an urge to repeat a personal trauma, as many anti-kink people might claim it must be. Nor do I engage in kink in order to reclaim and heal from traumatic experiences, as many in the pro-kink faction claim that they do. My kinks are first and foremost based in physical pleasure, derived from a combination of sensory and cognitive transport. I sub and sometimes bottom because I enjoy sensations that intensify my consciousness, whether complex and lingering or sharp and sudden.

Usually, I am very forthright about my identities. I identify as several kinds of queer: as bisexual, as one who partners with both transgender and cisgender people, as occasionally polyamorous and as genderqueer. I also identify as Chinese-American, as culturally Buddhist, as the child of immigrants and as an existentialist (how quaint, I know). Many times over the past few years, I've written and spoken publicly about transgender politics, being genderqueer and why good sex is important to transgender liberation. I've written about how bisexuality relates to my Chinese immigrant background. I'm openly sex-positive. I can talk freely about blowing a hot transdyke in the front seat of a parked Nissan and describe her strap-on sliding down my throat in great detail, at the drop of a hat.

I also avoid identifying as kinky and avoid kink communities, more generally, out of a sense of suspicion. I don't trust groups and communities, particularly racially homogeneous ones, in which power is eroticized.

Kink intersects complexly with race and racism. The "therapeutic" model of kink doesn't apply to me. Contrary to what one might gather from Amy Chua's *Battle Hymn of the Tiger Mother*, I did not grow up in an emotionally or physically abusive household. Indeed, my attraction to kink is sharply curtailed by the experience of racial violence. I grew up in a viciously racist New York City neighborhood. My section of Queens was mixed-income, with a core of homes owned by Jewish families and pockets of apartments with African-American, African, Caribbean and Puerto Rican families. My family was the first Asian-American household to buy a home there. Although we never experienced the high-profile racial murders of Crown Heights or Howard Beach, or an equivalent to Vincent Chin's murder, interracial hostility was pervasive.

This is what I remember:

- A Black student at my high school trying to pour garbage on me. I punched him in the sternum and he backed off.
- A White teenager—who thought I'd stolen his girlfriend—doing

a drive-by shooting at my home. The White police officers who responded never took my statement and laughed the incident off.

- The older brother of a White Jewish friend calling me "egg roll" and "fried rice" and trying to put me in a headlock whenever he saw me. I remember my friend being embarrassed and trying to get his brother to stop. I didn't understand the racial slurs at the time and I remember telling him that they weren't a big deal. I regret saying that now.
- A pair of White Jewish teens following me in the supermarket, yelling "Hey, are you Italian?" and other bizarre things as I bought, among other things, Italian bread.
- A Black teenager grabbing me at the front door of the library and demanding money in order to let me in.
- Older White teens at my high school screaming at me and grabbing me, while White teachers watching did nothing but stand there smirking.
- Groups of White and Latino kids hanging out in front of stores around the corner from my home, yelling at me, "Ah so! Chinky chinky!"
- An elderly White man stopping me in the street in front of my home and explaining to me that my family was "one of the good ones" in the neighborhood because we weren't Black or Puerto Rican.

I remember being very happy to leave.

In the 15 hellish years that I lived in that neighborhood, I learned a great deal about power. I learned that power, exercised through racial oppression, is a demon worshipped by both White people and People of Color. I learned that people who are weak-willed and hungry for any small scrap of power will gladly choose to become a demon's disciple. I also learned that although violence manifests along a spectrum—from a racial slur to a punch in the face to attempted murder—its fundamental motivation is always the pleasure of turning another person's life into meat.

In turn, my pleasure ends when kink practices begin to echo the "techniques" of racist violence. I cannot play with tops who use insulting or degrading language. Indeed, I often prefer to play in a meditative silence. Being grabbed, groped or slapped does not excite me; those particular types of physical manipulation are too reminiscent of the way my body has been objectified. Gags and other devices that prevent me from speaking hold no attraction.

I also have to admit that my history of violence prevents me from empathizing with doms and subs who seek to live in full-time D/s [Dom/sub] relationships. This is more my own limitation than a flaw in such relationships. I recoil from expressions of the desire for complete control over another and the surrender of will and agency to another. Both absolute control and absolute surrender too closely mimic the suppression of the human spirit that I see as inherent to racism.

For me, the pleasure of subbing is a tightrope walk. Certainly, my body is wired to enjoy many forms of sensation and power play. But my history has also hardwired me to fight, to treat touch as a prelude to aggression or exploitation. Both inside and outside of kink communities, I'm suspicious of non-Asians who are touchy-feely, initiating hugs and putting their arms around people. Those are signs that my racialized body will be treated with a casual intimacy that I've not consented to.

I do, in fact, think that kink communities have done important sexual-liberation work by challenging the perception of BDSM and related erotic activities as repetitions of patriarchal violence and sexual trauma. Kink has liberatory potential for exploring the senses, the human spirit and the mind. It can challenge oppressive norms for gender and sexual roles and for physical shape, ability and disability. But kink's liberatory potential is also limited by its risk of echoing racial violence and, in particular, the treatment of racialized bodies as prey. This limitation is neither easy to navigate nor something that kink communities have chosen. It is, I think, something that kink practitioners have inherited from a society that has not yet extricated racial difference from predatory violence.

Let me be clear about how I think this all ends. Kink communities will not be the ones to find a solution to racist violence, nor should they be expected to. If my Chinese-American heritage, queerness and kinkiness have taught me anything, it's the importance of patience, not in the sense of passive waiting, but in the sense of constantly pushing forward to create the reality one wishes to see in the world while understanding that any struggle—whether around queerness, race or sexual liberation—is multigenerational.

Nor, to be honest, do I think that talking about it (or holding "anti-racism workshops," as many progressives like to do) will accomplish very much. Only the slow social and institutional erosion of racism can change the terrain that racial histories have created, a transformation that far exceeds what any sexual minority can accomplish. In the meantime, however, it does not help the struggle for sexual freedom to pretend that kink practices do not have a complex and troubled relationship with violence. For me, in any case, kink is not a means of reckoning with my history of violence, but it must be carefully kept apart from it. I believe that for many of us, the encounter with violence has been etched into our spiritual bones; it remains there, an old and powerful poison that the alchemy of kink is not yet ready to transform. But the pleasure of kink also remains, awakening in blood, muscle and skin.

Richard M. Juang is a writer, activist and crazy cat lady in the Greater Boston Area. His work also appears in the anthologies Getting Bi: Voices of Bisexuals Around the World *and* Transgender Rights.

by anton petterson

So,
then.
I was told
I remember it well
very well
yes, very well indeed
that I was in love
I was told this at an early age
I was told that I loved, and
that which I loved had a name
Its name was woman.

And that's fine.

But I also loved
I loved by myself, and like the music that comes
unbidden
this love was unbidden, and for a long time,
it was shunned
and unwelcome.
I hid it,
I hid it well
very well.

I had almost forgotten it.
Yes, it was almost forgotten,
but never gone,
never quite absent.
It was a slight tapping on my shoulder
or a small little man in my stomach
calling out
through my mouth.

I thought it would go away.
It did not.

Here I am today.
It is difficult,
sometimes,
to say why
(that is, most of the time)
But here I am today
and I love freely,
And I love greatly,
And I love simply,
and there is no more
no more about that love
no more about that love
that can be said.
Free,
Great,
and Simple.
That is my love.

Anton Pettersson is a bisexual man living, working and studying in Gothenburg, Sweden.

bodies and embodiment

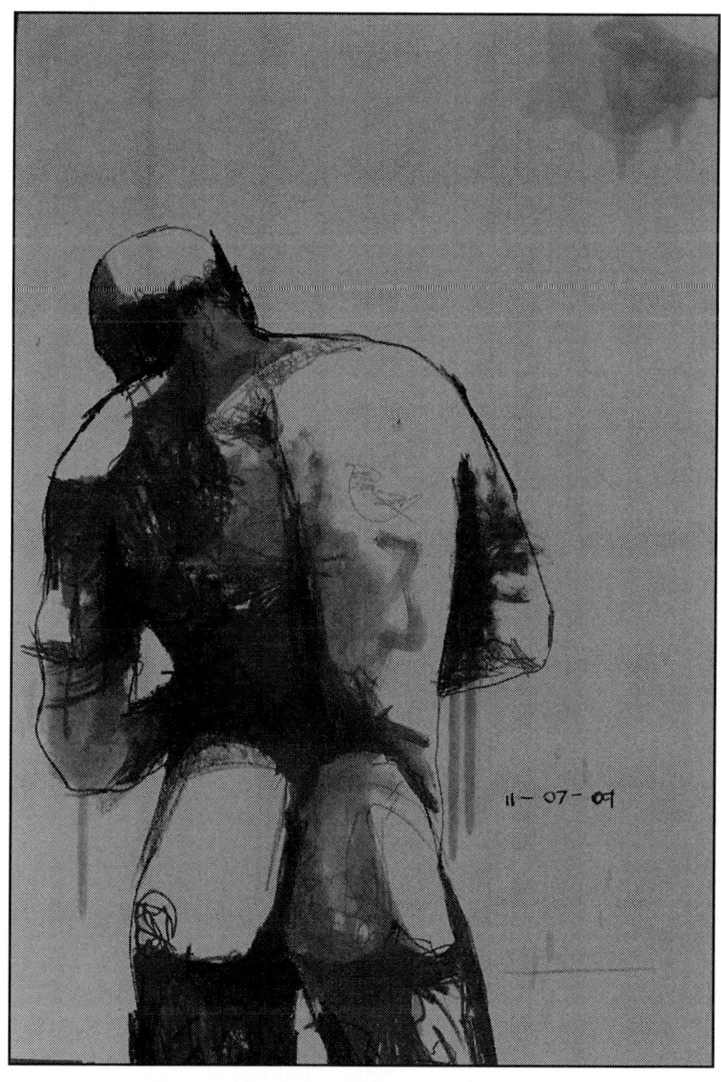

"untitled 1; from the witchcraft from the margins series"
--mixed media on paper, 2009-2011, by j. christopher neal

more fully

by james hawkins howard

My body is a very important thing for me
It is the point at which I enter the world,
The way my feet and fingertips feel and
respond to the world's buzzes and pulls
It is the place that my irregular
heartbeat thuds
Pumping blood throughout my body
Keeping me
Alive.
It holds the skin, with white and red complexion,
the dots and freckles on my body.
My white skin that privileges me, it is the body that locates
On the land we call America
That connects me to the history of my ancestors
As Europeans, as colonizers, as settlers.

The body is the place where I love
And fear
And fear to love
As a person who is a man who has male genitalia
I was taught to love, but also oppress, women
As a man.

MAN meant power . . . oppressive, dominating power.

Don't show your vulnerability.

Don't show your weakness.

Dominate women sexually and NEVER be sexual with a man.

(These were lessons somewhere deep inside my consciousness).

I regret that men like me weren't taught enough by our
fathers about how to love men (or not fully)
For a good many years
My father and I
Never exchanged the words
"I love you"
I can't imagine a clearer message that it is not okay to love a man.

I feel like my anger, my violence, is something I've used to fill a void.
The meaningless word count I use to fill up a blank page.
Blankness is my seeming inability to love many people.
I think
That having been encouraged to love men would have
made this violence less prevalent in my psyche.

I am a man who chooses to love men.

I am also someone who will not give up loving women,
who is still learning to do so in a non-oppressive way,
As a man who grew up in a culture
That taught me to be sexist.

Sometimes I am afraid
Enticed, ashamed, proud, overwhelmed
By the implications of what it means to fully be me.

I'm still afraid to embrace femininity
As I live in a body with differing and complicated relationships
with gender.

What does it mean for me to embrace femininity in my own body?
The same body that has also degraded
Shamed
Been violent towards
Others for being feminine?

How can I learn to respect more fully femininity in myself and in others?

What would it mean for me to be in a body that experiences both
domination and submission sexually?
(and can these things be experienced in non-oppressive ways?)

I feel my body
Talking to me
Expressing spirituality, sexuality and pain in ways I did not think possible
In the shower
While working out.
Sometimes I cry, I am not ready
To embrace my body in this new way.
To take the courageous step to love myself.
I am ashamed and know I shouldn't be.

I remember the first time I ejaculated and the fear and confusion I felt
I was ten years old it came as a surprise
I cracked up in a nervous fit of laughter
I was waiting for this thing my body was doing to end.
I was eventually able to learn to embrace that part of my sexuality
And I console myself with the fact that I will be able to more fully
embrace this part of who I am as well.

I love my body
That looks as natural in a dress,
As it does in a pair of boxers or jeans
Or slacks.

Deep down
There is actually no confusion.
I already know who I am apart from how I'm seen by others.

I know I embrace different identities.
Femininity is an important part of me
And yet so is masculinity
(I feel them balancing one another out in a natural flow).
Much of my experience
Is outside of this dichotomy.
I know I am a person who loves people with different genders.
I feel I see spirits.

I thank many people
For knowing who they are
It inspires me
I'll reach out to you,
Not with very many words,
But with a smile,
An embrace of spirit
More fully.

James Hawkins Howard is an aspiring multi-issue activist and writer. He is a self-identified queer feminist bisexual faggot and a proud sped[1]. James studies Women's and Gender Studies at Wells College, New York. Some of James's interests include singing, dancing, interrogating his privileges, yoga, nature and love.

1 A mentally disabled person. From "SPecial Education" (Source: The Online Slang Dictionary)

by richard m. juang

female parts

Dr. Matthews, neat in her white lab coat,
a decade of experience in internal medicine,
as better things to do with her life,
than dispense Viagra and sex advice.

Something in the way she stands says, "Isn't there a life I can save? This isn't an episode of *ER*, but I didn't go to school to help boys get booty."

It is not an unreasonable position. But there I was.

Bisexual sexual histories are fun to read,
even more to recite.
And Dr. Matthews, neat in her white lab coat,
tries her best to take down just the facts, *Dragnet*-style, and ignores
my interjections:

Oh, and he was cute.
She was friendly.
They were really nice. I miss them.

Until I say,
". . . and now I'm sexually active with a transman."

"A what?" she asks.
"A transman," I repeat, keeping it short, ready to say, an FTM, a female-to-male transsexual, a man who's becoming male, a guy on T, a lean-bodied cutie, a studmuffin with hard rugged abs and a cute little butt,

. . . if she needs to hear it.

But she asks, "What parts does she . . . he have?"
When people talk about parts,
Pieces of chicken come to mind,
Breasts and thighs, deep-fried.
Yummy as he is,
The boy's not a buffalo wing.

She repeats the question, thinking I've not heard,
"Does he have female parts?"
And this is where I pause,
Because, yes, my man's got female parts.
He's got a liver and lungs,

and a back that stays ramrod straight.
Because height matters when you're a man.

Yes, he has female parts. He's got a chest,
smooth and flat,
with two rough scars, symmetric,
from two careful cuts.

He's got these hands, rough on one side, smooth
and just a little furry on the other.
He's got feet that get cold at night,
calluses where his hiking boots chafe.

And have I mentioned that he's got a cute round butt?

Yes, he's got female parts.

No, he's got no female parts.
Because his chest is smooth and flat,
And when I spend the night on it, listening to him breathe,
There's nothing missing there.

No, he's got no female parts,
Nothing I would name,
clit, *cunt*, or *pussy*.

Yes, Doctor, our sex is high risk,
Just last week I rolled over on his cat.
Mister Grumbles is still mad at me.

Don't worry, Doctor, our sex is low risk,
When I told him about the cute butch in the corner office,
He just smiled and straddled me.

Yes, Doctor, he has all the parts,
all of his own
and all of mine.

Richard M. Juang is a writer, activist and crazy cat lady in the Greater Boston area. His work also appears in the anthologies Getting Bi: Voices of Bisexuals Around the World *and* Transgender Rights.

by miki r.

phallocentrism and bisexualinvisibility

The online Spanish bisexual group, STOP Bifobia, recently posted a video in which Manu Sánchez, a popular comedian from Seville, reads on his television show a letter in which a boy describes having sex with a girl and another boy. The girl came and ejaculated on them and ended up very "satisfied." He and the other boy remained very aroused, so they cuddled up and had sex with each other until they both came. Very sweet. Now they are asking themselves, Manu and the world: "Does this make us gay?" The bisexual community might respond, "Why not bisexual?" I have some ideas about that.

It is easy to receive the gay membership card if you're a boy. You touch a cock, and that's it. You're gay. Forever. Easiest certification I ever got in my life. To be honest, I didn't even have to touch a cock to get it. All I had to do was to say, "Hey, I wouldn't mind touching one." And that's it. They gave me my membership card on the spot! From that moment on, nobody ever disputed my gayness. I can be gay if I want to be. And even if I say I'm not, everyone knows I really am. It's only disputed that I'm bisexual.

I could never be heterosexual. Not that I'd want to be, but even if I wanted to, I couldn't. I've hooked up with boys and that disqualifies me. I've sucked a guy's cock. He came over my face. I came with him and I enjoyed it immensely. That disqualifies me from being heterosexual. But while I may have sucked a cunt and enjoyed it as well, that does not matter at all. That will never disqualify me from being gay.

If I requested the heterosexual membership card, I'd get the application returned with the stamp: "DENIED." Yet I will always be eligible to request the gay membership card. In fact, I already receive it, and it says: "GAY, FULL MEMBER." I constantly have to return it and request the bisexual membership card by special delivery, only to have my application returned to me along with a very polite letter:

Dear Mr. Gay: Given that it would be wholly unreasonable to print new membership cards (as this would require us to recognize the validity of an identity that would be alienating to our members who label themselves queer; validate a binary vision of sex/gender which we homosexuals, as our own name plainly indicates, absolutely cannot abide by; exceed the ASCII character limit to which our database is bound by a lack of free memory; and gravely violate the stipulations of the Kyoto Protocol; and as we are certain, good sir, that you would agree with us that protecting the Amazon is an issue of the utmost importance), we should be pleased to formally request that you consider yourself and your "bisexuality" already fully covered, included and integrated in the gay community by virtue of this document. You're welcome, honey.

The gay male identity is so very easy to acquire and you can also rest easy once you have earned it: once granted, nobody will ever take it away from you, no matter what you do. At most, you will be considered to be closeted or repressed. But gay you will remain. A bisexual male, for most people, even if they admit that we technically exist, is just another flavor of gay because the defining aspect of us is that we touch dick.

Bisexual women, on the other hand, though also eternally suspect, are subject to a form of harassment in which the authenticity of their attraction to women is questioned. Unlike us, they are suspected, not so much of being secretly homosexual, but rather of being undercover heterosexuals.

The defining characteristic of bisexual women, too, is that they touch dick. Everything else is secondary. Part of the English-speaking lesbian-separatist movement has developed a very simple explanation for why this is the case, which they articulate as follows: "Dick contaminates." Given that this definition of bisexual would include a large number of lesbians, it is controversial and generates conflict even within lesbian separatism. The conflict between lesbians who have never had sexual contact with men, called always-lesbians, and the "contaminated," known as ex-heterosexuals, testifies to the singular importance of the contamination question in lesbian separatism.

This same ideology is also followed in heterosexual separatist communities (heterosexual separatism, as it is considered "normal," is politically invisible). Heterosexuals have a special name by which they call women who are not contaminated by dick: "virgins," synonymous with "pure," "unspoilt" or "unused." Women who are contaminated are often seen as "sluts" or "whores" and men who are "contaminated" by dick are known by feminizing names like "faggot" or "poof" (degradation through "contamination" being seen as intrinsically feminine). In most of the Spanish-speaking world, less enamored of sex-segregated insults, we are also known as "sluts" and "whores"—the male-gendered forms of "whore" mean "faggot." That is not a coincidence.

Given this irrational panorama, I find it difficult not to conclude that, in *machista* culture, the sexuality of all people is determined on the basis of their relationship to dick and that both the very being and sexual relevance of women are denied. Consequently, I believe all of the sexual categories currently considered most important are phallocentric.

I've found, to my amazement, that people seem incapable of talking about or imagining sex between males without "tops" and "bottoms." They get to understanding "switches"—changing roles as you like—but that's as far as they get. That sex could happen without these roles is neither conceived nor allowed. Just as there are people who state, with absolute honesty, "I cannot imagine how two women could have sex without a penis," there are people who state, applying the same ideology, "I cannot imagine how two men could have sex with their penises without a dominant and a submissive. One of them retains his masculinity and the other one loses it." Both statements share more than a simple lack of imagination; they share a fundamental ideological premise. With a cunt nothing happens, because it is inherently passive. Something happens only with a dick, because it is inherently invasive.

Society as a whole does not see the subtleties that LGBTQIA people do. It sees simply men who are either "faggots" or "not faggots" and women who "let themselves be fucked by men" or who "do not let themselves be fucked by men." So the two boys referenced at the beginning of this article touched each other's dicks and asked, "Are we gay?" Of course. What else? Since a cunt "doesn't count" for anything, how could someone's relationship to cunts possibly determine their sexuality and not their relationship to dicks?

All things considered, I think Manu Sánchez, when he gives his take on the letter, does all right with this. He basically says, "No, not necessarily. But if you are gay, so what? Be gay, and happy." This response is—at first sight—the only sensible one. Yet it does not escape from the phallocentrism that motivates the original question and the bisexual invisibility it drags along with it. Nobody thinks to ask what, for we bisexuals, is a question so obvious in this situation that we find its absence incredible: "Might you be bisexual?"

Curiously, it is then argued in the video that, unless the boys start texting each other and saying "I love you, honey," they are not gay. Yet this broader method of determining sexuality, inclusive of affection rather than fixated on genitals, once again exclusively centers the emotional relationship that the boys have with each other.

If they are gay, it is because of the affection they feel toward each other; if they are heterosexual . . . it is because they feel no affection toward each other. Nobody suggests that the affection they may or may not feel toward the girl may determine their sexuality.

The girl is totally invisible. It is as if she lacks gravity. Because dick contaminates, it is dick and people's relationship to it that determines everyone's "authentic sexuality." Contact with cunt does not matter. Since each aspect of the relationship between the questioning boys and the girl—sexual, intellectual and emotional—is considered irrelevant and made invisible, bisexuality is likewise ignored.

The end of bisexual erasure requires that we recognize the existence and relevance of women. I suspect that something very similar must also happen to erase lesbian invisibility.

So I believe phallocentrism leads, or greatly contributes, to bisexual invisibility.

Miki R. is an out bisexual male from Madrid, of mixed Puerto Rican, Dominican and Slavic heritage, who was raised in Brooklyn, New York. He is active in the Spanish bisexual and feminist movements and interested in exploring meaningful connections between the two.

by juba kalamka

ambi (righthand)

This song, "Ambi," is both a literal and metaphoric exploration of masturbation and a tongue-in-cheek indictment of lazy binarist assessments of bisexual identity by many monosexually gay and lesbian theorists, many of which extend from and overlap monogamy fascisms and slut-shaming narratives. I had a lot of fun with the engaging Afrofuturist conversations on both the performative positionalities and real-life sexualities of various porn performers and archetypes in the descriptive of the jerk-off fantasy. The structure of the song and repetition of the chorus is taken from a line from the song "Grammatology" from my former group Deep Dickollective ("unapologetic about the terse verse/I hijacked Webster's dic with my left hand [righthand]") which poked fun at the often obtuse language of postgrad academia. The title refers to the colloquial notion of bisexuals "going both ways" but also to Ambi brand "fade cream" (read: skin lightener), which has been popular in U.S. Black communities since the mid-twentieth century.

Dial five digits to grab
The lands end on the flab of my abs
And maybe arc if I ain't took time to spark
It's getting dark
I think I'm turning Congolese
I think I'm turning Congolese
Stop/Freeze/Move/Suck It
Ah fuck it/wadding up the tissue in the bucket
Along with my issues around missing you
I'll man handle it
A candle in my ass will make it faster
But I wanna make it last, so I count backwards
Twist the wrist around, grab the stack of mags
Snaps of actors whose careers are flagging
and sagging and tanked
makes for great wanking
you can take that to the bank
yanking crank or smoking dank?
I like the former, leaves me warmer
And there's no one left to thank
It's just me moi and I/and this tear in my eye

Sometimes some butter and no other
is the thang that I try
So why ask why?
I seen them laugh and then cry
Almost always on demand
And there's no need to lie
I rock without a band

Chorus (12x)

With my left hand, right hand
(right, man)
I'm so pretty
I need my emollients when I'm rolling it
So much soul when I be holding it
(He don't need no music)
just a dab of lube'll do it
(lay down a sucking sound and run right through it through it)
("get involved, and get into it!")
check your fluids whether tube or a can
hanky panky with a blanket
plan of action if you jillin' or jackin'
cumming on your stomach or your back and
on your clit and in your crack and
(spit) there's a little bit of spit
I need to help me out a bit
with the glycerin be glistening
so listen to the slickness
it's so pretty when its pistoning
and emissions all end,
new dehiscence begins
if you're rolling in late, Joani got it on tape
with all the talk about the fate of my colored chalk
that's writing the lines, mano-a-mano designs
crafted is what my Shaft did
and he risking his neck for the brothers' respect
he come to rip it from the script
and catch a grip when he can

Chorus

Now lemme see what we got:
Some hot porn and popcorn, with some Kristen Bjorn,
Jeannie Pepper and some F.M.

Bradley want them badly
Ain't it cool I can reference them?
The fantasy warms when Bobby Blake
Hems me up in a corner
And in third person terms
starts to give me his bird and I squirm
'cause I been waiting my turn and I turn
the Rolodex that's in my head to the place
where Angel Kelly rubs my belly
and she sits on my face
and I'm tasting the funk
from the spunk in my eye
and there's that spot I feel that knot
that's in the back of my thigh
it's almost time I'm climbing, barely writing the rhyme
its getting tight in my chest
I'm short of breath, I might be miming the rest
And I guess there's no one home
So they won't hear me moan
Or yell, scream or spell your name
while writing this poem
So it's on, but yo it's all the same
its part of the game, if you're ready I'm willing
Take a chance, baby, fill your feelings with feeling

Chorus

Chicago-born Juba Kalamka is an intersectional multimedia art activist focused on HIV/AIDS healthcare and prevention education and sex workers' rights. He lives in Oakland, California with his partner, their daughter and a neurotic standard poodle, practicing polyamory both globally and locally. His music can be found at http://jubakalamka.bandcamp.com.

reactor

by zane hannan

I crossed your arms across my chest,
you lay upon my back
and waited.

The thousand little beatings of
your pulses in my veins
removed all apprehension and
relayed the consolation of
your body's weight on mine.

I moved your hips against the bed
then pulled your fingers through
my hair you willed my mouth
to open move towards
you clasp me tighter
tighter until still
the same we are.

Down our bodies'
boundaries breaking
of desire this
in our moment
fused to yours
my nervous system is

Zane Hannan is a 45-year-old South African bisexual writer who spent his formative years in Zimbabwe. His life has included periods as a student, actor, Anglican seminary administrator, optometric practice manager and activist. He is currently teaching English in London.

religion and spirituality

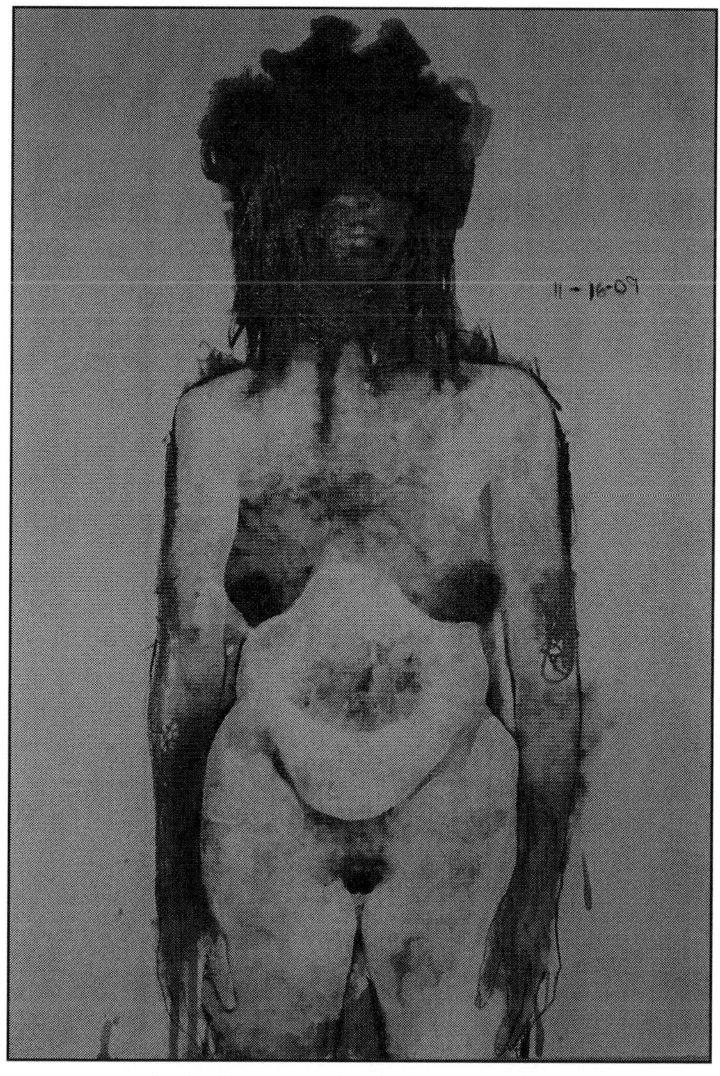

"untitled 1; from the witchcraft from the margins series"
--mixed media on paper, 2009-2011, by j. christopher neal

some reflections

by diego d.

E pluribus unum
One planet, two hemispheres. One planetary system, two
celestial bodies. One starship, at least two television series.
Three branches of government, one country, under
God. One God, three persons. One person of the
Trinity for each branch of federal government?
One mansion, many rooms. One room, one or more fireplaces.
One chimney, many fireplaces, with lots and lots of wood.

How to us, we are perfectly normal
In some places the manioc is called cassava, and in others, yuca.
It stews, fries, bakes and boils (a versatile vegetable). Its multiple
associations do not detract from its underlying indivisibility.

Cumulus, or, living the whole of a bisexual sexuality in the bedchamber of otherly married
A cloud. He has lain down in riverbeds and enveloped the spires of the cordillera, drifted across prairies and meandered through cities. Joyfully, he and a moist valley have discovered each other; here he nestles, bringing with hints and touches of all he is and all he has known.

Diego D. is a pastor in the Church of Christ.

by muhammad ali mendha

people of the book

Here a former me
Bound in the ties of a hijab[1]
Many stripes, colors and patterns hiding away
The fierce person that exists

Me, my person, I

Hidden away from the world
In a place that used to be safe
Or so I believed in my naivety
With my eyes just a small window into the world

Covered by clothes
My beauty hidden from eyes
As if it were a shame to be this creature
Only a creature, blissful and content

Once I dwelled among the modest People of the Book
People with hurtful thoughts against the dimensions of this world
Which they were ignorant of
Or turned blind to

Dimensions of free souls and minds
Where the rules of the Book were of old
A relic long lost or forgone
A new world encouraging free thought

Upon my realization of my residence
In a dimension not with the faith

1 head covering

I broke the many ties that cover *mayra chehra*[2]
To walk in forms Islam considers deplorable

With my face shed of its former jail
To take on colors of new
With lips and eyes open to what came
Flesh exposed to the sun in ways it never hoped for

Considers me bare and shameless
For I am not concerned with the bondage of yesterday
For I am living for the day
Not for the *Jannat*[3] in the afterlife

2 my face
3 paradise, heaven

Muhammad Ali Mendha is an undergraduate studying Biological Anthropology at Texas A&M University. He was born in Karachi, Pakistan, but has moved between Texas and Pakistan several times.

by rev. james semmelroth darnell

being a bi pastor in the bible belt

St. John United Church of Christ (UCC) didn't set out to make national headlines when they called me to be their pastor in August 2011—but eventually, that's exactly what happened. St. John Church is a small congregation in St. Clair, Missouri, a rural, working-class town of 4,000 people, only 55 miles from St. Louis, but mentally and culturally much farther. The only other time this community has made national news in recent history is in reporting about our county's meth problem.

I came to St. Clair being entirely clear that I am an out bisexual person. I made sure that people knew before they voted that I am a pastor who happens to be bi. I was clear that this was as much a part of my identity as being German-American and an uncle. When the congregation here called me to be their pastor, the vote was not unanimous—and a few families left the congregation in anticipation of my arrival. Nonetheless, it took chutzpah for St. John UCC, rural Missouri church that it is, to call an openly bi pastor. On one of my first pastoral visits to a local nursing home, a parishioner quoted Leviticus 18 (one of the so-called clobber passages, supposedly forbidding male-on-male sexual activity) to me and stated, "Of course you know it's an abomination." It was an auspicious start.

Serving openly in St. Clair has not been easy. But I have never been one to hide who I am. I came out as bi to family and friends when I was 16, growing up in Peoria, Illinois. I have been passionate about BGLT rights ever since. Prior to seminary, I served as an intern with the Human Rights Campaign and was a research assistant for a paper on same-sex marriage for Interfaith Alliance. I was out in seminary and in the congregations I served in metropolitan Washington, D.C. and through the ordination process of the United Church of Christ.

In fact, I came to the UCC from another Christian tradition because I knew of its bold stance on BGLT rights, beginning in 1969 with its support of the eradication of anti-sodomy laws and the ordination of its first openly gay minister in 1972. Ever since I've been in the UCC I have been out and open about being bi and have felt welcomed and affirmed as a bisexual Christian—so much so that I have been able to serve openly as a bisexual pastor.

But St. Clair is a community that really does value the notion of "don't ask, don't tell." The congregation I serve, though mostly inclusive, does represent this view to an extent. Previously they had an interim pastor who was a lesbian, though not out. She would tell those who asked, but those who didn't want to put two and two together, didn't. But when I came out openly, it really shook up some people's worlds. This is a community with few minorities—in our last census there were only 32 people of color in the city proper. Few people here understand what it is like to be a minority in this rural town. But some, especially those with BGLT children, have stretched themselves to understand and to be vocally supportive. My closest ally here has been our 71-year-old church president. Like many others, his family settled here generations ago, but having lived much of his life on crutches and in a wheelchair because of post-polio syndrome he gets what it's like to be an outsider.

When I arrived at the church from the East Coast, the news that the church had called a bisexual pastor was already circulating through the town rumor mill. The Southern Baptist Church threatened to picket St. John's, though this never actually happened. Behind my back, parishioners with hang-ups about sexuality would whisper, murmur and gossip to one another—but none had the courage to openly ask me their questions about my sexuality. A small group even attempted to have me removed from the church after only three months—an attempt that failed, but that placed undue emotional and physical stress, not only me, but also on the leadership of the congregation.

After a few months had passed, just prior to softball season, the league commissioner asked our church's softball coach if the rumors about my sexuality were true. When our coach confirmed this, three teams immediately refused to play against our church, even though I had nothing to do with the softball team. Our coach decided to back out of the league in response. The congregation seemed more upset about not being able to play than about why they couldn't play. The general response was to not make a big issue of it. However, my sense of justice knew that if we were to just let it go, it would only allow small-minded bigots to think that they could get away with such behavior and perpetuate prejudice in our community.

So I reported the story to local news media. While the local newspaper initially declined to report it, the *St. Louis Post Dispatch* ran a first-page story the next day. Within 24 hours it had made national headlines and was covered by the Associated Press and Fox News. Many in the community were not pleased that I chose to go public with the story, but it shed light on the ignorance and small-mindedness that continues to be prevalent in places like St. Clair. I received over 100 emails telling me what an abomination I am, and exactly how damned to hell I am certain to be. People in the congregation asked what good it did. The following Sunday some were afraid to attend church for fear that we might potentially draw protesters. There were no protests. In fact, things died down pretty quickly after that. Most people in town and in the congregation act like it never happened.

What made it worth speaking out were two emails I received from middle-aged gay men from St. Clair. Both had grown up in conservative churches in this community, and both had moved across the country in order to find welcoming places where they could live their truths openly. They both thanked me for my work in their old hometown, for bringing some inclusivity to St. Clair. I think of them often when the work here is difficult or frustrating. I hope that what I do here as a pastor makes a difference in the lives of bi kids in this community who are wrestling with who they are.

It's not easy being an out bi pastor in rural Missouri. It has many challenges, and can be lonely and isolating. But if just one person sees from my example that even a pastor can be bisexual and a faithful Christian and that it's possible to own both of these identities at once then it's all worth it.

James Semmelroth Darnell is a United Church of Christ minister serving, at the time of this writing, in St. Clair, Missouri. He has a Bachelor of Arts in Theatre History from Illinois State University and a Master of Divinity from Wesley Theological Seminary.

no longer letting life pass me bi

by travon free

I am a son. A brother. A comedian. An Emmy-nominated writer. But above all, I am a person. And my sexuality will never diminish that. Three years ago this January was when that truly sank in for me. Then I did what at the time felt unthinkable. I let go of the burden of keeping my bisexuality a secret. I wasn't sure when, where or how I would do it, or where, kind of like planning to propose to someone. And ironically, coming out comes with the same potential for mortification if you find yourself rejected for your declaration. I landed on writing a piece on my blog that would leave almost no question unanswered about what I was saying about myself and it eventually spread across the internet like a mild flu virus, far enough to be impactful, but not enough to need a press conference from the health department. Below is that piece from January 11, 2011. I hope it inspires.

It's been the best of times; it's been the worst of times. Dickens couldn't have summed my life up any better. This is the tale of two lifestyles, if you dare. A rollercoaster ride it's truly been. I've always been one to follow my heart and feelings and lately I feel I've been called to do what I'm doing now. Coming out.

I've constantly pushed my friends and strangers who read my writings and social-network posts to live truthfully, honestly, authentically and with love and compassion and I feel the world needs more authenticity. I need it from myself. So this is me practicing what I preach. Hopefully this inspires someone to live a more authentic life as well, or at least not to want to kill him or herself for being different.

This moment has been 11 years in the making. Five of those years were spent trying to gain an understanding of who I really was, and the other six spent growing into it. Now that I am 25 years old, I feel I have learned enough to finally express what had initially plagued me my entire adult life, but would turn out to be nothing more than a tremendous blessing.

I've been a lot of things and done a lot of things in my life. Brother, son, student, athlete, fraternity boy, writer, comedian, actor, and dare I say, I've done these things while remaining quite handsomely charming and humble. Almost all of them make me extremely proud of who I am and what I have become. But most of my teen and adult life there was one thing that I wasn't so proud of. In fact, I spent many years painfully ashamed of it. That thing being the fact that I am bisexual.

From the time I began to develop my sexuality up until the age of about 20, my life felt like oil in a world made of water. Couple that with the fact that the religion I was brought up in wasn't very gay-friendly, I felt like a prisoner in my own body. I felt like God had made a mistake. Because I knew I had not chosen the things I felt on the inside. I had always been attracted to girls but around the age of 14 I noticed things I had never felt before. I noticed that I was also attracted to other boys. I can say that now but at the time I didn't really understand what it was, due to the fact homosexuality isn't openly discussed in the Black family home as often as it is in other communities and when it is, it's not usually in a good way.

Being a young teen, I was deathly afraid to mention my feelings to anyone, given the fact I was the basketball player who spent most of his time around other boys. I didn't want to make anyone uncomfortable nor did I want to face the rejection and ridicule that would come along with thinking I might be anything other than straight. I knew I couldn't be gay because I knew I was attracted to girls sexually, but I knew there was more to me than I could understand at the time.

For many years I lived in an internal hell, because I believed that's where I would end up for feeling the way I felt. I tried suppressing my feelings or pretending they weren't real or weren't there and maybe I could pray them away. The first adult I ever confided in about my feelings was a pastor at a church retreat I went to when I was 19. I remember him telling me that I wasn't gay or bisexual, but I had these feelings because my father wasn't in my life and it caused me to seek his love from other men. Not surprising that would be his response since he himself is a "reformed" gay man who was cured by God. Well, that made me feel good for about a week, but I knew it wasn't true. It was actually complete bull. But at 19 you don't know that yet.

As I got older leading up toward college I became more fearful because I just wanted the feelings to go away so God would love me. Needless to say, they didn't. For the first two years of college I was at mental war with myself, to the point where it drove me away from church and God. I couldn't imagine how God would make me this way and then reject me. I couldn't listen to preachers tell me I was going to hell any longer for something I couldn't control. Finally, around the time of my twentieth birthday, I said that I would no longer go against the grain of who I felt I was (at least internally and privately) because it was killing me inside. I finally accepted me for me. And for the first time in a long time I felt good. I felt really good. I had reached a point where I felt if God didn't need me I didn't need God.

My freshman year of college I met one of my best friends, a beautiful girl by the name of Sacha. I didn't know she was gay when I met her; I was just a college basketball player who wanted to be friends with hot girls. Though I waited until I graduated college to tell her, I wish I had done it sooner. It probably would have helped me a lot. She has been nothing but instrumental in the maintenance of my sanity for the past four years of our eight-year friendship.

After spending so many years in spiritual turmoil, sometimes not believing in a God at all, I saw Michael Beckwith on *Oprah*. He was talking about God in a way I had never heard before. The God he talked about loved me. It was as if everything he was saying was being downloaded into my soul and my spirit had begun to awaken again. I found my way into a place that was more conducive to my spiritual growth.

I was still a little skeptical because in my 23 years of life to that point, I had never heard anyone talk about God, love and homosexuality in the same sentence without mentioning hell or repentance. I had to know where he spoke or taught and it turned out Sacha had been attending his spiritual center for a while and took me to visit. This was nothing short of divine intervention; the true nature of what the idea of "God" seems to be, calling me to where I belonged.

After leaving there, it felt as if my soul had reawakened from an extended hibernation and that "God" didn't hate me; hell, I can't even say with 100 percent certainty that God even exists, just like you can't, so why should I continue to torture myself? But something blessed me with a compassionate spirit that I don't think I would have, had I not been born this way. I think if more people could see the world through the eyes of any person or group of people who have ever been mistreated or oppressed simply for being who they were born to be, we would live in a much more compassionate, loving, caring world. You would think the Black community, if any, would understand that more than any. They don't.

Do I believe the Bible and religion is doing just as much harm, if not more, than good to people and the world? At this point in time, absolutely. You have an entire group of people who alienate and persecute a minority group of people because of one Old Testament verse while casually ignoring all of the other "abominations" in that same book on a daily basis.

Listening to a woman coworker who ultimately inspired me to write the book I wrote last year say such vile, hurtful, baseless things about someone because they were gay hurt so much to hear, especially knowing the person was a member of her family. What hurts the most is when someone says things like that, not knowing they're talking about you as well, and you feel you can't defend yourself directly and have to pretend to be taking a stand for "someone else."

I was fortunate enough to be blessed with the ability to mask the homosexual side of me, allowing me to avoid judgment from the outside world. But who are we to assume someone is straight or gay? There are so many kids and teens who aren't lucky enough to walk around wearing a mask of heterosexuality and they are being teased and bullied on a daily basis to the point where they are killing themselves. I feel I have a responsibility to do something about it.

In the U.S., in September and October of 2010 alone, over ten people as young as 12 years old committed suicide for being bullied for being gay and the saddest part is some of them weren't even gay; they were perceived as being gay. These bullies don't learn this stuff on their own. They learn it at home. And that's not even taking into account the hundreds of kids who are beaten up every year who drop out of school from fear of being bullied, some of whom have to go home and be further bullied by family and parents.

Writing my book took me on such a deep journey into myself that I believe it was God's way of truly opening me up to who and what I really am because I learned so much more about the world and myself. I was afraid to write it initially because I wondered, "Well, what if people ask, 'Am I gay?' or what if it forces me out of the closet." But I kept writing anyway. When I reached the end I knew I had done a great thing and that people needed to read what I had written. It helped me truly love myself for the first time in my life, and had I not done it, I probably wouldn't be writing this.

After reading the stories of such brave young men and women who had been beaten or killed or suffered through brutal attacks, I felt it was time for me to step up to the plate. The heaviest stone I have carried my entire life is finally being put down as if Atlas was finally able to take the world down from his shoulders.

My sexuality has always been on a need-to-know basis and for the larger part of my life, since I've come to understand who I am, I learned that most people don't or didn't need to know. It just provides another reason to cast judgment. I've listened to the things some people in my family have said as it relates to the issue, so it didn't really help with the coming-out process. There have been times when I heard Christian family members say some pretty "un-Christian" things about gay people.

If I did want to marry a man, they don't think I should be able to, that's for sure. They say once you find out there's a gay, lesbian or bisexual person in your family, everything changes. But I've learned through research for my book that sometimes that change is for the worse. There have been times on holidays where I would want to just do the stereotypical thing and tell everyone. Part of me wouldn't care what anyone thought but a part of me still would. This past Thanksgiving, listening to a lengthy dinner-table conversation, it was very close to being that day.

You always curse the process while you're going through it but you're so thankful for it when you feel you've reached the lesson. My adolescence was no walk in the park but I made it. I figured out who I was and I'm very comfortable with it. The French author Ana?s Nin said, "And the day came when the risk to remain tight in a bud was more painful than the risk it took to blossom." That day has come for me and I can no longer remain bundled up. I've wanted to do this for a long time; I just didn't know how.

Now I can truly say I'm in a place of spiritual liberation. I think it's no coincidence that my name translates into "free love." I've always lived my life in a loving, carefree manner and people have always tended to like me, almost with little effort on my part. It wasn't forced or strategically planned; it was just me being me. Loving people and living my life freely.

My favorite quote is by Voltaire, who said, "God is a comedian, playing to an audience too afraid to laugh," because it speaks volumes about the people in society. We've done nothing but label and separate each other throughout history and used God as reason or evidence or justification, but what most people don't realize is God has made it very simple while man has made it very complicated. People have used God to do all kinds of destructive and hurtful things to other people when the message is simple: love each other. But because religion and the Bible have been so terribly abused, people like me have to go through life feeling like our existence is a mistake. I just wish all the people who killed themselves before they got a chance to see the process through to the end had another chance.

I believe in a universal power and religion, but it's nothing like traditional Christianity. It's not based on any man-written book or collection of rules or guidelines. Because the "God" I know is love and that love is unconditional, and my religion is just that: mine. It's not based on a verse in the Old Testament, a book of laws that no one still follows, yet the one law people insist we still obey is the one that promotes exclusion and hate. I'm willing to assume you've eaten shrimp or lobster in your lifetime, worn clothing made of multiple fabrics, touched or eaten pork or done at least one of the many things Leviticus calls an abomination and punishable by death. Call me an Atheist with an asterisk if you want, but I'm not on board for many reasons.

But there's a reason we don't kill people as they walk out of Red Lobster or murder the NFL players as they leave the field on Sundays. It's because we are modern individuals in modern times and the laws of the land shift with the time as knowledge is gained by the masses. I can assure you that you won't find a single mention of Jesus Christ denouncing being gay in the New Testament. But you will find him teaching love, compassion, charity, peace and many other positive equality-based teachings.

It's not until we decide to become educated beyond the Bible that we learn that homosexuality has occurred in nature as far back as recorded natural history. I believe that the Bible was not meant to be taken literally; it was meant to teach lessons and be taken seriously; otherwise I think we need to revisit my Red Lobster idea. For the sake of argument: if you believe with all your heart that God pretty much detests gays, can you prove to me he does? Can you prove to me that God even exists? Can you prove to me that the Bible is really the actual true word of God? No one alive today was there when it was first written. But the difference is faith. We believe because we choose to. Religion is a choice, being gay isn't.

I'm sure when you were presented with Christianity at whatever point in your life if you're Christian—or whatever religion you may be—you didn't ask for proof that everything they told you was true. You just believed it. It's a matter of faith and why should gays and lesbians be excluded from society based on something no one has any real concrete proof of? By the way, the man who commissioned the Bible to be made, you may know him as King James or read from a King James Version Bible; well, he was also a gay man. Funny how it all works out, right? So to teach your children that a group of people are bad or wrong is no different than what White people did to Black people all throughout early American history. Why continue a cycle of hate when we can foster a culture of love and equality?

All Jesus ever talked about was love and peace for everyone. It's funny how most Christians miss that part. I think the true God, if you want to call it that, teaches living life based on love and equality, not fear and exclusion. If given the choice today, I don't think Jesus would even be Christian, the way people try to spread hate and discrimination in his name. Living your life based on the Bible is no different and just as much of a choice as me picking up a Harry Potter book and choosing to live by its contents.

If you truly believe that when God judges how you lived your life, no matter how great it was and how many great things you did for people, that he will say, "Well, too bad, you did it while being gay so I don't care, it doesn't count," then I feel sorry for you. All religions share a common thread: they teach us to use love in order to live the best life possible and that there is a higher power that guides us along toward a better place.

I feel good that I've made it this far and done this much in my life. Sometimes I wonder how differently things would have turned out had I not kept being bisexual a secret. It's a lot more complicated than just being gay because bisexuals live like unintentional double agents with one side always in the closet depending on whom they date. But I'm no different than anyone else, really. Bisexuality doesn't affect my driving habits, my vision or when my bills are due. If external details of my life offer no incentive to come out, my inward life cries out for it. Most of us grow up presumed straight until "proven" gay, and it may take years to realize that neither label really fits who you discover you are.

A bisexual identity can be difficult to maintain because unless I date both sexes at once, people will use my current relationship to define my sexuality, and that isn't something I want to be defined by. I want to be defined by me and by the things I do and the type of person I am. To hear someone say you can't be gay and masculine when I've done it for 25 years kind of makes that notion a bit false. Most people are so hung up on the stereotypes about gay people that they forget they are actually real people who look and act many different ways. To my knowledge, no one has ever looked at me and thought I was anything other than straight. Is that not proof enough?

It doesn't make sense to have to come out all the time and everywhere. And contrary to popular belief about bisexual people; yes, we do exist; no, I don't get a sexual smorgasbord, an open relationship or a lavender Toyota Prius. I just get peace of mind: the comfort of resting in who I am and knowing that no matter what anyone says I have every right to be me. Quite frankly, what other people think of me is none of my business. I couldn't have said that five or ten years ago. Over the years I've come to learn that in light of my strengths and in spite of my weaknesses, I am doing a beautiful thing with my life and at this point I couldn't be happier.

I was fortunate enough to not have to deal with being bullied for being perceived as gay, and not many people pick on someone six foot seven and 250 pounds, so I can only empathize with that experience. But I can relate to the self-hatred, nights spent crying wishing I was different, being terrified of someone finding out, asking repeatedly, "Why me, God?" but as I got older I began to realize: why not me? I am a true minority in every sense of the word: I'm one of the 13 percent of Americans who are Black; I'm six foot seven, far from the average height of a human being; and I'm bisexual, which represents approximately ten percent of the population. So, I can assure you, my life experiences are and have been unique.

If trying to out someone is considered a form bullying, then I might fit into that category, given that one of my college teammates somehow caught wind of my secret and tried to tell anyone who would listen. He didn't care if they were on or off the team. He's the kind of guy who would probably try to scratch the S off my SAG [Screen Actors Guild] card and replace it with an F. Fortunately for me, my track record with women along with his lack of evidence wouldn't allow anyone to believe him. I found out about this a few months after graduating college because no one came to me for verification. He claimed to have a photo of me at a gay club; problem was at that point in time I have never been to one. Sucks for him.

The part that made me feel good, though, in retrospect after finding out that people were told this behind my back, was that given the fact that most of my team had been told I was gay, none of them treated me differently or acted weird around me, proof or no proof. Earlier this year after I came out to him, my closest friend on the team at the time—who was also my roommate—said that the reason he didn't ask me was because he thought it would be disrespectful to me and he loved me like a brother so it didn't matter either way. That was both shocking and great to hear, because I don't want people to love or accept me because they think I'm straight or gay. I want people to love me for me because it's the right thing to do. For now that's just wishful thinking and I remain the eternal optimist.

In the book *A Course in Miracles*, Dr. Helen Schucman writes:

> *The escape from darkness involves two stages: First, the recognition that darkness cannot hide. This step usually entails fear. Second, the recognition that there is nothing you want to hide even if you could. This step brings escape from fear. When you have become willing to hide nothing, you will not only be willing to enter communion but will also understand peace and joy. Holiness can never be hidden in darkness but you can deceive yourself about it. This deception makes you fearful because you realize in your heart it is deception and you exert enormous efforts to establish its reality.*[1]

I spent many years of my teen and adult life trying to deceive myself and the world to try and establish the darkness as a reality in my life. At one point I thought I would take it to my grave, but as you get older and mature and meet people and fall in love that becomes impossible. It's when you become willing to hide nothing, that you truly enter into a communion with God, Spirit, the Universe, or whoever you praise, and truly understand peace and joy.

1 Dr. Helen Schucman, *A Course in Miracles*. (Foundation for Inner Peace, 2007)

Michael Beckwith said, "We shall be the angels and agents of change in our society . . . honoring and respecting one another, calling forth the highest and best in each other. Unique configurations of infinite possibility . . . that together we shall continue to build a kind and just global society."[2] This has been the message that has lived inside of me my entire life, from birth, even before I recognized it. I have always been a kind, helpful and compassionate person and I go out of my way to help friends and strangers alike, and sometimes I say things that help people tremendously and I don't even know where it came from but I know it was right and what they needed to hear.

Through this process I have come to learn that the butterfly doesn't contradict the caterpillar. The butterfly is the next stage of the caterpillar's development after it has surrendered to its next level. And much like the caterpillar, I was resistant to that transformation, but you can only resist for so long before nature/God pulls you, the caterpillar, the rest of the way. Because what the caterpillar and the butterfly want are two totally different things. The caterpillar is okay with walking around slowly, from place to place, living a somewhat mundane life eating leaves all day. But the butterfly wants to spread its wings and fly, showing off the silent beauty that has been created.

I've spent my life doing everything and getting everything I wanted, never having to use anger or violence, and I think that speaks volumes about who I am and the power that lies within me. I am a natural-born agent of change, though it took some time to come to know that, and now I know the proper use for my life and my gifts, to heal people through my work, be it comedy or acting or writing. We're all here to leave our marks and heal the world, leaving it a better place than we found it. Unfortunately, we all don't wake up to that fact in this lifetime. I now know that it doesn't matter if I am Black, White, blue, green, straight, gay, bisexual or a motorcycle, as long as I live my life according to the will of God/the Universe as I understand it and its intention for me.

At this point, I am no longer concerned with acceptance. My life will be my life, and I have to live it for me. I will not fight to change anyone's beliefs; I merely offer up an alternative way of seeing things, something not traditionally done in the Black community, seeing how religiously we're set in very old ways. Believe for me what you want, wish for me what you will but I already know the great things that are in store for me. You don't have to like who I am, you don't have to love who I am, but regardless of how you feel, I'm going to be me. You can choose to stay a part of my life or if you disagree with who I am then don't. I would much rather you be truthful about your feelings for me as a friend than

2 *The Answer is You*, PBS Special, December 2009.

be fake. I'm four years from thirty; I'm a big boy now. I can take it.

I'm not telling anyone how to run their family, raise their children or what to teach them is acceptable, but I know for a fact my child will never be taught to hate or dislike anyone simply because of who they are or claim to be or what some book tells them. Hate and separation have never solved anything in this world, but love, unity and equality have created the world as we know it today. I do know that when Blacks were fighting for equal rights the Bible was used to defend not granting those rights and left up to the people to vote and decide, Blacks still wouldn't have rights today. But it took a brave man in President Lyndon Johnson to recognize that telling people they weren't equal because they were born a different color was wrong and what was being done to Black people was wrong and he signed the Civil Rights Act on his own volition.

Today people like myself all over the world are in the middle of our very own civil rights movement fighting once again against religion and the Bible to be seen as societal equals and 50 years from now when history books tell the tale, those young people will read in disbelief that the same wrongs were perpetrated twice when the example was already laid forth on how to prevent it. A lot of people will find themselves on the wrong side of history. Ironically, even after the Civil Rights Movement only 50 years ago, the entire Black community might find itself there as a whole.

Some may wonder why I chose today to do this, though I've been hard-pressed to do so in the wake of all the bullying and suicides taking place. As funny and trivial as it may seem, I had been receiving a lot of "signs," if you will, pushing me to this point. So today when I received an email from Wordpress.com for the "Post a Day 2011" challenge and today's topic was, "Write about something you've never told anyone and explain why," it seemed pretty compelling that today was the day, don't you think?

So to my friends and family, including my awesome sister and mother who already have the privilege of knowing this information, I would like to say, "Thank you very much for your love and support throughout this process because I couldn't have done it without you." And to my friends and family just learning of this, I just say, "Accept me as I am, as you've known me my whole life, or don't. Because if I have proven anything to you, I have proven that LGBT people are just as normal, kind and talented as anyone else in the world and whom you love makes no difference in how you live."

How does this affect my comedy and acting career? Will it stop me from booking clubs or getting hired for acting jobs? Who knows for sure? But I believe the added element of truth will make it a whole lot easier to be myself, write funnier material, write truthful material, and that's good enough for me. Hopefully my story, work and life can serve as hope to someone else because the world could use a lot less people in the closet, that's for sure. I just pray that my ultimate truth takes me to the place and places where I truly belong.

I hope I can make one more chip in the wall of homophobia in the world and especially in the Black community, where so many other people like myself suffer in silence or are banished from their homes and disowned by family because of who they are. It's a very big problem and I will spend my life doing what I can with the talents I've been given to strip the Black community of this illness. We can't continue to be moral, ethical and historical hypocrites in Black America toward the LGBT community.

A quote often attributed to Dr. Seuss says, "Be who you are and say what you feel, because those who mind don't matter and those who matter don't mind," and this is a lesson I now take to heart, because I have just committed to doing just that. If you want to stop being my friend then by all means do just that, but if you want to continue the friendship that we have, then by all means, do that as well. I will no longer live my life for other people or for the wrong reasons. I'm no longer letting my real life pass me by. I hope this finds you all well and I wish you all the most high blessings and love. Both supporters and haters, I love all you guys. No Homo.

Travon Free is a stand-up comedian and Emmy-nominated writer for The Daily Show *with Jon Stewart. He describes himself as "everyone's favorite Black friend."*

by olorin

being a pansoul

I didn't always know I was bisexual.

After all, when we are young we don't have words for what we feel and how we experience the world around us. But as I look back into the memories of my childhood self, I see a joyful soul eagerly seeking connection with everyone and everything around him. At around age seven I found that writing came naturally to me. This unlocked whole new worlds for me, as I could create anything I desired to experience in a story.

Then came the real world, and it was scary. I have always had an awareness of both the physical and invisible realms in which we exist, and at first that divide was a source of anguish for me. The religion of my parents was not a psychological comfort. Eventually I began to discover romantic feelings in the form of crushes, and they were even more confusing because I had them for many people around me: some boys, others girls. At that point I didn't have awareness of sexuality, but I have always had an appreciation for manifestations of male and female forms, as well as those that seem somewhere in between.

Around the age of 13 puberty struck, and it was even more chaotic. I began to have sexual dreams and their power scared me. It was like being caught in a fire between living and dying. In Boy Scouts I found myself admiring the energy of some of my peers, but I was frightened by the way the tough ones picked on me. I was shy but always looking to connect. Much to my dismay, my urge to connect was crushed in that environment. After a year, my parents removed me from Scouting; they saw the other boys as a bad influence on my brother. One of them had introduced him to Internet porn, a major problem as my brother had an addictive personality. I grieved, for despite my shyness I had a few friends in the Scouts, but I moved on.

As I grew into my teens I discovered girls. They were both alluring and unreachable. My insecure adolescent self had no concept of being worthy of romance and pleasure of any kind, and my parents' homeschooling had taught me to "wait for the right one." I kept my sexual fantasies private, including my erotic readings and writings, and my exploration of nudity was limited to classical art. I had deep emotional infatuations with a few girls, and my heart was bruised by rejections. I had no clear idea of what was blocking me from successful intimacy.

Fast forward to my early twenties: I was still living with my parents and still a virgin. It was then, in the summer of 2009, that I found a path to paganism and Wicca, belief systems with which my soul had always been aligned but which had remained unnamed. As I studied the lore of primal, nature-based spirituality, I began to understand the balance of the masculine and feminine in the world and within myself.

With newfound motivation, I struck out into the wilderness beyond that which I had known with my family. I went to community college, met with local Wiccan gatherings, and experienced the variety society had to show me. By the end of that first year I had moved out into my own place, 30 miles from where I had grown up, and continued my studies both academic and spiritual. However, on the emotional side of life I still needed a mother, someone to whom I could be subservient, and so I was drawn in by a female witch who had no moral compass and played on my insecurities to run my life. I let it happen for six months, as this woman used sex and manipulation to keep me in line. Finally I had enough; I found the courage to end the unhealthy relationship, determined to keep growing and determined to conquer my fears.

As I look back on that humiliating first pairing, I realize that all that pain was something I had to go through in order to understand what is good and true. Now I am a quarter-century into my life and I know I have so much farther to go. But the adult me can now look back on that scared, wounded boy who just wanted to be one with his surroundings and have compassion. I realize he is where my gifts come from and only by embracing the whole me, with every experience both harsh and blissful, can I be happy and loving.

I have made friends of all ages, both male and female, and I've let good people influence my life. My best buddy is a gay man a couple years older than me who is a social activist. This year I met a wonderful girl whose energy is a magical complement to mine and, as we get deeper inside each other's souls, I am learning something vital. We all have both the God and the Goddess in us, to varying degrees, which shows up differently in each individual. The key to relationships is finding the people whose energies sync with ours. For this bisexual man, that is one of the beautiful mysteries of life. My mate and I switch back and forth in our energy expression: sometimes I am the masculine and she the feminine and at other times it is reversed. The organs involved are less important than the feelings we experience during our interaction.

Now for the shocker reveal that could catch me some criticism but I don't care: the truth is I have never sexually engaged with a man. The reason for this is simple: I have not yet met a guy where the emotional closeness and friendship reached a physical consummation. I sense that such a bonding will happen in my life, and it will come exactly when my heart is ready to receive it. One thing I do understand is that there are many kinds of love and many ways to connect with our brothers and sisters on this Earth. As a pagan practitioner I intend to remain open to such blessings. The only thing that makes life worth living is love: how much we give unconditional acceptance and embrace the interconnected nature of all things in the Universe.

Olorin is a California native who grew up in the Midwest near the Mississippi River. He never attended public schools until college, studying at home where his imagination was given free rein through writing. He has a full-length fantasy novel looking for the right publisher.

traveling

"sleepy subways," gymnos alithea

journeys over time

by james donald ross

Years. . . so many years,
  waiting on the heart,
the mind, the society around me,
        all around me.

Echoes of masculinity, of men,
  Nothing though, nothing but
orders from others, orders that must
  be obeyed.

No, you cannot love another,
  another boy, another man.
No . . . no . . . no!

God will hate you
God will punish you

How my heart and soul yearn,
  desire that woman
AND . . .
man of my dreams.

Can it be I want both?
Can it be I LOVE both?
Of course! Of course!

From 12 to 20
  21 to 30
  31 to 41 . . .

Collective years in silence,
  dreaming, wondering, growing,
infinite questions streaming forward.

  Suddenly,
A cloudburst, rain, sleet and hail
  burst forth.
Then silence, no words from
  one that I love. Gone forever.

Again, heavens open.
  Sunlight. Rays of heat.
Burdens lifted.

Disappeared are pressures,
  regulations, smirks, loveless smiles.
Religion has no hold
  No hold

Love both, I cried
  Confessions, not to clergy,
not to authority...

But to my own love
  My love . . .
Full of acceptance.
  complete of heart.
Passionate and clear.

Be yourself
  Come out
Love her, love him.
  Love the PERSON

42 to 45.
  Grand illusions in view.
No pressures, smiles abound

Intense love of my wife,
  of many years.
Passionate love for men,
  no room for tears.

Bright future

James Donald Ross is an American bisexual man of 47 years who finally had the courage to come out after 33 years of religious, social and familial pressure to conform. He thanks his wife, Ann, and his partner, Liberty, for all their support.

tripping out

by cameron kude

Thursday, August 18th, 2005

I had just been fired from my first job as a laundromat attendant. It wasn't the end of the world, but I was an 18-year-old fat kid who'd been living in the suburbs of Southern California with George W. Bush as president since puberty. My only skills were getting high and folding clothes. Every day seemed like it could be my last.

I had these two tabs of acid I'd been saving for a special occasion. They'd been burning a hole in my Buddha box for months so I figured my newly wide-open schedule was sufficiently special. I'd never done acid before, but I was no stranger to psychotropics. A few years prior, in an adverse reaction to ingesting an eighth of 'shrooms on an empty stomach, I had unzipped my pants and begun masturbating in a room full of friends, all of whom, unfortunately, were also 'shrooming.

There are certain things a person does in life—even if they can't remember doing them—that they will never forget. I could never remember doing this. I will never forget doing this. My actions had never cleared a room so quickly and one of my friends, in fact, never spoke to me again after that night. Subjecting my friends to nonconsensual visuals of me fondling myself must have had a traumatizing affect on some of their trips. Clearly though, I had a high tolerance for embarrassment if I was willing to continue experimenting with hallucinogens.

I was with two of my best friends, Felix and Alexis. Alexis was one of the friends who bore witness to my masturbatory blunder but she had a great sense of humor about it, probably because she was a Scorpio and was exuberantly ruled by her genitals. She'd been dating both boys and girls since middle school and was a *Rocky Horror Picture Show* regular. Felix was a professional gay at 17 and the two of us were regularly mistaken for boyfriends, mainly because whenever we were together we were giggling uncontrollably. The three of us had been spending this brilliant afternoon in his backyard, which was like an unsupervised smoking patio on San Francisco's Castro Street.

We were fully stocked with booze, pot, cigarettes and sunshine. Felix had the house to himself for the whole three-day weekend and Alexis was expecting a boy she was crushing on to join us in our debauchery. I didn't have a plan in the world.

I put the acid on my tongue. Instantly my whole being started bubbling. It was a feeling like queasiness, but I knew it couldn't have been a physical reaction to the acid—it had barely started dissolving. No, something was surfacing. I couldn't get my mind off of how ridiculous I felt after that awful 'shroom trip. What had caused me to lose control like that and expose myself, I wondered. Maybe I was keeping too much to myself. Maybe, I thought, I needed to expose myself in a different way.

"I'm bisexual," I blurted. It was something I had known for a long time. For the span of my high school career I had been secretly screwing some jock from a rival high school. I didn't think I was gay because I enjoyed being sexual with girls. In fact, the first time he and I fucked, I couldn't bring myself to orgasm without imagining that he was a woman. Thankfully, his bedroom walls were plastered with posters of Sports Illustrated models.

My understanding of bisexuality was heightened by another secret. I was a boy who had developed breasts during puberty. This was a secret I shrouded for years with the help of excessive weight gain as a justification for my "man boobs," and a good excuse to keep my shirt on. Looking back, this may be the reason I waited as long as I did to come out. These were a lot of sex and gender issues for a teenage boy to deal with. Having a female chest was not fun nor was it easy to hide, but I managed to keep the mortification to myself. The previous year I'd inherited a bit of money from a dead relative, and I wanted to spend it on corrective surgery. I broke down and told my mother, the only person I knew who could give me a lift to "Hollyweird" for the reverse boob job that would make me feel normal. It's not something the two of us talked about much, and I never sought counseling. I quietly went under the knife, recovered and went about my life.

"You are??" Felix and Alexis spat simultaneously. It was the only time I ever saw Felix turn the music down without being asked first.

"I am . . . I mean . . . yeah! I'm bisexual." And that was that. I told them how I perceived them, my beautiful friends, carefree and confidently queer. It was time I joined their club.

The typical questions commenced. How long have you known? Have you been with any boys? Details, details, details! I was pretty tight-lipped at first. Not because I didn't want to talk about it, but because I was paralyzed with relief. Golden light was flooding my body, mind and soul. I showed them the scars on my chest. I was having a religious experience.

To this day, I still feel like the acid just happened to be there and that the event would have been just as impactful and special while sober. I'll never know for sure, but I wouldn't have wanted it to happen any other way. It was the most defining moment I had ever experienced. Within an hour of my trip (which lasted, oh, about a month) I was spouting all kinds of craziness about God and the universe and the sun and the moon and the meaning of it all. Most of the specifics have escaped me but the profound feeling stuck like a tattoo.

I told everyone I knew that I was bisexual with pride and ease. I was done with secrets.

That day, in one life-changing sweep, I stopped smoking cigarettes and eating fast food, junk food and soda. I started exercising regularly. Over the next two years, I lost 150 pounds. For the first time in my life I was able to stop seeing myself as a victim of circumstance and recognized myself as the powerful force that I am.

Another result of that experience is my bisexual advocacy. Bisexuals are a niche of the LGBTQ world that is vastly underrepresented yet transcends both the queer and straight populations. Some say the term bisexual is outdated or unnecessary, but for a teenage boy with tits, living in the suburbs in a pre-Tumblr era, knowing that there are other people out there who aren't exclusively gay or straight or male or female and having a word like bisexual can be lifesaving. It wasn't until my twenties that I learned about terms like *genderqueer, pan-gendered* or *homo-romantic*.

To be bisexual means something slightly different for everyone who identifies this way. For me, it's not just a reflection of my sexual attractions but also a way to describe my biological history. I'm a complex and peculiar creature and I am very fortunate to have an identity that encompasses me, a label that reflects me and a community that embraces me.

Cameron Kude is a bisexual community advocate, film student and nonfiction writer. He's lived as a total cliché in Portland, Oregon since 2011.

by glenn shiflett

aventuras!

The story of what my life had been like, what happened and what it is like now for me as a bisexual man is a bit complex, but I can sum it up best by way of a real-life parallel: in May of 1993 I was on a 750cc BMW in Mexico, returning from a great trip to Zacatecas in the central highlands. The terrain at one point in the trip was high dessert between the East and West Sierra Madre mountain ranges. And it was hot, hot, hot, with nothing but sagebrush, mesquite, cactus and desert sand as far as the eye could see. I was wearing the usual good protection: helmet, leather jacket, long jeans, boots and leather gloves and I was looking for something cool to drink. I happened to go through one of those little towns along the way that looked like it was a movie set for a Western when I saw a sign that said "Refrescos."

I stopped the bike over on the sand, got off and trudged across the scorching black asphalt strip to the wood-sided shop across the road. On the porch were two old guys who got up and went inside with me. One got me a Coke, but the other guy, his face deeply lined and tanned by the sun and dry climate, asked "Donde está la señorita?" pointing to the back of the bike. "No, no, no," I replied. He thought for just a moment. "Aha" he finally responded, a twinkle in his eye, "Aventuras!" *Aventuras* is Spanish for adventures.

What It Was Like

I had always thought of myself as a straight guy: married, two kids, not particularly sympathetic to gays and lesbians, middle-class, Midwestern/urban, educated in applied science. Nonetheless, I had experienced what Paul Simon in one of his songs called "incidents and accidents, hints and allegations." As a kid, I had been sexual with my best (male) friend and, as a young engineer working on location, I was shocked when I experienced sexual arousal when propositioned by a man my age. My life was like that motorcycle I rode across the desert—dusty, hot and interesting—but I was parched.

What Happened

In 1977, I tried LSD-25 and in the first several minutes of the trip experienced acute fear. I had done research into how to do acid safely and the book said, "Whatever you experience, just go with it." So I relaxed a bit. Immediately a crystal-clear thought entered my mind: "You're gay." Taking the book's advice I had no problem with the rest of the drug trip, but I awoke the next morning a worried man.

Over the next few years, I attempted to work out the meaning of this seeming revelation. Eventually, I met a man who identified as gay and found that being sexual with a man seemed to be okay. The fact that I still felt sexual toward women was confusing. I was living in what I call, these days, "the 1/0 world": you're either gay or straight. Luckily, the Bisexual Organizing Project (BOP) in Minneapolis and associated BOP individuals allowed me to make distinctions that I previously had been too immature to see. Finding a way to express the full dimensions of my own self was like finding that *refrescos* shop in the high desert: relief.

What It's Like Now

I can, of course, speak only for myself, but becoming honest, open and willing to accept the reality of who I am has made a tremendous difference in my life. It has opened up the world for me in ways I never could have imagined. The biggest psychological change I've experienced is that I no longer divide up the world into polar opposites: straight/gay, right/wrong, love/hate, liberal/conservative, etc., but rather see a kind of melding of events and ideas. That is a very big deal.

Another major shift has been my acceptance and tolerance of other human beings. I've come to realize that the people who oppose the LGBT community are running scared. We have no reason to fear them. Truth and openness are on our side; we are willing to see the world as it is, not as others would like it to be or believe it ought to be.

Best of all, I've come to live a life that is full of *aventuras!*

Glenn Shifflet is an old married guy with three children and three grandchildren. He is a retired designer, an avid motorcyclist and a national and world judo champion (Toyko, 2003/Vienna, 2004).

by andrew milnes

the heart as a foreign country

"The past is a foreign country—they do things differently there." —*LP Hartley*

We sat on the sand, he and I facing each other under the hot tropical sun, a smile passing between us as our legs lightly touched. The three of us enjoying this beautiful beach—me (a White guy in my thirties), with him (a Black man in his twenties) and my neighbor (a White woman in her late fifties)—could well have caused locals to take pause and wonder: what was the relationship between us, and particularly between him and me, given that close friendships between White men and local men in this part of the world were quite rare. The friendship between him and me must have for them lived in this vague unspoken region between friendship and more, in the realms of both *whiteman's bisnis* (as the private lives of expats were often called there) and that of many men and their secret (emotional) lives. But he and I both knew exactly what it was and what it meant, this inner world that we had both discovered in each other's bodies, minds and souls.

I was 35 when I left my homeland, Australia, and lived for one year in Papua New Guinea (PNG), a culture and society vastly different from my own. In this wild, rugged, mysterious and diverse land I experienced many insights that transformed me and my life. I write about this now because one of the major changes that I experienced was in perspectives on sexuality, race, gender and in ways of perceiving one's identity within a culture.

I identified as bi before I went to PNG; the country and culture did not change that, in and of itself. What it did change, though, was ways of looking at that, ways of perceiving my sexuality and the centrality of it or not to my identity. I have also chosen to write particularly about this experience now because I have written in the past about my thoughts on sexual identity as a bi man, but that was before this experience and I want to honor my changed perspective.

The first and most obvious way it changed my perspective on life, love and sexuality was that I met and fell in love with a soulmate, the last thing I expected at the time. The relationship since its inception (nearly six years ago) has been transformative for me in terms of emotional self-discovery and growth. I also strongly believe that I have, because of the challenges of having a "cross-cultural" relationship, gained immense strength and insight; my partner taught me different ways of being a *man*, different modes of masculinity, of feeling and of expression than I could have learned through many men from my own culture and I believe it was some of those qualities that drew us so strongly together.

I also still firmly believe that many Western (White) men have much to learn from men from other cultures, including deprogramming ourselves around some of the destructive patterns of masculinity we have learned (such as taboos around touch and expressiveness, obsession with rationality and control, and distrust of intuition).

I don't want to idealize attitudes toward sexuality (or gender) in PNG. There are many current problems with attitudes towards homosexuality, for example, based upon prejudice that has been fueled by years of missionary influence. During the time I was there I lived in a closet of sorts, which was frustrating. But apart from an element of unspoken don't ask/don't tell tolerance, I found there lay underneath a deeper issue of what constitutes identity in PNG. In a fundamentally tribal society, the average Papua New Guinean's identity was their culture, their language and their land. In my view, that was what defined them. In contrast, postmodern categories of identity (like sexuality) seemed very ephemeral and secondary. The idea that whom you loved or slept with was a central characteristic of who you were would seem strange to many Guineans. Western influence is changing this, including seeding the development of a nascent queer-identified community; but even within that, the tribal and community elements of the culture can still be detected.

While PNG culture is partly embracing elements of post-modern identity, the influence of missionary Christianity and modern Western culture did not erase all the old tribal, pagan and warrior cultural remnants. So, like many Pacific nations, PNG has a local tradition of cross-gender/transgender people—named *girly-girls*—men who dress and behave as women. These people are found in some PNG cultures and are part of a tradition that long predates Western contact. Polygamy of various forms (mostly unofficial, but sometimes semi-official) still exists in many parts of the country, particularly the Highlands. While I found polygamy as practiced in PNG often problematic (with a misogynist or gender-imbalanced element), finding it so prevalent did make me question the presumed naturalness of monogamy as it is framed by Western societies (in my case, Australia). Also, getting to know girly-girls made me think more deeply about our culture's obsession with binary views of gender (and binary categories in general) and the limits of this.

Even beyond this, being in PNG, like being in any culture very different from my own, gave me the unique vantage point of being an outsider. I have always had degrees of this living in my own culture (being queer; being bi within that too—a minority within a minority) but having it in PNG was unique because in a certain sense I lived for a while suspended between two cultures. Not only was I suddenly the exotic other for once (and getting quite a bit of attention from the ladies and the lads because of it, I might add!) but I was also in a kind of limbo between cultural expectations. The old rules of home were no longer all applicable. While obviously I had to conform to some of the rules of the new culture (particularly the important ones), being a *Taubada* (White man) meant I was given cultural leeway and freedoms that others in the culture were not allowed. For example, I could criticize authority (e.g., my dysfunctional boss who bullied some of the other local staff I worked with) in a way locals often would not (or could not)—the cultural taboo against embarrassing a higher-up *big man* was too great for them, even if his behavior was egregious. Whereas I, being a *stupid whiteman* who didn't know the norms, could "get away with it" sometimes.

Living in a culture with different norms was quite challenging but also quite liberating, allowing me to ask questions about myself outside the constraints of my culture: Who am I really? What do I want? What is really important to me? I became aware of the complex way our personalities are formed in a nexus between the individual and society. I also became aware of how society programs in us ideas around desire and attraction. I came to believe that, like me, many of us have the shifting potential to have and express all kinds of qualities, that human nature can be quite plastic, but some qualities are encouraged and others discouraged by community and culture. I was aware how even intimate desires can be repressed or controlled or, on the other hand, tolerated and even celebrated by the society you are in. I also had the vantage point of coming back to my own home culture afterwards and seeing it, partially, as an outsider of sorts—an experience that was strange, fascinating and disturbing, but also very illuminating.

For example, while I am generally in the middle of the introverted/extroverted scale, I found myself becoming much more extroverted in PNG, partially because that is encouraged in the society (Melanesian people tend to be friendly, open and outgoing), but also because I was such an anomaly (the only White man on the bus, for example) and therefore never able to be anonymous or have much privacy. I was constantly being approached and contacted. I also became more generous—as much of the culture is about sharing, with kin, relatives near and far, members of one's own tribe, which the people there had to do to survive and which was still a strong cultural obligation (much of PNG traditionally had what anthropologists call a gift economy rather than a market economy). Living there, I became less clingy and fussy about material things and my own possessions and more focused on relationship and connections with people.

So what does that mean for me now in terms of my sexuality and identity? Well, like any personal growth, sexualities are works in progress; there never is or will be (for me, at least) a point of, "That's it, I've discovered it all!" But the lasting legacy of my time in PNG is the ability to look at my cultural programming a bit more objectively, including programming around sexuality and gender, and see it for what it is: a set of human categories and ideas that are culturally specific, not universal truths. That realization allows me to break through some of those limited categories—whether they be about the way a real man should be, or whom you should love or lust after, or how many partners you should have or ideas about what gender means—to make new definitions that make sense for me in accordance with my own desires and needs. It is about unlearning some of that deeper cultural programming, and finding new discourses (if you want to take a queer theory/postmodern perspective) or ways of thinking and being that give me fulfillment and happiness in life, and that are closer to who I really am.

Andrew Milnes is a queer, bi-identified man living and working in Melbourne, Australia. He has worked in a range of media and marketing roles in the community sector and is a musician, writer and activist interested in travel, languages and spirituality. He worked for a year in an Australian Volunteers International placement for a local community organization in Port Moresby, PNG, doing development work. This involved training local staff in a range of different skills and working with local groups in the slums of Moresby.

by big sky bi

coming home to myself

As I sit down to write about the moment in which I came out to myself as a married bisexual male, I find myself extremely nervous, scared to the point that I am shaking but invigorated by the opportunity to finally tell my story.

I am now 28 years old, married for four years now to my amazing wife to whom I am out and completely faithful. I come from a very narrow-minded and homophobic family and I have spent the majority of my life in Montana.

Growing up, I always knew that there was something unique about me that I could never put my finger on—that is, until my freshman year of high school. For the first time in my life I became acutely aware of my attraction to men, and not just any man: I realized I was attracted to my best friend. Despite my blatantly obvious attraction to another male, I was not ready to accept the fact that I was anything other than straight.

I pushed the realization of my attraction to my best friend as far out of my memory as possible and moved on with the rest of my life. I went through high school completely denying my attraction to men as—just like my friends—I intermittently dated girls.

At the age of 21, I met my wife while at college in Illinois. I dropped out of college a semester later and returned to Montana to work while she finished school in Illinois. Throughout this part of my life, I never allowed myself to entertain the fact that I was anything but straight. We married two years later and were it not for a life-changing experience, I would most likely still be in denial regarding my sexual identity.

We had been married for two years when I returned to school studying through an online program through a university in Nebraska. I was working full-time and going to school full-time and I truly felt that with my new degree program I had found my calling. As a result of my academic success, I had the opportunity to join a scholars' program, which required that I study abroad in a program which they paid for.

Now, as I have previously mentioned, I have spent most of my life in Montana around my homophobic family. The opportunity to go out and see the world for five weeks was a frightening proposal at first, but my wife and I determined that it was something that I needed to do and that it would be academically beneficial to me.

This is the point at which my life was irreversibly changed in the most positive of ways.

I arrived in Amman, Jordan as a 27-year-old man who had never seen much of the world other than Montana. I had never truly thought for myself due to the hold my family had over me, although I had last thought that I might be something other than straight when I was a 15-year-old high school freshman.

I vividly remember first meeting the other American students with whom I was to study and thinking to myself, "Two of the guys in my group are *gorgeous!*" As quickly as that thought presented itself, I dismissed it. I was then introduced to the leader of our program in Jordan, a Jordanian male, married, in his mid-thirties, with skin more beautiful than I had ever seen. His aroma was of the sweetest cologne I had ever smelled and his personality was compelling. Once again, despite the countless signals that were now shouting to be heard, I dismissed the idea that I could truly be attracted to another man.

The first two weeks were beyond anything I had imagined. The group that I was studying with experienced the wonders that Amman had to offer. We swam in the Dead Sea. We snorkeled in the Red Sea. We toured the ancient city of Petra. This was the first time in my life during which I had no contact with my family other than email. I had no one telling me what was right, what was wrong or who I was.

It was during the first two weeks that I became increasingly aware of the fact that not only was I noticing how beautiful the Jordanian women were, I was noticing to an even greater extent the beauty of the Jordanian men. I found myself getting nervous around the two handsome men who were in my group, and my eyes were drawn to the European men who lay on the beach at the Red Sea. I was finally seeing the world through the eyes of a man who did not have his family censoring his every thought and action.

My family's lifelong stifling of my true self was crumbling around me, bringing me to the most glorious revelation of my life: I was bisexual.

I remember sitting alone in my bedroom that night in Amman and telling myself—very quietly so as not to wake up the other group members in my apartment—that I was bisexual. Fear, terror and panic filled my mind as I thought about what my wife would say, what my family would say, what my friends would say—and what my new future would hold. But as I continued to sit alone in my room, evaluating my newfound self, a calm came over me as I finally allowed myself to accept that this was who I had always been.

I sat on my bed laughing as I thought about the first instance in high school when I realized I was attracted to my best friend and how incredibly foolish I had been to think that this was somehow immoral.

I allowed myself to fully embrace the fact that I was indeed very much attracted to the two handsome men in my group as well as the Jordanian group leader. I went to bed that night feeling a level of freedom I had never before experienced.

As the final three weeks of my time in Amman wound down, I allowed myself to freely embrace my bisexuality as I made up for 27 years of never acknowledging my attraction to men. Everywhere I went in those last three weeks, I found myself noticing men: their physiques, their aromas. I took in everything about them.

Traveling back to Montana from the Middle East, a completely new man no longer worried about how others might view my sexual identity, I found myself astounded by just how much I had missed in life by blocking out my attraction to men. On my flight from London to America, I noticed men from all over the world. I noticed men at the airports, and for the first time I did so completely without shame.

I returned home truly feeling I had a new lease on life. For the first time, I had experienced other parts of the world; I had relied solely upon myself for thoughts and perspectives; and I had, at last, come to embrace myself and my sexuality. It was the most accomplished I have ever felt: I realized that in taking the risk to leave what was comfortable, I had finally found my true being.

After arriving home, it took a week to build up enough courage to come out to my wife. That night, as we were getting ready for bed, I told her that I had something that I needed to talk to her about. She listened patiently as I explained what I had experienced while abroad. I told her that I had found myself attracted to my best friend in high school and had been very much attracted to other guys with whom I had played college basketball. I told her that being so far removed from the overbearing presence of my family for five weeks had allowed me the opportunity to finally come to terms with the fact that I am bisexual.

My wife has been my strongest supporter since I came out to her and for that I am eternally thankful. We have encountered bumps in the road as we have hashed out exactly what my sexuality means regarding our marriage and our future. Even as we encounter those occasional hurdles, I could not be happier that I am out to her. She loves me for the man who I am and for how I treat her, regardless of my sexuality. The love we have has only been strengthened by my honesty.

I am tremendously grateful for having had the opportunity to share my story. I cannot imagine the burden that I would still be carrying had I not come to terms with the fact that I am a bisexual male. I find myself becoming increasingly integrated into the LGBTQ community, I am far more confident than I was before I came out and I can finally say that I am living a life in which I am 100 percent true to the real me.

Big Sky Bi is a 27-year-old married bisexual male living in Montana with his wife.

journey to

by muhammad ali mendha

I am rushing upon this voyage
As darkness engulfs the sky
The sky is split in two
One still filled with the hopes of a day
The other swarming with the fears of the night

My journey takes me to a place of the past
A place I thought I belonged
An old me used to belong

Now it is a foreign landscape
The people know my name but don't know me
They loved me once
Loved me for who I was
Loved for who they thought I was
Loved me for who I thought I was

I make this frequent trip to appease the ones I still love
Ones who I wished embraced me
But this was a futile effort of a caterpillar, now a butterfly

Muhammad Ali Mendha is an undergraduate studying Biological Anthropology at Texas A&M University. He was born in Karachi, Pakistan, but has moved between Texas and Pakistan several times.

relationships

"men kissing," efrain gonzales

conversations with parents

by l. ramki ramakrishnan

When I was eighteen, Amma said
it's ok if you find a wife on your own
just make sure you find someone
from Our Community
[you know, a nice Tamil Iyer girl
preferably someone comely,
with waist-length hair
who sings like MS Subbulakshmi]

By the time I was twenty-one, Vibha
Had come into our lives
And endeared herself to all,

Before deciding she wanted space and time
And moved back home to Pune
Appa said, well, at least she was Hindu
And showed respect to elders, not like
Some of these other Modern Girls

When I turned twenty-three, they said
Now that you're going abroad
Just make sure you find a girl
Who is Indian, don't go with those
Foreign women:
their ways are different

But I came back for my first
Christmas Break
with photos of Wendy and me
from our trip to the Smokies
They thought for a while,
and said, good that she is vegetarian
And, you know, Jewish culture
Is a lot like ours, really

Twenty-sixth birthday, I celebrated
in Chennai, with Appa, Amma
and Ahmed, French-Algerian
condensed-matter physicist
who made dosas for them
in perfectly concentric
circles of batter, and lit up
the room with his gentle smile

And they sighed, and said
Nothing you do
surprises us
any more
Happy birthday, son..

L. Ramki Ramakrishnan is a biologist, public health professional and classically trained musician based in Chennai, India. He has been involved in bi/queer organizing since 1996 in the U.S. and in India, and currently volunteers with the collectives Orinam and the Chennai Rainbow Coalition.

This piece first appeared in Trikone Magazine *March 2006 issue Vol. 20/21 No. 4/1, and has been reprinted with permission*

à la mode de kahlo: the lovers

by d.e. green

Is that a dead hummingbird on your necklace of thorns
    or are you just Frida Kahlo?
Am I supposed to put my Diego on ice, to see the real you
    behind the peasant mask and striking poses?

Sometimes love feels like incest, we get so close we merge,
    like the Cyclops eye I see when lovemaking brings us face to face.
What is a gay man doing in a lesbian's bed? we've wondered
    and yet found no hearth nor home in other arms.

Oh, we do imagine others' lips and sheets, phantom romance,
    the kind the airport novels offer, all heaving bosoms and protruding packets.
But we still fly home, fall into the familiar indentations, and move our fingers
along the old well-worn grooves and levers, maneuvering

like rusty ancients on old red tractors. That's love—
    though you wouldn't think so to see us ride. If love's perennial
survives, its seeds fall in the end on untilled soil, weeds springing
    despite the unpromising and unseasonable weather.

You shouldn't have loved me, love, because I don't like
    hummingbirds, alive or dead. There's no Diego worth this show,
though your Kahlo imitation has its pleasures. Before the end,
    we will sit side by side for our portrait: the thorns drawing our blood

siphoned by arteries from your heart to mine, cross-sections of my brain
    revealing monkeys of pleasure, a lemur wrapped around your neck
and staring back at me. That's love, my love, entwining us upon the operating table,
    Siamese twins joined at the groin, the despair of the hovering surgeon.

D. E. (Doug) Green teaches Literature, Creative Writing, Composition and Gender and Queer Studies at Augsburg College in Minneapolis, where he was also faculty adviser to the LGBTQIA student organization for its first 18 years. He has been writing and publishing poems, essays and scholarly articles for three decades.

the great pugachev

by d. dolnick

Sunlight through a window, shafts of mote-speckle dance between gaps in heavy drapery. Darkness deepens protectively. A man, alone, tangled in the sheets on the bed. He flails, pulling the stained and sweat-damp fabric over his head, blotting out some rank, malodorous injustice. Failing, it does not cut off the light. A few heartbeats, four or perhaps forty, and the covers fly back. A coughing gasp for air, eyelids clenched and moist. Somewhere, elsewhere, a quiet sob, then all is stillness save the ragged breathing. Himself? Another? It doesn't matter anymore, it is less than the dust, disturbed now and fleeing into the corners again. He curses, breaching the silence again, an imprecation at the light and its obscene route vilification of its journey, all 93 million miles now damned in a breath. Then it begins, as the years, the decades, leak out and trace a path well worn. They mark anew a cheek, betray this man with lachrymose letters, solitary missives for the flailing and self-sequestered. A bed, a room, somewhere else, some-when else, perhaps? A question dying in the afternoon. How? He asks the uncaring dust, how can one forgotten now resurface? How can this be the cause of such? As always, silence. And yet, here I am to tell the tale, as it were.

I do not believe in ghosts, nor in ghouls, nor in the things that men call spirits, nor in a soul or a spirit of men. How can it be, then, that I am haunted? And to come in such a manner, by the hands of long-dead Pugachev? Absurd, that. A thief of names from the dim reaches of a life descending should never wield such power. The name was never his, he stole it, adopting it, if you will, and abandoning another to do so. He seemed to me to garner mirth and strength in equal measure by styling himself after such, an impostor mirroring an impostor. Why choose a charlatan, a rebellious peasant born in ignorance who died a traitor? Why pay homage to one beheaded in a public square in Moscow, not far from the Kremlin, but still only a minor gathering of streets? The end that befitted his life in every manner conceivable. How could a faithless deserter reach through time to inspire such devotion? How can a man who betrayed and abandoned children, wives, armies, clans, nations and, ultimately, the truth, inspire anything other than mockery? Why that name of all possible names? But there it was. Pugachev he named himself, Pugachev the Hero. I laughed and asked hero of what? On a summer day, so long ago, when I was bright and beautiful, he laughed in turn, but there was no reply.

On that bright day, in the sunlight, I am younger, so very much younger. I am tall and slender, if not completely straight (oh no, not straight at all, he giggled). A curve to my back, an imperfection that cannot be concealed, but still, I am beautiful, or so I am told. He said to me once that it is our flaws that make us beautiful, but I do not know this, not truly. I hear it, much as I heard it often before, in a dark age long ago. There/then, in darkness, bounded by staring gaze and moistened lips, bordered by darting tongues and flaring, widened eyes, the pupils expanded, all the better to see in the dim shadows. My entrance, then, anywhere, brought punctuation. Sharp, biting inspiration. Breath quickened with the sharp tang of fear, seasoned by desire and hunger, hunting in the fringes of light. I was always protected, then, sharp words at my back, covering me, but all made of harshness and edges. Leave him alone, they would say. You do not touch him, they commanded. He is a child. I see the dark umbrae and the lights that bound them, and I know of the danger, and of the fear, and of the revulsion. Turn away, I am told, we will go elsewhere. We will go over yonder. Where is yonder, I wondered, a child yet not. I've never been to yonder, all these many trips to find it. Where is yonder, I ask. He smiles at me, it's right around the corner, next to the delicatessen. You know. . . .

But I do not. The delicatessen is across the street from the cafeteria. And next to that is the liquor store. That's where One came for me, and almost caught me there, a boogeyman kind of man. I saw him, next to the liquor store. He didn't touch me, not that time, not there in front of the cafeteria, across from Yonder. I stood in the delicatessen where dead eyes looked at me from the case, filmy and milky, held in fishy heads, they stared at me, like to those outside. Different, not different, always staring. There I was, across the street from Yonder but not knowing where it was. He came towards me there, or perhaps he didn't, but someone thought he had, and stabbing words came swirling in the night, razors slashing across the concrete, swords penetrating, forged of hardness and tempered by loathing born of fear. I wasn't afraid: I knew that what lingered in the darkness there didn't want to hurt, only to see. To see what I was, to see the lightness I could become. But it could not be, not then, not ever. It cannot be, it was not meant to be, and it should not be.

Like all memory, those days are legacies that blur but never fade; they are available to be born anew as the need arises. The colors remain if the outlines are softened, and it is really from those we repaint the world anew each time we visit it there. Two dozen years later, I find that same canvas with Pugachev, and the colors are as vibrant as ever. But, as now, I cannot quite make out the subject of the work. Like me, he had beautiful hands. Like mine were, they are delicate with long thin, sensitive fingers. The hands of a reader, a musician, a painter, perhaps even a writer.

I have a picture from those earlier times, I don't look at it, not any more. I remember it, though, a picture of me, staring at the camera. My right elbow rests on something, a table? My forearm vertical into the air, the hand limp at the wrist and horizontal, pointing languidly at the viewer, with the index finger slightly raised. Why? I do not know, could not say, not any more. A beautiful man-boy, sculpted with lovely hands. A beautiful face, cast with sensual lips. Were I not myself, I could kiss those lips, caress that face. My wife, or the one I was with at that time, took the picture, had it printed and framed. My wife, the one I am with now, displays it for some reason. It was taken in the bookstore, in Pugachev's. It was taken a lifetime ago, or perhaps only a few years—it all blurs—but my hands are no longer beautiful, not as they once were.

In the picture, the lights are dim. It was a long exposure, there was no harsh flash to jar the edges and define the darkness. I was odd, and out of place. In those days, brightness ruled and enlightenment flowed, but in the picture, one sees none of that. Perhaps that is why it pains me. It presages the battles to come, foreshadowing. You see, the picture is not actually of me. It is, in reality, a portrait of the darkness, that which is the absence of me. I am only there to define that darkness, and thus it could only have been taken in Pugachev's. That was where the border lay, the seam where darkness and the light could meet and rest together, where they could sit on the divine divan in peace, conversing amiably before they went back out, returning to their timeless battle, back to defining yonder by that which is not-yonder.

I first met Pugachev there, at a store, his store, a bookstore. Musty, dusty, old and decrepit, the shelves creaking with wisdom and folly. On Colorado Boulevard, where the flowers march every year. It reeked of decay, a demesne of silverfish and of quiet. But the sun would come down through the window in the afternoon, and it would stir the dust, and Pugachev would laugh. See, he would say, the dust stirs for the want of learning, and yet the learning is all here. The light would strike his desk, weathering the old leather writing pad, a pad on which nothing was ever written, but it weathered all the same, and Pugachev would laugh at the colors that the sun brought in, colors that were not there in the darkness.

He was as short as I was tall. I had strolled into his store one day quite by accident, on lunch, on a hunch, looking up at the shelves on shelves followed by shelves. It was a place made up of all I wanted. Nothing tawdry or cheap was ever allowed, the books were never paperbacks here; all were bound in hardness, firm covers confining the pages and the words. The wisdom was cataloged in some inscrutable system, a method only known to Pugachev. He was afraid of someone stealing his essence he said, of pirating the wisdom he collected in that place. But you never read them? Never, he said. These are for the others. Mine are back at home.

Would you like to see them, he asked me one day, and I assented and ascended the stairs at the back of the store. The mezzanine was his loft, long before those things became fashionable and trendy and expensive. It was his sanctuary within his abbey, a concealment in plain sight. He played a game I understood all too well, then and now. The hunter's blind, you see, is never actually out of sight; it is simply so ordinary and unremarkable that it isn't worth the notice. Unseen, even at the end of what happens, it is nowhere. It is, always, over yonder.

The first time I was there, I wandered the aisles as he watched. I could see the eyes in the shadow, hear the inspiration. I posed for him, playing the dance out in my head. A game of chess, more than he ever knew; we each saw the other, knew the steps, the path. I saw more, concealed within my blind, I saw him within his, in the open yet not in the open at all.

I like your hands, he remarks one day, later, not long after. Tell me, is all of you as long and slender? A hitch in his breathing gives him away and sings to me what he wishes and wants and desires. I toy with leaving, with staying, and smile in indecision, and in that, deciding. It has been so very, very long since I was who I am with someone like me, but he is not like me at all. He is one pole of the magnet, and Catherine is the other: they are a bar with two ends. And I am neither, I am a sphere, the perfect sphere with an imperfection. A concept made real, I have no corners. I lack the sides that define, the one against the other, and so I am neither and yet both but not of any kind at all. And still as we attract, or repel, I am there, and then I stay. And thus it began, not long after my first time there. In beginning there is also ending, or a recognition of ending already forged but yet reserved for the future.

He would rise and stand, striding over to me, straddling me as I sat on the couch. Ah, no, I forgot for a moment, it was on the divan. You should never, he would declaim, never call such a magnificent sculpture seating, such a work of art, merely a "couch." You can couch your words, he preached in a fever, or your meanings, but you could be seated only upon a divan. A divine divan, he christened it, as certainly it once belonged in the best salons in Paris! Voltaire himself would have sat upon such a divan, and Diderot's library would have surrounded it. It was stolen from the Hermitage itself, he would boast, the spoils of victory, a medal of the Enlightenment, captured. Brought to Russia by Catherine the Great, Champion of the Progress, Empress of All the Russias. She herself had bought it, had it shipped from Paris in the reign of Louis, the Fifteenth of that name. It was the first of her acquisitions, a gift from the King of Poland maybe, or perhaps from Potemkin, or from Panin, Pugachev was not certain on this point. All had been her lovers, in their time. And Pugachev, standing there, astride the world, or perhaps merely astride me, would entwine his fingers in my hair. He would wrap his fingers through it, and we were entranced in the light of the day and of the afternoon. And later, then, in those afternoons, his fingers wrapped themselves again, as did mine. And we passed them, the afternoons and evenings in succession, the books, the music, the afternoons, the meals and the evenings. We spoke of the world, the one where he now lived, and the one he claimed to have left. We spoke of his family, of his father. The uneducated son of Cossacks spoke of learning and of wisdom with the son of rabbis and of professors. We spoke of mine, and of yonder and of the streets. And he wept for me. And I wept for him and for Catherine.

Remember your history, he would proclaim, remember it well! George, King of England and the Third of that name, asked his cousin but not-cousin, Catherine the Great, for 20,000 Cossacks. George needed them to help pacify his troublesome colonies. Facing threats at home from Turkey and from Prussia, she refused. She needed her troops. George needed his colonies and had turned to her, a fellow German, both on thrones, but both on thrones that were not German. Catherine's Pugachev, the one of history was dead by then, two years past. She, who had corresponded with Voltaire and who had thought to bring Mozart to Moscow (it never happened, or history would have changed again), she could not purge her memory of Pugachev. Of this we spoke often, of the history of his name. Pugachev had stolen the name of Catherine's husband, the husband whose death allowed her to ascend the throne and become Empress of all the Russias. Pugachev the impostor. Of this, we spoke, he astride me, me on the divan. The sun fading through the window. The dust stirring. The light playing games as it faded into the evenings, and as Yonder loomed large in the distance, behind the delicatessen in the lights of the streets in the night. And Catherine refused her fellow monarch, and the Cossacks stayed at home. Because of Pugachev, dead barely two years then, Catherine refused George, and George turned to the Hessians, and the Hessians were defeated, and here we were, now, in their legacy. And there we were then, and thus he became, simply, Pugachev. And Pugachev haunted Catherine. He haunted her and, when Louis' grandson went to the guillotine, it was the memory of Pugachev that rose like bile in her throat, and the Enlightenment in Russia ended. And the Catherine of that Enlightenment was no more.

And how could Pugachev frighten Catherine so? What kept the Empress awake, all those nights, was the thought that a ragtag army of Cossacks and serfs and deserters and thieves could ever take Kazan. Capturing with barely a fight the largest Tatar city in all the Russias, and Catherine is caught by surprise. The Empress of All the Russias could do nothing to prevent it. Catherine, you see, loves many men. As do I. And we, my Catherine, not the one of history but the one I married, we loved each other, or so we told the tale. But Pugachev, my Pugachev of the books but not the one of history, he loved himself. He loved to play the great game of it all. Pugachev, the one of history, rebelled. He gathered his Cossacks, he marched on Catherine. He could not abide her, and he stole from her. He stole her husband's name, and that was me. He became her long-dead husband to raise an army and to take Kazan, and when she rejected him, she cast away much of the light she had brought to herself, to me. There would be no freedom for the serfs, no change in the feudal structure for Catherine of Russia. And there would be no Cossacks in America, not for many years. And me, I am taken by this present Pugachev while my Catherine, the one who married me, feigns surprise and disbelief. While she was loving many men, so was I. And so was Pugachev.

And I was the beautiful boy, the boy with the lovely hands. Pugachev asked me about them when first we met. Long fingers, he observed, fine and delicate. Like something else, he asked, you know what they say, don't you? Is it long and delicate as well? Artless, direct, compelling to a boy with beautiful hands, a boy who lived only to love and to be loved. And Pugachev loved me. And now Pugachev is dead. And the sun blasts through the window, stabbing into the room, piercing my comfort. And my Catherine, she is gone, she tired of the games and she has left me, now many years ago. And so I cover my head and weep for the loss of Catherine, and for her news of the death of Pugachev, though he was gone from my life for many years. I cocoon myself in the sheet, but it is too confining, too stifling. I hurl the covers off, gasping. . . .

D. Dolnick was born and raised in Chicago, but has lived in Southern California for the last 38 years. He has written for a variety of business and professional publications and hates labels.

wonder

by justin adkins

People see me, I'm a challenge
to your balance, I'm over your heads
how I confound you
and astound you
to know I must be one of the wonders
—*Natalie Merchant, "Wonder"*

"What, I don't understand?" A phrase I have heard so many times in my life, I've lost track. People don't understand how I ever worked as a christian missionary and now identify as buddhist. People don't understand why I transitioned, because I was a "good-looking woman." Then, most stunning, was the day a gay male friend said that phrase when I told him that I like men and women.

The question came a couple weeks after I separated from my wife. I moved to Massachusetts in 2004 specifically to get married: same-sex marriage was legal here. This was a few years before I transitioned so we were married as a lesbian couple. I was proud of being a lesbian, a dyke. I was proud of all of the strong women who I surrounded myself with who paved the way for me to be out and proud. However, I had no interest in lovin' my "womyn-lovin' self." In fact, I had no interest in being a woman.

When I left my career as a missionary and started my journey to find myself, I thought that my "issue" was that I was attracted to women. I always had been. I had been hurt by so many men, I wasn't sure if I had relationships with them because I wanted to, or because I had no option of anything but straight in my chosen career. In one quick intense move, I came out as a lesbian, shaved my head, and started working at a lesbian, feminist, separatist, pagan bookstore. Never one to do anything half-assed, I was OUT!

It was at this time that I met my ex-wife. We both identified as christians and shared a deep concern for the earth. She challenged me mentally and we had fun together. I was in love.

In 2004 the thing to do, if you were a same-sex couple in love, was to get married. We met during that short month when San Francisco Mayor Gavin Newsom issued a directive to the county clerk to issue marriage licenses to same-sex couples. We missed the short window, but marriage was on our minds. Though I don't think marriage is a good idea for anyone because it gets the government involved in your relationship and grants some people benefits solely because they are coupled, you couldn't escape the excitement; it was palpable. Moving across the country also brought me to a new phase in my life: a place and time in which I could safely explore my gender.

As a lesbian couple in Western Massachusetts, we spent a lot of time with other lesbians. The women who mentored us were scared of trans* guys. They were scared that all of the butch lesbians would become men. They had little understanding of what it means to be trans*. These women challenged me. They challenged me to think about why I wanted to medically transition. This was not an easy experience but it was formidable. Their "I don't understand" questions were actually helpful. At first, the questions hurt; over time they helped me articulate who I am.

After I started testosterone, my ex-wife asked me the question that is all over the female-to-male transsexual blogs, "Will you start being attracted to men now that you are on testosterone?" It was a particularly tough question for me because I never stopped being attracted to men. I was a failed lesbian. Also, I work better in a monogamous relationship, and in my vows I had committed to monogamy. Her real concern was that I was going to cheat on her, not that I was "still" attracted to men. Cheating was the furthest thing from my mind.

For a variety of reasons, our relationship ended after five years of marriage. And it was then that I encountered the double whammy: that day that my gay male friend said, "I don't understand." His confusion was, why did I transform my body if I like men? Why not just "stay a woman" and be straight? I wanted to say, "Honey, wake up. Gender and sexuality are different things. I can be bi and trans*!"

That sexuality and gender are different is a simple fact and confusing to a wide swath of the population. As an LGBTQ community we also regularly confuse the two. Hearing coming-out stories, person after person describes their childhood spent playing with the "wrong toys" and desiring to dress in the "wrong clothing" as the root of their homosexuality. The fact that "we" describe drag as a gay thing and associate lesbians with short haircuts and Subarus does not help the matter either.

Both sexuality and gender are social constructs; that is, they are constructed by society. What are considered the behaviors associated with masculinity in the United States are very different from the behaviors associated with masculinity in India. This is gender. There is the gender you see yourself as, and then there is the way you express gender (gender identity and gender expression, respectively). The two may or may not line up. I understand why people are confused. Gender is confusing! To add to the confusion, not all theorists even agree.

Your sexuality, by contrast, is to whom you are attracted. There is sexual behavior, sexual orientation and sexual identity. Your behavior is what you do. Your orientation is the pattern to your attraction. I am attracted to butch men and high-femme women, for instance (not that there are only two sexes or genders). Your sexual identity is the label that you use. So, you could identify as a straight man and still have sex with men. You could be a bisexual man married to a woman. When you combine it all together you could identify as an intersex woman (your sex and you gender identities, respectively) with straight identity and omnisexual sexual behavior. The possibilities are really endless.

The difference between sexuality and gender is why people find me so confusing. My friend seems to think that being gay is "hard" or "less than" being straight. His internalized homophobia came to light when he questioned me that fateful day.

I have no interest in being straight. I am more than happy for all of my straight-identified friends, and I support them in their identities and relationships, just as I would like them to support me. However, straight just isn't me. Even if I end up in another long-term relationship with a woman, I will not be straight. We would most likely be perceived as straight walking down the road, but that's a matter of perception. Sexuality is not always what it appears to be.

Queer, in all senses of the word, is probably the best word to describe me. Queer is political. Queer is something "off the norm." Queer is sexual and gender minorities. Queer rejects traditional sexual and gender identities. Queer is outside the bounds of normal society. Queer is breaking the rules for sex and gender. One can be queer and bi. For that matter, one can be queer and straight.

For the longest time Natalie Merchant's song, "Wonder," has been "my song." It describes me. Its message is that you might not understand me, and that is okay. God clearly had a higher purpose for my life and though there is no explanation for why I am trans* or why I am bi, I know that it's okay. I know that it is a wonderful thing just to be me. I know that there are people who don't "believe" in bisexuality and that there are people who don't "believe" that transsexuality is real either. I say to them, "Hello, my name is justin and I am a queer bisexual transsexual."

justin adkins is a radical trans activist living in Massachusetts. He works at a small liberal arts college, where he coordinates programming, supports students and advises on policies focusing on gender, sexuality and activism. justin gained national attention for his participation in Occupy Wall Street and the mistreatment he received from the New York Police Department because he identifies as transgender. He loves traveling around the U.S. speaking about trans* and LGBTQ issues and making sure that schools and organizations go beyond policy and instead focus on LGBTQ people being embraced and thriving in society.*

in the direction of greatest courage

by erik moore

"Life rewards those who move in the direction of greatest courage." — *Franklin Veaux*

The checkout lane at the grocery store is an odd place for a story to begin, but then, this is an odd story. I hadn't noticed her in the store, but when I got to the checkout, she was in front of me and for a few moments, I didn't notice anything except her. No more than two inches shorter than my own five foot nine, which would put her head at the perfect height to rest on my shoulder when cuddling. Straight hair past her shoulders, so black it almost looked blue under the lights. And curvy in a way that would have had Rubens or Titian falling over themselves to find a paintbrush. She looked back for a second, and I could see the pale, freckled skin on her face and the thin-rimmed glasses sitting in front of her bright, green eyes.

After she paid and left, I noticed she'd left her cell phone. The clerk hadn't noticed it because it was in front of the little credit machine where he couldn't see. I turned to call for her, but the doors had already closed, and I didn't see which way she went.

So I grabbed it and slid it into my pocket. Don't ask me why. The smart thing would probably have been to give it to the customer service desk to hold until she came back looking for it. But I knew how lost I'd be without my phone, and who knows how long it might be before she realized it was missing. She'd have to backtrack all her steps to find it, and I didn't want her to have to do that.

Besides, if I could figure out how to get in touch with her, it would give me a chance to learn her name and hear her voice. So I'm selfish. Sue me.

I didn't wait to get home before I called. I would have lost my nerve by then. As soon as I got into the car, before even turning the key, I fished out the phone and flipped it open. Fortunately it wasn't password locked or anything, so I brought up the phone book, scrolled down to the entry I knew would be there, and pressed, "Send." Four rings later, a generic answering machine voice piped up telling me to leave a message. I hadn't thought this out very well. Of course she wouldn't be home yet; she just left the store.

"Hi," I said after what I hoped wasn't too long a pause. "My name is Jason. You—left your phone at the Kroger's today. Give me a call when you get this, and I can get it back to you." I left my cellphone number, hung up and drove home.

Do you know what it's like to stare at your phone, trying to will it into ringing with the awesome power of your mind? Most people do, I think. Unsurprisingly, this has a spectacularly high rate of failure, so I really can't be blamed for nearly falling out of my chair when my phone rang after only 7,000 years of staring. Or it might have been 20 minutes. I didn't check.

"Hello?" God, I hoped I didn't sound as nervous as I felt.

"Is Jason there?" A female voice I didn't recognize. My stomach did a couple of back flips.

"This is he."

"Hi, you left a message saying you found my phone? Do you work at the store?"

"Um, no, actually. I—" Shit, this was embarrassing. "I was standing behind you in line."

"I see. And how did you get my number?" Wary, and possibly a little angry. Shit, shit, shit.

"Just about everyone has an entry in their phone list marked *Home*. I hope you don't mind," I said quickly before she could respond. "I figured the store would hold it and make you come in for it once you realized it was missing, and by then you might not know where you left it."

There was a pause, and I was sure I was screwed. She'd call the police and report me for theft. Worse, she'd start yelling, and I couldn't stand the thought of that pretty, freckled face twisted up in anger. But after three hours (or two seconds—again, I didn't check) of listening to the soft hiss from the phone, she said, "Wow, thanks. I really appreciate that. Can I meet you somewhere to pick it up?"

I let out the breath I was holding. "Sure thing. I don't know how far you are from the store, but we could meet at the Starbucks in that same shopping center."

"Sounds good. Are you okay with doing this now? I'd really like to get my phone back ASAP," she answered.

"Yeah, no problem. Should take me about 15 minutes to get there," I told her, trying hard not to sound too eager to see her again.

She chuckled, and I wondered how badly I'd failed to hide my enthusiasm. "You'll probably beat me, so I'll look for the guy with two phones."

“That’ll be me,” I agreed. “See you there.”

My fifteen-minute drive took me nine-and-a-half minutes. I’m fairly certain I broke several laws of motoring (if not laws of physics) to pull that off, but my mind was too focused on the destination to notice much of the journey. Fortunately, no police officers or physicists witnessed the feat, so I wasn’t stopped.

I sat down in the Starbucks at a table with a clear view of the door and waited. The only paper lying around was *USA Today*, which I hate because it doesn’t have a funnies page. I looked at it anyway and realized it was a day old, which I suppose made it *USA Yesterday*. Still, it was something to keep me occupied instead of checking the door every three seconds. It didn’t work. My neck was on the verge of repetitive stress disorder from all the up-and-down motions by the time she arrived.

She picked me out immediately, and it was flattering to have been remembered. “Jason?” she asked, stopping in front of my table.

I stood up and offered her a hand. “Yep, that’s me.

She shook my hand politely and smiled. “Hi. I’m Beth. Thanks again for this. I’m totally lost without my phone.”

“I know the feeling.” I fished her phone out of my pocket and passed it over to her. “And don’t worry; I didn’t go through it or anything.”

Beth quirked an eyebrow. “Too bad. I think I still have some nude shots saved on here. Guess you missed out.” She must have caught the stunned expression on my face because she suddenly laughed. “I’m kidding. Here, let me buy you a coffee to thank you. That is, if you don’t need to rush off right away.”

I managed to find my voice again. “My life is phenomenally boring, so I’m not especially anxious to rejoin it just yet.”

“Not just boring, but phenomenally boring? We’ll have to see what we can do about that.”

Before I could quite register I was being flirted with, Beth turned away and started toward the counter. She ordered like a pro, rattling off her drink options with a practiced ease.

I only caught “double shot” and “soy milk,” but the barista didn’t bat an eye at the litany. Then, as if to emphasize the relative mundanity of my own life, I meekly asked for a tall black coffee to which I added very small amounts of cream and sugar myself.

“You didn’t have to get the cheapest thing on the menu,” Beth said to me once we were seated back at our table.

I shrugged. "I never got into the whole "frappe-mocha-latte-cino" thing. I've tried it, but it's not for me. I like my coffee to be coffee."

"Fair enough." She took a long drink and sighed. "So, now that you're settled with your coffee, I have a confession to make. I sort of—left my phone behind intentionally, hoping you would find it."

My cup paused halfway to my lips as I tried to process that statement. "You wanted me to take your phone?"

Beth blushed a little and looked down. "Well, no. I wanted you to call me, and this seemed like the best way."

"And what if I had turned it into the lost and found at the store?"

"Oh, I'd have swung by in the morning and grabbed it."

"But—" I was stammering, and my mind was racing. I took a sip of my coffee and forced my thoughts in order. "But what if I'd just—taken it?"

Beth thought about that for a moment, and then shrugged. "Sometimes, you have to take a big risk to get a big reward."

I shook my head. "I'm sorry, what parallel universe did I wake up in this morning where I'm a big reward?"

She whapped me playfully on the shoulder. "No putting yourself down. That's rule number one around me."

"Really? And what's rule number two?" I asked with a smirk.

Beth mirrored my expression. "Guess you'll have to take me to dinner and find out."

It took a little negotiating with schedules, but we finally agreed on the following Friday night for dinner. We talked a little more, mostly boring stuff that needs no reproduction and my mind neglected to adequately record, being so giddy at having a date after a long dry spell. I didn't really check back into the conversation until Beth said, "Oh, so you're not surprised when you pick me up, I'm married."

I'd heard the phrase *my heart dropped into my feet* before, but never understood the feeling until right at that moment. "You're looking for an affair," I said numbly.

"Oh, no, it's not like that!" she replied quickly. "We have an open marriage. He knows I'm here with you, and he knows why. He knew even before I left my phone. He was in the store with me, but he went to the car before I checked out so you wouldn't see us together."

This was too much weirdness for one conversation, and I clenched my eyes shut as I tried to digest it all.

"So, you're—what? Polygamous or something?"

Beth made a non-committal sound. "Polygamy is a legal term that deals with marriage. We prefer *polyamorous*, which has more to do with relationships and love." I still hadn't opened my eyes, but I suddenly felt her hand atop mine. "Hey, Jason, if that's an issue, I understand, and I'm sorry for not saying something before I asked you out. We can just go our ways, no harm done."

I took a deep breath and let it out slowly before looking at her. She was visibly upset by my reaction, and my chest ached at the hurt in her eyes. "This is all very new to me," I said carefully. "I've never done anything like this before, never even knew anyone who did. But, like you said, it takes a big risk to win a big reward, right?"

"And I'm a big reward?" she asked, almost echoing my tone and inflection from earlier. But her expression instantly relaxed and softened.

"Powerball jackpot big," I told her, earning myself a laugh and a blush. We shared a little more polite small talk while we finished our drinks, and then headed out, she home to her husband, and I back to my empty apartment and microwave dinner.

I love the Internet. The biggest storehouse of information in the history of the world, some of it even accurate. I spent quite a few hours between meeting Beth and our date that weekend searching the Internet for information on polyamory. There was a lot more than I'd expected. This wasn't some hippie free-love cult or fundamentalist Mormon idea. I was finding articles from all kinds of people, and from all over the world.

Even armed with all this information, though, I was completely unprepared when I knocked on Beth's door and a man opened it. And a damn fine-looking one at that. He was taller than me by a good five inches, with short-cropped white blond hair and piercing blue eyes. Athletic without being overly muscular, this was a man who would have been right at home on the cover of a fitness magazine, yet here he was between me and my date. I couldn't speak. No, I mean, I literally could not convince my mouth to make sounds come out.

Fortunately, he seemed to sense my discomfort, because he smiled and offered a hand to me. "You must be Jason. I'm Geoff, Beth's husband. Beth's almost ready. Come on in."

I shook Geoff's hand. I only know this because I could see myself doing it. I don't remember making the decision to do it, nor could I feel my hand in his. I allowed myself to be led numbly through the foyer and into the main living room. The entire time, I was waiting for something to go horribly, horribly wrong. Geoff's going to punch me. A camera crew is going to jump out. The Large Hadron Collider is going to prove all the scientists wrong by creating a black hole that swallows the planet. Something.

And then something did. I tripped. The sitting area in the living room was sunken, and I missed the step down. I threw my hands out, and was rather surprised when they contacted Geoff's chest rather than the ground. He'd moved quickly and caught me around the waist before I'd pitched forward very far at all. It took me a moment to steady myself, admittedly longer than absolutely necessary as I couldn't get over the feel of his chest under my hands or how incredibly good he smelled. I'd already begun picturing myself stripping off his shirt and running my tongue along his breastbone when the thought, "You're becoming aroused by your date's husband" managed to confuse my libido enough that I was able to step back.

"And what's going on here?" asked Beth.

I spun around (almost tripping again) and saw her coming around the corner of the stairwell. "Oh! Um, I tripped."

"Don't listen to him," Geoff said, clucking his tongue. "Your date was throwing himself at me. We're in love and are flying off to Massachusetts to get married."

Beth put her hands on her hips and flatly stated, "That would be bigamy."

Geoff nodded and laughed. "I know! I think it's big of me, too, considering we only just met." He walked over to Beth and bent down to kiss her quickly on the lips. She coiled an arm around his waist and goosed his ass. The easy familiarity between the two of them instantly made me irrationally jealous. Which was doubly stupid because I was the interloper here.

"Have fun, you two," Geoff said once they disengaged. "Nice meeting you, Jason."

I swallowed and nodded. "You, too." He started for the stairs, and I couldn't help stealing a glance at him from behind to complete the picture in my mind. He had the ass and thighs of a Tour de France cyclist. I stopped myself from envisioning him in skin-tight spandex and forced my attention back to Beth.

She looked amazing. She was wearing a frilly white peasant blouse casually falling off one shoulder and a gauzy purple skirt stopping just above her ankles. Her hair was piled on top of her head, only a few strands falling down to frame her face. If she was wearing makeup, it was subtle enough as to be unnoticeable. She said something to me, but I was too caught up in admiring her to notice, so she repeated, "Ready to go?"

I looked down at the dark blue jeans and simple black collarless button-down shirt I was wearing. It was a nice enough outfit—they were both relatively new pieces—but I suddenly felt underdressed anyway. "Sure. Just as soon as I run home and change into something nicer."

Beth laughed. "Oh, you look fine. I love that shirt."

"Um, thanks. You look incredible." That made her blush. It went all the way down her neck, which I thought was adorable, and told her so.

"You're sweet. C'mon, let's go. I'm hungry." She walked over to me, slipped an arm around mine, and led me toward the door.

I don't remember where we went, just that it was one of those fake "roadhouse" places where they give you a basket of peanuts and encourage you to throw the shells on the floor. We both ordered Guinness, agreeing with each other on the similarities between domestic beer and having sex on a beach (they're both fucking close to water). Beth ordered a thick t-bone and ribbed me good-naturedly about coming to a steakhouse and ordering fish, but the cedar plank grilled salmon was too tempting to pass up.

The conversation was casual, most of it the usual getting-to-know-you stuff of any first date. I found out she was a Capricorn, worked as a court stenographer, loved lilies but hated roses, and believed *Tommy* was a better rock opera than *The Wall*. (I made a mental note to convince her otherwise on that last one.)

What made it a little surreal was Geoff's invisible presence throughout—every question I asked, Beth answered for him as well. For the record: he's also a Capricorn, drives an ambulance for a living, likes carnations and prefers Baroque opera to rock opera.

Over the apple pie à la mode, I finally got up the courage to address the elephant in the room. "So, how long have you and Geoff been doing the polyamory thing?"

"We've only known the word for the past three years," she replied after a little thought. "But for the first four years we were married, we had agreements that outside relationships were okay, mainly because, even while we were dating, it was no secret we were both bisexual. We decided we wouldn't restrict the other from exploring that other side of their desires. And when we learned about polyamory, we discussed it and realized it was silly to restrict outside relationships to same-sex only."

My ears started ringing when she mentioned the B-word, and I barely heard the rest of her explanation. "Did you say Geoff is bisexual, too?"

Beth nodded. "Does that bother you? I mean, it's not like he's going to jump you or anything. I'm here because I like you, not because of anything to do with him."

I realized she'd misunderstood my question, thinking I was grossed out by thoughts of man-touching. I should have expected that; God knows I've run into that attitude from other people often enough. I cleared my throat, trying to think of the best way to put her at ease on that score. "Well, um, that's kind of a pity, since I thought he was pretty fucking hot."

Her eyes widened as her mouth formed a tiny "O" of surprise, and she slapped the table, laughing loudly. "I thought I noticed you checking him out!" she exclaimed happily. "I didn't want to say anything in case I was wrong."

I exhaled slowly, feeling a knot of tension at the back of my neck suddenly release. "No, you noticed right. I did actually trip, though. I just—wasn't unhappy he was there to catch me."

"Yeah, I hate that step. I can't count the number of times I've forgotten about it, either going up or down. And not always with Geoff there to grab me. But, seriously, you're bisexual?"

"I am," I told her, feeling oddly exposed to be making such a statement in a public place. The din of conversation and loud music meant no one beyond our table could have heard, but emotion is rarely persuaded by things like logic. "For a few years now. I've just never met anyone, male or female, who was okay with it."

"There's definitely a healthy portion of biphobia from both the gay and straight camps, that's for sure," Beth agreed. "But you don't have to worry about that with me."

"Whew," I said, wiping imaginary sweat from my forehead. "That's good to know, because my neck is getting a crick from having to sneak looks at our waiter's ass without you noticing."

She laughed again, and her eyes lit up like fireworks. "Oh, God, I know! It's like they painted the denim right over his skin! Rawr."

I laughed with her and made some remark about bouncing quarters off it.

It felt so incredible to be able to share that with her, to give her that piece of myself I'd held back from so many others. I fell just a little bit in love with her right then.

When the check came, she offered to pay since the restaurant had been her choice, but I refused. We compromised: I paid the check while she left the tip. We decided between the service and that tight ass, the waiter had easily earned eighteen percent. She threatened to write my phone number on a napkin and leave it with the tip for him to find, but I managed to steer her away from the table before she could find a pen.

I stared at the text message for several seconds before the meaning fully registered. "Geoff says he wants 2 date u 2. Call me. Beth."

I swear to God, my first thought was, "Why would Geoff want to date an Irish rock band?" It really didn't register that he might be interested in me. Besides which, date me "too"? Since when were Beth and I dating? We'd only been out the one time, three nights before. Sure, we'd had a quick goodnight kiss and agreed we wanted to get together again, but did that count as dating? I was obviously more out of practice than I'd thought if the basic terminology was tripping me up.

I fired off a quick reply: "How would that work?"

I had this horrible image of some bizarre joint custody situation where I'd see Beth one weekend and Geoff the next. I'd seen enough after-school specials to be fairly sure nothing good could come out of that. Inevitably, the competing would start, and the pressuring me to make a choice, and no matter who I picked, it would tear the two of them apart, and that was the last thing I wanted, and—

My mind was jumping around way too fast for me to deal with at that moment. I finally put the brakes on the whole train of thought. I was in the middle of debugging a finicky security subroutine at my job, hardly the best time to try to make sense of open relationship protocols. I got so wrapped up in it, as a matter of fact, I didn't see Beth's answering text—"How do u want it 2 work?"—until I was finishing up for the day, several hours after pretty much everyone else had gone home.

It wasn't too late yet, so I gave Beth a call as I was heading out of the office toward my car. As it turned out, both of their days had run long as well, so they were getting ready to have a late supper. Beth suggested I come on over and join them so the three of us could talk. The pot roast she'd had in the slow cooker all day sounded better than the grilled cheese and tomato soup waiting for me at home, so I eagerly agreed.

The entire house smelled like beef and vegetables, and it was mutually decided eating first was the best idea. You know it's good food when no one feels the need to speak during the meal, and this was very good food.

It wasn't until after dinner when we'd all moved back into the living room—I managed not to trip this time—that the conversation actually started.

Geoff started things off. "I guess the important question is, would you even be interested in dating both me and Beth?"

"Seriously? I hadn't really thought about it," I said. "It didn't even occur to me as a possibility. I guess it would be an elegant solution to the whole bisexuality issue, but how could something like that work?"

"Don't worry about that right now. Assuming we found a way to do it, would it be something you would want?"

It wasn't easy to think about the answer to that question without thinking about the logistics of such a thing, but I tried. Would I, in a perfect world, have interest in relationships with not one, but two funny, intelligent, interesting, and downright sexy individuals? Put that way, it wasn't too difficult a decision. "Yes, it definitely would be."

Beth nodded her head. "Then we'll find a way to make it work. It's that simple."

"Have you ever both dated the same person before? At the same time, I mean?" The mere concept boggled the mind.

"Nope. New territory for us all, I guess. But Geoff and I have met a long-term triad before, so it's certainly possible for it to work."

"I've also seen a guy break through a stack of cinder blocks with his head," I pointed out, "so it's certainly possible. It doesn't mean I'm lining up to take a shot at it." I could almost hear Beth's voice in my head from our first meeting. Sometimes, you have to take a big risk to get a big reward. Because, man, to be able to have something like this work had the potential to be epic. So I took a deep breath and went for it. "But hell, if you guys are willing to try, I say let's go for it."

Geoff laughed suddenly. "You realize what this means, right, hon? Jason's our Hot Bi Babe."

That got Beth laughing, too. "Holy shit, you're right!"

I crossed my arms, aware I was the punchline in some inside joke, and let the two of them laugh it out. "So, as much as I enjoy providing comic relief," I said when the giggles had run their course, "I have work tomorrow and should probably get at least a few minutes of sleep. You guys want to get together this weekend and see how things go?"

Beth patted me on the knee. "It was a compliment, I promise. But, yes, this weekend would be great. Geoff's off Saturday, so he can maybe grill steaks and we can have dinner and a movie night. Sound good?"

"That works for me," I replied, already relieved at being spared the awkwardness of going out with two people at once. I stood up, and the two of them walked me to the door. Beth gave me a hug and a quick kiss as she had on our date, but then Geoff did the same, which left my mind reeling with possibilities and ensured sleep was a long time in coming.I'd like to say the rest of the week was a blur, but the fact is it plodded along with all the insistence of a geological event. On the other hand, nothing that happened in those several days was in the least bit remarkable—unless reconfiguring firewall settings fills you with ecstasy—so on to Saturday. I had absolutely no idea what to expect from the evening. Normally, that would have been enough to make me cancel, but I'd been taking chances left and right since meeting these two. Now the potential reward had increased, and the question was whether or not I was going to fold.

Beth greeted me at the door with a hug and a beer and led me through the house to the backyard. The unmistakable scent of meat cooking over fire hit me the second we stepped outside. Beneath that was the crisp tang of chlorinated pool water and the sweetness of honeysuckle far enough away not to be overwhelming. The sun was just starting to drop, taking the heat of the day with it. If there exists a more perfect summer day, God kept it for himself.

Geoff was manning the grill, but spared me a quick salute with his tongs before turning his attention back to the steaks. "Good timing," he said over his shoulder. "A couple more minutes, and these'll be perfect."

We ate outside since it was so beautiful. Geoff's talent with the grill was considerable; the steak was one of the best I'd ever had. I'd expected the situation to be awkward, but somehow, it wasn't. We talked, we joked, and it was all perfectly normal. This was the first chance I'd had to really get to know Geoff, and it quickly became apparent he and I had at least as much in common as I did with Beth. I probably shouldn't have been surprised, but I was.

At the same time, there were differences. I guess I'd always assumed a married couple would agree on just about everything—isn't that how you know you've found "The One"? But that wasn't the case, at least not here. As it turned out, my movie preferences were closer to Geoff's while my tastes in music were more like Beth's.

Maybe it sounds obvious to some people, but for me, someone who had never managed a serious relationship, this was a major revelation. "I feel so unbelievably naïve," I told them at one point. "I'm not that much younger than you two, but it's like you two are in honors calculus while I'm still mastering basic arithmetic."

Geoff laughed and touched my arm. "We're still learning all this ourselves, Jase. God, don't think that we're some kind of experts on relationships. We have fights like any other couple. Being married doesn't change who you are. Besides, how boring would it be to agree with someone on everything?"

When it started getting dark outside and the mosquitoes began to swarm, we moved inside and relaxed on the sofa, Beth sitting between Geoff and me. We debated over a movie to watch for a few minutes before settling on some mindless romantic comedy with Hugh Grant, mainly because we all agreed he was hot.

We'd all seen this particular one before, but that was okay because the jokes were still amusing, Hugh was still hot, and we all ended up quoting the same lines back at the screen. About two-thirds of the way in, though, I noticed they didn't laugh at what I thought was one of the best bits in the whole movie. I looked over at them and realized they were kissing. My head snapped back toward the television so fast my neck cracked. I wasn't uncomfortable with it, exactly. I felt jealous, turned on, and whatever that emotion is where you see a happy couple out somewhere and think "Aww, aren't they cute," all at the same time. Still, that's a lot of conflicting feeling to be dealing with at once, and I wasn't sure what to do about it.

I heard some low talking and glanced back to see Geoff whispering something to Beth, though I couldn't hear what. It became pretty clear a second or two later, though, because Beth shifted in my direction and slipped an arm behind my neck. I don't remember ever making the conscious decision to kiss her, but suddenly, I was. None of my fantasies of kissing Beth had included her husband sitting three feet away, but the knowledge he was there didn't hamper my enjoyment of the experience.

Beth tugged me closer, and I wrapped my arms around her. She kissed the way I like to kiss, with lots of tongue action, back and forth between our mouths. I was so wrapped up in it that when I felt something on my arms, I was briefly startled. I opened my eyes and saw Geoff sitting behind Beth, watching us kiss. It was his fingernails I was feeling, sliding gently up and down my arms, making me shudder.

Beth noticed the shift in my attention and broke away from my lips, trailing kisses along my jaw and down to my neck instead. I held eye contact with Geoff for several seconds, but then Beth started nibbling at my collarbone, and my eyes rolled back in my head. I blindly groped for Geoff's arm and felt the shifting of the sofa. A shadow fell across my field of vision, and suddenly Geoff was kissing me, too. He was more of a gentle kisser, briefly brushing his tongue against mine in between peppering my lips with short kisses.

The dual sensations were driving me nuts. I tightened my grip on Geoff's upper arm as my other hand slid up and down Beth's back. Beth started unbuttoning my shirt and kissing down my chest, and I just—stopped thinking. I stopped thinking about how strange this all was, or what this was going to mean tomorrow, or how I was ever going to make sense of any of it. I shut all of that away and let myself be carried away by the passion of the moment.

Geoff slid off the couch and knelt beside it instead to continue kissing me without so much strain on his legs. Beth looked up from my chest and gasped. She actually gasped. "Oh, God, that's fucking hot."

I pulled back from Geoff and asked, "What? Us kissing?"

"I've never watched Geoff kissing another man before," she explained.

"Seriously?"

Geoff nodded. "This is actually our first threesome."

The word broke the spell I'd been under. All those thoughts I'd let go came crashing back, and they brought friends: Is that what we're doing? Having a threesome? Do people actually do that? Threesomes only happened in porn videos, and never involved two guys kissing. Or such was my experience at that time.

Beth sensed my hesitation and sat back. "Are you freaking out?"

"A little," I admitted.

"You want to stop?"

"I—don't know. Not really. I mean, it felt great, and I've definitely thought about being with both of you. Just—never at the same time, you know? It never even crossed my mind."

"We don't have to do this," Geoff said as he brushed his fingers through my hair. "We could put in another movie. Or one of us could go upstairs, if you want. We don't mind."

I shook my head. "No, it wouldn't be fair to ask either of you to do that. And the fact is, you're both turning me on so much I couldn't choose anyway."

"How about we all three go upstairs to the bedroom," Beth suggested, "and see how things go? You get too freaked, you just say stop, and we'll stop." She slid her hands up and down my thighs as she spoke. She probably meant it to be a soothing gesture, but it actually turned me on even more. (Then again, that might have been exactly what she was going for, too.)

I mean, what was I really worried about? That I wouldn't like it? That I'd like it too much? Just like that, everything I was thinking felt silly.

"All right. I still reserve the right to freak out, but I want to try this."

Three years later, Beth, Geoff and I are still together, and I haven't freaked out yet.

Erik Moore describes himself as a bisexual, polyamorous switch (or, if he's in a hurry, "greedy") and tries to bring positive aspects of all three into his writing, without becoming a soapbox. The unabridged version of "The Direction of Greatest Courage" is available through Storm Moon Press (http://www.stormmoonpress.com).

in the dark

by david b.

It would always be a weekday afternoon, in the couple of hours leading up to 5:30—sometimes an hour, sometimes two, depending upon when he could leave work without drawing attention.

He'd park his car in the street, a door or two down from my house. I'd leave the downstairs door unlocked so that he could let himself in. The shades would be drawn; music or the TV would be on to keep my housemate from hearing our voices or anything else, should he happen to come home early.

I'd watch for him from the living room window, or wait for him in the bedroom. From the moment he arrived, there'd be a sense that the clock was running, counting down the minutes until six, when the house would no longer be my own. He'd climb the stairs, walk in to find me waiting, offer a "Hi, how are you," and we'd exchange a couple of moments of platitudes about my day, his day, breaking this off when I'd kneel before him and fumble with his clothes. The clock was running. There was very little time.

His name was John. An Air Force veteran (shoulder tattoo to prove it), a decade out of the service, now spending his days in a human resource department's cubicle farm. Married? Attached? Something like that; the specifics I didn't know. There was a female involved, somewhere, at least part of the time. The relationship, never spoken of, always came into the room with him, a mist surrounding his mood. The only things I ever knew about her were that she knew about me, if only in the abstract, and that per her agreement with him, there were some things he would not do.

I was single. Bland semi-young semi-professional, presumed straight, presumed between girlfriends, presumed capital-N Normal, with an anxious desire that this perception should never change. He never learned much about me beyond that; my first name, possibly my last name, my general occupation (which he'd only asked about to be polite). Never talk of family or friends or hobbies, certainly none of pasts or futures, both of which were presumed effectively not to exist.

We had met through Craigslist. BiWM seeking discreet NSA, and so forth, followed by an initial in-person appraisal near a drab and generally ignored statue in a public park. He was to watch for the black jeans and jacket, I for the blue windbreaker with the automotive insignia.

This, followed by coffee in a deserted seafood restaurant, followed by a first quick visit to my house, followed by the first act-like-nothing's-happening, we-don't-know-each-other period of silence thereafter, finally broken by an email with a suggested day and time.

And there we'd be: Another weekday afternoon at my place. Linens changed. Visible areas furtively, if halfheartedly, cleaned. A few beers in the fridge, some lube on the nightstand, the stereo or the TV refracting off the plaster walls. He'd come inside, we'd speak for a moment or two, then fall silent, his hands on the back of my head, him in my mouth, me listening alertly for the sound of a door opening downstairs above the music.

It had happened once, months earlier with someone else, during a rainstorm: I'd heard the door open, footsteps in the hall. It had happened while I was face down, with him inside me. My name, shouted from the foot of the stairs. I did my best to ignore it, until it was shouted again. And again. I'd twisted away, pulled on my clothes, flushed, sweating, embarrassed. "Just a MINUTE. Hang ON." And, "please, don't say anything. . ."

I had almost been caught. If my housemate had known, everyone would have known, and in as much sordid detail—real or imagined—as he would have been able to muster. As it was, he was left with suspicions, the sort that made themselves evident in my subsequent treatment: a little less friendly talk, a little more reserve, a new edge of sarcasm and what seemed like a measure of insinuation.

I couldn't let it happen again. Hence, the rules: done and out by 5:30. John, subject to rules of his own, was willing to be accommodating. So for a few months we had our intermittent weekday ritual. It wasn't all we wanted, but for the time being, it was enough. Late afternoon sex with music playing, cued by an email 24 hours in advance.

Late fall became winter. The indoor air was cool and dry, and by the time we'd finish the light would have drained from the sky behind the blinds. He'd lie on his back, my head on his shoulder or chest, leg twined around his, my hand between his legs. He'd rest his hand on my shoulder. Through the door, we'd hear the music playing; through the window, the December wind. When the green LED clock neared 5:30, he'd rise to go, pull on his clothes, let himself out, always sure to look out the window first: no pickup truck in the driveway.

Sometimes I'd pull the blinds apart, watch him as he made his way down the sidewalk to the little Japanese car that I'd never ridden in. I'd get up, switch off the music, and lie back down on the bed in the dark, feeling the space he'd occupied cool and then go cold.

David B. is a writer, occasional musician, father and full-time corporate drone living and working in a frequently intolerant corner of the American Midwest. His passions include fiction and film, noisy guitar, graphic design, his family and occasionally men; preoccupations include navigating reactionary corporate environments as a camouflaged interloper.

by silenus zarkoff

my kind of bi

I'm writing this to create a data point. I am not propounding some theory of bisexuality, just setting forth my personal experience and feelings. But I insist that any explanation of bisexuality must include me and people like me. I want to share how I am bisexual, recognizing that my way is just one of many ways I've observed men being bi over the years. My hope is that if enough men write their data points, it will dispel some of the stereotypes and utter nonsense about male bisexuality that is perpetrated by both academics and media pundits.

I like sex with men and women, but I am not Het Guy who goes into a phone booth and changes into Gay Guy. My dichotomy is not gay/straight but mono/multi. That is, when I meet someone I'm attracted to, my question is, "Are they bisexual or monosexual, polyamorous or monogamous?" In bed, my preferred genders are all at once. I can make do with one at a time, but I really like something up my butt and my cock in an orifice at the same time. I don't care if the cock is meat or silicone. I don't care what gender the orifice is either. It can be an asshole, cunt, mouth or hand. I do want my lovers to be people I feel a rapport with, and prefer to be sexual with my long-time partners with whom I have a strong emotional connection.

For over 52 years, I have been with a woman to whom I am legally married and love unconditionally. We have run several businesses together, raised two children and are working on two grandchildren. I continue to have devastatingly satisfying sex with her. Over the years, we have practiced polyamory, swinging, BDSM and miscegenation. We are a racially mixed couple who married in 1964. At that time our marriage was illegal in 16 states. My wife and I have had a few male lovers in common. For a few years we had another husband, who lived with us. We still keep in touch with him, and care for him deeply. My wife identifies as straight, but has, on occasion, played with me and some of my female bisexual partners.

Our ex-husband identifies as straight. He tried once to penetrate me, because he knew how much I would like him in me, but he just couldn't. I was OK with that. I love him, and a sex act one way or another doesn't make much difference to that. Our wife liked to watch us doing 69 and getting hard for her. Our most exciting sex was penetrating her vaginally at the same time. The feeling of her cunt squeezing our cocks together was incredible. Otherwise we took turns until we were exhausted. One time, driving up to Seattle from Portland in an old station wagon with bedding in the back, my ex-husband and I took turns driving and making love with our wife for about 140 miles. Later our ex, who had been a long haul trucker, told us he hung behind some of the 18-wheelers in just the right spot so they could get a good look at us in their rear views. We all had a great laugh about that.

I am more attracted to women than men. A bi woman who has been my very dear friend for 20 years and is mainly attracted to women, feels the same way about men as I do. We are not usually visually attracted to men—e.g., men we see on the street. But every once in a while a guy comes along who clicks with us on an intellectual/emotional level. Then we can be very attracted. I don't get much from gay porn, but that is because it usually doesn't depict men who look like my lovers, or sex the way I like to do it. And it rarely attempts to depict any emotional connection.

Growing up in the 1950s, I didn't learn anything about gay sex until I was in my twenties. Although I had played with my own butt since my early teens, I was 39 before I had any sexual contact with a man. I did know that to be "queer" or "homo" was bad. I knew that an effeminate boy in my high school was disparaged, bullied, and, I think, sexually used by some of the "jocks." I didn't understand why they did that. I didn't like it, but I didn't understand how to help, either. I had a "steady" girlfriend who was stereotypically attractive, so I didn't get gay bashed much. The "jocks" did aim homophobic slurs at me, just to try to provoke me. I was on the receiving end of teasing because I was a "brain," not an athlete. I knew that some parents didn't want me dating their daughters because I was Jewish. My Catholic girlfriend's father, in fact, once threatened to shoot me for that reason.

Since my parents moved to an all-Gentile suburb and didn't have many ties to the Jewish community, I didn't fit in well in either social milieu. I also found myself puzzled by the sex-negative attitudes that pervaded the 1950s. When I was assigned books like *The Scarlet Letter* or *Ethan Frome*, or read some of my dad's popular novels, I couldn't understand what the fuss over sex and adultery was all about. My parents never said much, and the one hour of sex ed I got in the fifth grade was fraught with misinformation. My generation got its sex education from *Peyton Place* and from dog-eared French porn some of my friends' fathers had brought home from World War II.

Although I might not have articulated it that way, I began to see that I had no stake in the social mores of the dominant culture. This probably made it easier for me to "question authority." Each fun-filled transgression of puritanical mores lowered the energy level needed for breaking the next taboo. If that's the slippery slope, I did much better on it than poor Ethan Frome.

I had some near misses with man-man sex. When I was 16, my father invited a visiting New Yorker he knew from business to a cocktail party. He was 40-something, dressed in a three-piece suit, had slicked-back black hair, and, I thought, beady eyes. He made a point of suggesting I visit him in New York soon. I was creeped out without really knowing why. In the late 1960s, I was in graduate school in Seattle and already polyamorous. When I saw an ad in our underground newspaper, *The Helix,* which had been placed by a couple who were "looking for Lucky Pierre," I angsted for days, then dialed their number. Alas, their teenage son answered, and informed me that they were no longer interested in Pierre, or me either. He who hesitates . . .

My first sexual experience with a man happened in 1981 at a workshop on sexuality. About 100 people, couples and singles, bi, gay and straight, were in attendance. Early on in the workshop people were allowed to remove their clothes, and most did. While no activities were forced on attendees, there were a number of exercises where we were encouraged to find a same-sex partner and explore their body to the extent we were both comfortable. We chose partners by milling around the room and making eye contact with people. My partner was about my height, barrel-chested, hirsute and of Mediterranean descent. When my turn came to explore him, I was a little apprehensive, but also a little giddy with desire. As I moved my face between his legs, I caught his scent, yeasty, like new baked bread. When I took his cock into my mouth, gently, a little worried about doing it "right," he stiffened. So did I.

In the early 1980s, my wife and I and our ex were part of a polyamory group in Portland. One bi man in the group wanted to take a number of us down to the gay baths. I was intrigued, but my wife felt very uncomfortable with it. I acquiesced to her misgivings and didn't go. There is no doubt in my mind that I would have had my brains fucked out. And what I have heard about the baths over the years still makes me wish I had experienced them. But today I am alive, and that bi friend died of AIDS around 20 years ago.

Most of my sex with men has been oral, me going down on them. I love filling my mouth with cock and I love the way men smell, some better than others. Frankly, I've only enjoyed being on the receiving end of oral sex a few times in my life, and that has mostly been with women.

I've only had one lover who I fucked in the ass, but he was a world-class athlete. Perhaps I made up in quality what I've lacked in quantity. And I've only been fucked by a man once in my life. I was playing with a couple I like a great deal. He took me anally while she took my cock in her mouth. Altogether a lovely afternoon, but just the prelude to a gang-bang I'd organized for her at a local club. I must be frank and say that HIV is the main reason I haven't had more anal sex with men. I might have taken that risk for myself, but I did not want to expose my wife and other long-term partners to any risk. Not only the risk of infection, but the risk of having to take care of me during a long, arduous, expensive illness. And I have children and grandchildren to think about.

The most intense orgasms I have are with anal penetration. With the exception noted above, I get butt-fucked with strap-ons, pegged, as Dan Savage would say. Mostly the strap-ons are wielded by women, but a few times I've been taken that way by men. And I like to use anal toys, my favorite being the Aneros butt plug that gives great prostate stimulation.

I've always joked that gay men avoid me because they can't stand the smell of pussy on me. Among my close gay friends, there are a few I've enjoyed playing with, mostly BDSM stuff. I dated one gay man for a while, until he moved to San Francisco. But mostly I'm not attracted to most manifestations of gay culture, with the definite exception of leather bears. One time, at a pansexual play party, a gay man I knew slightly walked up to me and, by way of greeting, grabbed my crotch. I understand this might be considered polite behavior, at least in some gay circles. But I was startled, and then pissed off. "Shit!" I thought, "If I'm going to fuck men, I want to be treated like a lady."

Since the mid 1980's, almost all my significant lovers, men and women, have been bi, my hopelessly straight life partner being "grandmothered" in. Bi men appreciate my attraction to women, and are sometimes attracted to my wife or another of my female partners. Bi women understand my attraction to men, and are sometimes turned on by being with me and a male partner. The only downside of having bi woman lovers is that sometimes they have been more interested in my wife than me. Alas, they have generally been disappointed. I've also had a few flings with transgender women, and I certainly would be interested in a transman lover, if the right guy came along. In short, I'm happy with the way I've been bi for the last 30 years. My bisexuality is certainly not a way station to or from gay or straight. I enjoy men when they come along, which is not often, but I'm not driven to find men for sex. And at 70, I'm somewhat less driven by any kind of sex than I was a few decades ago.

It both saddens and infuriates me when I hear straight or gay people pontificate about bi men. Ideas like bi men don't exist, or that they are just afraid to come out as gay, are intellectually lazy at best and mean-spirited advocates of a political agenda at worst. There needs to be better understanding of the finely nuanced diversity of the ways bi men incorporate multiple genders into their intimate lives. Just as I know many straight and gay people are bewildered by the way I desire all genders, I have trouble understanding why anyone would use gender as a criterion to reject pleasure and intimacy with an interesting person.

Silenus Zarkoff has been a sex-positive activist and breaker of sex and relationship taboos since the late 1950s. His academic training was in molecular genetics, but his career wound up being in the arts, with a few years spent working for civil liberties and public interest groups. Although the author feels it is very important to be out, he has used a nom de plume to respect the privacy of his dear friends.

i wanna be in the middle

by dan barry

When people see a happy couple, a natural reaction is to want to murder both of them. Especially if you're single. You watch them kiss in public and talk about dinner, oblivious to the misery they're inflicting upon the world. They force you to stare—it's their fault, not yours—and you feel prematurely disappointed in your next relationship, which can only fail to achieve similar levels of cuteness.

Most of the time when I see couples I get jealous—either of the entity as a whole, or of the less-attractive member standing between me and my object of desire. I have a lot of objects of desire. If you pick any two random people, chances are one of them is an object of my desire. In the case of Ryan and Emma, both are.

Ryan and Emma are about my age. They've opened a little storefront called Seventh Seal Music in downtown Waterbury, Connecticut. It caters mostly to punks, hardcore kids and metal heads, but they also sell a lot of DIY crafty stuff, which, if you think about it, is punk as fuck. I think their store is so cool. I want to see it become huge. But I grew up around here, so I know what's going to happen. Everything in Waterbury fails, so I know their business will and eventually their love will too. Still, I have never been so excited to get on a sinking ship.

So I bring Ryan my records. While sorting through the record collections I've inherited, I find plenty that I don't like. Some are just awful. Others aren't necessarily bad, but they're not up my alley. I figure someone out there can love them more than I will. Ryan and I sell those on consignment. Sometimes I bring him one that I thought was mediocre, but he gets really psyched about it because it's some rare old hardcore band. I let him keep those for himself. Thus far it's working really well. I just let him keep the cash and I take store credit instead. I use the credit for vinyl I know I'll like. Ryan gets some cool records from me, Ryan's customers get a better selection and good prices, I get some neat vinyl, and Seventh Seal gets a few extra bucks in its register.

Emma has big cheekbones, but the rest of her is small and skinny. She knits and makes all the cool little crafty things that they sell in the shop. Someday soon if I get up the courage, I'm going to take some of my crafts down there to see what she thinks of them. I have this mobile I'm making. Well, it's more of a plant holder. Actually, it's kind of both. To make the plant holder part, I heated up old records in the oven until they were soft, and draped them over a metal bowl to make smooth concave shapes. I want to hang these lovely Sailor Moon pencils off of it. The problem is, I don't have any way to connect the vinyl bowls together, or hang the pencils from the bowls. But I know Emma could do it. She has yarn.

When Ryan and Emma are together you never feel like you're in the way of their relationship. Ryan makes a mess of the store counter every single day and every day Emma cleans it up. Sometimes she comes down in her pajamas from their apartment above the shop. One time she told me about the bread maker they just got from the Goodwill store. Ryan laughs and tells me about the morning after they got it. Before he was even awake, she got up to check on the bread that had been baking overnight. She was so excited that she dove back into bed with him, still in her underwear, forcing these huge fistfuls of cheddar bread into Ryan's mouth.

They agree the bread was really good.

Meanwhile I am thinking: I want to bang them, jointly and individually. I want to be in their relationship. I imagine myself in the bed between them. We're all bunched up in our underwear, nestled together for warmth now that fall is here, tearing big chunks off of the square-shaped loaf from the bread machine. We kiss each other and think about how we'll open our record shop for business whenever we damn well feel like it. Everybody wants the same thing.

It wasn't the first time I wanted a couple. It happened to me when I lived in Boston, too, before I moved back home to Connecticut. I had a job doing real estate. I was showing apartments to this couple who was relocating from Seattle. He was an actor going back to school at Boston University, and she was an administrator for Starbucks. They both had the loveliest handwriting you've ever seen. I wish I had scanned in their rental applications and lease so you could see their handwriting. All loops. They rented an apartment from me—which was no small victory, because, although I wasn't horrible, I certainly was not destined to be a realtor—and they drove a U-Haul all the way to Boston from Seattle. I fidgeted in anticipation. I did little things for them I never did for any other clients. I visited their apartment before they arrived to make sure it was clean. I put a six-pack of local beer in their fridge as a housewarming gift. I dropped in while they were moving, asked if everything was OK, and helped them with some of the heavy stuff. We all searched together for their new laundry room.

I had secretly hoped that, after discovering the six-pack, they would see me at the door of their new apartment, invite me in, abduct me, tie me to the bed and do me. Just like that. I always envisioned it starting out really sweet. "Oh hey, it's you! How've you been?" they would ask with sincere interest. And I come inside, and there'd be pleasantries and hors d'oeuvres, and then their sinister ulterior motives would dovetail perfectly with my forbidden desires. (I could never quite figure out how that would happen, but it definitely would.) And then it's the next morning, and I'm walking bow-legged to my car, all bruises and rope burn, laughing to myself like I've just won the lottery.

Although, if you want to get technical, even they weren't the first couple I've ever wanted. For that, we'd have to rewind a couple years further back to the guy who made me admit that I was bi. He was a gorgeous ruddy Norseman—athletic build, sandy hair. We met in a college class about Buddhist poetry. His in-class journals were thoughtful and imaginative, and he dug mine, so we started hanging out. He invited me over to his off-campus apartment. I still lived in the dorms, and it seemed so cool that he had his own place. There, he introduced me to tons of amazing underground hip hop. There was this one evening when we sat on his front stoop, eating BBQ ribs and drinking brews, watching the sun set over town. I felt like a lizard, basking in the glow of his attention. There was no way to deny myself the obvious: I had a crush on him. It felt too similar to every other crush I'd ever had. I started thinking, "I guess this means I'm bi."

We finished up our meal because he had plans with his girlfriend that night. She arrived just as I was leaving. She had brilliant blonde hair and, as I met her for the first time, she gave me a big, friendly smile. She too was a stunner and she was nice to me. As if it wasn't enough of a struggle to admit to myself that I was crazy about a guy, now my libido started going apeshit. I was envisioning these two gorgeous humans, both of whom seemed like genuinely good people, in bed and the resulting scene was like some kind of sexual Clash of the Titans. I wanted in.

All of which is to say: the first time it could have just been part of my coming-out process. The second time it could've just been an incredibly charismatic couple. But now, living back in Connecticut where I grew up, a few years into being out as bi, this third time clinched it. I had to admit it. I wanna be in the middle. I like guys, and I like girls and I like couples.

I'm still trying to figure out the differences between liking guys and liking couples. Whenever I go up to Seventh Seal's counter and talk to Ryan, my mouth goes dry. I mispronounce simple words, and it freaks me out because I hear myself talking and saying it wrong. Inside, I say to myself "What are you, drunk?" and I don't know if he notices or not, so my heart races, and my thoughts get wilder. ("Should I say it over? What if I fuck it up a second time? Should I just finish my sentence?") It took me weeks to figure out what was happening. Sometimes, the fact that I'm bisexual still surprises me. If Ryan were a girl, I would have known what that dry mouth meant in an instant.

I wonder about Emma a lot. Her eyes are sparklier than Ryan's, but you can see a little trouble in there, too. I think that she's doing what a lot of women do, which is supporting a man who has a vision and an artistic gift at her own expense. Seventh Seal was Ryan's idea, and Ryan owns the business. He started it by selling off rare records from his own collection. I want to ask her what her dream is, but there was only one time when it was just her in the shop, and I was only able to talk to her for a minute or two before she went down to the basement to get Ryan.

Then one day Emma isn't there anymore. I ask Ryan what happened, and he explains briefly that Emma was crazy—actual-for-real crazy—and had to move back home to Georgia. Ryan doesn't even seem particularly sad about it. It was creepy. It was like the government disappeared her or something.

Meanwhile, Seventh Seal isn't doing so hot. Ryan complains about customers coming in, looking at records, writing down the musicians' names, and then going home to download those exact same tunes. He starts trying anything and everything to get people into the store. He hosts concerts; he does cheapo DVD rentals of cult stuff not easily available online; he starts selling pipes and bongs in addition to music merch. I notice a subtle shift in his mood. I think he's started sleeping around a lot.

The end comes with all the grace of a dump truck. Ryan gets his new girlfriend pregnant. He starts talking about how he's gotta make more money in order to be a good provider. Seventh Seal tanks not long after, a victim of music piracy and Waterbury's slummy economy.

Ryan seems to have made it out all right. He married that girlfriend, they had a daughter, and he works at an auto parts store. The last time I saw him, he told me there were a bunch of my old consigned records buried in his garage, which now contained the ruins of Seventh Seal's inventory. I thought I had gotten all of them back before the store went under. Still, he invited me to sort through, so I stopped by his apartment. I saw a couple records that looked familiar, but never encountered a big stack or anything. He told me that if I brought him some Taco Bell sometime, he'd help me pull out all the record bins and really scour them. That was a couple years ago now.

Since then, I've learned that what I was doing has a name: I was trying to be a unicorn. Also, I was doing it all wrong. And even if I had been doing it correctly, the prognosis for unicorn-based relationships is pretty grim. Seeking a couple to be their unicorn—and the companion behavior on the couple's end, "unicorn hunting"—is a laughable, newbie mistake among polyamorists and folks who practice open relationships.

Unicorn-based relationships often end in spectacular wipeouts and, while there are a variety of reasons, they share a common thread. Unicorns usually idealize the couple they want to join, and the couple idealizes the unicorn, so disaster ensues when the complexities of a three-way love affair come calling.

I know I idealized Ryan and Emma. I idealized all of those couples, really—I didn't know the slightest thing about their relationships, if they were healthy, or how they worked. What's worse, to my knowledge, none of them were even looking for a third partner. If they were, they almost certainly would've had a bi female partner in mind.

I've also learned about polyamory and kink, and being in touch with those communities has allowed me to meet people who are actually looking for partners like me. I've learned that I don't have to keep experiencing the ache and the letdown of pining for a (probably straight, probably monogamous) couple to take me into their relationship, into their bed. I've learned that I don't have to make inarticulate advances, hoping someone will see a sweet gift as a sexual invitation. I've learned that I don't have to hope for a chance to fit the pieces together for me, as they do for the characters in so many books, movies and games. Chance won't bring me the love I want.

I look back on my old self—the voice at the beginning of this piece—and he sounds reckless and naïve. He sounds like he was taking his Smiths and Soul Coughing records a little too seriously. He sounds needy and bitter at the same time, dying for affection but also convinced he doesn't deserve it and can't find it. He seems petulant and narcissistic.

He wishes he could have his way. His three-way. I, for one, am kinda glad he never found it.

Dedicated to all the other bi male unicorns. I see you.

This is a true story, but due to the sensitive nature of the topic, I did not seek consent from the people I've written about. (In fact, in most cases I can't seek consent. I don't even have leads on contact info for most of the people in this story, and in a few cases I don't even have names anymore.) Therefore, the names and places have been changed to avoid consent issues and give the people in this story (if not me) a shred of privacy.

After a seven-year stint as a music critic, Dan Barry finally stopped writing about other peoples' art and started making his own. He enjoys practicing massage therapy, playing video games, attending conferences, watching artsy-fartsy films and playing house with his partner. He still listens to tons of underground music.

floating

by d. dolnick

It is morning. I am parked on the street, across from the strip mall. Two of its storefronts gape like empty eye sockets in a skull, and the doughnut shop closed hours ago. The sad Chinese buffet competes with a nail salon for scraps of attention from the occasional pedestrian. You would need to want to be here, to require this place for some reason, and so few ever come here by accident. Those who do leave quickly. There is a pervading odor of despair, the musk of lost dreams coupling with the spicy notes of bitterness and disappointment. It assaults those who walk by, encouraging them to hurry along. There is no allure, and they always quicken their pace, eyes averted and heads hunched down. It is that kind of a place.

Today there is a couple—a boy and a girl—leaning against the wall, artfully arranged in slouching stances, postures that speak of an assertive, hopeful avoidance. It is that which draws my eye, the mixture of receptive and engaging with a cautious awareness, ready to flee or to bluster at the need of the moment. It is easy to read, anticipatory, abject and accepting. Neither stands with the inner power or any evidence of a will of steel. There is no crying out against an uncaring world, only the beginnings of a weary resignation to fate, long battled but now triumphant and clearly overcoming the optimism of youth.

He is an enigma, a young man-child lounging against the brick. She is a slender shaft of youth, all hips and tits and ass. His shoulders are taut and artfully hunched forward, his head slightly down. Her dirty jeans are too large. They both reek of want, and of a neglect that arose through necessity and a simple lack of options. He stares at the ground for long moments, focused and fascinated by some minor irregularity, his eyes flickering up and out every few minutes, casting around, preternaturally bright. She looks around, knows and sees all but gives no signs. They know I am here, but neither will ever look this way. When I get close enough, I see their eyes, pupils enlarged far too much for even this cloudy daylight. Hers are dark and beckoning, but his stance, his posture, is not. Edward Hopper would love this scene, and title the portrait "Hustlers."

I leave the car, stroll nearer. From across the lot I can feel the fine hairs on his neck: they tickle my nose. I can breathe in his unwashed tang, the sharp stabbing of cheap cologne that is all wrong for him. I would bathe that off, but leave the rest as it is. She will be vanilla and cream, grease from the fryer and the warm smell of potatoes. Neither of them is musk or spice and certainly not the bitterness of the street. There is something so very familiar here, but it evades me. She approaches, smiling, while he frowns and looks away. He is confused, he cannot understand that there is nothing about them that is individual to me. They are unitary, singular and indivisible. I once heard bisexuality described as reaching into your lover's pants and being delighted with whatever you find. I find two, and that astonishes him. There is no fear.

I've never been with them. I would remember. How to do this? I imagine that I approach. He looks me over with disdain, slouching further against the bright graffiti that justifies itself by holding the bricks together. He mumbles a number, an astonishing number, it is too much. His hands thrust deeper down into his pockets, dragging the waistband of his jeans down an inch, two. The taut line of his boxers emerges below the black t-shirt, a red slash of agony against his pale skin. I am anathema, I am desire. I am want and I am plenty. He cannot resolve this and resumes his study of the sidewalk, wishing me away, pushing me back, needing me there. I oblige, she takes the offering. His need and his hunger resonate within me. I am become predator. A spring compressed with the force of waiting, I need the chase. I need them far more than the ending of the hunt, which as it always must, comes far too quickly. It is the act, not the terminus point, which defines me.

We leave, but it is too early for action. He is tense, and yet not, and shows nothing. Dark, lank hair hides his face. She sits beside me, he in the back seat. Sequestered, he is no longer anyone I know. We go home, the three of us trembling, quiet, shaken in our hunger. We anticipate, and in that are yet empty. My heart aches for, and of them. We turn a corner, he slides down on the seat and I cannot see him in my mind and all is quiet for a moment. Then, his touch, his breath and I come back. We are there, inside, and I run my hand up his back, so thin, the muscles are whipcord yet the skin is too smooth to be real. I want to ask if they would like something to eat, but only later. Yes, I will ask, but she will not indulge that of me. She never dines with anyone, it is too intimate, too vulnerable. They will leave hungry, gaunt. We will not kiss. None of us.

It is afternoon, and I lie in the warmth, the sun streaming through the transom above the door. A window is open a bit, but the air is still and heavy in an August sort of way, and the quiet and the heat begin their magic. I drowse, slipping into the sheets, between them, naked in the coolness of shadow. The music breaks in, disturbing and shaping the room for its own purposes. A piano, slow, sad and bright begins the Nocturne number 1 in B-flat minor (Chopin, of course). I allow it to wash over me, and with each breath, my ties to the room, the house, the city are released. I am hot taffy being stretched too thin on its pulling machine, each of them an arm. Round and round they rotate, kneading me, as I needed them. I sag into the membrane of life a bit, rise into the air, lifted on a fog, fading as I lift, in dreams, from the divan. Ah, my affectations, calling it a "divan," even in my own thoughts and home. It is a sofa, simple and easy, but I wish more of it, and it is, after all, mine to name.

As the Nocturne descends in a slow, minor trill it severs the last connections stunning me, slicing through the ether, and I suddenly can turn, rising above myself, pivoting in the air and seeing, truly seeing, for the first time since we three arrived. The light in the room is yellowing with the waning of the day, shadows lengthening, but the heat remains, the warmth envelops me in a womb of comfort, and yet I am freed of my body. Free to float, to soar.

In days before electricity, winter was a time of rest and hibernation, when the setting of the sun meant the ending of the day. Unable to sleep for 14 hours of darkness, we would enter a twilight restful waking, a dream world. In that place was inspiration birthing poems, operas, pictures. We have lost that; our sense of it has changed in this world of immediacy and of gratification and we have become sensory gluttons, unthinking and drunken from our continual stimulation, insensate by overload. Our reality can neither be ignored nor controlled, although it is entirely of our own making. It is a Frankenstein that will destroy us, and we will never know that it has done so. Perhaps it already has.

Somewhere in the distance, there is a noise, a grunting, a base and ordinary sound I imagine must come from a wild boar or feral pig. I look but see nothing, the Chopin wafting through the open window competing with those more earthly voices. The sound disrupts, cries of pain or passion, I cannot tell. I must find the source of them. The air turns smoky and dense, acrid and bitter with sweat and other things best unnamed. I remember those all too well from the gym when my father would take me. Such a pretty boy they would say. Over and over, they repeated it, sweating, clutching. I smell that now, and it frightens me. I cannot see them anymore, those two, but I know I must go and find them now, save them. Will they still be there, slouching against the wall when I return? I can see where she was, standing there, against the wall. I can see his shoulders tight and rigid; his head was down. I wonder what he saw, on the pavement. Does he even know? Did he really see me? I drift, seeking them until darkness arrives and gives me rest. Rest, for a while, but only until the dawn returns.

D. Dolnick was born and raised in Chicago, but has lived in Southern California for the last 38 years. He has written for a variety of business and professional publications, and hates labels.

the worst feeling

Arriving home from work, I could instantly feel it in the air. Something was wrong. The silence and stillness of my apartment congested my stomach with caution. Calling for my girlfriend. "Babe?" Hearing the sound of wrestling coming from the bedroom caused me more concern.

"Babe?"

Swinging open the door to my bedroom, the discovery of my girlfriend crying escalated my bad feelings. She was curled into a fetal position. Rushing to her body, I reached out to touch her, "What's wrong?" My touch made her flinch. Her body jerked away from my hand. Her sniffling evolved into sobs. I was overwhelmed by confusion and fear. "What's wrong? Talk to me."

It took her a while to collect herself. Something traumatic had just occurred. A myriad of morbid possibilities raced through my mind. Had she received bad news? Had there been a death in her family? Had she been attacked? No matter how tender, my touch was causing her great discomfort.

With her face against a pillow, her voice struggled through the tears and mucus, "I—"

My fear and imagination joined forces to haunt me. What happened while I was away? She was falling apart. Her voice trembled again, "I—" The message lodged in her throat was choking her. "I—found something."

My heart dropped. My stomach collapsed. My thoughts of robberies, rapists and tragedies were all exchanged for something much worse. Playing stupid, I asked, "What did you find?" I knew exactly what she had found in the back of my linen closet.

She looked at me for the first time. Her brown eyes were bloodshot. She knew I knew what she had found. Her voice matured to the point that it was ancient: "Just tell me it isn't yours. I'll believe you, I won't bring it up again; just tell me it belongs to a friend or your brother or something. Please."

Two words—"It's mine"—stank up the room with shame and regret.

My head became too heavy to lift my eyes from the floor. It had finally happened. Someone had finally stumbled upon my secret self. This was the worst feeling. A cardboard box turned me into a monster. Men's magazines. DVDs and VHS tapes of gay porn. I was no longer decent. A cardboard box reversed everything I'd ever done with her.

I was at a loss for words. All I could say was, "I'm sorry. I'm sorry. I'm sorry." In that moment, anything I would have said would have been a lie to comfort her—and myself.

Soon after her discovery, I started to realize the true impact of that day. Every time I'd ever said "I love you" became another lie to add to her list. During every intimate act between us, she assumed I had men on my mind to fuel my erection for her.

I began to see just how contradictory she felt it was for me to have ownership of both that cardboard box and her heart. There was no turning back.

New author Forbidden Light has a knack for chronicling his sexual exploits. On the surface, he appears to be shamelessly broadcasting his dirty thoughts and even dirtier activity, but there's more than what meets the eye. In his blog and new book, Journals of an Intelsexual, *each erotic experience becomes a landmark along his path towards maturity.*

by nate taylor

speaking my truth, even as my voice shakes

This is the worst story I have to tell.

In 1997, I met the man who would become my first serious boyfriend. I was 19 and, like bright young things of that age, a delightful mix of well-informed and clueless. He was 25, a seasoned world traveler, out and gay and fabulous. I had in fact never had a proper queer role model to speak of prior to that point. I'd known gay men, of course, but their relationship to me had always been one of teacher or family friend, and their contributions to how-to-be-a-person never really stood out above those of others. Moreover, it was only a year prior to that that I even had heard of the concept of non-binary sexual orientation.

I am about dead center on the Kinsey scale. Experiencing my adolescence in a small town in the Midwest and being unambiguously, enthusiastically attracted to women, I just assumed I was straight and deliberately ignored the equal degree of strong physical and emotional attraction I experienced toward men. That was the kind of stuff that earned you a beatdown when expressed, so I just didn't. But when I first heard the word bisexual my entire world shifted on an axis I hadn't been aware existed.

So when, in my newly-adult life, this charming, witty, handsome, urbane gay man expressed interest in me both as a person and as an object of desire, I was not only flattered but tickled beyond words. At the time, I was in a monogamous relationship and engaged. My ethics have always forbidden me from pursuing a physical or romantic relationship outside the bounds of existing rules, implicit or explicit. But we became fast friends. It wasn't long before I fell very much in love with him. We had a ball together and I learned more about queer culture with him than I had even guessed existed.

Sometime later, after I had married my fiancée and he had moved away, my wife and I opened up our relationship. I was disappointed that my first sexual experience with a man was not with him and at some point I think I even told him so. When he moved back to the area in 1999 or 2000, our friendship shifted almost seamlessly into being lovers.

There had always been something of an inherent power imbalance in our relationship. In addition to being older and well-traveled, he also had a good five or six inches and fifty-odd pounds on me. It was always apparent that should he wish to do so it would be trivially easy for him to physically overpower me. I think he always worked that body language angle to some degree, although at the time I was blinded to this by my affection for him. Things felt good and I loved him without reservation, and basically did not see anything negative in any of our interactions.

One evening, though, I went to his house and he seemed rather off. We were supposed to have dinner together and enjoy each other's company, but his affect was very flat. We ate and were hanging out on the couch watching TV. After a show ended, he turned off the TV. There are some gaps in my memory here, but the next thing I clearly remember was that he was talking in this incredibly unsettling, high, lilting voice that was wholly unlike his and he was holding a very large knife in his hand. As soon as the knife came out, I panicked. In a split second he ceased to be the big, sweet, cuddly bear in whose arms I felt safe and nurtured and became an immediate threat to my safety.

In that moment my will and self-direction broke entirely. I thought only about how to escape the situation without violence. He actually handed me the knife and I just set it aside. It was an irrelevancy. Even with it, between his size and strength and my total emotional vulnerability to him, I would not have been able to stop him from doing whatever he wanted. That much had been clear to me long before the situation arose. And so, as he disrobed and removed my clothes as well, I did not resist in the slightest. I rode the situation out and waited for him to come and to fall asleep. When I got out of his house and got to my car, I panicked anew; he had parked me in. His Jeep was right behind my car and his keys were somewhere in the house. I did not know where they were, but having gotten out of there without being stabbed, I was not going back in for any reason. I wiggled the car around, drove over the neighbor's bushes and got about ten miles away before completely melting down in the car.

There's this overwhelming societal image in the Midwest, especially among men in my generation, that rape is something that happens in dark alleys, perpetrated by unexpected strangers, much the same way as a mugging. In health class at school, they talked about this at length and recommended rape whistles, Mace and self-defense techniques as possible defense against it. Implicit in this is the injunction that you have to fight in the moment or else you probably wanted it. This is rape culture. And it doesn't even begin to touch what happens when it's someone you love and trust implicitly, who does violence to your psyche without leaving a mark on your body, someone who takes from you with the threat of force what you have given them freely.

I had some very broken relationships with men after this point and then none at all for a very long time. It's only recently and after much therapy that I am beginning to reclaim this part of myself, to put the pieces back together into some kind of cohesive whole. I hope that at least one person who has had a similar experience will read this and feel less alone. We have a social climate in which rape too often goes unexamined and unreported. I believe we can build a better world, and I believe that one of the ways I can help that come to pass is by standing up and speaking my truth, even as my voice shakes.

Nate Taylor is an engineer, father, musician and inveterate nerd. He has identified as bisexual for much of his adult life, although recently he has eschewed this in favor of the term "queer" as he feels that it does not falsely imply a gender binary to which he does not ascribe.

rules

by richard m. juang

for Sean

Try to be tidier,
You told me while we undressed,
    Don't leave my underwear on the floor.

I like it when you use that rule-making voice,
Half social worker,
    half dog trainer.

Woof.

I should warn you, though,
    It's the rules that turn me on.
I like the way you like things neat,
    The way the bananas in your kitchen are lined up by ripeness,
    in the order you plan to eat, 7 bananas for 7 days.

        Sometimes when you're not looking I eat Wednesday
        even though it's only Monday,

And I wait for you to get mad, when you find me in your kitchen, mouth full of banana, chewing slowly, dangling the peel in my hand.

And when I say whoops, I'm sorry I've been bad,
    you know that I'm not sorry at all.

  Bad doggie.

  But the bigger rules, I never break.

After our first night together, while I was still wet
    and barely able to stand,
    You hopped out of bed and showed me
    the sterile space you keep,
    on a short brown table.

Syringes, bottles, and sharps container,
inside a perimeter,
washed down every 4 days.

No coffee mugs, Kleenex, or fingerprints,
you told me, serious like a submarine commander explaining where the launch codes are kept.

Even half-asleep, I remembered everything.
The bigger rules I don't need reminders for.

In four weeks,

You plan to show me how to clean a three by three square,
On the hard muscle of your left leg,
Force air out of a syringe, pump a plunger, find the precise dose,

And break through skin, in one fast motion.

In four weeks, my hands will be scrubbed and dry.
All the boundaries that keep you safe,
will be clean and hard,
and nothing will be out place.

The bigger rules I never break.

Richard M. Juang is a writer, activist and crazy cat lady in the Greater Boston Area. His work also appears in the anthologies Getting Bi: Voices of Bisexuals Around the World *and* Transgender Rights.

offworlder

by polyhedon

The lawsmiths held their banquet in the Alba Hall. It was the night before the war began. I met Beka at that party.

The entrance was higher than the floor, so new arrivals had to descend a broad staircase. This layout imbued each entrance with a certain pomp. Heads turned at each arrival.

And so I saw Beka on high, descending stairs of marble and jade.

He was all-over exotic. His jacket was black with gold trim, and his eyes were a shade of blue not found in nature. Not on my world, anyway. Those eyes were framed by tattoos—red swirls made of calligraphy in an alphabet I'd never seen before.

Every inch of him screamed "offworlder." He was achingly dashing.

In that moment, I resolved to get close to him.

When I saw him next, he was dancing with a beautiful pneumatic vision in a cream-white gown and a coif of gold chain. Some shadow-clerk in my head tagged her as a princess of one of the nearby city-states.

I saw him with three more partners in quick succession, all women. I marked him as unavailable.

Near the end of the ball, he came to me. He asked if I wanted to go out for some air.

We wandered far from the Alba Hall.

"How can you make yourself go up in that thing?"

We were at the city's spaceport, standing on a vast platform under the stars. Beka's ship crouched there, its engines arching out to the sides, like a dragon in chrome.

Beka looked at me. His eyes seemed more natural with every glance. "Have you never been offworld?"

"Gods, no," I breathed. "Space is death! Pure, unalloyed death!" I gestured at the heavens. "And you go out in it, with only a few inches of metal to protect you!"

He grinned. "It's about freedom. I can go anywhere." He turned to stand beside me, behind me. He set a hand on my waist, and I trembled. I hoped he noticed.

Beka pointed up into night sky—at a star. I couldn't tell which one.

"I've heard the nation-choirs greet the dawn on Dhento." He pointed at another star, then another. "I've swum with whales on Earth! Skipped from mountain-top to mountain-top on tiny Sphika, where gravity is so faint, you can reach escape velocity with one good jump."

He turned to me and took my hand. His other hand was on my back. "I've walked the battlements of the Survivors' Wall."

I traced the arcane curls of his tattoos with my eyes. There was a shimmering life to them, and I imagined them cavorting about on his skin when no one was watching. The eyes themselves were deliciously terrifying.

I murmured, "But where is your home?"

He kissed me. I slid my arms around his shoulders, and felt his words against my ear.

"The universe is my home," he whispered. "Promessa, Earth, Dhento, Sphika—they're all my home. I can go anywhere."

He kissed me again, and I felt myself swelling against him. I hoped he noticed.

Polyhedon is a computer technician in Toronto. He has a background in computer science and is a fan of all things fantasy and science fiction.

resources

mapping sexual orientation

by robyn ochs

To state the obvious: human beings—and our sexualities—are complicated. Each person has a unique experience of self and sexuality. Yet we have a need to organize, classify and categorize things in order to make sense of our environments, turning chaos and randomness into perceived order. When we encounter something unfamiliar—an object, event or person—we sort it through our systems of meaning and respond to it as a member of a "preformed category." "Oh, he's a whatchamacallit," we say to ourselves, and then we filter our understanding of this newly encountered person through the associations we have with that category.

Which categories of identity are important to us and what they mean are based upon our own experiences, assumptions and prejudices and are culturally specific. In present-day United States, for example, salient categories may include gender identity, sexual orientation, race, nationality, class status, age and so on. Thus we make assumptions about people we meet based upon their perceived group membership within these categories. It is important to remember that the menu of possible identities within a category is also culturally specific. In some languages—Vietnamese, for example—the word "bisexual" does not exist. And the same word may be assigned negative, neutral or positive value, depending upon context.

Ascribing identities to others also has its down side: we can over-generalize and ascribe to people labels with which they do not, in fact, identify. In other words, we can misread them.

How does this apply to sexual orientation?

When we encounter people for the first time, we "read" and classify them based upon the limited information available to us. For sexual orientation, in the absence of evidence to the contrary, we usually assume that people fall into the dominant category, heterosexuality. Heterosexism and heteronormativity have created the illusion that heterosexuality is superior and that it is pervasive. But not everyone is heterosexual, and we usually fail to recognize those who are not. Within queer community, a similar dynamic is in play, with homosexuality being the default presumption.

And we tend to assume that sexual orientation categories are binary, clearly defined and mutually exclusive. But in reality, many people's sexualities are complicated. We are complicated in terms of whom we desire, the specific sexual acts that turn us on and the types of relationships to which we aspire. And to further complicate identities, our actual behavior or experience may or may not align with our desires. We may, for example, have powerful similar-gender attraction, but no similar-gender sexual experience.

In addition, we do not all use the same criteria to categorize our own sexualities or those of others: Is that which we understand to be our "sexual orientation" based upon behavior, desire or fantasy? Is it defined by our current experience, by our recent experience or by our experience over the course of our lives? How do we decide which experiences, desires or fantasies "count" and which do not? How much same-gender attraction, experience or fantasy does it take to push someone out of the identity category "straight" and into another category? How much different-gender attraction, experience or fantasy does it take to push someone out of the category lesbian or gay and into a different category?

To complicate things further, these spaces of attraction do not have universal labels. The authors in *REC*OG*NIZE: The Voices of Bisexual Men—An Anthology*, who all occupy what might be called the "middle sexualities," define themselves using a multitude of labels; so do you, our readers; and so does everyone else.

There is no simple solution to the problem of labeling. Labeling is a complex process constantly negotiated through individual experience and social context. It is mediated by our various intersections of identity: geography, social class, gender, race, ethnicity, age and so on. A 20-year-old university student in a large Northeast city in the United States is likely to have a different identity vocabulary than a 67-year-old rancher in rural Oklahoma or a 34-year-old Evangelical working at a nursing home in suburban Mississippi.

Some researchers have taken on the challenge of mapping sexual orientation. Below are three models, with a brief discussion of their strengths and weaknesses.

First published in *Sexual Behavior in the Human Male* (1948), Alfred Kinsey and his research team provide a measurement tool called the Kinsey Scale. In it, sexuality is placed on a linear continuum, with one end of the continuum representing exclusive heterosexuality and the other exclusive homosexuality.

In 1980, Michael Storms graphed sexual orientation on a two-dimensional map with an X and Y axis. This scale draws a conceptually different map, presenting sexuality more as an open field, and allowing for asexuality (0, 0 or a very low number on the graph) and takes into account the reality that people are varying degrees of sexual: some people are more sexual than others.

The Storms Sexuality Axis

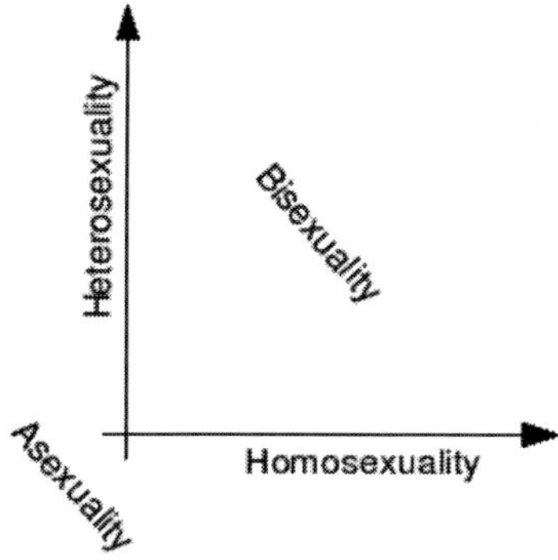

In his 1987 book, *The Bisexual Option*, psychiatrist Fritz Klein expands upon the Kinsey scale with a model called the Klein Sexual Orientation Grid (KSOG) which utilizes a 7-point continuum similar to Kinsey's (heterosexual only, heterosexual mostly, heterosexual somewhat more, heterosexual/homosexual equally, homosexual somewhat more, homosexual mostly/homosexual only but also assesses 7 different aspects of sexuality and incorporates the factor of time. Participants are asked to map themselves according to the past (from early adolescence until one year ago); the present (during the past year); and "ideal," an aspirational category (where would you place yourself on this scale if you could choose?). This 21-point scale obviously results in a more complex picture of sexuality.

Klein Sexual Orientation Grid

On the Klein Sexual Orientation Grid, people rate themselves on a 7-point scale as follows:

1. Other sex only
2. Other sex mostly
3. Other sex somewhat more
4. Both sexes equally
5. Same sex somewhat more
6. Same sex (G/L) mostly
7. Same sex (G/L) only

Variable	Past	Present	Ideal
Sexual Attraction			
Sexual Behavior			
Sexual fantasies			
Emotional preference			
Social preference			
Het/Homo lifestyle			
Self-identification			

These are crude tools, as they ask broad questions that could be interpreted in multiple ways and sexuality is so much more than that which is measured on these scales, but they nonetheless shed some light and are helpful for introducing the concept of complex sexualities.

Keep in mind that all three of these models rest upon the presumption of a gender binary and conflate sex and gender and they are therefore structurally problematic. To their credit, Kinsey, Storms and Klein created these models at times (1948, 1980 and 1987, respectively) when there was a near universal cisgender assumption (at least in the United States and other Western nations) that there were two—and only two—sexes, and during which the terms gender and sex were conflated and used interchangeably. For those unfamiliar with the difference between these terms, sex describes our biological makeup; gender is a social construct. The conflation of sex and gender remains largely the norm even today, though increasing numbers of people are coming to understand both that gender is not the same as sex, and that there are significant numbers of people who fall outside of the binaries of each. (This could be compared to sexual orientation?)

For one of my educational workshops, in an attempt to update these models, I have created an exercise that—rather than assuming a sex/gender binary—puts "different sex or gender attracted" and "similar sex or gender attracted" as the two ends of the continuum, with *similar* signifying people who more or less share your gender (or sex) identity; and *different* being people with a different gender (or sex) identity than yours. For example, if you identify as a man, different could be woman or genderqueer or any other gender identity that is not man. I also ask workshop participants to decide together whether we will be doing the exercise based upon the category sex or upon the category gender, so that we are all answering the same questions. Some people—especially those with non-standard sex or gender identities and/or attracted to same—might answer the questions very differently if the answers were based upon the category sex than they would if the answers were based upon the category gender.

Different-gender attracted						Similar-gender attracted
0	1	2	3	4	5	6

Among other questions, respondents are asked to chart their sexual attraction, sexual behavior and fantasies, before age 16, in the past year and during the past month. The final question asks, "What word or words do you use to describe your sexual orientation?" It is from seeing the responses of thousands of participants that I am convinced that sexuality is wonderfully complex. The labels straight and heterosexual usually cover at least the first three numbers on the scale (zero through two), and occasionally extend even farther. Those who identify as lesbian and gay usually cover four through six. Bisexual is usually two to four—occasionally even one to five—and so many other labels are reported: omnisexual, fluid and pansexual (usually the same range as bisexual), queer (usually two to six), asexual, "no label" and more. The introduction to this book lists the sexual orientation identities of the authors whose work appears within the covers of this book.

Thus, our categories each cover a broad range of space, and furthermore, they overlap. Thus, a given bisexual might be gayer than some gay men or lesbians, or straighter than some straight people.

One of the "bonus questions" I often include in my workshop exercise is "How many sexual orientation identities have you had—so far—in your lifetime?" Invariably, several people in the room report "two" or "three," and often there are a few who report "five," "six" or more. The default assumption is that everyone is straight, so most of us likely start there. But what happens next is often no simple story. Many of us use different labels at different points in our life or identify with multiple labels simultaneously: after all, labels—when self-selected—are tools for understanding ourselves and for communicating information about ourselves to others. Thus it is possible that we might use different labels when with our closest peer group from what we might use when speaking with an elderly relative or a co-worker.

In conclusion, sexuality is complicated, identity is a journey and mapping sexuality is no simple process.

robyn ochs interviews
aleta baldwin, m.a.;
jessamyn bowling, m.p.h.;
and brian dodge, ph.d.

a bisexual q & a

Wondering what social scientists had to say about bisexual men, I contacted three researchers from Indiana University's Center for Sexual Health Promotion in Bloomington, Indiana. Here are some data-driven, research-based responses to commonly asked questions about bisexual men.

What is the average age at which men come out as bisexual?

One way to approach this question may be to consider when people first become aware of their sexual attractions and desires, in addition to the age at which people come out as bisexual. There is quite a bit of research surrounding "identity trajectories," or whether there are common milestones shared by men and women on their way to identifying as gay, lesbian, bisexual, etc.

Among men who identified as either gay or bisexual, one study found that the average age at which they became aware of their same-sex attraction was between 11 and 12. The average age at which these men first self-identified as gay or bisexual was between 18 and 19; however, they didn't begin *identifying to others* until their early twenties.[1]

Other studies have found that the ages of first attraction and first identification were earlier: one study found that the mean age of first same-sex attraction was 7.7 years old and first self-labeling was 16.5 years old.[2] Still other studies have found that the first attraction is anywhere between 9 and 12, and first identification as gay or bisexual occurs between 14 and 16.[3 4 5]

While these studies each have slightly different numbers, which may be due to differences in study samples or differences in the structure of the questions, none of these ages are unusually early or late.

Unfortunately, few of these studies also ask (where applicable) at which age participants are first aware of their other-gender attraction or desires. Too few researchers are interested in sexual identity development in people who identify as heterosexual, as it is structured as the norm in our society. But it is safe to say that men and women who report same-gender attraction and desire first begin to recognize these feelings at roughly the same age that we all begin to understand our sexual attractions.

How is this changing generationally?

One sociological study of bisexuality from the 1980s found that the men experienced their first same-gender attraction around the age of 13, only a little later than contemporary researchers are finding.[6] Though there is still stigma associated with non-heterosexuality, and still discrimination against LGBT individuals and communities, one reason why people may report bisexual attraction or identity at younger ages could certainly have to do with the increasing acceptance of diverse sexualities over the past few decades. However, as yet, there is a lack of scientific research on the "coming out" experiences of bisexual men and women, in general, and virtually no research has focused specifically on bisexual young adults.

I notice that gay and bisexual men are grouped together in the data that you cite. Do we know whether there is any difference in average coming out age between these two groups?

In short, there has been an absence of scholarly attention to the lived experiences of bisexual individuals when compared to homosexual and heterosexual individuals across the board, including their experiences of "coming out." Research on behavioral and self-identified bisexual individuals has been largely absent from scientific literature, including those studies that examine relationships of sexual orientation and identity with health and wellbeing. Most previous research on health issues among "lesbian, gay and bisexual" and "same-sex-attracted" populations has not distinguished bisexual individuals from lesbians and gay men.[7] The number of articles that present relevant information specifically to bisexuals in terms of health is a miniscule proportion of the published literature on sexual orientation and health. This body of research is already problematic given that operationalized classifications of sexuality (i.e., "LGB," "same-sex attraction," etc.) vary widely among studies. This is concerning because although it has been established that bisexual individuals may share with lesbians and gay men some challenges on the basis of their sexual orientation and identity, particularly in regards to their same-sex practices and desires, bisexual individuals may also face additional stressors specifically on the basis of their *bisexual* behaviors and/or identity. The existence of "biphobia," or the stigma and discrimination experienced by bisexual individuals from both heterosexual and homosexual individuals on the basis of their bisexual orientation and/or identity, has been extensively illuminated in activist and, more recently, scientific literature. Researchers have finally begun to investigate how bisexual individuals may experience such "double discrimination" from both heterosexuals and homosexuals and how biphobia may impact the lives and, in particular, health of bisexual individuals.

Overall, it is critical that future research on health and well-being among sexual minority populations be based on more diverse populations of bisexual, homosexual and transgender individuals—which will require sincere efforts at recruiting and engaging participants in research beyond traditional "convenience sampling" techniques in gay-identified locations. Public health research on "non-heterosexual" individuals was long based solely on samples of men and women who happened to be present in "gay-identified" venues, including gay bars, clubs, parades and community centers, resulting in samples that were highly skewed in terms of their potential representativeness in terms of age, race/ethnicity, socioeconomic status, income, sexual identity and other factors. Generalizing to all non-heterosexual individuals from previous samples of primarily young, White, well-educated, upper-middle-class, self-identified lesbians and gay men is dangerous as results may be misleading and simplistic. Recent studies have shown that many bisexual individuals have little or no interaction in "gay" social spaces. Few researchers have made attempts to specifically recruit bisexual individuals outside of "gay" spaces from which "LGB" samples are often drawn. Future research may benefit from the development of innovative strategies to locate, recruit and examine bisexual individuals who may not frequent "gay-identified" venues.

For what percentage of men is bisexual identity "just a phase" and for what percentage is it an "enduring" identity?

There is a lot to unpack in this question. First, we know from Alfred Kinsey's work from the 1940s and 1950s that not all identities—be they gay, straight, bi or whatever—are always enduring. [8] For many people, the direction of our attraction and behavior is subject to change throughout the life course. When it comes to identity there is a stereotype about bisexual men in particular, that bisexuality is "a stop on the way to gay," or that for women, bisexuality is just a phase. A component of this bi-negativity is that rarely are bisexual people equally attracted to men and women. Should a person have a same-gender primary partner and then later an other-gender primary partner, this shift contributes to the idea that their identity is somehow untrustworthy or unstable.

Most of the data we have on changes in sexual identity over time focuses on young people. One of these studies found that there was no significant difference between the number of men who consistently identified as bisexual throughout time and the number of women who consistently identified as bisexual.[9] This finding poses a direct challenge to the idea that all bisexually identified men are actually gay, and that their bisexual identification is transitional. Nevertheless, these findings are not always consistent among studies. While studies of bisexuality in young adults have found that some are likely to later identify as gay or lesbian rather than bisexual, this should not be taken as proof that bisexual identity is just a phase. Rather, it can be seen as evidence that sexual identity is not unidirectional or stagnant, that people's erotic lives and the meanings they attach to their feelings and experiences are varied. As far as percentages go, it is difficult to find numbers. However, the studies mentioned above, which tracked sexual identification throughout time, found that about 70 percent of youth who identified as bisexual at the start of the study identified as bisexual at the end of the study.[10 11]

One final reason why bisexuality might not be seen as enduring is because the standard of monogamy in our society makes bisexuality invisible. If a bisexual person were to enter into a long-term relationship with a same- or different-gender partner, our tendency would be to define them by that relationship, (i.e. see them as "really gay" or "really straight") rather than acknowledge that the gender of their relationship partner doesn't necessarily undo their sexual identity.

I've heard said, "Everybody is bisexual," and I've also heard said, "No one is bisexual." What's the truth?

The "truth" is that the concept of sexual orientation is complex, and many researchers who are interested in sexuality have noted that there are a number of issues and challenges associated with the term. One issue is that sexual orientation includes multiple dimensions, for example behavior, attraction and identity. However, many individuals do not identify consistently as a single orientation across all of these domains (for example, a person's identity may not reflect their behavior), and many do not map consistently across all these domains *and* across time. In terms of identity labels, there *are* many people who identify as bisexual, and this alone contradicts the statement that nobody is bisexual: identity matters. This is the key issue in determining how many people are "actually" bisexual; individuals determine this for themselves. The idea that no one is bisexual stems from the misconception that those who self-identify as bisexual are in transition to being gay or straight. For a variety of reasons, many individuals do not experience an equal attraction to men and women, or engage in intimate partnerships with men and women at the same time (or ever). Additionally, the lack of visible identity for individuals (including physical presentation, social movements, and subculture) may lead them to participate in gay or straight cultures, causing further invisibility.[12 13]

Conversely, the idea that everyone is really bisexual reflects the idea that rarely does an individual only ever feel attraction toward, or engage in sexual activity with, either men *or* women for all of their lives. In the same way as saying nobody is really bisexual, to categorize everyone as bisexual negates one's individual choice in identity, and erases the subjective experiences of people who understand themselves to be entirely gay or straight.

There's a myth out there that bisexual men are by definition incapable of monogamy. Do we have any data with which to respond?

The idea that bisexual men are incapable of monogamy comes from multiple places. First, there is the idea that all men, regardless of their sexuality, are incapable of monogamy. Masculinity, in our society, is tied to being hypersexual: the idea is that men always are, or should always be, ready for sex. This stereotype of hypersexual masculinity is compounded by the conception that bisexual individuals are even more sexually insatiable because their erotic potential is not limited by gender. There is an assumption that a bisexual person won't be satisfied without having sexual relationships with *both* men and women.[14 15 16] Bisexual people are therefore seen as incapable of monogamy.[17] These ideas falsely limit the agency of bisexual men to have committed relationships.

Statistics on bisexual men's relationship patterns are limited, and in particular we lack studies that separate "non-monogamy" (which is consensual, and may include polyamory or open relationships) and "infidelity" (cheating). Consistent with statistics collected in the 1990s, one more recent Australian study found that many bisexual men choose non-monogamy, by engaging in open relationships for example, while still having one primary relationship partner.[18] Sixty percent of bisexual men in this study had one primary relationship partner but negotiated open relationships, while 25 percent were in exclusive relationships. One way to interpret these findings is that 85 percent of the bisexual men in this study were in long-term and loving relationships with one partner, and many had developed ways of being in successful relationships without violating an expectation of monogamy. There is a great need for future research that explores these issues in diverse samples of bisexual men.

Unfortunately, not much research is conducted on relationship formation among bisexual men. We do know, from research on bisexual women, that infidelity may be linked to biphobia. One study found that bisexual women who were unfaithful were more likely to have more internalized biphobia.[19] We don't have data on the reasons for, or prevalence of, bisexual men's infidelity.

Is there a correlation between bisexual identity and bisexual behavior? Is bisexual behavior more common than bisexual identity? Do we know what percentage of all men are bisexual?

Yes. From what we know, bisexual behavior is more common than bisexual identity. We have known for a while that one's sexual identity doesn't necessarily describe one's sexual behavior. For example, lots of heterosexual-identified people engage in sexual activity with same-gender partners, but may not identify as bisexual for a number of reasons—perhaps they are more attracted to other-gender partners, perhaps the same-gender sexual behavior was situational, or sadly, perhaps they have internalized the stigma surrounding same-gender sexual attraction or bisexuality. People have many reasons for how they sexually identify, and behavior may not always be the most salient reason.

Some researchers estimate that 1.4% of men (ages 18 to 44 or 18 to 59) identify as bisexual.[20] This estimate comes from an analysis of studies conducted in the United States, but also internationally. In terms of differences between behavior and identity, one recent nationally representative study of sexual behavior in the United States found that among adult men, 4.2% identified as gay, and 2.6% identified as bisexual.[21] However, rates of same-sex sexual behavior reported in this study were much higher than 6.8%. Up to 14.9% of men reported having received oral sex from another man, and up to 10% reported previously performing oral sex on another man. Reports of engaging in receptive anal intercourse were between 9.5% and 10.8% depending on age. So, we know that plenty of men engage in sexual behavior with other men who may not necessarily identify as gay or bisexual.

Since the 1980s, the concept of the "down low" or "DL" man appears from time to time in the media advancing the idea that certain ethnicities are more bisexual than others. Is that the case and what is the relationship between the "down low" and bisexuality?

Although a proliferation of mass media has drawn attention to "the new down low phenomenon" (presumably "secretive" bisexuality among Black men) over the past few decades, relatively little scientific research has explored bisexual behavior and identity among ethnic minority men in the United States or elsewhere until recently. Although the study of bisexuality in Black, Latino and other ethnic minority men in the U.S. is significant in its own right, disproportionate rates of HIV/AIDS among these men make the current lack of scientific information even more urgent and concerning. From the very beginning, the popular construction of the "new down low phenomenon" has been fraught with complexities and contradictions. First, a clear and consistent definition of the "down Low" has been noticeably lacking. The term arose in African-American vernacular to describe any sort of "secretive" behavior. In the late 1990s, the term was heard in rhythm and blues songs as an indicator of male infidelity—as seen in R. Kelly's 1996 hit, "Down Low (Nobody Has to Know)." The term also appeared in other forms of pop culture, primarily in Black male rap songs, as a marker of a man "keeping his business to himself." The sudden ominous image of a "straight" Black man engaging in "secret" sexual activity with male partners was a relatively new and more limited characterization of the down low. Along with the construction of this phenomenon, men started to adopt "down low" (or "DL") as an identity label, used, for instance, in self-descriptions in personal ads on the web, where DL indicates both a desire for privacy as well as serving as a marker of masculinity and sexual positioning.

Additionally, the recent construction of the "down low" has been yet another portrayal of bisexuality as a "new" concept, similar to *Newsweek's* "discovery" of "Bisexual Chic: Anyone Goes" (1974) many years ago. Although the existence of male and female bisexuality has been well-documented across cultures since ancient times, the "down low" was portrayed as a new phenomenon. However, the cyclical erasure, stigmatization, re-erasure and re-stigmatization of bisexuality, particularly among men, is hardly "new." As opposed to media depictions from recent decades, however, this time bisexuality was not exposed as a glamorous trend among pop stars and supermodels. Rather, it was a shameful "secret" which put innocent people (women in particular) at risk for disease and death. Indeed, the down low was suddenly exalted by some to the status of the "driving force" of the HIV epidemic in the Black community. Oprah Winfrey, in a highly publicized episode of her TV show, explicitly linked the down low phenomenon to HIV transmission, as did a panicked report in *The New York Times Magazine*. Although down low men seem useful scapegoats for the disproportionally high prevalence rates of HIV among Black women, any direct empirical evidence regarding the role of the down low phenomenon in the HIV epidemic among African Americans was lacking. Also, research on Black male bisexuality and its associations with HIV transmission has not yet adequately described the complexity of these men's sexual behaviors and associated risks, for themselves and their partners.

Last, current discourse surrounding the down low suddenly characterized "secretive bisexuality" as being all but exclusive to Black men. Interestingly, early studies of bisexuality in the U.S. focused heavily on White men and women. When acknowledged at all, early images of the potential role of a "bisexual bridge" from bisexual male to (presumably heterosexual and monogamous) female partners also promulgated the stereotype of the "white picket fence," i.e., the White, married man as a vector of disease transmission. The public discourse on the Down Low in the mid-2000s brought with it an abrupt about-face in terms of racial/ethnic focus. This has resulted in renewed demonization not only of bisexuality but of Black male sexuality. In a scientific presentation shared at Indiana University in 2007, our close colleague Dr. David Malebranche summed it all up by saying, "(D)emonizing Black male sexuality has been a staple of American culture since slavery, where our role was to work and breed, and the Mandingo stereotype of a hyper-sexual Black man with an insatiable appetite for White women was created...we distort the truth about HIV in the Black community to divert our attention from the real 'down low' issues of oppression, racism, low self-esteem, sexual abuse, substance abuse, joblessness, hopelessness, and despair." We explored these matters from scientific and theoretical perspectives in a special issue of the journal *Archives of Sexual Behavior* (2008) focusing on Black and Latino male bisexualities.

In my Beyond Binaries workshop, I use a modified seven-point Kinsey Scale. Workshop participants are asked, "Where would you put yourself on this scale, overall?" Another question asks, "What identity words do you use to describe your sexual orientation?" What I see consistently is that people who identify as "bisexual" most often place themselves on one of the three middle numbers of the continuum and some self-identified bisexuals may be as high as five or as low as one on the continuum. "Straight" people usually cover the first three numbers, and "lesbian" and "gay" people the last three. That means that there is considerable overlap between the different identities, and that a "bisexual" person might be at the same point on the continuum as someone who identifies as lesbian, gay or straight and, in fact, might even be gayer than a "gay" person or straighter than a "straight" person. Is there any related research?

This question points to a key problem in comparing research on sexuality across studies; different researchers may make arbitrary divisions in this continuum, which other researchers may alter, incorporate or entirely disregard. There is no one standard scale for measuring sexuality, though the Kinsey Scale is the most widely recognized.[22] Typically, identity, behavior, and attraction are considered the main components of sexual orientation, but we lack all-encompassing tools to capture these concepts easily, especially when we acknowledge the change in these different dimensions over time. The Klein Sexual Orientation Grid measures additional dimensions of sexual orientation (including whom you feel emotionally close to, and whom your sexual fantasies involve).[23] Importantly, the Klein Sexual Orientation Grid also includes time period (past, present and ideal). This way of assessing sexual orientation may be more comprehensive, but takes longer to complete and is not widely used. The differences in these two measurement tools also points back to the variability in how we understand orientation to begin with.

Another thing to consider is how two people who may have the same amount of same-gender attraction and same-gender sexual behavior might subjectively rate themselves in two different places on the scale because of the meaning they attach to their sexual feelings and experiences. Additionally, some measurements of sexuality look at same-gender sexual attraction and behavior *relative to other-gender attraction and behavior* (To whom are you mostly attracted? With whom do you mostly engage in sexual activity?). Therefore, two people may have the same amount of *same-gende*r attraction and behavior, but one might have more *other-gender* attraction and behavior. If these two men both identify as bisexual, is one really "less" bisexual than the other because he experiences less *other-gender* attraction? By which dimension(s) will we measure how gay/straight/or bisexual someone really is? One must question the relevance of comparisons of sexuality across individuals, as this is not how most people think of their own identity.

I also see from the data provided in these workshops that there are many different identity words out there. Relevant to this book are pansexual, omnisexual, heteroflexible, homoflexible and fluid—which cover similar areas of the continuum as bisexual—and queer, which in my experience usually covers the five highest numbers on a seven-point sexuality continuum.

One of the reasons why we have seen a proliferation of sexual identity categories recently is because we have begun to recognize that sexuality isn't a byproduct of a two-sex/gender system. The word bisexual—as it is most commonly understood—implies that a person is attracted to two (but not more than two) genders. But we know that there are more than two genders, and that there are a number of ways of doing gender. Therefore, some people who may have once identified as bisexual might choose to identify as something they perceive to be more inclusive (queer, pansexual, etc.), and others have re-defined the word bisexual in a way that does not assume a gender binary. As well, people whose sexual identity is not determined by the gender of their sexual partners now have a lot of freedom in determining which language best represents how they understand their own sexuality.

Because traditional sexual continuum scales place two sex/genders at opposite ends, some of these sexual identity categories which aren't organized around partner sex/gender don't fit anywhere on them (such as queer). Unfortunately, these sexual identity labels have yet to gain much traction when it comes to research, because there are so many potential categories and a large group is needed for any one of them to be statistically significant. A number of studies end up excluding participants who identify as something other than gay/lesbian, straight or bisexual, because there are too few. This is one reason why we don't have good numbers when it comes to how many people actually identity within these categories. However, just because they might not be statistically meaningful, doesn't mean they aren't meaningful at all.

References

1. Floyd, F. J., & Bakeman, R. (2006). Coming-out across the life course: Implications of age and historical context. *Archives of Sexual Behavior,* 35(3), 287-296.

2. Savin-Williams, R. C., & Diamond, L. M. (2000). Sexual identity trajectories among sexual-minority youths: Gender comparisons. *Archives of Sexual Behavior*, 29(6), 607-627.

3. Herdt, G., & Boxer, A. M. (1993). *Children of horizons: How gay and lesbian teens are leading a new way out of the closet.* Boston: Beacon Press.

4. D'Augelli, A. R., & Hershberger, S. L. (1993). Lesbian, gay, and bisexual youth in community settings: Personal challenges and mental health problems. *American Journal of Community Psychology, 21*, 421-448.

5. Rosario, M., Schrimshaw, E. W., Hunter, J., & Braun, L. (2006). Sexual identity development among lesbian, gay, and bisexual youths: Consistency and change over time. *Journal of Sex Research*, 43(1), 46-58.

6. Weinberg, M. S., Williams, C. J., & Pryor, D. W. (1995). *Dual attraction: Understanding bisexuality.* New York: Oxford University Press.

7. Dodge, B., & Sandfort, T. G. M. (2007). A review of mental health research on bisexual individuals when compared to homosexual and heterosexual individuals. In B. A. Firestein (Ed.) *Becoming Visible: Counseling bisexuals across the lifespan* (pp. 28-51). New York: Columbia University Press.

8. Kinsey, A.C., Pomeroy, W.B., Martin, C.E., & Gebhard, P.H. (1953). *Sexual behavior in the human female.* Philadelphia: W.B. Saunders.

9. Dodge, B., Schnarrs, P. W., Reece, M., Martinez, O., Goncalves, G., Malebranche, D., Van Der Pol, B., Nix, R., & Fortenberry, J. D. (2013). Sexual behaviors and experiences among behaviorally

bisexual men in the Midwestern United States. *Archives of Sexual Behavior, 42*(2), 247-256.

10. Diamond, L. M. (2000). Sexual identity, attractions, and behavior among young sexual-minority women over a 2-year period. Developmental Psychology, 36(2), 241-250.

11. Rosario, M., Schrimshaw, E. W., Hunter, J., & Braun, L. (2006). Sexual identity development among lesbian, gay, and bisexual youths: Consistency and change over time. *Journal of Sex Research*, 43(1), 46-58.

12. Clarke, V., & Turner, K. (2007). Clothes maketh the queer? Dress, appearance and the construction of lesbian, gay and bisexual identities. *Feminism and Psychology*, 17(2), 267-276.

13. Hayfield, N., Clarke, V., Halliwell, E., & Malson, H. (2013). Visible lesbians and invisible bisexuals: Appearance and visual identities among bisexual women. *Women's Studies International Forum*, 40, 172-182.

14. Rust, P. C. (2000). *Bisexuality in the United States: A social science reader.* New York: Columbia University Press.

15. Rust, P. C. (1996). Monogamy and polyamory: Relationship issues for bisexuals. In B. A. Firestein (Ed.), *Bisexuality: The psychology and politics of an invisible minority*. Thousand Oaks, California: Sage Publications.

16. Spalding, L.R., & Peplau, L.A. (1997) The unfaithful lover: Heterosexuals' perceptions of bisexuals and their relationships. *Psychology of Women Quarterly, 21*(4), 611-625.

17. George, S. (1993). *Women and bisexuality*. London: Scarlet Press.

18. McLean, K. (2004). Negotiating (non) monogamy: Bisexuality and intimate relationships. *Journal of Bisexuality*, *4*(1-2), 83-97.

19. Hoang, M., Holloway, J., & Mendoza, R. H. (2011). An empirical study into the relationship between bisexual identity congruence, internalized biphobia and infidelity among bisexual women. *Journal of Bisexuality*, *11*(1), 23-38.

20. Gates, G. J. (2011). How many people are lesbian, gay, bisexual and transgender? *The Williams Institute, UCLA School of Law* 2011. Available online: http://wiwp.law.ucla.edu/wp-content/uploads/

Gates-How-Many-People-LGBT-Apr-2011.pdf. Accessed 02/09/2014.

21. Herbenick, D., Reece, M., Schick, V., Sanders, S. A., Dodge, B., & Fortenberry, J. D. (2010). Sexual Behavior in the United States: Results from a national probability sample of men and women ages 14–94. *The Journal of Sexual Medicine*, *7*, 255-265.

22. Dodge, B., Reece, M., & Gebhard, P. H. (2008). Kinsey and beyond: Past, present, and future considerations for research on male bisexuality. *Journal of Bisexuality*, *8*(3/4), 177-191.

23. Klein, F. (1978). *The bisexual option.* Binghamton, NY: Haworth Press.

by robyn ochs

understanding biphobia

Many of the bi-identified people I have met come laden with painful stories of rejection by heterosexuals and also by lesbians and gay men.

A primary manifestation of biphobia is the denial of the very existence of bisexual people, attributable to the fact that many cultures think in binary classifications, with each category having its perceived mutually exclusive opposite. This is powerfully evident in terms of sex and gender. Male and female, and heterosexuality and homosexuality are seen as opposite categories (such as, "the opposite sex"). Those whose sexual orientation defies simple labeling or those whose sex or gender is ambiguous may make others profoundly uncomfortable.

Thus, bisexuals create discomfort and anxiety in others simply by the fact of our existence. We are pressured to "pick a team" and remain silent, as our silence allows the dominant culture to exaggerate the differences between heterosexual and homosexual and to ignore the fact that human sexuality exists on a continuum. It is much less threatening to the dominant heterosexual culture to perpetuate the illusion that homosexuals are "those people, way over there," very different from heterosexuals. If "those people" are extremely different, heterosexuals do not have to confront the possibility of acknowledging same-sex attractions within themselves and possibly becoming like "them." There is considerable anxiety in being forced to acknowledge that the other is not as different from you as you would like to pretend.

Because of the cultural erasure of bisexuals, bisexuality tends to become visible only as a point of conflict. Given that studies reveal that only a small percentage of bisexuals are simultaneously involved with men and women and that we tend to assume that a person's sexual orientation corresponds to the sex of his or her current partner, it is difficult to make our bisexuality visible in daily life. As a result, most people usually "see" bisexuality only in the context of uncomfortable situations: a closeted married man contracts HIV from unprotected sex with another man and his wife contracts the virus; a woman leaves her similar-gender partner for a male lover. Often, when bisexuality is given attention in public discourse, it is portrayed as a transitional category, an interim stage in a coming-out process, usually from heterosexual to homosexual. This erasure has the effect of associating bisexuality in many people's minds with conflict and impermanence.

The word bisexual itself may be seen as a product of binary thinking and, therefore, problematic. Many people struggling to understand bisexuality can only imagine bisexuality as a 50-50 identity. In their minds, if bisexuality exists, then it must fall midway between heterosexuality and homosexuality and have clearly defined, unchanging parameters. Using this measurement, they will find that there are very few "true" bisexuals, and indeed, if bisexuality is overdefined in this way, it can become rare. Many people also assume that a bisexual person must by definition require a lover of each sex to be satisfied, raising the specter of non-monogamy, another hot button for many.

This association of bisexuality with non-monogamy is a source of biphobia within heterosexual communities, especially since the arrival of HIV and AIDS. In the minds of many, bisexuality is strongly identified with images of married, closeted men bringing HIV to their wives and children through unsafe sex with other men, and these stereotypes are amply reinforced in the media. This has been a common theme since the second half of the 1980s and has included a frenzy of media attention about men on the "down low"—African-American men who have sex with men and with women but who identify publicly neither as bisexual nor as gay. (It is interesting to note here the confluence of racism and heterosexism evidenced by the intense media focus on African-American men when, of course, there are ample numbers of closeted men in every ethnic/racial category.)

Biphobia directed at bisexuals by gay men and lesbians is complex. Its roots lie in the dynamics of oppression and the particular historical contexts affecting the growth and development of individual gay, lesbian, bisexual, transgender and queer (LGBTQ) communities. Coming out and living openly as gay can be very difficult. Many gay men and lesbians have experienced a great deal of hurt and rejection, and shared pain is one of the foundations on which many so-called lesbian and gay communities have historically been based. External oppression may create a sense of not being safe and a strong need to maintain a clear boundary between "us" and "them." Bisexuals are by definition problematic in this regard, blurring the boundaries between insider and outsider. And further, the visibility of bisexuals and people with other non-binary identities within LGBTQ communities calls into question the myth that there is a monolithic lesbian and gay community with a single set of standards and values, composed of individuals who all behave similarly and predictably.

Lesbians and gay men may also fear that they are unable to compete with the benefits accorded to those in different-sex relationships, believing that those who are perceived as having a choice will ultimately choose heterosexuality. Many lesbians and gay men believe that bisexuals have less commitment to "the community," and that whatever a lesbian or gay man might have to offer to their bisexual partner may not be enough to outweigh the legal and social benefits offered to those who are in heterosexual relationships. There is some realistic basis for this fear: heterosexual relationships are privileged, and many bisexuals—like many lesbians and gay men—adopt at least a public front of heterosexuality to avoid family censure and to develop careers and raise children with societal approval. However, I also believe that this line of reasoning shows some internalized homophobia. Many bisexuals, even with this perceived choice, still are in same-sex relationships. What gets lost in the fear is the fact that same-sex relationships also offer benefits not available in heterosexual relationships: the absence of scripted gender roles, freedom from unwanted pregnancy, the ease of being with someone with more similar social conditioning and so on. Most important, we don't fall in love with categories but with individuals and the psychic cost of denying one's love for a particular person can be astronomical.

And finally, I suspect there are few bisexual men who have not been told by at least one gay man, "Oh, honey, you just think you're bisexual. I went through a bisexual phase too before I realized that I was really gay. You'll get over it. You'll see." There are men—perhaps many—who identify as bisexual for a time before coming out as gay. If you are a teenage boy and you have a crush on another boy, does that mean that you won't ever have a crush on a girl? Perhaps. Perhaps not. For some people coming out, the category bisexual is broad enough to encompass various possible outcomes and may indeed serve as a transitional identity. But it is a mistake for gay men—or anyone else—to universalize their own experience and assume that others will necessarily share their identity trajectory, thus invalidating other people's identities.

Internalized Biphobia

Biphobia does not come only from the outside. Internalized biphobia can be powerful, sometimes overpowering, and the experience of isolation, illegitimacy, shame and confusion felt by many bisexuals can be disempowering, even disabling. Even today, with modest improvements in this area, bisexuals have few role models. Due to bisexual invisibility and the paucity of bisexual role models or bisexual community, most bisexuals develop and maintain our bisexual identities in isolation.

Many bisexuals spend a majority of our social lives in the community that corresponds with the sex and sexual orientation of our romantic partner. As a result, we may experience a sense of discontinuity if we change partners and our partner is of a different sex, or if we shift back and forth between differing communities over time. Other bisexuals have a strong social affiliation with either a heterosexual or LGBT community. This can result in another set of conflicts: if our partner is not of the sex expected by that community, then we may feel guilt or shame for having "betrayed" our friends and community. Because of these potential difficulties, many people privately identify as bisexual but, to avoid conflict and preserve their ties to a treasured community, choose to identify publicly as lesbian, gay or straight or to stay silent, allowing others to presume that they are lesbian, gay or straight, further contributing to bisexual invisibility.

Therefore, it is not surprising that some bisexuals find their bisexual identity more a burden than a gift. They may feel a pressure or a wish to choose between heterosexuality and homosexuality to make their lives easier and avoid internal and external conflict. Many desire the ease they imagine would come with having one clear, fixed, easy to explain and socially acceptable identity.

Another challenge is that the behavior of individual people who are members of a stigmatized group is frequently seen as reflective of all members of that group. Thus, a bi-identified person may feel a sense of shame when any bisexual person behaves in such a way as to reinforce existing negative stereotypes of bisexual people. And we can feel an even more profound sense of shame when our own behavior happens to mirror one of the existing stereotypes of bisexuals (such as practicing polyamory or leaving one relationship for another). Although some bisexual people do behave in ways that conform to stereotypes about bisexuals, it is actually the dynamics of prejudice that cause others to use such actions to generalize about an entire group. Are some bisexual people polyamorous? Of course some are! And so are some straight, lesbian and gay people. But when straight people are polyamorous, their behavior is not seen as reflecting on all straight people.

Ironically, bisexual individuals in monogamous relationships may also experience difficulties, feeling that their continued maintenance of a bisexual identity constitutes a double betrayal of both their community of primary identification (straight or gay) and of their partner. Alternatively, the bi person's partner may feel that a bi person's decision to continue to identify as bisexual, despite being in a monogamous relationship, represents a withholding of full commitment to the relationship and a holding out of the possibility of other relationships. This overlooks the fact that one's identity is, in actuality, separate from particular choices made about relationship involvement or monogamy.

So, how do we make things better? Given so many obstacles, both internal and external, discussed above, how can a bisexual person come to a positive bisexual identity?

Understand the social dynamics of oppression and stereotyping. Get support and validation from others. Join a support group. Subscribe to an email list. Attend a conference. Read books and blogs about bisexuality.

Get a good bi-affirming therapist. Find a friend (or two or twenty) to talk to.

Silence kills. I encourage bisexual people to come out as bisexual to the maximum extent that you can do so safely. Life in the closet takes an enormous toll on our emotional well-being. Bisexuals must remember that neither bisexuals nor gays and lesbians created heterosexism and that as bisexuals we are its victims as well as potential beneficiaries. Although we must be aware that we, as bisexuals, may—because of the gender/sex of our partner compared to our own gender/sex at a given point in our lives—be accorded privileges that are denied to gays, lesbians and to transgender people of any orientation, this simply calls for us to make thoughtful decisions about how to live our lives. We did not create the inequities, and we must not feel guilty for who we are; we need only be responsible for our actions.

Bisexuals, along with lesbians, gay men, queers, transgender people and supportive heterosexuals, must open our hearts and minds to celebrate the true diversity among us. Our success lies in creating a space where the full spectrum of our relationships is respected and valued, including those that are unlike our own. We must remember that each person is unique and also that we have much in common. Labels can unite us, but they can also stifle us and constrict our thinking when we forget that they are merely tools. Human beings are complex, and labels will never be adequate to the task of representing us. It is impossible to reduce a lifetime of experience to a single word.

If biphobia and heterosexism are not allowed to control us, we can move beyond our fears and learn to value our differences as well as our similarities.

Bibliography

Allport, G., *The Nature of Prejudice* (1954). Reading, Massachusetts, etc.: Addison Wesley Publishing Company.

Lorde, A., *Sister Outsider* (1984). Freedom, California: The Crossing Press.

Rust, P., "The Politics of Sexual Identity: Sexual Attraction and Behavior Among Lesbian and Bisexual Women," in *Social Problems*, Vol. 39, No. 4. (Nov. 1992).

Thompson, C. and Zoloth, B., "Homophobia" (1992), a pamphlet produced by the Campaign to End Homophobia. Cambridge, Massachusetts, 1990.

resources for mixed-orientation marriages

by betti schleyer, ph.d.

I am a therapist who works with LGBT individuals and couples. In my experience, bisexual issues, in particular, tend to be marginalized, and most of the information that can be found is full of bias and stigma, so there is a need for positive resources for those in mixed-orientation marriages where one of the partners is bisexual. I hope you find these helpful.

Positive online discussion groups:

Making Mixed-Orientation Marriages Work (MMOMW) is for those who are in mixed-orientation marriages. This group includes straight spouses with gay or bisexual partners and also married gays and bisexuals themselves. The group welcomes all those in this situation no matter how they have decided to deal with this within their own marriage. http://groups.yahoo.com/group/MMOMW/

Hope Understanding Growth Support Couples (HUGS) is a list for couples of mixed sexual orientations working to keep their relationship strong and growing. It provides a positive environment where these couples can express their concerns, share their successes and give and receive support and encouragement. http://groups.yahoo.com/group/HUGS_Couples2/

Monogamous Mixed-Orientation Marriages (MMOM) is a support group for either or both members of a mixed-orientation marriage or relationship working to remain monogamous. "Mixed orientation" means that the sexual orientations of the two persons involved do not match. This includes any combination of GLBTQS persons (gay, lesbian, bisexual, transgendered, questioning, straight). "Monogamous" means that the partners are sexually exclusive with each other. https://groups.yahoo.com/neo/groups/mmom/info

Living Fabulous is a positive website for bisexuals, which also has a discussion site for those in mixed-orientation marriages. http://livingfabulous.org/

Transcending Boundaries has a good description of the basics of making a mixed-orientation marriage work, with links to resources. http://www.transcendingboundaries.org/resources/mixed-orientation-marriage.html

Patrick RichardsFink has written a positive article on coming out as a bi man, with links to resources. http://www.huffingtonpost.com/patrick-richardsfink/for-bi-guys-thinking-of-coming-out_b_2530612.html

Books showing that long-term, happy mixed-orientation marriages are possible:

Hill, Ivan, Editor (1987). T*he Bisexual Spouse: Different Dimensions in Human Sexuality*. Barlina Books, Inc.

Ochs, R., and Rowley, S. (2009), editors. *Getting Bi: Voices of Bisexuals Around the World, Second Edition*. Boston: Bisexual Resource Center. Chapter 6, Relationships, pp. 115 – 133.

Orndorff, K. (1999). *Bi Lives: Bisexual Women Tell Their Stories*. Sharp Press.

Suresha, R.J., and Chvany, P., editors (2005). *Bi Men: Coming Out Every Which Way*. Binghamton, New York: Harrington Park Press.

Weinberg, M. S., Williams, C. J., and Pryor, D. W (1994). *Dual Attraction: Understanding Bisexuality*. New York, Oxford University Press.

Research that shows that stable, satisfactory mixed-orientation marriages are possible:

Brownfain, J. J. (1985). A study of the married bisexual male: Paradox and resolution. *Journal of Homosexuality*, 11(1/2), 173-188.

Coleman, E. (1985). Integration of male bisexuality and marriage. *Journal of Homosexuality*, 11(1/2), 189-207.

Edser, S. J., & Shea, J. D. (2002). An exploratory investigation of bisexual men in monogamous, heterosexual marriages. *Journal of Bisexuality*, 2, 7–43.

Jordal, C. E. (2011). *"Making it work": A grounded theory of how mixed orientation married couples commit, sexually identify, and gender themselves* (Doctoral dissertation). Retrieved from http://scholar.lib.vt.edu/theses/available/etd-05112011-160023/unrestricted/Jordal_CE_D_2011.pdf

Matteson, D. (1985). Bisexual men in marriage: Is a positive homosexual identity and stable marriage possible? *Journal of Homosexuality*, 11(1/2), 149-171.

Wolf, T. J. (1985). Marriages of bisexual men. *Journal of Homosexuality*, 11(1/2), 135-148.

Theoretical background:

Gustavson, M. (2009). Bisexuals in Relationships: Uncoupling Intimacy from Gender Ontology. *Journal of Bisexuality*, Vol. 9(3-4), 407-429.

Research reviewed by Patrick RichardsFink, a bisexual activist, husband, father, student, and blogger in Central Minnesota. http://www.huffingtonpost.com/patrick-richardsfink/

Dr. Schleyer has more than 30 years of experience as a therapist. Among her specialties are treating members of LGBT populations, as well as working with couples in mixed-orientation marriages and families struggling with transition and coming-out issues.

selected online resources

American Institute of Bisexuality: Offers grants toward research and publications related to bisexuality, publishes Bi Magazine. http://www.bisexual.org

BiNet USA: Nationally-focused U.S. umbrella organization that facilitates the development of a cohesive network of independent bisexual and bi-friendly communities; promotes bisexual, pansexual and bi-inclusive visibility; and collects and distributes educational information regarding sexual orientation and gender identity with an emphasis on the bisexual and pansexual and allied communities. http://www.binetusa.org

Bisexual Organizing Project (BOP): A nonprofit organization committed to building the Bi, Pan, Fluid, Queer, Unlabeled and Allied communities of the Upper Midwest (focusing on the greater Twin Cities Metro area of Minnesota). They host the well-known national conference on bisexuality, BECAUSE. www.bisexualorganizingproject.org

Bisexual Resource Center: The oldest national bi-specific organization creates resources, provides support, and helps to foster a stronger sense of community for bi/pan/fluid people across the U.S and beyond; raises awareness and builds bridges within the LGBT and ally communities; and fosters bi-supportive social and political space wherever it can. Publisher of the 42-country anthology *Getting Bi: Voices of Bisexuals Around the World* and *REC*OG*NIZE: The Voices of Bisexual Men—An Anthology*, the book you are currently reading. http://www.biresource.net

Transcending Boundaries: Provides education, activism and support for persons whose sexuality, gender, sex or relationship style do not fit within conventional categories. They host an annual conference in the Northeast U.S. that brings together sexuality, relationship and gender minorities for three days of education, activism and community building. www.transcendingboundaries.org

Bisexual Community on Tumblr: Largest English language bisexual community on Tumblr bisexual-community.tumblr.com/

Bisexual People of Faith Facebook Page: www.facebook.com/pages/Bisexual-People-of-Faith/122630744589878

Bisexual People of Color Facebook Page: www.facebook.com/bipeopleofcolor

Non-Monosexual People of Color Facebook Page www.facebook.com/pages/Non-Monosexual-People-of-Color/296563900470373

recent publications by the editors

Robyn Ochs

Robyn Ochs and Sarah Rowley, eds. *Getting Bi: Voices of Bisexuals Around the World*. 2nd ed. (2009). Boston: Bisexual Resource Center.

Robyn Ochs, editor, *Bi Women Quarterly*. Ongoing. Available online at www.biwomenboston.org.

Robyn has published numerous essays in bi, women's studies, multicultural and LGBT anthologies. You can find some of them on her website: http://www.robynochs.com.

Dr. Herukhuti

Dr. Herukhuti, editor-in-chief, sacredsexualities.org

Herukhuti, *Conjuring Black Funk: Notes on Culture, Sexuality, and Spirituality, Volume 1*. New York: Vintage Entity Press, 2007.

Loraine Hutchins and H. Sharif Williams, eds., *Sexuality, Religion and the Sacred: Bisexual, Pansexual and Polysexual Perspectives*. London/New York: Routledge, 2011.

Dr. Herukhuti has published numerous essays, poems, and academic articles as well as co-edited academic texts under the name H. Sharif Williams and Herukhuti.

so many words: a glossary

As stated in this book's introduction, there has been an explosion of labels, monikers, handles, representations and identities used to describe non-binary, non-monosexual or middle sexualities: bisexual, pansexual, omnisexual, polysexual, panromantic, fluid, queer, questioning, heteroflexible, straight-with-a-twist, gayish, same-gender-loving (which doesn't necessarily preclude simultaneous different-gender loving), MSM (men who have sex with men) or, as Robyn likes to say, PSP (people who have sex with people), etc. The possible ways to describe the middle sexualities are as limitless as our imaginations. Concomitant with this trend is the simultaneous explosion of gender binaries with various possibilities such as transgender, genderqueer, genderfuck, gender fluid, agender, etc.

Our decisions about how—or even whether—to label are highly personal and are informed by our context: the intersections of our cultural genealogies, socioeconomic statuses, geographic locations, ages, temporal contexts, relationships to global phenomena like colonialism/imperialism and a host of other factors. There is no "correct answer" and we are not promoting the use of any particular label, and we hope that you will respect each individual's right to self-definition.

Further, we understand that there is no singular definition for any of these terms and that one person's definition of bisexuality may differ dramatically from another's.

It is also clear to us that many of our readers are familiar with only some of the terms used in the book, and we present below some terminology along with at least one possible definition for each. If you have a different definition of any of these terms: good for you! We hope you find this helpful.

AMBISEXUAL: see bisexual

ANTHROSEXUAL: sexually attracted to humans

BDSM: short for Bondage/Discipline, Domination/Submission, Sadism/Masochism

BEAR: term used by queer men to describe mature, hirsute, large men and the community of these men and their admirers

BI*: (pronounced "bi star") refers to the constellation of different identities used to describe non-binary sexual orientations (e.g., bisexual, pansexual, queer, omnisexual, heteroflexible, etc.)

BI-ERASURE: identifying someone as gay, lesbian or heterosexual despite their self-identity as bi* or in dismissing the ways bisexuality exists in their lives

BISEXUAL: someone with the potential to be attracted—romantically and/or sexually—to people of more than one sex and/or gender, not necessarily at the same time, not necessarily in the same way, and not necessarily to the same degree

BIPHOBIA: prejudice, fear or hatred directed toward bisexual people

BODEME: concept from the Dagara people of Burkina Faso and Ghana for people whose gender and sexual practices transgress social norms because of their spiritual gifts; also called gatekeepers

BUTCH: masculine woman

CISGENDER: describes a person whose gender identity is the same as that to which they were assigned at birth

DOM: the dominant partner in a sado-masochistic relationship

DOWN LOW: pejorative used to describe men who have sex with other men but do not talk openly about these experiences

DYKE: lesbian

FEMME: someone who identifies with femininity or behaves in a strongly "feminine" way

FLUID: a sexual orientation identity understood to be malleable over time

FTM: female to male transgender person

GENDERFLUID: a gender identity understood to be malleable over time

GENDERQUEER: self-identity for someone who identifies as other than "woman" or "man"

HEGEMONY: political or cultural dominance or authority over others

HETEROFLEXIBLE: having a mostly heterosexual orientation but open to other attractions and/or experiences

HETERONORMATIVITY: a cultural standard that says that the only acceptable romantic and/or sexual partnering is between one cisgender man and one cisgender woman.

HOMOFLEXIBLE: having a mostly homosexual orientation but open to other attractions and/or experiences

HETEROSEXISM: a form of discrimination that privileges

heterosexuals over people of other sexual orientations

INTERSECTIONALITY: a way of understanding how the multiple social identities we carry, as individuals and members of social groups, interact to affect the unique ways we experience oppression and how our relationship to oppression will shift depending upon the context we are in at any given moment.

INTERSEX: a general term used for a variety of conditions in which a person is born with anatomy that doesn't seem to fit the typical definitions of female or male

KWEER: coined by Dr. Ibrahim Farajajé to refer to LGBTQ people of African ancestry and their cultural production

MIDDLE SEXUALITIES: any/all of the identities used to describe a non-binary sexuality

MISOGYNY: hatred of women

MONOSEXUAL: someone who feels romantic and/or sexual attraction to members of only one sex

MONOSEXISM: structural inequality and violence that privileges heterosexual, gay and lesbian people and relationships over non-monosexual people and relationships

MSM: men who have sex with men

MTF: male to female transgender person

MULTISEXUAL: having the capacity to be attracted sexually to people of any gender

OMNISEXUAL: having the capacity to be sexually and/romantically attracted to people of any sex or gender

PANROMANTIC: romantically attracted to people across the gender spectrum

PANSEXUAL: sexually attracted to people across the gender spectrum

PHALLOCENTRISM: a cultural and social system that privileges maleness and masculinity

POLYAMORY: being open to more than one simultaneous sexual and/or romantic relationship, with the knowledge and consent of those involved

POLYSEXUAL: attracted to people of multiple genders

POMOSEXUAL: short for "Postmodern sexual"; someone who does not want to be put into a conventional sexual orientation category

QUARE: coined by Dr. E. Patrick Johnson to refer to Black LGBTQ people in the United States as a way of highlighting the distinctions between their experiences and those of White gay men

QUEER: originally a pejorative term, now often used as an umbrella term encompassing all non-heterosexual sexual orientations; sometimes used as a term embracing difference or non-normative sexualities

SAME-GENDER LOVING: coined in the 1990s as a Black culturally-affirming identity to describe gay or bisexual people

SUB: the submissive partner in a sadomasochistic relationship

SWITCH: someone who takes more than one role in sexual play

T: testosterone

TRANS*: (pronounced "trans star") term for the constellation of different non-standard gender or sexual identities

TRANSGENDER: someone whose gender identity is different from that to which they were assigned at birth

TRANSMAN: a transgender or transsexual person who identifies as a man

TRANSPHOBIA: prejudice, fear or hatred directed toward transgender people

TRANSSEXUAL: someone who identifies as a sex different from that assigned at birth

TRANSWOMAN: a transgender or transsexual person who identifies as a woman

TWO-SPIRIT: umbrella term used to describe North American, Native American and Canadian First Nation individuals who adopt non-traditional gender roles; these individuals have been viewed by certain tribes as having two spirits in one body.

ZHE, ZHIR: gender-neutral pronoun, meaning "the person" (gendered equivalents are "he" and "she"; "his" or "her")

about the artists and artwork in this anthology

Gymnos Alithiea: Classic Tracks Nasty, on page 37; Sleepy Subways, on page 201.

Gymnos Alithiea is not his name assigned at birth, but rather one man's super-hero cloak. It is at once a thousand clouded veils, and the persona stripped down to its essence: Naked Truth. What started as a handle in the early days of pseudonymous email tags and instant messaging, "NakedGuyNYC" grew to encompass a renegade nudist seeking expression in a concrete jungle. The initial Flickr account, in need of little more than an avatar and a collection of photos, transformed when Facebook arrived, and with it the growth of social networking; the requirement for a first and last name morphed the Naked Guy from nickname status to cultural persona—and so Gymnos Alithiea is brought to digital life with every upload of a photo, with every keystroke of a camera-enabled smart phone.

Efrain Gonzalez: Nobody Knows, on page 1; Men Kissing, on page 219.

A native New Yorker and a photographer since high school, Efrain Gonzalez has studied at the School of Visual Arts. Published in The New York Times, Time Out and the Village Voice, Efrain presently has two photos in the permanent collection of the Museum of the City of New York and is working on a book about the old Meat Packing District of New York back in the 1980s.

J. Christopher Neal: Untitled 1; from the Witchcraft From the Margins Series—mixed media on paper, 2009-2011 (female) on page 179; Untitled 1; from the Witchcraft From the Margins Series—mixed media on paper, 2009-2011 (male) on page 163.

Originally from the 'D' (Detroit, MI), living in Brooklyn, NY, J. Christopher Neal (Chris) is an artist, educator and the originator of an upstart organization, FluidBiDesign, an advocacy and support community for fluid men of color.

Hew Wolff: Sex Symbols, on page 59.

Hew Wolff is a software engineer and occasionally published writer whose main distractions include painting, garlic and the work of Joss Whedon. See also www.hewwolff.org.

index by topic

This index is a resource for readers to find contributions by topic or characteristic of contributors (e.g. age, ethnicity, or transgender identity). The page numbers refer to the pages upon which the contribution begins.